DRESSED FOR SUCCESS

Tarawe slung the feathered blanket around her shoulders like a cape and fastened the headdress around her forehead. Then she sent another call to the wind. *Bring me the birds*, she told the restless air. She sent a call to the high winds. *Bring me the clouds. Bring me the cooling rain.*

"Wait," Ana said. Reaching into her bag, she pulled out a handful of tiny, glowing lights. She whispered something over the tiny teardrops and threw them at Tarawe. Where they touched the headdress and the multicolored cape, they clung. They lit the shifting feathers like a sparkling, starlit night. "Go now, Storm Caller," Ana said.

Tarawe moved as quietly as she could across the lava.

By Carol Severance
Published by Ballantine Books:

REEFSONG

Island Warrior
Book One: DEMON DRUMS
Book Two: STORM CALLER

STORM CALLER

Carol Severance

A Del Rey Book

BALLANTINE BOOKS • NEW YORK

A Del Rey Book
Published by Ballantine Books

Library of Congress Catalog Card Number: 92-97262

ISBN 0-345-37447-9

Manufactured in the United States of America

First Edition: May 1993

Acknowledgments

The author would like to thank Bud Krames, Pele, Leilani, Shaka and Kona for sharing their Dolphin Quest world at the Hyatt Regency Waikoloa. Special thanks are also due to Richard Curtis, Vonda N. McIntyre, Caralyn Inks Reed, Craig Severance, Shelly Shapiro and Fred D. Stone for their help in creating the Storm Caller's story.

The story itself is for all the mothers of the world, most especially for the two very best:

Dorothy Joan Wilcox
and
Lucile Day Severance

☙ Chapter 1 ❧

THE great clam's brilliant blue mantle shimmered along the edges of its opened shell. Decades of coral encrustation had turned the creature into a jewel as bright and colorful as the reef itself. The clam pulsated slowly as it syphoned sun-warmed seawater through its massive folds.

A short distance away, a scuttling crab lifted a plume of fine sand. It hung suspended for a moment, then settled. A few small reef fish fed nearby, and feather worms slid in and out of their tubed homes to sway in gentle currents, but nothing larger disturbed the quiet surrounding the giant clam.

"The sea is calm, gentle friend," Iuti Mano sang softly.

She squatted near one end of the huge, hinged shell, taking slow, careful breaths from the tube vine attached to her shoulder. She had set a weighting spell on herself earlier to prevent her from floating upward with each breath she took. A thin stream of bubbles bounced along with her calming words toward the surface.

Iuti was dressed much more plainly than the clam. Her shirt and trousers were faded and worn, torn after weeks of searching through the treacherous coral for this particular site. Her white hair was tied in a tight warrior's knot atop her head. The only ornament she wore was a large shark's tooth hung from a thick necklace of braided, human hair.

"The water is sweet and warm," she sang. She flexed her fingers to keep them from stiffening around the hilt of her bared sword. "Relax, generous friend."

The great serrated shell stretched open another finger's width.

Save for the slight movement caused by the clam's rhythmic syphoning and her own breathing, the water remained still. Iuti took another breath of slightly sour air and glanced up to where

1

Tarawe sat in their small canoe. The girl was watching through a glass-bottomed bucket. She grinned as their looks met. Iuti blew a stream of bubbles and grinned back.

Iuti's chant affected only the clam itself. It was Tarawe who was keeping the water calm. With her newfound water and wind magic, the girl was holding the sea so still it hardly seemed to move. The surface gleamed like polished glass above where Iuti crouched. Even the clouds were being kept at a distance so that none would cast a shadow over the light-sensitive clam.

Tarawe had spelled a protective shield around the clam as well, to keep out any sea creatures whose movement might startle the mindless creature and cause it to retract and close itself inside its massive shell. That wasn't something they wanted to happen while Ho'oma'eva was deep inside.

Iuti returned her full attention to the clam. The sea mimic, in his guise as a long-armed octopus, was just dipping out of sight again into the great clam's maw. Ho'oma'eva had spent the long day hovering over the ever-widening mouth of the clam. His rusty orange body contrasted sharply with the clam's brilliant blue. He sank slowly and lifted, sank and lifted, each time brushing the tips of his tentacles against the sensitive surface of the clam's shining flesh.

In the beginning, the fluted folds of azure had shrunk back from his touch, retracting from where they were spread over the outer lips of the shell. Sometimes the shell itself would begin to close. Then Iuti would whisper another word of the calming spell, Ma'eva would lift away, and after a time the clam would relax fully open again.

They had been working with the clam since morning, and after so many hours of quiet, it had grown tolerant of Ma'eva's gentle probing. Now it only shivered slightly and shifted away from his teasing touch. The massive shell remained steadily open.

At long last, Ma'eva nudged a gelatinous fold aside and the object of their long search was revealed. Iuti tensed, then quickly forced herself to relax again as she stared at the Great Pearl. It was much larger than she had expected, larger than an overripe coconut. It glowed milky white against the clam's deep-blue flesh.

Even in their wildest childhood speculations, back when she and Ma'eva had playfully seeded the clam with a fingertip-size pebble of coral, they had never imagined such a prize as this.

Of course, they had never expected to wait twenty years before harvesting it.

Iuti smiled. This harvesting of the Great Pearl held more meaning than the simple gathering of the stone. Her agreement to make the attempt had been a long-standing mating challenge between her and Ma'eva in his human form. The sea mimic's sinuous movements around the gleaming pearl reminded her of the many pleasant hours of lovemaking they had shared in celebration of the end of their childhood challenge.

Ma'eva bumped the pearl closer to the center of the widely spread shell. The clam shivered slightly. The shell moved.

Iuti sang the charm again, hiding her excitement behind the soft calming words. "The sea is calm, generous friend," she sang.

She tightened her fingers around the hilt of her sword. She knew she couldn't stop the massive creature from closing, as it surely would when Ma'eva began pulling the pearl free. But by wedging her weapon between the two halves of the hinged shell, she hoped to give him time to lift the pearl and escape before the shell's strength overcame her own and closed completely.

If they failed to retrieve the pearl today, it would be weeks, perhaps months, before they could try again. After being disturbed in such a way, the clam wouldn't relax again soon. Iuti had made Ma'eva promise to leave the pearl if he couldn't get both himself and the great gem out in time. If the sea mimic were to become trapped inside, he might well be a pearl himself by the time Iuti could force open the shell and get him out.

"The sea is calm, generous friend," Iuti sang. Ma'eva slid a trio of tentacles around the pearl.

A few more careful touches. A few more calming words. Then the prize would be theirs. Iuti took a breath and sang the calming charm again through smiling lips.

Suddenly a shadow slid across her shoulders. A cloud? she thought. It couldn't be. Tarawe would never allow such a dangerous distraction at this critical moment.

Something large splashed into the water behind Iuti. She looked up and back to see a streak of gray sweeping toward her.

Shark! she thought, but knew instantly it was not.

It was a dolphin!

How could a dolphin have broken through Tarawe's shield? Even the shark god Mano Niuhi hadn't been able to do that.

There was no time to warn Ma'eva. Iuti could only hope he had felt the vibration of the splash from his position deep inside the clam. It was clear the clam itself had sensed the disturbance. It shivered and began quickly sliding in on itself.

Iuti rammed her sword into the swiftly narrowing crack of the hinged shell.

She ducked as the dolphin swept past her. It crossed directly over the rapidly closing shell and brushed its tail across the clam's flesh, as if deliberately urging it to retract.

"Mano's bloody teeth!" Iuti muttered. Where had the dolphin come from? What was it doing? Why hadn't Tarawe stopped it?

There was no sign of Ma'eva. Iuti leaned forward and saw him deep inside, caught in the retracting mantle's folds. His tentacles were still tangled around the pearl.

"Leave it!" she cried. "Get out, Ma'eva!"

Bubbles bounced upward along her cheeks as the closing shell reached the metal edges of her sword. It ground to a halt. Iuti held the blade level with all of her strength. Its razor-sharp edges sliced easily through the clam's soft flesh. They chipped away flakes of pearlized shell, marring even the coral-hardened outer edges of the great clam's home. But the heart muscle of the clam was far stronger than she. The sword's hilt began to twist in her hands. The shell began, slowly, to close again.

"Get out, Ma'eva!" she called. She could say no more, for her air was gone. She groped with her mouth for the tube vine while continuing to watch Ma'eva struggle upward with the pearl. He had almost reached the outer edge of the shell. Iuti sucked in a breath of warm air and used the strength it provided to hold her sword steady.

As suddenly as it had come the first time, the dolphin swept over her again. It caught the air tube in its mouth and yanked it away from her shoulder. A quick glance showed the vine dangling just out of reach. Iuti cursed as the shadow of the dolphin passed on and disappeared.

Her footing was still firm in the treacherous coral, but despite her own great strength, her sword continued to twist slowly in her hands. Her wrists burned with the strain of trying to keep it from snapping vertical and releasing the shell to close entirely.

Ma'eva had maneuvered the pearl to the very edge of the shell. He was trying to turn it to fit through the narrow opening. The egg-shape gem was obviously heavy and there was only one way it would fit through the opening now. Ma'eva tugged and twisted and turned.

Iuti's lungs felt as if a knife were passing through them. Her arms trembled. Leave it, Ma'eva! she cried silently. It's not worth your death! Her vision began to grow fuzzy.

Still Ma'eva did not release the pearl. He slid part of his body out of the shell. He used four of his arms to brace himself against the outer shell, and for an instant, it looked as if he might be able to lift the pearl free.

Then a sudden racing current knocked away Iuti's sure footing. The dolphin again! This time it brushed its broad tail against the backs of Iuti's legs. She fell and her sword was wrenched from her hands. She had time only to curse the dolphin's flashing form again before landing hard on the razor-sharp coral. A blue-black cloud spread suddenly over the great clam.

Iuti scrambled up, blinking away growing darkness, denying the overpowering urge to surface for air. She stumbled back toward the clam, surprised to see that it had not yet fully closed. A handful of coral rubble had washed into the narrow crack where her sword had been. The stones had stopped the shell from closing entirely, but as she watched, the porous coral crumbled into sand. The great shell slid tightly closed.

Iuti could see nothing of Ma'eva through the spreading ink and her own desperate need for air. Had he escaped? Had he been caught, or crushed in the final closing of the shell they had worked so long to keep open?

There was nothing she could do without air. The sea all around her had turned dark; she wasn't even certain which way the surface was. Only an image of Ma'eva trapped between the closing jaws of the great clam remained clear in her mind. She could hear nothing but the pounding of her own heart.

She felt swift motion, warm water sliding rapidly across her skin. The dolphin! she thought.

Go ahead and kill me, Dolphin, she tried to say, I can't do anything to stop you now. But her lips wouldn't form the words and she had no air to force them free. Her arms and legs felt as if they were stones.

Suddenly bright light struck her eyes. Sunlight! The water slid away from Iuti's face, and in her shock, she gasped and sucked in a deep, painful breath of afternoon air. Then another and another until her vision cleared and she could feel and hear again.

"Ser Iuti!" It was Tarawe's voice. "Ser, come! We have to help Ma'eva."

"Ma—" Abruptly Iuti came fully conscious. "Where?" she

rasped before choking on a mouthful of splash from her own flailing arms. "Is he alive?"

"He's caught in the clam. Come!" Tarawe dove straight down. Iuti took three deep breaths, then one more to bring luck to the dive, and followed.

The ink Ma'eva had released was dissipating quickly. A large stain had settled over the upper edges of the clam. With air in her lungs, the seawater was clear to Iuti again and she almost called out in relief when she saw a writhing mass of tentacles at the top of the great shell. Ma'eva was alive!

Iuti motioned for Tarawe to bring the air tube near. The girl did it without leaving Iuti's side, using her water magic to carry the tube to them. Then she closed and opened her left hand, and the water all around them grew calm again. There was no sign of the damnable dolphin.

As quickly as Iuti touched him, Ma'eva grew still. He slid three of his long arms around Iuti's left arm and clung with sucking tension to her water-soaked skin.

"I'm here, good friend," she said. "I'll get you free."

A fourth tentacle snaked around her wrist and held her close. Iuti managed a smile as Ma'eva's rubbery head relaxed against her fingers. She pulled in a breath of air from the tube vine and bent to examine Ma'eva's other arms. Only two were caught in the closed shell, but they were caught firmly, about a finger's length from their tips. There was no sign of the pearl.

Tarawe brushed Iuti's shoulder and pointed to where her sword lay on the coral. Iuti nodded. There was only one way to free Ma'eva, since he chose not to free himself. The tendrils around her arm squeezed tighter.

Tarawe swam to pick up the sword herself, not trusting her untrained water magic to bring it to them as safely as the tube vine had come. She had learned the hard way that human-made items weren't as trustworthy as those of the sea. She handed the sword's hilt to Iuti carefully, then bit her lower lip and moved back.

Iuti didn't hesitate. As soon as the blade was in her hand, she sliced it across the shell's upper edge, cutting Ma'eva free. He clutched her hand tightly for just an instant, then hung limp. The natural suction of his mimicked body kept him wrapped firmly around her arm as she swam swiftly for the surface.

Tarawe reached it first. "Is he—"

"He'll be all right," Iuti said as soon as she had air. "We need to keep him in the water, though. If he changes back to his human form now, he'll carry the injury with him, and there's no way to know if that was two fingers or a whole hand I just cut off.''

"Or a foot," Tarawe said. She stared wide-eyed at Ma'eva.

"Aye," Iuti muttered. "Or a foot." She hoped Ma'eva had sense enough to remain in his present form until the tentacles could regenerate fully. He had promised, before she had agreed to this plan, that he would if the need arose.

He also promised to leave the pearl behind at the first sign of danger, she reminded herself. Fool mimic. She thought for a moment, then decided against placing a binding spell of her own on her injured friend.

To her relief, Ma'eva remained limp and fully an octopus while she climbed into the canoe. She scooped up a bucket of seawater, peeled Ma'eva from her arm, and set him into it. She licked two fingers of her right hand and said a soft word while dipping them into the water beside the sea mimic. His color mottled, then brightened again. He relaxed onto the bucket's bottom. Iuti wasn't certain the small healing spell would work—she had never had occasion to treat a mollusk's injuries before—but she knew it would do no harm.

Tarawe lifted herself aboard in silence.

"What happened?" Iuti asked. She was surprised at the depth of her disappointment. They had come so close.

Tarawe dropped her gaze to the sea. She brought it back slowly. "I don't know. The dolphin—"

"How did it get past your shield?"

"I don't know! It just came. I tried to stop it, Ser, but all of a sudden it was there. I couldn't stop it from scaring the clam."

Iuti frowned. Tarawe had no reason to lie about what had happened. And she certainly had no reason to want the pearl harvest to fail. The pearl had been promised to the birdfolk in return for their help in the recent battle at Fanape. Tarawe considered the debt as much her own as it was Iuti's or Ma'eva's.

"How could a simple dolphin break through your shield when Mano Niuhi himself could not?" Iuti asked.

Tarawe straightened. "I did just what you said. I watched all around and didn't let anything bigger than a fingerfish move in the water near you and Ma'eva."

"Then how—"

"I told you! It just *came*! There was a big splash and then it was there! I thought it was a bird at first, but then I saw it wasn't."

Her words made no sense. "What did the dolphin do after it first startled the clam into closing?"

"It circled back and knocked the air tube away from you," Tarawe said. "I tried to turn it in the water, but nothing happened. I mean, the water turned, but the dolphin just kept moving through it. Then it knocked you down and—"

"Was it you who washed the coral stones into the shell to keep it from closing?" Iuti asked.

Tarawe nodded. "It was all I could think to do. It didn't work very well."

"It worked well enough to save Ma'eva's life," Iuti said, glancing into the bucket, "and most of his limbs. What did the dolphin do then? Where did it go?"

"I don't know. I was too busy trying to keep the shell from closing and then getting you to the surface for air." Tarawe's shoulders slumped. "I'm sorry, Ser. It was my fault. I should have seen it coming and strengthened my shield, or . . . something."

That didn't make sense either. Tarawe's water and wind skills were for the most part still untested, but the one thing Iuti knew the girl could do well was set a proper shielding spell. There was no way any sea creature could have broken through her guard. The dolphin couldn't even have jumped over the shield, because Tarawe's control of the air was even stronger than that of the water. Only the strongest of the birds could break through.

A chill ran along Iuti's arms. "By the gods!" she whispered. She glanced up and around. Except for a few scattered clouds, the sky was completely empty. Not even Tarawe's friendly gull was nearby.

"It must have been a flying dolphin!" Iuti said.

Tarawe caught her breath. She looked quickly up at the sky, then down again at the sea. Her face turned very pale. "A flying dolphin?" she said in a very small voice.

Iuti set the bucket containing Ma'eva into the bottom of the narrow hull. "Only a bird could have broken through your shield. The flying dolphins are as much airfolk as they are creatures of the sea. There's nothing else it could have been."

"But why would it come *here*?" Tarawe cried. "Why would a flying dolphin want to stop us from harvesting the pearl?"

"I don't know." Iuti slid her paddle into the water and began pulling the canoe toward the small island where they had made their camp. But she did know. Or at least she had a good idea. The way Tarawe fumbled as she turned in her seat, the tenseness of her back as she slid her own paddle into the sea, made it clear that the girl knew, as well.

"Revenge," Tarawe whispered.

The word scudded like a wind-damaged gull across the quiet lagoon.

✇ *Chapter 2* ✇

TARAWE gripped her paddle tightly as they moved away from the great clam. The wood was rough and dry, warm after its day in the hot sun. Tarawe didn't need to paddle. She could easily have moved the small canoe by moving the water itself, but she was afraid to use her magic now. Afraid she might make another mistake and bring more trouble than they already had.

"I never meant to kill the dolphins," she whispered into the wind. "I never meant for my magic to kill anyone."

But it had.

Tens of humans and uncounted seafolk, even birds, had died in the great storm Tarawe had mistakenly called just a few months before. The girl squeezed her eyes shut against remembered pain and matched her strokes to those of Iuti Mano at the back of the canoe.

They had been paddling like this the night she had called the storm. They had traveled through an entire sun-drenched day without pausing, without water. When they had finally stopped, and while Ser Iuti slept, Tarawe had sung to the wind. She had used a chant she had once heard the Fanape Island sorceress sing when the island needed rain.

Tarawe had been excited at first, delighted when the winds began answering her call. Soft breezes and teasing eddies tumbled toward her, carrying the unmistakable scent of approaching rain. But in the end it was much more than a simple rain squall that came. The winds grew in power and swiftness. The swells began running deep and long. Soon the waves were lifting high enough to be ripped into glistening spray by the ever more powerful wind.

Tarawe had known no way to stop it. Calling the storm had been her first use of true magic. She had never before used anything more than a simple healing spell, and that only on herself and in the company of her mother. Tarawe had been completely helpless in the face of the gathering storm.

Many weeks passed and many lives were lost before Tarawe found a way to harness the air and the water and return them to calm. In the meantime, the lands and coral reefs affected by the storm had been devastated. Tarawe herself had nearly been destroyed as her untrained mind was forced to absorb the death thrust of every life her storm took.

Most painful of all had been the deaths of the flying dolphins. The evil sorceress Pahulu had forced two of the magical creatures into the maelstrom at the storm's center. Worse yet, she had forced the flying dolphins to herd their cousins, the sweet-faced true dolphins, into the storm before them, and thus lose their own souls as they died in the act of killing their kin.

As the dolphins were torn to shreds in Tarawe's raging seas and screaming winds, the sorceress had absorbed the power released by their innocent deaths. Tarawe, completely unpracticed in the ways of power, had absorbed only the pain. The horror of the dolphins' deaths still lay like an icy splinter next to her heart.

"I never meant for you to lose your souls," Tarawe whispered. She pulled her paddle from the water and bent forward to press her face against her knees. The canoe stopped. It dipped and steadied. A hand touched her shoulder.

"Are you all right?" Ser Iuti asked.

"It came because of me," Tarawe said. "It came because of what I did."

"We can't be sure of that," Iuti said. "It might only have been drawn to us because of the magic in your shield. It didn't try to hurt us, and it could have easily."

"It hurt Ma'eva," Tarawe said.

"Ma'eva could have escaped safely if he'd swum out of the clam right away," Iuti said. "All the flying dolphin did was stop us from taking the pearl."

"Why would a magic dolphin care about a stupid pearl?"

"I have no idea," said Iuti. "Maybe it wasn't interested in the pearl at all. Maybe it was just playing, or curious, or thought we were hurting the clam. I've heard they're very protective of the lesser seafolk."

Tarawe looked up. Ser Iuti was watching her in that steady, calm way of hers that revealed nothing of what she might be thinking inside. Her hair, still bleached white from her disguise in Sandar City, had slipped from its knot to hang in long, wet strands across her shoulders. The scars on her right cheek looked dark against her golden-brown skin.

Tarawe met her look and said, "That dolphin was protecting the pearl, Ser."

Iuti sighed. "Aye, so it seemed. Well, there's nothing we can do about it now. It'll be months before that clam will relax enough for us to try again. We'll just have to wait for Ma'eva to return to his human form and ask him. Maybe he'll know what happened."

She started back toward her seat at the back of the canoe. "Or maybe your gull would know. I wish the birds would tell us why *they're* so interested in the pearl. They may change their minds about wanting it when they find out how big it is. I doubt any of them will be strong enough to lift it."

"My gull said she's not supposed to talk about the pearl," Tarawe said. She suspected the great clumsy bird wasn't supposed to talk to her at all, but they'd become friends since the Teronin War ended and the bird seemed to enjoy her company. She had mended the gull's wing, injured during the storm, and then taught the great bird to fly again by providing supporting air currents for it to ride.

"Where is your gull anyway?" Iuti asked.

Tarawe picked at a splinter in her left palm, wishing she didn't know. After a moment, she said, "She flew off this morning to find the other birds and tell them we were harvesting the pearl today."

"Mano's teeth," Iuti muttered. "That's just what we needed. They'll be upon us first thing tomorrow demanding their payment. Without Ma'eva, we'll have a hard time explaining why we don't have it."

Tarawe glanced back toward the bucket where Ma'eva lay coiled. His formerly bright-red color had faded to a mottled gray. He looked limp and lifeless. "I'm sorry he got hurt."

Ser Iuti smiled. "Don't worry about Ma'eva. This isn't the first time he's lost part of a leg while taking the octopus form. It's one of the ways octopus escape being eaten. They grow their lost limbs back very quickly, and I've set a healing spell that should help."

"Why didn't he break free of the clam on his own?" Tarawe asked. "Why did he wait for you to come back for him?"

Ser Iuti's smile faded. She started paddling again. "He claims I can heal any wound I cause him," she said. "And he likes being rescued by me, even when it's not necessary. He has a strange sense of humor, the sea mimic has. Come on, let's get back to the island.''

"I wish using magic wasn't so dangerous," Tarawe said before turning forward again and sliding her paddle back into the water. Ser Iuti grunted. In agreement, or with the effort of paddling, Tarawe couldn't tell.

Kala Atoll was small, little more than a ring of coral sandbars set in the middle of the wide western sea. They had made their temporary camp on the only islet large enough to sustain a few coconut palms and a single, struggling breadfruit tree. The rest, although they stayed above the high water mark in calm weather, were swept too often by storm tides to provide a base for more than hermit crabs and an occasional grabber vine. It was a lonely place, far distant from any of the populated atolls, and until today, Tarawe had felt safe there.

She had lived in fear for many years on Fanape, never speaking out, never daring to try the healing spells her mother allowed her to learn without ever formally teaching her. Most certainly, never trying the spells the visiting warriors showed her. She remembered feeling magic in the air all around her; there had been days when her fingers had itched with the desire to touch it. But the dark presence of the island sorceress and her mother's adamant warnings had always stopped her.

Even on the day Pahulu had stolen her mother's soul and sold her empty body to the Teronin warriors, Tarawe had remained silent—frozen with fear and a fury that she could control only by saying and doing nothing. By then, she had understood that the sorceress was drawn to any use of magical power, that she fed on the souls of those who dared to set any spell within her realm.

It wasn't until Tarawe had left Fanape that she began experimenting with the magic she'd learned from watching her mother and the others. Ser Iuti said it shouldn't be possible for her to use such borrowed spells, but while they didn't always work precisely, Tarawe found that by changing and combining the charms, she could turn most of them to her use. Iuti said that shouldn't be possible either.

Maybe I should stop using other people's magic, Tarawe thought as they approached the island. Maybe I'm not supposed to use it, and that's why things keep going wrong. She glanced down at her hands—her wind hand on the right, her water hand on the left. With the exception of that first wind-calling charm, she hadn't borrowed *that* power. She was certain of that.

The touch of the wind and the water felt like a part of her own body. Even as unpracticed as she was, she could move either the air or the water with little more than a thought. The danger arose when she *didn't* think, Tarawe knew. She had spent most of her time at Kala simply studying the natural movements of the air and ocean currents, so that she could learn to alter them without endangering anyone or anything nearby.

Her mind had once been nearly destroyed by the death thrusts of the many killings she had done, with her own hands and with her storm. She knew she dared not kill again and still hope to survive whole.

When they reached the beach, Tarawe helped Iuti pull the canoe onto the sand and unload their few supplies. Ser Iuti picked up the window bucket holding Ma'eva and a short, thick length of bamboo holding the last of their day's water ration. "Ma'eva's going to be hungry when he wakes," she said.

"Do octopus eat roasted breadfruit?" Tarawe asked.

Iuti laughed. "Ho'oma'eva will eat almost anything, but I think hermit crabs might suit him better than breadfruit right now."

"I'll go find some," Tarawe said. She tied her carry pouch to her waist.

Iuti nodded. "Check the rain pots first. I'll set a fire and open the oven. The food should be well cooked by now."

They had left breadfruit and a large parrot fish baking in an underground pit while they were away. Tarawe's stomach rumbled in anticipation. It had been many hours since she'd eaten, and then it had only been the soft insides of a newly picked drinking coconut. She felt as if she could eat a pair of breadfruit, all on her own.

After carefully stowing the paddles and bailer and tossing away the limp tube vine, Tarawe ran inland to their freshwater catchment roof. The lean-to of woven coconut fronds was set at a shallow slope against a pair of trees so that rainwater could run off it into a row of halved coconut shells.

Tarawe had seen two rain squalls pass near the island that day and was relieved to find that at least one of them had passed directly over it. All of the shells were filled with clean drinking water. Tarawe could easily have nudged the clouds closer, using her wind magic, but she had promised Ser Iuti that she would keep her entire attention on the harvesting of the pearl. The warrior woman also insisted it was best not to use magic unless it was truly needed. "There is always a price to pay," she said. Tarawe thought of the sleek dolphin that had prevented them from harvesting the pearl and suspected Ser Iuti was right.

Tarawe carefully transferred the water into bamboo storage logs. She sealed each length with a wad of breadfruit sap before tying them into a bundle and replacing the empty shells under the catchment roof. She carried the logs, along with a coconut shell still three-quarters full, back to where Iuti was opening their earth oven. The nutty fragrance of roasted breadfruit sped her steps.

"Four!" Iuti said when Tarawe arrived and sat the water logs beside her. "We *did* have some good luck today. Did you drink yet?"

The question surprised Tarawe. Simple courtesy dictated that their water supply be divided by the leader of their small group.

Ser Iuti looked surprised when Tarawe shook her head no. "You make a good traveling companion, girl," she said. She nodded toward the coconut shell. "You drink that. I'll finish what's left from the canoe."

"You weren't able to drink all day," Tarawe said. "You need more. I'll take what was left on the canoe, and there's water still sitting in some of the fallen breadfruit leaves. I'll drink that while I look for crabs. You'll get sick if you don't drink enough tonight."

"You sound just like Ho'ola. Always telling me how to take care of myself." Iuti muttered the remark, but she took the coconut cup from Tarawe's outstretched hand.

"Auntie Ola's a good healer," Tarawe said. "If she were here, she'd make you drink more than that."

Iuti laughed and motioned her away. "Go find some crabs for Ma'eva. We'll open a pair of drinking nuts with our dinner, all right? That would satisfy even Auntie Ola."

"Drink the water," said Tarawe.

Iuti drank the cup dry.

Tarawe returned to the catchment roof to set the cup carefully back into line with the others. Then she scrambled through the brush to the beach. The sun had dropped near the horizon and Tarawe hurried through the growing shadows. She wasn't afraid of the dark; she was just eager to find Ma'eva's dinner quickly so she could get back to her own.

She kept her gaze on the ground as she scuffed through the coarse sand near the brush line. Before she had gone far, she caught sight of slow movement just ahead. She quickened her steps to reach a large hermit crab crawling across the sand. Its shell was almost as big as her own fist. She picked it up carefully. The crab pulled inside as she lifted it, then when she did nothing to startle it further, began crawling back out again. Before its questing claws could reach her fingers, she tapped it with her other hand to frighten it back inside.

"Why are you carrying such a big house, little crab?" she asked, for the shell was much larger than a hermit crab this size warranted. The crab must have just recently moved into the shell. He began crawling out again, as if to answer her question. She laughed and tapped it back inside before stuffing the shell into her woven waist pouch. As she started walking again, the shell shifted. There were scrabbling sounds as the crab tried to scratch its way free.

"I'm sorry to interrupt your dinner," Tarawe said to the next crab she discovered; it was dining on a sliver of decaying sponge shell, "but Ma'eva needs to eat, too." She dropped the surprised crab into the pouch with its cousin.

She found a third and then a fourth crab and was about to pick up a fifth when a splash drew her attention to the water. She turned her look to the sea. There was another splash, closer this time. Something large moved in the shallows. Tarawe moved carefully toward it.

A sudden flash of bright blue-green brought a grin to Tarawe's lips. It was the parrot fish again, the one she'd been trying to catch for days. It was a magnificent creature, fat and shiny, iridescent where it caught the direct rays of the setting sun. It had swum so close to the shore that for a moment Tarawe thought it might beach itself in the shallows. She wished she'd thought to carry her fishing nets the way Iuti Mano always did when she walked along the shore.

But there were other ways to catch a fish. Slowly, so as not to startle the parrot fish, Tarawe began pulling off her shirt. If she could get close enough . . .

She threw herself forward and scooped the fish into her outflung shirt. The fish thrashed in sudden panic. Tarawe stumbled and fell. The parrot fish slipped and slid inside her improvised net.

"I've got you!" Tarawe cried, and then choked as their combined splash filled her opened mouth with seawater. The fish slid upward in her arms. Its head came through one of the shirt sleeves. Their excited looks met.

"What . . . ?" For an instant, the fish's expression looked entirely human. Tarawe almost let it go. Then she remembered that it was tomorrow's breakfast she held and tightened her grip around the creature's belly.

It was a mistake. The parrot fish had slid just far enough forward in her arms so that her squeeze gave it the force it needed to break free. Tarawe's shirt sleeve ripped open and the fish burst away from her in a flash of iridescent blue.

Tarawe sat, stunned, staring after it.

She started to laugh. "You're a tricky one, you are, friend fish." She looked ruefully down at her shirt. At least it had split along the seams, she'd be able to repair it without too much difficulty. A handful of scales, each as big around as a human eye, were tangled in the fabric. Tarawe picked them free and stuffed them into her waist pouch, along with the frantically scrabbling hermit crabs. She stood and tapped the side of the pouch to encourage the crabs back into their shells.

"I'll get you next time," she called after the fish, then blinked in surprise when she saw it swimming back toward her, almost to within her reach.

Tarawe took a step toward it. It veered and raced away. Then it returned again.

"What's wrong with you, fish?" Tarawe said. "Do you *want* to get caught?" That thought made her more cautious. She considered using a bit of her water magic to entice the fish into her hands, but then thought of the flying dolphin again. She left the magic untouched.

The fish swam up to her, then swept away again, staying in water almost too shallow for its size. It swam around the curve of the island that led to the open ocean side. Another hermit crab caught Tarawe's attention. She walked up onto the beach to add it to her collection. She had almost enough now to provide a good meal for Ma'eva.

Tarawe glanced back at the water and was startled to see that the parrot fish had returned yet again. As quickly as she noticed it, the fish darted away, stopped, then turned half back. It was almost as if . . .

"Do you want me to follow you?" Tarawe asked.

The fish raced off once more.

Very cautiously, staying in shallow water, Tarawe followed it around the island to where she could see the open ocean.

"I'll come," she said. "But don't think you can fool me into—"

Tarawe stopped. She caught her breath and froze.

Across the coral shallows, a sailing canoe was just cresting the waves at the outer edge of the reef. Sunlight flashed on the high decorative prow, revealing a fiercely grinning image. It was a war canoe!

⚔ Chapter 3 ⚔

THE canoe swept inward with the lifting swell. It settled with barely a ripple into the shoulder-deep water near the edge of the reef flat. Two men scrambled to drop the sail, while others paddled to carry the outrigger forward and away from the surging danger of the following waves. These sailors were obviously well skilled to have succeeded at so dangerous an approach to the island.

Before Tarawe could step back, or even squat to make herself less visible, someone on the canoe shouted and pointed her way. Paddles flashed again and the canoe sped toward her.

Tarawe turned and ran. She splashed from the water, crossed the shadowed beach at a run, and raced back through the brush. She slipped back into her torn shirt as she ran. Her waist pouch bounced against her hips.

"Ser! Ser Iuti!" she called. "Someone's coming!" She shouted only loud enough to alert Iuti Mano. She didn't want the men on the canoe to hear. "There are warriors on the reef!"

Iuti was already up and strapping a sword onto her back when Tarawe ran into the breadfruit-fragrant clearing. "How many?" the warrior woman demanded. She slid a second sword belt—a death gift from a Teronin she'd killed—around her waist.

"Only one canoe with six men." Tarawe panted, trying to catch her breath. "They brought the canoe right through the waves onto the reef. I've never seen—"

Iuti grabbed up her shield, another war gift. "Did they see you?"

"Aye," Tarawe replied. "They're wearing feathers, Ser, and—"

"Bring Ma'eva!"

Iuti began running back the way Tarawe had come.

Tarawe hurried to the bucket in which Ma'eva lay. He was smaller than before, although not by much. He must have wakened long enough to have changed his form at least a little. He was still gray and mottled, deep in whatever healing sleep Ser Iuti had set. Tarawe scooped up the bucket and ran to join her.

Iuti was standing in the brush that bordered the beach, so still in the deepening shadows that she looked like a shadow herself. A slight movement of her hand was all that alerted Tarawe to her presence. She motioned Tarawe close and they both peered through the leaves to watch the approaching warriors.

The men had stopped their canoe in waist-deep water. Two of them anchored it, fore and aft, with lines tied directly to the coral, while a third rolled the stepped sail into a tight bundle. Two others shifted mats and travel gear onto the beach. By the ease with which they handled the bundle of water logs, Tarawe judged the containers to be empty. All the men wore sheathed weapons and headbands of cowrie shells and bushy gray feathers. *Gull feathers*, Tarawe thought, and that made her angry.

A sixth man sat motionless at the center of the canoe while the others worked. He, too, wore a feathered headdress, but unlike the others, it had long, black feathers stretching high above its bushy base. Tarawe tried to imagine a bird with feathers so long and smooth and silky black, but could not. Like the others, the warrior wore a vest of knotted cord and polished tortoiseshell plates. A necklace of shark's teeth hung around his neck.

Tarawe glanced toward a movement beside her and saw Iuti's hand tighten on the hilt of her sheathed sword. She met the woman's look and Iuti bent toward her.

"Get Ma'eva into the water the first chance you get," Iuti whispered. Tarawe could barely hear her over the soft rumble of the distant surf. The men near the canoe made no sound at all. If Tarawe hadn't seen them coming, they could have come ashore in complete secrecy.

"Shall I take him back to the lagoon?"

Iuti shook her head. "It's too late for that. They'd see you. Then they'd know it's not an ordinary octopus you carry. Just free him as quickly as you can without alerting them." She licked two of her fingertips and ran them along the scars on her cheek—the scars that had been made by the shark god's own teeth—then she held the fingers out to Tarawe.

"Touch them," she said when Tarawe hesitated. "You have to be able to wake Ma'eva from my healing spell or he'll be eaten by the first hungry crab that finds him." She lifted Tarawe's free hand and pressed their fingertips together. "Be sure to use this hand when you lift him from the bucket. Understand?"

Tarawe nodded—not understanding, but knowing what she must do. Ser Iuti straightened again.

"I could set a shield—" Tarawe began.

"No shields," Iuti said quickly. "No war magic at all. These men are as skilled at it as I am. They'd crush you if you tried. And there's the dolphin to consider. We must avoid a fight if we can."

"Who are they, Ser?"

Iuti lifted a hand to silence her. The warrior in the tall headdress had moved. He slid his long, bare legs over the canoe's side and stepped into the water. He lifted a massive war club from the outrigger platform and began walking toward the beach. As he came closer, Tarawe saw that he had three dark lines painted along his right cheek.

Iuti Mano touched the scars on her own cheek, then motioned Tarawe to follow her as she stepped into the open.

"Welcome," she said just as the warrior in the tall headdress stepped onto dry sand. Her voice was soft, but the warriors all heard. They started and reached for their weapons. The one carrying the water logs dropped them with a splash into the shallows.

"Join us on this island and be at peace," Iuti continued.

Tarawe recognized the greeting as one ranking southern warriors often shared. But if these were southerners, why was Ser Iuti so obviously expecting trouble?

All of the men stared at Iuti for a shocked moment. Then suddenly, recognition touched their eyes. The scars on Iuti's face, and her white hair, made her appear very different from the way she had before. Tarawe was surprised these men recognized her as quickly as they did; they must have known her well at some time in the past.

"Let our weapons rest as brothers," Iuti finished.

The man in the tall crest took another step forward. Then he stopped. He looked Iuti up and down slowly before spitting on the sand.

Iuti glanced down at the glistening spittle. "Your manners haven't improved a bit, Kuwala," she said.

He glared and pointed his weapon at her. "You killed Mano Niuhi and you speak to me of *manners*!" His voice was low and gravelly, filled deep with anger. And thirst, Tarawe suspected.

The man who had dropped the empty water logs had already scooped them back up and dropped them into the canoe so they wouldn't float away. The clatter of their landing inside the wooden hull echoed loud across the otherwise quiet reef flat.

"Mano was the one who chose the battle," Iuti said.

"*Mano* was our *brother*!" Kuwala shouted.

. . . and suddenly Tarawe understood. A chill ran along her arms and she gripped Ma'eva's bucket tighter. This powerful warrior was Mano Kuwala, Iuti Mano's eldest brother. Iuti had warned Tarawe that someday she would have to face her family to explain why she had killed the shark god. She would have to face her mother's and her brothers' anger at being deprived of their totem's special protection. But Tarawe was sure Ser Iuti hadn't expected the meeting to come so soon, and certainly not on this deserted isle.

"Mano had swum into the dark side of evil, Kuwala. The deed had to be done," Iuti said.

"You had no *right*!"

"He left me no choice but to destroy him," Iuti said. Her voice was tight, but she made no move to draw her weapons. She would not, Tarawe knew, unless she had to to defend herself.

"He'd have taken my soul with him into the dark if he could have," Ser Iuti said. "He almost did. He had already taken many others."

The other men had gathered close to Kuwala and now Tarawe saw the resemblances among them. They all carried themselves in that same erect way Iuti Mano did. They all had the same dark eyes and hair as black as a moonless night where it showed beneath their gray feathered headbands. Only Kuwala and one other wore the painted sign of the shark god on his cheek.

Those two were brothers, Tarawe decided. The others must be cousins.

"You stole the shark god's power from us ten years ago," Kuwala said. "Now you return to the Western Isles in shame, just as I predicted. Did you really think we wouldn't find you here at Kala? We all knew this was your childhood hideaway."

"I didn't expect you to be looking," said Iuti. "You could have saved yourself a long voyage if you'd waited for me at Kiholo."

Kuwala laughed. "You? Come voluntarily to face your mother and the clan you destroyed? We'd all have been dead of old age before that happened, *sister*."

Iuti Mano sighed. Tarawe glanced up at her, then quickly back at Kuwala and the others.

"What is it you want from me?" Iuti asked quietly.

"I want to kill you," Kuwala muttered.

"Does your anger and jealousy run so deep, brother, that you would give up your own soul by murdering a kinswoman to take your revenge?"

"My anger runs deeper than—"

The second man wearing Mano's marks on his cheek stepped to Kuwala's side. "We've come to take you back to Kiholo," he said. His voice was not so deep as Kuwala's, nor was it so fully filled with hate. But his eyes were dark with anger.

A small smile touched Iuti's lips. "Anele," she said. "It is good to see you well, brother. You've grown into a man since we were last together."

Anele didn't return the smile. "Our mother wishes to hear from your own lips what happened at Fanape," he said. "We all do."

Not all, Tarawe thought with another glance at Kuwala. He only wants to kill her. By the look of the others, Tarawe was certain they would aid him without hesitation if Iuti gave them any excuse to attack. The air was leaden with tension. Something had to be done or the battle Kuwala so obviously wanted would soon begin.

Tarawe glanced down at Ma'eva, swallowed hard, then took a step forward. "We have food prepared," she said, her voice sounding small among all these powerful warriors. "And fresh water. You're welcome to share them with us."

Kuwala's look snapped her way, then returned to Iuti. One side of his mouth turned up into a mocking grin. "We've come to tell you we want you dead, and your servant offers us guest right?"

"The girl isn't my servant," Iuti said. "She's an eastern islander, with *manners*."

The grin slid from Kuwala's face.

"We need water," the man by the canoe said. "It's been two—"

"Shut up, Pali!" Kuwala shouted without turning away from Iuti.

"We *do* need the water," Anele said. "Don't let your anger blind your good sense, Kuwala. Tumaki, go inland to the fire and see what they have. Bring what's useful back here." One of the men hurried away.

Anele turned back to Iuti. "Understand, sister. We do not accept guest right from you. Only from the girl."

Kuwala glared at Tarawe. "What's in that bucket? Bring it here."

Tarawe bit her lip. She glanced up at Iuti, who nodded very slightly, and took another step forward. "It . . . it's an octopus, Ser. I . . ." She glanced back at Iuti again. "I was just coming to wash it in the sea when I saw your canoe. Sh-shall I clean it now?"

Kuwala motioned her forward again so he could look into the bucket. His brows lifted and he glanced back at Iuti. "You haven't forgotten your fishing skills, I see. You always could catch the prizes of the ocean." He pushed Tarawe toward the water. "Clean it. We'll eat it with the breadfruit I smell cooking."

"Go deep enough so the taste of the war canoe doesn't taint it," Iuti said as Tarawe moved into the shallows.

"You never change, do you, Iuti Mano?" Kuwala said. "Always on the watch for some evildoing, when you yourself are the center of evil. Pali, stay with this girl whose name our kinswoman has so carefully not given. Be sure all she does is clean the animal. I want no sly war play going on behind my back."

"She's not a warrior," Iuti said, which was true enough, despite the many warriors Tarawe had killed. "She knows nothing of war magic." That, of course, was a lie. Tarawe carefully kept her eyes on the bucket.

The man called Pali laid his broad sword on the outrigger platform and came to stand in waist-deep water at Tarawe's side. She lifted Ma'eva from the bucket with her right hand, carefully pressing the fingers Iuti had touched into his limp flesh. She bent forward as if to begin cleaning his ink sac.

Pali slid a hand across her lower back.

"You wouldn't mind a little woman's play behind your back, would you, Kuwala?" he said. "This is a sweet morsel, this one is."

A shudder as cold as death ran through Tarawe's body. She stepped away, but Pali followed. His breath smelled of too many days without fresh water. Wake up, Ma'eva, Tarawe pleaded silently. The sleeping sea mimic hung limp in her hand. She left the bucket to drift and began kneading Ma'eva's tentacles as if to soften them for the cookpot.

"Is it true an eastern island woman can grip her man so tight he can't escape until she sets him free?" Pali said. He touched

Tarawe's back again, then before she could move away, snatched the comb from her hair.

"Leave her alone," Iuti said.

Tarawe's thick, dark hair tumbled down her back as she pushed away from Pali. She had rubbed fresh coconut oil into her hair that morning. Its sweet smell lifted around her. Ma'eva, she cried, wake up and escape. I can't let this man touch me. She didn't understand why the man's hands brought her such shuddering horror. She was sure he wouldn't do *more* than just touch her here in this public setting. Not with his kinsmen watching.

Other women have put up with far worse than a man's pawing hands to protect those they love, she thought. But when Pali stepped toward her again, she let Ma'eva loose in the water and stumbled away, gagging in revulsion. He laughed and reached for her again.

"Leave it, Pali!" It was an order this time. Ser Iuti had moved forward onto the beach. For the first time since leaving the bushes, her hands were on the hilts of her weapons.

Pali hesitated. Fear touched his eyes for just an instant. But at a word from Kuwala, he grinned again.

"She offered guest right, cousin," he said, "and I have a powerful hunger. Where better to feed it than here at the edge of the sea, with my family all around to provide protection."

"Surely you can do without your little eastern island consort's services for one night, sister," Kuwala said. "Even a woman of your reputed appetites needs a rest sometimes."

Iuti took another step toward him. Pali's grin widened.

They're using me for bait! Tarawe thought. The other three warriors had fanned out around Iuti. They were trying to make her fight, so they could kill her despite their mother's wishes. Even Anele, who had stopped his brother before, had circled behind Iuti. If a battle started, he would take part.

As Pali reached for Tarawe again, she fumbled in her waist pouch. "Here!" she shouted. "Feed your hunger with this!"

She thrust one of the hermit crabs at Pali's mouth. The crab was still partway out of its shell, and its strong claws snapped closed around Pali's lower lip before he could bat it away. His startled cry and flailing movements as he dislodged the crab brought shrieks of laughter from the other men. Even Kuwala.

Iuti took another step forward.

"Don't!" Tarawe called. "Don't let them trick you, Ser."

"Finish your work, girl," Iuti said without looking away from her brother.

Suddenly Tarawe remembered Ma'eva. She looked quickly around and spotted him lying in an unmoving lump near Pali's sandaled feet. His two shortened tentacles were stretched limply to one side. Tarawe met Pali's look. He was staring at her, wiping blood from his lip with one fisted hand.

"Come get it, little girl," he said. He held his bloodied hand out, palm up. He flexed his fingers. "Come take your dinner from between my legs. I'll show you a *western* man's strength." There was another laugh from the beach.

"For the sake of the gods, Pali," Iuti shouted. "Have you no pride? This is a family matter. Your quarrel is with me. Leave the girl alone."

"What gods, sister?" Kuwala shouted in return. "What gods do you believe in now that you've killed your own?"

Pali lunged at Tarawe. She evaded him by squatting and twisting to one side. She reached for Ma'eva. *Why doesn't he wake up?* she thought. *Why doesn't the magic work?* Pali's unexpected kick caught her in the stomach. She doubled over, retching, still reaching for Ma'eva.

Pali touched her again and she heard Iuti's war cry and the teeth-grating clang of steel striking steel before Pali rolled on top of her and forced her head under the water. When their looks met through the sweet, warm sea, she knew the man was no longer teasing, no longer toying with her to draw Iuti Mano into battle. That job was done. Now he was playing for real. Tarawe retched again.

I cannot! she thought in cold terror. *He must not!*

Her outstretched fingers touched something soft, pliable. A strong, smooth tendril slid around her wrist, attaching itself with sucking tension. Ma'eva! *Go!* she cried silently, squirming in Pali's strong grasp, screaming inside her soul that she could not let this happen. *Hurry. Ho'oma'eva! Swim away!*

Pali laughed and pulled her upright so they could breathe.

"Go, Ma . . . !" Tarawe choked off her cry before she could say Ma'eva's name aloud. If Ser Iuti wouldn't say hers, then she certainly must not use Ma'eva's. "Go," she cried again, and this time she was weeping. Pali tore at her already torn shirt. His hard hand slid through a rent in her trousers and touched her thigh.

Suddenly, nothing mattered to Tarawe but that she stop him. Not the battle sounds from the beach, not the angry shouts and striking metal. Not even Ma'eva's escape. Most certainly not Ser Iuti's warning against using magic in front of these men. Magic was all Tarawe had.

She fisted her left hand and twisted it through the water toward Pali's side. A current of racing water formed around her fist and struck Pali with such force that he was knocked away. He had a tight grip on her hair, however, and he pulled her with him across the rough coral. What was left of Tarawe's shirt shredded as they rolled over and over across the razor-sharp coral. She tasted blood in the roiling water. Pali's and her own.

Still he didn't let her go. She brought the water swirling around and between them again. He coughed and choked, as did Tarawe herself.

"End it, cousin! End it now or Kuwala dies."

Iuti's hard voice came from only an arm's length away. "Let her go!"

Pali jerked and lifted his focused attention from Tarawe. She thrust herself away from him. Ser Iuti stood in waist-deep water with Kuwala firmly in her hold. His war club was gone from his hands and one of Iuti's swords was held tight across his throat.

"Get back to the beach," Iuti ordered. It took an instant for Tarawe to understand that Ser Iuti was talking to Pali. He pulled a long, thin knife from his belt.

Suddenly Ma'eva slid from Tarawe's right hand. She whispered, "Go, you're in great danger here," into her left palm and quickly washed the message into the sea. She was afraid for a moment that Ma'eva might change back to his human form, or some other, to try to help. But then he stiffened and was suddenly engulfed in an inky black cloud. He squirted away, right between Pali's legs. Pali stabbed his knife into the water, but succeeded only in unbalancing himself. Tarawe aided his stumble with another quick shift of currents and he splashed to his knees.

"Kill her!" Kuwala cried. He struggled, but could not break Iuti's hold without forcing her blade deeper into his throat. His right hand hung limp and he pawed at Iuti ineffectively with his left. The other men, all but Pali, had backed away. "Kill her!" Kuwala shouted again.

"If anyone dies tonight, it will be you, brother," Iuti said. "Anele, if you treasure your brother's life, get everyone back to the beach. Now. My patience is gone."

"Kill her!" Kuwala screamed. "If she murders me before she dies, she'll lose her soul! *Kill her, Anele!*"

"Cut the canoe loose," Iuti snapped, and this time Tarawe knew exactly whom she meant. She stumbled toward the anchored war canoe. "Bring it close behind me. Quickly," Iuti said.

"No!" Kuwala cried.

Anele took a step into the water. "I won't allow you to leave," he said. "I won't allow you to run away from this."

"Then our brother's blood will be on your hands," Iuti replied. Tarawe sawed at the fore anchor rope with Pali's sword.

"You said you came here to bring me back to Kiholo," Iuti said. "You said that was our mother's wish. If you force me to kill Kuwala here tonight, his death will rest as heavily on you as it does on me. It is you who will have to face our mother with the news."

Anele hesitated.

The anchor rope split and the canoe swung toward Iuti. Tarawe stopped it with a flick of her fingers. She scrambled to the other end of the hull to release the second anchor line.

"She'll never kill me," Kuwala shouted. "Can't you see that? She's afraid. You must *make* her—"

Iuti shifted her sword in a quick move and cracked its hilt along the side of Kuwala's head. He slumped in her arms, dazed, unable to move or speak. Before Anele or the others could reach her, she had the sharp edge of the blade back at Kuwala's throat.

"The canoe is free, Ser," Tarawe said just loud enough for Iuti to hear. She held the hull steady just behind where Iuti was standing.

"Do you have the pole?" Iuti asked.

"Aye," Tarawe replied. She was holding the long straight length of mangrove wood braced against the reef as if she were using it to keep the canoe in place. There was no need to reveal more of her water magic than she already had. Pali had backed away when she moved the canoe, but had not yet returned to the beach as Iuti ordered. He kept glancing down at the now-still water. He glared at her.

"The center seat is just behind you," Tarawe said to Iuti. She allowed the gunwale of the canoe to brush lightly against the backs of Iuti's legs. Carefully, still holding her blade to Kuwala's throat, Iuti stepped backward into the hull.

"I won't let you take him with you," Anele said, moving forward again. Kuwala stirred in Iuti's arms. "I won't let you steal away another of my brothers, only to kill him in the end."

"The last thing I would steal from you is this fool brother of ours, Anele," Iuti said. "Here, take him!"

She shoved Kuwala forward. As he fell away from her, she scrambled aboard the canoe and grabbed up a paddle. She thrust deeply over the side, shoving its tip against the hard coral. At the same instant, Tarawe pushed her pole against the sea floor with all her strength. The canoe surged toward deeper water.

Kuwala woke as the shock of water struck his face. He spluttered and flailed to his feet. The long feathers of his headdress hung limp and sodden. "Stop her!" he screamed.

The other warriors raced past him, chasing the canoe. Anele flung his sword.

Ser Iuti ducked away. The blade struck the outrigger beside her and flipped inside the hull. Iuti gasped, and a second later, Tarawe tasted the sharp tang of freshly spilled blood on the air.

"Quickly, girl," Iuti said. "Take us beyond the breakers before they reach us." She caught her breath and leaned forward. She jerked and Tarawe heard the dull thunk of metal against the bottom of the hull. Then Iuti gripped her paddle again and thrust it back into the water. She moved quickly, but her strokes carried little of the power they always had before.

Tarawe glanced back. Pali was only a short distance behind, his knife raised to throw. Tarawe moved her left hand, calling up a quick current. Pali's feet were swept from under him. His curse was cut off as the water swallowed him. Tarawe moved her hand again, causing another swift current to form, this time under the canoe. They surged forward at doubled speed.

"You won't get away!" Anele called after them. "We'll find you, Iuti Mano!"

"You will die!" Kuwala roared.

They had almost reached the breaking surf. Tarawe braced herself to turn the incoming swells so the canoe could pass through safely. The crash of the swells breaking against the reef's edge all but drowned out the shouts and curses of the men giving chase.

The tumbling waves split easily at Tarawe's silent order. They spread just wide enough apart for the canoe to pass through.

"You are already dead, sister!"

Kuwala's deep voice lifted over the crashing surf.

"You murdered our god, Iuti Mano! You destroyed our clan. You are the last of Mano's line! You are the *last*! Do you understand me?"

The paddle slipped from Iuti Mano's hands. It tumbled away

in the surf as she bent forward, hugging her knees. "By the very gods," Tarawe heard her moan just as they slid through the last of the surf onto the calm, open sea.

Behind them, the water slammed back across their path, swallowing all sound but its own.

⁂ Chapter 4 ⁂

IUTI held her breath and pressed her hands over the long, deep cut Anele's tumbling sword had left in her right calf. She tried to focus on a healing spell, to stop the bleeding, to control the pain. Kuwala's last cry still screamed through her mind.

You are the last of Mano's line!

"How can he hate me so much?" she whispered. The blood ran hot and heavy across her fingers.

"Ser. Ser Iuti."

Iuti felt the slight dip and bob of the canoe as Tarawe crawled forward. She must have called up one of the deep-water currents to keep them moving swiftly because neither of them was paddling now, and the sail was still furled. The sail, Iuti thought. We must put up the sail.

"We're free of the reef, Ser." Tarawe climbed onto the outrigger beside Iuti. "What shall . . . ? Ser, what's wrong?"

She stopped suddenly.

An instant later, Iuti felt Tarawe's small, strong hands tugging at her own.

"Let me see," Tarawe snapped when Iuti didn't immediately remove her hands from the wound. "I can't help if I don't know what's wrong."

"You're sounding like Ho'ola again," Iuti said, and blessed Tarawe for removing Kuwala's voice from the forefront of her mind. She tried again to focus on what must be done.

"Ayiii," Tarawe said softly as Iuti lifted her hands.

"We must set the sail," Iuti said. She started to get up but Tarawe pushed her back.

"My current is carrying us faster than any sail could," Tarawe said. "We need to fix this—"

"We need the sail, Tarawe," Iuti insisted. The girl's face

31

went out of focus. Iuti squeezed her eyes closed and said a word to steady herself. "If they see it set, they won't know we're using magical means to escape."

"They already know," Tarawe said. She held the gash on Iuti's leg closed with one hand. With the other, she yanked off the shreds of her shirt and began wrapping them tightly around Iuti's calf. "I moved the canoe very fast over the reef, and they saw us pass through the surf."

"It was almost dark and they know my reputation for strength," Iuti said. "You pretended to be poling the whole time, didn't you?"

"Aye, but—"

"It all happened very fast. They won't even be thinking of magic. Set the sail, Tarawe."

"Your leg—"

"Did you hear what Kuwala said, there at the last?" Iuti said. "He would never have called me the last of Mano's line unless . . ." The air around her turned dark and Iuti leaned forward again to hang her head between her knees. "Just do it, Tarawe," she whispered.

Tarawe's hands left her leg. The outrigger dipped as the girl moved to where she could reach the furled sail. A few moments later, the canoe dipped again as Tarawe braced the mast at the bow and lifted it into place. The outrigger lifted as the great triangular sail swung wide on the opposite side of the hull.

"Shall I call a wind?" Tarawe said.

"Aye, but only enough to make it look like we're moving naturally with the trade winds," Iuti said. "When we're fully out of sight of the atoll, call up your currents again and move us as fast as you can."

"Which way?" Tarawe asked. "Ser Iuti?"

"I hear," Iuti whispered. It was all she could manage. She needed to set a deep healing spell quickly or she was going to bleed to death right here in her brothers' canoe. "Take us southwest with the trades for as long as they can see us. The Akana archipelago is that way; they'll think we went there."

"And then?" Tarawe said.

"Then?"

"Ser Iuti. Wake up. Which way should I turn the canoe after Kala is out of sight?"

Iuti pulled in a ragged breath, wondering why this wound, serious though it was, should cause her such exquisite pain. Because it was Anele's blade that struck me, she thought. My favorite brother. The only one who ever truly loved me. The only one who wished me well when Mano Niuhi and I left for the Teronin Wars.

"West," she forced out. "Due west. And Tarawe, throw the swords overboard. Anele's and Pali's. Do it before we change course."

"Shouldn't we keep them in case—"

"Those men are both from my family. Do you want to chance carrying another of Mano's blades?" Iuti asked.

Tarawe dropped the two swords overboard without another word. She washed her hands thoroughly in the sea before returning to face Iuti in the canoe's narrow hull. "Do you have a healing spell that can deal with this?" she asked.

That made Iuti smile. She'd once asked the same question of Tarawe. "Aye. I can deal with it, though it would be a kindness if you would help me clean it."

Tarawe immediately began stripping the rags from Iuti's leg. The bleeding began anew. "Hold it closed," Tarawe snapped. Iuti did as best she could while the girl washed the rags in the sea. Before retying them, Tarawe blew softly across her left palm and pressed it against the wound. She met Iuti's look.

"It's not really magic," she said. "It's just for good luck. One of the warriors who came to Fanape showed me how to do it."

Iuti nodded and whispered a strong, very real, healing spell of her own. Her eyelids grew suddenly heavy. "I'm sorry you missed your dinner," she said. "The breadfruit was roasted to perfection."

Tarawe remained silent.

"Don't let them catch us," Iuti whispered. Tarawe was still tying the last of the cloth strips into place as Iuti slid into deep, healing sleep.

Iuti woke to bright light. Sunlight, she thought without opening her eyes, although it didn't feel as if she were lying directly in it. It took her a moment to remember where she was. She opened her eyes and tried to sit up.

Her head bumped something soft. A mat, she saw with some confusion. Then she realized it was the sail, or a piece of it. She was lying on the outrigger platform. Tarawe must have braced the stiff folds of woven pandanus above her to provide shade. Out the two open sides, she could see sunlight glaring off a great expanse of open water.

Tarawe's face appeared around the edge of the makeshift hut. There were dark circles under her eyes. "You're awake," she said. Tension drained from her expression.

Iuti rubbed her hands over her face, forcing the last of the sleep away. "Almost," she said. "Where are we? Is everything safe?"

"Everything's fine," Tarawe said. "Except I'm hungry. I don't know where we are."

She crawled into the shade beside Iuti. "I'm sorry I had to cut the sail. I didn't have anything else to cover you with and I didn't want to move the clouds around more than I had to."

"The sail doesn't matter," Iuti said. "We can mend it if need be. But a few hours of sun wouldn't have hurt . . ."

Something in Tarawe's expression stopped her. "How long did I sleep?"

"Almost three days, Ser."

"Three days!"

Iuti leaned forward and lifted the bandage from her leg. There was only a light strip of cloth, a piece of her own shirt, spread loosely over her calf. The gaping wound was gone. Only a vivid red scar remained. From the pinpoint marks bordering it, Iuti realized the gash must have been sewn closed for a time. She looked up at Tarawe.

"It wasn't healing properly, Ser," Tarawe said. "Auntie Ola told me once that a deep wound has to be closed from the outside sometimes, before the healing spells can begin closing it from the inside. So I sewed it."

Iuti ran her fingers along the scar. It tingled, sensitive and still very sore. "How?" she asked. What could there possibly have been on this, her brothers' canoe to give the girl the means to do such a thing?

"I carved a needle from a hermit crab's shell that I had in my pouch," Tarawe said. "I used one of your swords. I think I dulled it a little."

"Where did you get thread? That from our clothing wouldn't have been strong enough."

This time Tarawe hesitated slightly. "I used one of the braided strands from your necklace, Ser. I was going to use my own hair, but . . . Well, I thought since Kunan was a warrior, his hair might be stronger than mine—for sewing a war wound, I mean. I'm sorry I had to cut it, Ser, and for using your sword without asking."

She reached under a pile of matting beside Iuti and pulled out a small handful of black threads. "I only needed one strand, and I saved the stitches after I took them out." She handed the small bits of braided hair to Iuti.

Iuti stared at the remnants of Kunan's hair, then back at Tarawe. What did I ever do to deserve this girl? she wondered. There was no hair of greater strength in all the world than that of Kunan Iliawe, and there was likely no wound but her own that it could have healed so quickly and well.

"I am most grateful for your care, little sister," she said. "Your presence is a gift from the gods. I think even Kunan must be smiling from somewhere in the land of warrior's dreams."

Tarawe's grin held only a touch of shyness. Her pride in having done the right thing was refreshingly evident. Iuti tucked the bits of hair into her trousers pocket.

"We have water," Tarawe said. "The wind brought us rain this morning without even being called. I caught it in the sail and filled the water logs Pali left in the hull. We don't have any food, though. There was some preserved breadfruit in the hull, and some pounded taro wrapped in ti leaves. But they were blood-soaked and going rancid by the time I found them. I threw them overboard."

She brushed a hair from her face. "I caught a small butterfish yesterday when it swam near the canoe. I scooped it up with my water magic. I hope that was all right. I was really hungry and it was the first fish to come near. I think the current is keeping them away."

Iuti stretched, taking care not to jar her injured leg. "Just let me wake the rest of my body and then I'll see if I can call a couple of flying fish or maybe a good, fat tuna near. Here, help me to the side. My bladder is about to burst."

She fumbled with her trousers. "Mano's teeth," she muttered. "It's times like these when I wish I were a sea mimic." Tarawe giggled and turned politely away while Iuti peed into the sea.

When Iuti was finished, she had to lie down again to stop the spinning in her mind.

"You lost a lot of blood," Tarawe said. The worry lines had returned to her face.

"I'll just rest a minute," Iuti replied, panting to catch her breath after the simple movement. For ten years, the shark god Mano Niuhi had helped her absorb any pain or weakness caused by the injuries she took in battle. She had forgotten how difficult it could be to suffer them on her own.

"Here's water, Ser." Tarawe was back at her side. Iuti drank gratefully, directly from the water log. The rainwater tasted slightly stale, no doubt because the logs had been empty for some time before Tarawe refilled them. Or maybe because her own mouth tasted so foul. She scooped up a handful of seawater, rinsed it through her teeth, then drank again from the log.

Then she lay back to rest again.

"Maybe you'd better go back to sleep," Tarawe said.

Iuti shook her head. "Not yet. We both need to eat first. I'd prefer something other than raw fish right now, but it'll have to do. I'll call something close and then you bring it aboard as you did before." Tarawe helped her to sit upright again.

"Take down the shade," Iuti said. Tarawe had the stiff mat down and folded in an instant. The pandanus weave carried one of her mother's designs. Iuti frowned at that. It meant that her mother had, indeed, sent her brothers to find her.

"Do *you* know where we are?" Tarawe asked. She stood in the hull now, at the canoe's center.

Iuti lifted her gaze from the mat and stared out at the empty ocean. There was nothing but mirror-smooth swells visible in any direction. The only clouds were small and distant. "We must be far out onto the Empty Sea," she said. "I won't know for sure until I can see the stars. Have we been traveling west all this time?"

"Aye, I think so," replied Tarawe. "It was hard to tell at midday and sometimes I fell asleep, but I think the current is moving in a straight line."

Iuti looked around again. "I understand now why they call it the Empty Sea. I wonder how far it stretches."

Tarawe looked startled. "Haven't you been this way before?"

Iuti laughed. "No one comes this way, girl. No one who wants to live. There's nothing out here."

"Then why . . . Oh, you think they won't follow us here."

Iuti nodded. "By the time they've searched the Akana archipelago, the taste of your magic will be gone from our path, and even if they do decide we've come this way, they'll have no way to follow us."

"Are we going to stay out here forever?" Tarawe asked.

"Not forever," Iuti said. "Just until my leg heals. By then, we'll think of somewhere safe to go."

Tarawe looked up and around. The fingers of her right hand twitched and a fresh breeze brushed across Iuti's face. "I wouldn't mind staying," Tarawe said. "I like it here. I could practice my wind and water magic without anyone getting hurt."

"There'll be plenty of time for that. Right now, we just need to call our dinner." Iuti frowned suddenly and leaned forward. "Is that a piece of the sail you're wearing?"

Tarawe looked down at the band of woven matting she had wrapped around her waist. "My shirt was too torn to fix, so I used it for bandages and to patch my pants. This piece of sail was scratchy at first, but it's soft now. If I had some shells I could make it look nicer."

Iuti smiled. "It looks fine, Tarawe. You're very skilled at keeping yourself well dressed."

"I'm hungry," Tarawe reminded her.

Iuti moved to the edge of the deck. She whispered a simple beckoning spell into her palm. Glancing up, she caught a flicker of disappointment slide across Tarawe's face.

"Oh, all right, girl," Iuti said. "I guess you deserve to hear it, and it's a good spell for you to know. You're so much a sea person, it'll probably work better for you than it does for me."

Tarawe grinned.

Iuti said the spell again, aloud this time so Tarawe could hear, then washed the call into the sea.

"How long will it take?" Tarawe peered over the side of the canoe.

"Not long. Watch in front of the outrigger platform, that's where the fish will come." Iuti's exhaustion caught up with her again. She lay back, closing her eyes.

"Are you all right?" Tarawe said immediately. "Shall I—"

"Just keep watch," Iuti said. She listened to the rush of water along the side of the hull, to the brush of the outrigger float skimming across the tops of the swells. The air was dead still except for the light wind caused by their own movement. The swells were wide and shallow. Barely a ripple disturbed their smooth ride.

Doldrums, she thought. Without Tarawe's magic, they wouldn't be moving at all. Her brothers would need a full crew of paddlers to follow her across such a calm sea, and they couldn't keep moving long without rain to bring fresh water. They would also need someone aboard who could call food to them directly from the sea, and only the women in their clan carried that magic. Iuti felt almost safe.

"Something's coming," Tarawe said. She kept her voice low

so as not to scare away their potential catch. "Oh, good, it's a sugarfish. A big one. No, two! Shall I catch them both?"

Iuti lifted her head to watch. "We only need one, but if they're swimming together this far from land they must be a mated pair. One can't live without the other. It would be kinder to take them both."

"I'd rather just let them go, then," Tarawe said. "We can wait—"

"They both answered my call, Tarawe. We need to eat, so take them both. What we don't use, we'll give back to the sea. Someone will make use of it."

There was a flash of movement under the canoe. Iuti peered through the cracks in the decking to study the sugarfish pair. They were fine, fat fish, shining silver with bright yellow eyes. "Honor to you, fine fish," she murmured. "Thank you for answering my call. I apologize for taking your lives."

Tarawe moved her left hand. She cupped it palm up and raised it gently. Below them, just ahead of the outrigger platform, the two sugarfish lifted near the surface of the water. Tarawe snapped her hand shut and scooped it upward. The water surrounding the fish followed her movement and lifted into a sudden wave, higher than the outrigger platform. The swiftly moving canoe sliced through the wave. Tarawe opened her hand and the wave collapsed and drained quickly away through the cracks, leaving the sugarfish slapping and flailing on the slick bamboo deck.

Tarawe reached for them both. One slipped from her grasp, but Iuti stopped it from falling back into the sea. She brought it to her mouth and bit it hard just behind its eyes. It immediately went limp in her hands. Tarawe did the same with the second fish, although she hesitated for just an instant before biting down. She shuddered slightly as she laid the dead fish beside its mate.

"Does the killing disturb you?" Iuti asked.

Tarawe glanced down at the fish. She rubbed her hands together, looked at her palms, then bent to rinse them in the sea. "I know it shouldn't," she said, "not when I'm only doing it for food, but . . ."

Tarawe met Iuti's look again. "I'm afraid to kill, Ser. I'm afraid if I do it just one more time, I'll slide over the edge into darkness. Killing has that taste to me now. I don't want to go to that dark place, Ser."

Iuti nodded. She found it hard to hold Tarawe's open, honest look. The healer Ho'ola had trained Tarawe as best she could to withstand the painful thrusts caused by violent death, but the girl had never learned to control them entirely on her own. She was a child who had never been meant to kill other living creatures, yet she had already been forced to kill more than many warriors did in a lifetime. Iuti licked the salty taste of the fish from her lips.

"I'll clean them," Tarawe said. After politely asking Iuti's leave, she used one of the swords to slit open the largest fish's belly. She scooped out the soft innards and dumped them back into the sea.

A gift, Iuti sang silently to the calm ocean, *in return for a kindness given.*

With quick, smooth movements, Tarawe sliced thick fillets from the fish's sides. She handed the first to Iuti. "It would be better with limefruit," she said.

"I'm so hungry right now, it makes no difference," Iuti replied. She bit into the crisp, cool flesh. It was sweet and watery, and as soon as she swallowed, her empty stomach threatened to send it right back to the sea. She groaned and rolled forward, clutching her stomach. Only with the strongest effort of will did she force the fish to stay down.

"The second bite is easier," Tarawe said. Iuti glanced up to see Tarawe stuffing a large bite into her mouth. "I spit half of that butterfish back into the water yesterday before I finally got some to stay down. But afterward I felt better. You just have to get enough in to get your stomach working again."

Iuti's unexpected irritation at the girl's obvious enjoyment of her meal faded. She tugged off another bite of fish and forced it down. It took a long while before she began to feel comfortable.

It was almost sundown when she pushed the last of her meal toward Tarawe. "Give the rest back to the sea," she said. "It'll go bad if we try to keep it for later. I know there are creatures in the ocean that eat foul, rancid things, but I prefer to feed those who eat their meat fresh."

Tarawe, who had eaten more than half of the larger fish on her own, cheerfully scooped the remaining meat over the side. She yelped in surprise as something black and shiny swept up from the depths to snatch it away. "What was that?" she cried.

"I don't know," Iuti said. "But it certainly has a good nose. We'd best not trail our fingers and toes in the water near here."

Tarawe moved back from the edge.

"Ser Iuti?" she said after a while.

"Aye," Iuti murmured. She felt stronger now, although her

leg still pulsed with pain. She would have to return to a healing sleep again soon or this wound would cripple her for weeks.

"Why did your brother say that to you?" Tarawe asked. "About you being the last of Mano's line?"

A pain much deeper than that in her leg slid back into Iuti's consciousness. "It was Kuwala's way of telling me that my cousin Nelina is dead, or has had some accident that will prevent her having more children. It was his way of saying that he has sworn to kill me so that Mano's line can't go on past this generation."

Tarawe's eyes widened in surprise.

"My mother had no other daughters but me," Iuti said, "and with the exception of Nelina, Mother's sisters had only sons. Neli herself has produced only boys, six of them when I last counted. She was the one I was going to take you to, back before you became so involved in the Teronin War."

"The one with the taro farm?" Tarawe asked. Her nose wrinkled with distaste.

Iuti nodded. "Kuwala has daughters, as do others of my brothers and male cousins, but they belong to their mothers' clans." Iuti stared out at the Empty Sea. "Kuwala may well be right. I may be the last."

"You're not," Tarawe said after a long moment.

Iuti's look lifted back to her. "What?"

Tarawe had let down her hair. She sat stroking the long, black strands with her fingers. She was staring at Iuti.

"What did you say?" Iuti asked.

Tarawe's strong fingers slid the length of a single strand of hair. "You're not the last of your line, Ser." She let go of the hair. "While you were sleeping, I . . . Well, your healing spell wasn't working, so I decided to try one I once saw my mother use. But she always said a child-testing spell over the women she treated, to be sure she didn't harm any baby that might be growing inside. I . . . I'd never used any of my mother's strong spells before, except on myself, so I thought I should . . . Well . . ."

"What, Tarawe?"

Tarawe gave an apologetic shrug. "You're pregnant, Ser."

Iuti caught her breath.

"But I'm sure your baby is all right. I didn't want to make a mistake and hurt it, so I didn't use Mama's healing spell after all. I just sewed up your leg from the outside."

A child?

"Tarawe, are you sure?"

A look that reminded her of Ho'ola touched Tarawe's eyes. "If you didn't want one, Ser, you shouldn't have done that with Ho'oma'eva so many times. Especially in the water where the seeds could get mixed up so well."

Ho'oma'eva's *child*?

Iuti laid a hand on her stomach. It was hard and flat, the strong muscular stomach of a warrior. "By the very gods!" she breathed.

"Ser? I'm sorry if . . ."

Iuti began to laugh.

"Honor to you, little sister," she said. "You have given me a gift beyond price."

"*I* didn't give you that baby," Tarawe said.

That made Iuti laugh again. "I know where the baby came from, Tarawe. Your gift is the news of its presence."

Abruptly Iuti felt hot tears slide down her cheeks. She caught her breath in a sob, in tearing grief for her cousin, and for her mother and her brothers who carried so much hate. As she wiped the tears away, her fingers traced the ridges of Mano's scars. That grief, too, still lay like a raw wound along the side of her soul.

Her hands slid back to her belly. Ho'oma'eva's child!

"He will be so pleased," she said softly.

"Ma'eva got away safely," Tarawe said, as if following her thought.

Iuti nodded. "I saw. I apologize for my kinsmen, Tarawe. I never imagined they would use you that way."

Tarawe shifted on her seat. She paled and her look dropped to her hands.

"What's wrong?" Iuti said

A shudder moved over Tarawe's body.

"Is it the killing sickness?" Iuti said. She moved quickly to Tarawe's side. Too quickly. She gasped as her right leg bumped the raised gunwale. Tarawe lifted her look, tight with concern again.

Iuti waved her away from her leg. It wasn't reinjured, only made more painful. "What's wrong, Tarawe?" she said again.

Tarawe blew out a long breath. "Something happened when that man touched me. Something bad. I don't know what." She stared down at her fisted hands and shivered again. "I don't want to talk about him. I don't even want to *think* about him."

Iuti watched her for a moment, then nodded and returned to

her former place on the deck. There would be time enough to talk about Pali later. For now, Tarawe was safe from his touch, or any other's save Iuti's own.

"You should go back to sleep," Tarawe said after a while.

Iuti shaded her eyes with her arm and listened to the canoe's smooth passage through the water. "I'll sleep again after the stars come out," she replied. A small splash drew her attention and she turned to glance through the cracks in the deck.

Abruptly all her tension returned. Something long and dark was moving under the canoe.

⚙ Chapter 5 ⚙

TARAWE heard the splash, too. When she saw Iuti tense, she immediately joined her in peering over the side. Something was moving in the shadow under the hull. I hope it's not that thing that took the sugarfish, she thought. She kept her fingers well away from the edge.

She felt a faint vibration through the soles of her bare feet as whatever was beneath them slid along the outside of the hull. She lifted her look to Iuti's, but the warrior woman's full attention was on the sea. There was a flicker of light under the water and Iuti tensed again, but then quickly moved closer to the edge of the outrigger deck. She winced as the move jarred her injured leg.

"Stay back!" Tarawe whispered. She pulled Iuti's sword from the weapons rack inside the hull, but Iuti waved it away.

"What is it?" Tarawe asked.

"Wait," Iuti replied very softly. She leaned forward again just as a long, dark tendril slid from the shadows. It crept upward along the hull to the surface, then pulled away from the canoe with a wet, sucking sound. It stretched toward Iuti.

A squid! Tarawe thought. *Or an octopus!* She had never seen one so large. To her horror, Iuti Mano reached out to touch the questing tentacle. It was thick and deep red, lined with fat, round suckers. There was a pale-pink place at the tip. The tentacle twined around Iuti's hand and pulled, and if Tarawe hadn't been so startled by Iuti's willingness to touch the thing, she would have sliced the tentacle right off.

Suddenly Iuti laughed. "Don't pull me in, Ma'eva."

Ma'eva! Tarawe stared at the gigantic creature that suddenly separated from the shadows. More tentacles slid up the side of

43

the hull and along the outrigger's edge. Tarawe leaned back farther so they wouldn't touch her.

Iuti tugged on the tentacle still wrapped firmly around her hand. "Come up, friend mimic," she called.

The tentacle flickered. A second writhed close and nestled beside it, then the two began melting into one. Rusty red faded to ruddy brown and the boneless flesh wavered and took the form of a human hand and arm. It tugged at Iuti again.

"Don't pull me in," Iuti said again. "I can't swim right now."

Instantly the hand released its hold and the rest of the giant octopus flickered and re-formed into the shape of a man. Ma'eva's dark, handsome face lifted from the water. "Are you injured, friend Iuti?" he asked. His eyes were wide with concern. He'd made them blue this time, the same color as the sea. Otherwise, his human form looked the same as the one he'd used before—broad shoulders and narrow waist, the muscled thighs of a strong swimmer. He gripped the edge of the outrigger to keep from being left behind by the swiftly moving canoe.

"Only a little," Iuti replied. "Come aboard, good friend, so we can talk. No, I can't help you just now. Tarawe, can you . . . ?"

Before Tarawe could extend her hand, Ho'oma'eva lifted himself onto the outrigger deck as lightly as if he weighed nothing at all. Tarawe wished she understood why Ma'eva asked Iuti to help him so much when he didn't need help at all. Seawater glistened in his ebony hair and on his dark skin. He ran a quick finger along Iuti's cheek, then sucked in his breath when he caught sight of her leg.

"Ayiii," he said softly. "What happened to you, Iuti Mano? Did those big males at Kala—"

Suddenly he slid a hand across Iuti's stomach. "Is our child safe?" he asked.

Iuti's eyes opened wide. "How do you know about the child?"

Ma'eva blinked. "Its sweet taste has been on you since the day it was formed."

Iuti stared at him. "When did it happen? How old is it now?"

"Three full moons," he said proudly, "and a quarter more. It happened on the voyage between Fanape and Kala."

"How could you not know for so long, Ser?" Tarawe asked. "Even I wondered when you didn't bleed with the moons."

Iuti frowned. "I'm a warrior. My body is lean and hard. My

blood times often come many months apart.'' She looked thoughtful for a moment. ''All the while Mano Niuhi was with me, I chewed ilimi leaves to be sure no friendly companion would gift me with a child I couldn't carry, or care for, while I was fighting in the wars. I . . .'' Her look turned back to Ma'eva.

''I never thought it would happen so soon.''

Ma'eva pulled back his shoulders so that his broad chest appeared broader. Or perhaps he actually made it so. He grinned and ran his hands along his naked thighs. ''Sea mimics make good lovers. You said so yourself, Iuti Mano.''

Tarawe shivered.

Iuti Mano shook her head and motioned toward the sword Tarawe still held. ''You'd better put that away, Tarawe.''

Tarawe looked down in surprise. She'd forgotten all about the sword. She slid it back into the weapons rack.

''Would you really have killed me, Storm Caller?'' Ma'eva asked.

''I didn't recognize you until you started to change,'' Tarawe replied. ''You were awfully big. Much bigger than when you were in the bucket.''

''You need to be careful, Ma'eva,'' Iuti said. ''Even when you know it's us.''

''I had to be big to come this far into the Empty Sea,'' he said. ''It isn't so empty under the surface. If I'd stayed small, I'd have been eaten along the way.'' He looked around the deck and into the hull. ''Do you have anything to eat on this canoe?''

''If we'd known you were coming, we could have saved the extra sugarfish we caught this afternoon,'' Iuti said.

''You threw away a sugarfish?'' Ma'eva said plaintively.

''Something big and black and shiny came up and ate it,'' Tarawe said. ''I have two hermit crabs left, though. I caught them for you on Kala. They're still alive.''

Ma'eva looked hopeful for a moment, then frowned again. ''I think I'll wait. Hermit crabs don't taste very good to my human tongue.''

''Did your tentacles heal, Ma'eva?'' Iuti asked. She looked tired and pale, and Tarawe knew she needed to stop talking soon and return to her healing sleep. If she became sick again, Tarawe wasn't sure she could save her. With the baby there, she'd be afraid to try any more spells, and there were no herbs or medicines here on the canoe.

Ma'eva showed them a finger on his right hand, and a toe on his left, both with baby pink tips and new nails just forming.

Iuti kissed them both. Then she rested her head on Ma'eva's shoulder.

"You need to sleep again, Ser," Tarawe said.

"Aye," the warrior woman said. "And so do you. Ma'eva, are you so hungry you need to hunt now, or can you sit watch for a time?"

"Will the sleep make your leg heal faster?" he asked.

She nodded.

"I'll watch all night," Ma'eva said.

Iuti smiled. She glanced at Tarawe. "I'd like to wait until the stars come out, so I can tell where we are, but—"

"Go to sleep," Ma'eva and Tarawe said at the same time.

Ho'oma'eva grinned. Tarawe began to relax. Ma'eva would make sure Ser Iuti stayed asleep if anyone could. Tarawe was as tired as she could ever remember being. She'd only napped a few times during the long voyage, afraid that if she fell too deeply asleep, her current might slow, or something bad might happen before she could wake.

Ma'eva changed places with Tarawe so she could stretch out on the outrigger deck beside Ser Iuti. "The hermit crabs are in the pouch, there in the hull," she said.

He flicked his eyebrows in a quick affirmative. No doubt as soon as she and Iuti were asleep, he would revert at least in part to some sea creature who could enjoy the hermit's taste. Tarawe bade him a fair night and turned so that she faced Ser Iuti. The woman was lying on her right side, with her injured leg braced against one of the outrigger struts. Iuti whispered something Tarawe couldn't hear and instantly closed her eyes. She smiled slightly and slid a hand across her belly. Then she began snoring softly.

The light behind Tarawe's closed eyelids told her it was morning. She must have slept the whole night through. She felt heavy and languid, well rested—and hungry! Poor Ma'eva, she thought. She hoped he had gone ahead and eaten the hermit crabs the night before.

Ma'eva didn't sound distressed. He was singing merrily, something about a sailor making port in many lands. Judging from the sailor's many amorous exploits, Tarawe suspected Ma'eva had learned the song from the milimilis. The Lowtown whores had spent a lot of time whispering and giggling with the sea mimic while he was recuperating from the battle on Fanape.

They'd always stopped talking, but laughed harder, when Tarawe came near.

The words of Ma'eva's song, and the clever way he sang it, made Tarawe want to smile, but the sailor's groping adventures made her skin turn cold. They reminded her of Pali.

What's wrong with me? she wondered.

She knew what Pali had done—what he had intended to do—was not the same as the playful mating games of Ma'eva's sailor. Certainly it was different from what Iuti and Ma'eva had done together, rolling and tumbling through the sea. When they were underwater, Ma'eva had formed gills along the sides of his neck, so that when Ser Iuti needed to breathe, he could kiss air into her mouth from his own lungs. Tarawe remembered laughing and feeling happy as she watched them from various hiding places in the coral.

Now, when she thought of playing in such a way herself, she felt as if she had swallowed something evil. Not wanting to listen to Ma'eva's song any more, she opened her eyes, stretched, and sat up. Ma'eva broke off his song immediately.

"Greetings, Storm Caller," he said. "Did you sleep enough?"

Tarawe nodded, returning his grin. It was impossible not to. Ma'eva was as friendly and welcoming as the sun. She glanced at Iuti, but the woman was still in the same position she'd been in when she fell asleep the night before.

"She hasn't moved," Ma'eva said. "Her leg looks better though."

Tarawe lifted the cloth Ma'eva had laid over Iuti's wound and nodded again. "It's healing well now," she said. Much of the redness and swelling was gone, but the angry, puckered scar remained vivid against Iuti's golden skin. "I don't think the scar is going to go away."

"She told me once that there are scars no manner of healing can remove," Ma'eva said. He ran his hand over the scar on his own leg, a long, wide band, darker than his dark skin. "Perhaps hers is one of those."

Tarawe thought of the manner in which Ser Iuti had received her wound and who had given it, and thought Ma'eva was probably right. Although it might have just been the clumsy way I sewed it, she admitted silently.

"Are you still hungry?" she asked.

Ma'eva looked dubiously over the side. "Shall I go hunting? I haven't seen anything black and shiny, but . . ."

Tarawe knew very well that Ma'eva could change into any sea form he chose, from a starfish to a giant grouper, or even a shark if necessary, but if he didn't want to go back in the water here, *she* wasn't going to make him do it. Besides, she didn't want to be left alone on the canoe again while Iuti slept so deeply.

"Ser Iuti taught me a beckoning spell yesterday," she said. "Let's try that first. You sit here on the outrigger and catch whatever comes."

"Aye," he said. They exchanged places again and he squatted where she pointed near the front edge of the deck. Tarawe glanced away from his prominently displayed manhood. She took her own place in the hull, just behind Ma'eva, so she could catch whatever came if it slipped through his hands. Then she whispered the beckoning spell into her palms, checked the surrounding water carefully to be sure nothing black and shiny was near, and washed her call into the sea.

Almost before she lifted her hands from the water, a flash of color appeared. Not black this time, but blue. Bright blue and green, with streaks of pink, shining iridescent in the morning sunlight.

"Ayiii!" Ma'eva cried. "A parrot fish. You've called us a fine meal, Storm Caller. Even my human tongue loves the taste of a fat parrot fish."

It was a magnificent creature that had answered Tarawe's call, so beautiful she hated to take it from its watery home. But she was very hungry. She remembered, too, the wily parrot fish that had escaped her so many times at Kala reef. She'd likely never get another chance at *that* fish, but settling for its fat cousin would be just as satisfying.

"Get ready," she called. With her water hand, she pulled the water and the fish up into a wave, then braced herself as the canoe sliced the wave through. She released the water to collapse over the deck—and over Ser Iuti, she realized with horror. With a quick twist of her hand, she caught the water near the sleeping warrior and flung it away behind the canoe.

The parrot fish slammed directly into Ma'eva's arms.

He shouted and laughed, and wrestled with the thrashing fish, unable to get a good grip on more than its tail. He tried to slide a hand under one of its wide gills, but the fish sealed them tight shut against his probing fingers. Tarawe hadn't realized parrot fish were so smart.

"Help me!" Ma'eva called, still laughing. "She's going to get away!"

Tarawe grabbed up the sword and scrambled forward to whack the flat of it against the fish's head. Just before she struck, the fish flickered in Ma'eva's hands and he jerked it away from Tarawe's swing. She lost her balance and tumbled forward. The sword slid from her fingers and splashed into the sea.

"Ma'eva, what's the matter with you?" Tarawe cried. "Ser Iuti is going to be . . ."

She stopped when she caught sight of the parrot fish again. It still struggled in Ma'eva's grasp, but it was flickering madly now. Its iridescent scales shimmered blue and green, popping away by the handful. The pink, all but that on the very top of its head, disappeared. The fish grew thinner in Ma'eva's hands and something vaguely like a face—a human face— superimposed over the fish's rounded beak.

Not human, Tarawe thought. "Throw it back!" she cried.

But Ma'eva held tight and the fish, or whatever it was, continued to struggle and change. Fins extended and narrowed and became bony arms. The wide, flat tail split and stretched into legs with knobby, scarred knees. Tiny feet appeared. The toenails were painted bright red.

"What is it?" Tarawe asked.

"Shame on you, Ma'eva!" the thing said suddenly. It *was* human! "Scooping me up like that. You could have squashed me! Put me down!"

It was a woman! An *old* woman. The oldest woman Tarawe had ever seen. Her skin was pale and flaccid and scattered all over with small, dark spots. Like a spotted cowrie shell, Tarawe thought. Or a giant grouper with a skin rash. There was a rumpled bag hanging on a leather thong around the old woman's thin neck.

Her hair was as white as Iuti's, only not long and thick. It hung in tangled, dripping strands around her deeply lined face. Her eyes were the same blue as Ma'eva's.

The sea mimic gave the old crone a hug. "Mama!" he said. "What are you doing way out here?"

Tarawe gasped.

"Put me down, boy," the old woman said. "You're crushing my ribs." She pushed back from Ma'eva as he set her feet on the deck, but didn't pull entirely from his grasp. Her head reached only halfway up his chest. She reached up to brush a pair of scales off his shoulder.

"By all the gods of Ilimar! You look just like your father in his favorite human form," she said, then added over her shoulder, "If you don't close that mouth, girl, something big is going to fly in."

Tarawe closed her mouth and bit her lower lip to keep it that way. She looked down at her hands. Why does my magic always call such strange things? she wondered.

"Are you hungry, son?" the woman asked as if they hadn't just been trying to kill her for their breakfast. "I have some leftover sugarfish here somewhere. Now where did I put my purse?" She twisted around, searching the deck.

Ma'eva laughed. "It's around your neck, Mama."

"Oh, so it is." She pulled the bag forward without lifting it from her neck—it looked like a blowfish bladder, pulled up by a drawstring—and squatted to rifle through it. After a moment of digging, mumbling all the while, she pulled out a shining silver sugarfish. Its eyes were still bright yellow.

Ma'eva snatched it from her hands eagerly, then paused just before biting into it. He eyed Tarawe over its side. "Are you hungry, too?" he asked.

Tarawe looked at the wrinkled old woman, who was still muttering and rummaging through her sack. Then she nodded. She wasn't sure about eating something offered by such a strange creature, but if Ma'eva thought it safe, then it must be. She glanced at Iuti Mano, wondering how she could sleep through such a ruckus, wishing she would wake.

Ma'eva's fingers flickered and formed into long, sharp claws. He stripped the flesh from one side of the fish and handed it to Tarawe. She took it gingerly, careful not to touch his suddenly frightening hand. By the time he lifted the rest of the sugarfish to his lips again, he had returned to being entirely human. Tarawe sat on one of the seats in the hull and took a bite of the fish. It was crisp and sweet, obviously fresh. She licked the taste of salt from the corners of her mouth.

"We have water," she said when the old woman looked up again. Tarawe thought it only proper to offer guest right to someone Ma'eva called mother.

The woman had pulled a faded brown cloth from her bag and was wrapping it around her waist. She blinked. "Water?"

"Fresh water," Tarawe said. "For drinking. If you want some, I mean."

"Oh. Oh, yes. Fresh water. Yes, of course. Now, wait just a minute. I have some here in my bag somewhere."

"No, I mean you can have some of ours . . ." Tarawe began, but it was too late. The old lady was deep in her bag again. After a moment, she lifted out a calabash no bigger than her fist. She pulled out a stopper of carved shell and handed the container to Tarawe.

"You just drink all you like, dear," she said.

Tarawe stared at the tiny gourd. She didn't want to take the woman's obviously small supply of water, but neither did she want to disappoint the lady's obvious pleasure in offering it. A glance at Ma'eva offered no help. He was feasting noisily on the sugarfish, sucking the flesh from the sharp bones along the spine.

Tarawe drank. A small, cautious sip. Then she looked up at the woman in surprise. The water was cool and fresh, it tasted as sweet as if it had just fallen from the sky. "It's good!" she said, and was immediately sorry, because the woman insisted she drink more.

"Take as much as you like," the old lady said again. Then she turned her beaming smile on Ho'oma'eva. "*So* much like your father," she said. She patted his naked thigh.

Tarawe drank from the calabash again, deeply this time. Then she lifted one of their own freshwater logs from the bottom of the hull. She had just started refilling the gourd when the old lady turned back.

"*What are you doing?*" she shrieked.

Ma'eva dropped the fish.

Iuti Mano sat up with a jerk. In an instant the warrior woman had her hands around the old woman's waist and was wrestling her to the deck.

"Don't kill her!" Ma'eva cried. He scrambled onto the outrigger to grab Iuti's hands.

Iuti released the woman and the old lady scooted away from her into Ma'eva's embrace.

"Mama, are you hurt?" he asked.

Iuti sat back and stared. "Mano's teeth!" she said. "What is going on here?" She turned her astonished look toward Tarawe. "Tarawe, why are you dumping away our water?"

Tarawe looked down. She was still holding the calabash in one hand, the water log in the other. Fresh water was pouring from the log into the overfilled gourd and spilling into her lap. She yanked the log upright.

"Ma'eva, who is this . . . this woman?" Iuti demanded.

Ma'eva grinned. "Don't you recognize Mama, friend Iuti?"

Iuti leaned forward. The old woman backed away.

"Anali? Anali of Ilimar?" Iuti said. Then suddenly she smiled. "It *is* you. What are you doing so far from land, good mother?"

"Well, it's very nice to see you, too, Iuti Mano," the old woman said.

Ser Iuti actually blushed. "Ah, forgive me, Mother. I am still startled by your presence and my sudden awakening. You are welcome, of course. Can we offer you food? Well, we have no food, but water . . . ?"

There was a sudden silence on the canoe and Tarawe wished she knew a disappearing spell. Ma'eva and his mother and Iuti Mano all shifted their looks to the gourd in her hand. A drop of water spilled over its edge and drained away across her fingers.

"I was just refilling it," she said. It came out in a whisper. "She told me to drink from it, but there was so little. I didn't want to give it back empty so I was just refilling it, that's all."

"You were refilling it?" Ma'eva's mother asked.

Tarawe nodded.

"With fresh water?"

Another drop slid over Tarawe's trembling fingers. She nodded again.

The old woman crawled toward her. She snatched the calabash from her hand. She peered into it, tested the water with her finger, then drank from it. Her eyes grew round. "Water," she said, turning to Ma'eva. "She refilled my gourd with fresh water!"

Ma'eva nodded.

"I didn't mean to hurt it," Tarawe said.

The old woman peered into the calabash again, mumbled something Tarawe couldn't hear, then replaced the stopper and stuffed it back into her bag. Ma'eva grinned. Tarawe glanced toward Iuti, but the warrior woman only shrugged. Tarawe passed her the water log, being careful not to spill another drop.

After Iuti had drunk her fill, Ma'eva handed her the head of the sugarfish. "Mama brought it," he explained. His mother was rummaging through her bag again.

Iuti examined the fish carefully. "This is the same fish we threw away last night!"

"I didn't want it to go to waste," the old woman said. "And I wasn't hungry enough to eat it myself."

Tarawe looked down at the fish she still held in her lap,

then at the old woman. "How did you get it away from that black . . . ? Was that *you*?"

The old woman grinned. She patted Ma'eva's knee and ran a finger over the scar on his thigh. She looked even older as she leaned against Ma'eva's side. Her skin was much paler than his, mottled and weathered by the sun and sea. Her breasts hung like small, empty water flasks over her thin chest. The top of her head, where it showed through her thin hair, was the same pink as that of the parrot fish.

Tarawe had a sudden thought. "Was that you back at Kala, too?"

Iuti paused in her careful picking of flesh from around the sugarfish's beak. "At Kala?"

"She was a parrot fish," Tarawe said at the old lady's nod. "She led me to where I could see the war canoe crossing through the surf."

Iuti laid the remaining fish on the deck. "Then we owe you our lives, Mother."

"Who were those big males anyway?" Anali asked.

"My brothers." Iuti rubbed her injured leg.

"Brothers! But they tried to hurt you!"

Ma'eva frowned. "Was it because you killed the shark?"

Iuti nodded. "I warned you they would be angry."

"But to deliberately harm their own kinswoman would be foolish," Ma'eva said.

Ma'eva's mother patted his knee again. "Angry humans often do foolish things, son. Not even this one you've chosen to mother your child will always do the sensible thing when she's angry. Remember that."

"You know about the child, too?" Iuti said.

One thin white eyebrow lifted. "*All* the seafolk know about it, warrior woman. The conception of a sea mimic's child is a celebrated occasion. The birthing is even more so. At the moment a new sea mimic touches the sea, the water itself sings with joy."

She smiled as if remembering and squeezed Ma'eva's hand. He stroked her thin arms.

"I would be honored to accept your guidance through this pregnancy, Mother," Iuti said with a small bow. "Since you've already done this thing, perhaps you'll be willing to tell me how to do it right."

Ma'eva's mother sat up straight and brushed Ma'eva's hands

away. "Well, first off, you can turn this canoe around. These waters are not safe for a woman in your condition."

"The waters behind us are less so," Iuti said. "My brother's sword fell on my leg and cut deeply. The wound hasn't had time to heal properly. If we went back now, I wouldn't be able to defend myself, much less the rest of you."

"Facing your brothers might be a blessing, sharkwoman, compared to what you could face if you continue on into the Empty Sea."

"When Mano Niuhi died at my hand," Iuti said, "the ages-old bond between my family and the sharks was broken. My mother and my brothers and cousins have no god now. They have no special powers or protection. They feel shamed by the first, angered by the second. They want to kill me and end the shark clan entirely."

"Surely your mother will not allow—"

"My mother sent my brothers to bring me back to Kiholo," Iuti said. "She wove the sail that carried their canoe to the Kala shore. My mother was the most angry of all my kin when Mano Niuhi first chose me. She has never forgiven me for accepting Mano's bond. I don't want to believe that she would send my brothers to kill me, but—"

"But when she learns you're carrying a child. Her grandchild!"

"Angry humans do foolish things, Mother Ana," Iuti said quietly. "I won't risk Ma'eva's child by turning back now."

"Then you sail into unknown dangers, sharkwoman," Ma'eva's mother said. "No human has ever traveled farther west than where we are now. None, at least, who ever returned. Among the seafolk, there are rumors of islands made of burning stone and places where time does not exist. There are tales of powerful spirits and monsters beyond imagining."

Iuti's eyes, when they met Tarawe's look, were dark with the same kind of pain that Tarawe had once seen in the Demon Drummers' den. The warrior woman had been faced with an impossible choice then, too.

"Which way do the currents flow in this empty sea, little sister?" Iuti asked.

Tarawe felt a shiver of pride at the sharkwoman's trust. They both knew that Tarawe had only to turn her hand and the water would take them in any direction she chose.

Tarawe smiled slowly. "West, Ser. Due west."

❧ Chapter 6 ❧

"Only . . ."

"Only what, Tarawe?" Iuti asked. She wasn't surprised that Tarawe was willing to continue into the unknown. Better the danger you don't know than that of which you're certain. Besides, the girl seemed to like it here on this empty ocean. The farther from land they got, the happier she seemed to be. Iuti suspected it was because she could play with her newfound magic without fear of harming those around her.

"What are we going to do about the birds?" Tarawe asked.

Iuti stared at her. Mano's teeth, she thought. I forgot all about the birds.

She rubbed a hand across her eyes and cursed the moment in which Anele's sword had stolen so much of her strength. She needed to think clearly now, but all her mind wanted to do was go back to sleep. "We're going to have to convince them to take some other payment," she said. "Or else they're going to have to wait."

"They only want the pearl," Ma'eva said. "I already asked."

Anali was leaning against her son's chest again. Her eyes had drifted closed and she began snoring softly.

"Even if we went back now, we couldn't get the pearl," Iuti said. "Kuwala and Anele probably tried to follow us as soon as they found our canoe, but at least three of the others would have stayed behind. That canoe wasn't big enough for more."

Ma'eva nodded. "They found the canoe right after you left. They filled it with food—your breadfruit smelled good, friend Iuti—and coconuts. Then three of them put to sea. They used your water catchment roof for a sail, and they took some branches from the breadfruit tree."

"To carve another paddle and a better mast," Iuti said. "I

hope my cousins who stayed behind don't cut down the rest of
that poor tree to make another canoe. It's taken a long time for
it to grow strong enough to bear fruit. There's so little soil on
that isle.''

"Those men are dangerous to more than the trees, friend Iuti,"
Ma'eva said. "On the first morning, while they were searching
the rest of the island, they discovered the birds that had come
for the pearl. They threw nets and spears. That one who tried to
hurt Storm Caller killed one of the birdfolk."

Tarawe sucked in her breath.

"Not your gull," Ma'eva said quickly, "although she did
lose a few feathers. She's still awfully clumsy getting off the
ground. The bird they killed was a little o'u. The others are very
angry, both about the killing and the pearl."

Tarawe turned to Iuti. "Why would Pali kill such a small
bird?"

Iuti sighed. "Probably out of spite, because they were stuck
there on the island, while the birds could fly free. And for its
feathers. The o'u's yellow is rare in the Western Isles."

"Most of the feathers those men wore were *gull* feathers, Ser
Iuti. Do your kinsmen kill gulls, too?"

It was clearly an accusation. Tarawe must be closer to forming
a permanent bond with the gulls than she had realized. "I cannot
speak for my kinsmen, Tarawe," she said, "but I have never
killed a gull for its feathers. Nor any other bird, for that matter."
She had killed birds for food, of course—many of them gulls
just like Tarawe's friend, but she decided not to mention that.
Tarawe's right hand, her wind magic hand, was tight on the
gunwale.

"No one should ever kill the birds," Tarawe said. "They
should be free to fly wherever they want, without danger."

"The seafolk kill birds sometimes," Ma'eva said. "When
we're hungry." Ma'eva in his octopus form was very skilled at
chasing schools of flicker fish near the surface to lure small
birds. When they swooped low enough to scoop up the fish,
Ma'eva snagged them right out of the air. Then, at least when
Iuti was near, he re-formed himself into a human and shared his
catch. Iuti doubted Tarawe needed to hear *that* right now either.

"I'm sorry about the o'u, Tarawe," she said. "I apologize
for my kinsman and I'll do my best to see that he repays the
airfolk someday."

She turned to Ma'eva. "It'll be weeks before my brothers
reach the Akana archipelago and get a canoe back to my cousins.

We dare not return to Kala while they're there. But there's another reason we may not be able to get the pearl, good friend. That shell didn't close on its own. A flying dolphin broke through Tarawe's shield and swam close to startle the clam. Then it stopped me from bracing the shell open long enough for you to get the pearl out.''

Ma'eva caught his breath. ''A flying dolphin?''

Anali's eyes snapped open. ''What? *Who* saw a flying dolphin? Where?''

''At Kala,'' Iuti said. ''He came while we were trying to harvest the Great Pearl.''

Anali sat up straight. ''What Great Pearl?''

''The one Ma'eva promised to give the birds,'' Tarawe said.

Anali turned her sharp look on her son.

''I needed their help, Mama,'' he said in a small voice. He hung his head, like a child waiting for a scolding. The look was entirely incongruous on his strong, very adult human form. ''It was the only thing they would bargain for.''

Ma'eva's mother shook a thin finger close to Ma'eva's face. ''How many times have I told you not to make bargains with the birds, boy? They always trick you. They always take advantage of the seafolk.''

''Mother Anali,'' Iuti said before Tarawe could speak in defence of the birds. ''Ma'eva saved many lives, both human and seafolk, by what he did—and there was no other way he could do it. The pearl wasn't that great a price for the birds to ask. It's only a stone. We planted it in the clam ourselves, back when we were just children.''

''Only a stone!'' The bony finger appeared under Iuti's nose. ''Only a stone! Now just why do you think a flying dolphin would be interested in *only a stone*, warrior woman?''

Iuti backed away from the old woman's hand. She couldn't go far, she was already at the outrigger's edge. ''I . . . I don't know, Mother.'' She glanced at Ma'eva and was startled to see that he had turned very pale. It was, she was certain, not a deliberate color change.

''Ma'eva, what's wrong?''

''Ah, friend Iuti,'' Ma'eva said. ''That couldn't have been a pearl. I should have realized when it was so big.''

''Realized what?''

''You almost stole a flying dolphin's egg!'' Anali snapped.

Tarawe's right hand moved. A sharp, precise gust of wind slammed into Ma'eva and knocked him backward off the canoe.

Anali shrieked in alarm as her son splashed into the water. She began flickering and would have gone after him if Iuti hadn't held her arms and insisted she stay aboard. Tarawe swung her left hand up and the sea beneath them churned into sudden froth.

"Tarawe, stop it!" Iuti shouted over Anali's shrill cries and the rush of angry wind and sloshing waves. The canoe lurched. "Stop it right now!"

Tarawe jerked her look toward Iuti. "How could he do that?" she cried. "How could he take *me* with him to steal a flying dolphin's egg after what I've already done to those creatures? I thought Ma'eva was my friend. I thought *you* were my friend!"

"We are, Tarawe," Iuti said. Anali went slack in her hands but Iuti didn't loosen her grip. If the woman was anything like her son, she was full of many tricks and they needed no further confusion now. *A flying dolphin's egg, by the very gods!* Iuti wished more than anything that she could just go back to sleep. Her mind felt like a moldy sponge, her leg burned with pain.

"I'm sure Ma'eva didn't know," she shouted over the wind. "I didn't. We thought it was our own pearl."

Tarawe glared at her.

"Stop the wind, Tarawe," Iuti said. "This is not the way to use your magic."

Tarawe watched her for a moment more, then sat down hard and turned her look toward the distant horizon. She closed both hands into fists, then opened them again, palms down. The sea and the sky returned instantly to calm. The canoe settled into its steady westward movement.

"By the hairy spines of a thorny starfish," Anali murmured. Iuti let her go. After a long look at Tarawe, the old woman crawled to the side of the outrigger deck and spat into the water. "You can come up now, son," she called.

There was a flicker far below. A moment later, Ma'eva's dark human figure appeared, swimming rapidly toward them. "Is it safe?" he asked as his face lifted from the water. He was still flickering slightly, ready to re-form into something small and swift again if it should prove necessary.

"It's safe," Iuti said. She held out a hand and he let her help pull him aboard.

"*So* much like your father," Anali said.

Ma'eva shook the water from his hair and took a place on the outrigger deck as far from Tarawe as he could get. Iuti moved inboard to keep the canoe balanced. Anali dropped into a seat in the hull facing Tarawe.

"Are you the Storm Caller?" she asked.

Tarawe said nothing. She continued to stare at the horizon.

Anali turned to Iuti. "Well, is she? Is this little girl the one all the seafolk have been burbling about for the past many weeks? The one who called the great storm and turns the water at her whim?"

"I'm not a little girl," Tarawe said without moving.

"Ho, so you *can* still talk," Anali replied.

Tarawe turned on her. "Yes," she shouted. "Yes. I'm the Storm Caller. I'm the one who called the great storm that killed so many seafolk. *I'm the one who killed the flying dolphins!*"

Her tortured look lifted toward Ma'eva.

"I didn't know," he said. "I thought it was our pearl. It was the same clam. Friend Iuti, you saw the markings we made years ago. I know the pearl was bigger than we expected, but I don't know how big a pearl can get and . . ."

Iuti nodded. "It was the right clam, Ma'eva. There's no doubt of that. Mother Anali, why would a flying dolphin's egg be inside that shell?"

Anali was still staring at Tarawe. "To keep the birds from stealing it, of course," she said.

Tarawe's mouth dropped open, as did Iuti's own.

Anali looked surprised at their reaction. "The birds have been trying to capture a flying dolphin's egg for centuries," she said. "Didn't you know that?"

Iuti closed her mouth. Ma'eva crept closer and brushed a hand across hers. She turned her palm up and squeezed his fingers.

"Why?" Tarawe asked. Her voice was more frightened now than angry.

"Long ago," Anali said, "when the gods of the land and the air and the sea divided the earth's creatures among them, the air and sea gods fought over who would have dominion over the magical dolphins, just as the land and sea gods fought over the sea mimics. The dolphins, like the mimics, settled the matter by refusing to submit to either."

She glanced at Ma'eva. "The dolphins continue to be both air- and seafolk, although they chose to live primarily in the sea. But, if the birds can capture a flying dolphin's egg and hatch it in the sky, far from the water, it will become more bird than dolphin. Its loyalties will be with the airfolk."

"None among the seafolk can escape the magic dolphins if they choose to hunt and eat us," Ma'eva said. "If one of them should choose to start feeding its bird cousins . . ." He shrugged and shivered.

"Couldn't the other flying dolphins stop it if that should happen?" Iuti asked.

Anali met her look. "Aye, Iuti Mano. The flying dolphins could stop their own kin—if they were willing to lose their souls in the doing."

Tarawe moaned and lowered her face into her hands.

"They would never willingly kill one of their own," Ma'eva said. "There are too few of them. Each can bear only one true child during its lifetime. Like us, they are a dying people."

Iuti laid a hand on her stomach.

"Why can't people live together peacefully?" Tarawe said. She lifted her tear-stained face from her hands. "Why is someone from the land or the water or the air always trying to take more than their share?"

"Most do live peacefully," Iuti began. "It's only a few who seek power over—"

"Power!" Tarawe jumped up, taking care even in that swift movement not to tip the canoe. "*I* have *power*, Iuti Mano! I could kill you all if I wanted to. I can even kill flying dolphins with *my* power."

She collapsed back onto her seat, staring at her palms. "What good is *power*? I wish I didn't even . . . I wish I never . . ."

She stopped and closed her hands into fists again. She closed her eyes and breathed out a long, shuddering sigh.

Ma'eva's mother patted Tarawe's knees. "Now you understand a bit about power, my dear. You might not have sought it, but now that it's yours, you find it hard to even think of giving it up."

"I never meant to hurt anyone," Tarawe said.

Anali patted her again, harder this time. "Well, you're going to go on hurting people if you don't learn to control that temper of yours."

"Anali, don't—"

Anali waved Iuti to silence. "You go back to sleep, warrior woman. We'll figure out what to do about the birds later. And don't you worry about the flying dolphins, youngster. If they'd meant to punish you for the storm deaths, they'd have done it long before now. As long as their egg is safe, they're not likely to bother you again."

"Are you sure, Mama?" Ma'eva asked.

Anali glanced at him. "As sure as I can be."

Which means she's not sure at all, Iuti thought. A further slump in Tarawe's shoulders told her that the girl understood that, too.

"What are we going to do, Ser?" Tarawe asked.

Iuti stared at her for a long moment. "Do you want to go back?"

Tarawe looked up and around. "If it were just me, I'd stay out here with just the wind and the water forever. I . . . I'm afraid of the flying dolphins, but I wouldn't blame them if they came to kill me. And now the birds are angry with us, too. But I'd rather face all of them than go back to where so many people want to turn my power to their own ends."

"We could be stuck on this canoe for a long time," Iuti said. "I know of no lands west of here, and we'll no doubt get mightily tired of eating raw fish and drinking rainwater during the months it will take to bring this child to term." She patted her stomach. She knew there was a wealth of food in the sea, and with Ma'eva to provide for them, they would never go hungry. Still, it seemed a great price to ask Tarawe to pay.

"What will happen when the baby comes?" Tarawe said. "You can't give birth on a canoe."

Anali laughed. "When the birthing time comes, youngster, she'll give birth no matter where she is."

"In the water is best," Ma'eva said.

"True," Anali replied. "Although you'll need to stay near the surface in case it turns out to be a girl."

Tarawe frowned. "Why does a girl need to be closer to the surface than a boy?"

"So she can be brought up to the air quickly to breathe," Ma'eva said.

"Don't boy sea mimics need air?"

Ma'eva laughed. "Of course not."

"Then why do girl—"

"Tarawe," Iuti said before Tarawe's temper could rise again. "There are no girl sea mimics. Female offspring of the mimics are fully human. Only the boys inherit the ability to make the sea change." She wished now that she'd taken the time to explain this to Tarawe earlier. She'd assumed they would have many months, perhaps years, during which to talk before she became pregnant. She hadn't even been certain the girl would still be with her when the time came.

Tarawe turned to stare pointedly at Anali. "Then what is *she*?" she asked.

Anali had fallen asleep again, sitting upright on the canoe seat. Her head hung forward on her thin neck; it wobbled slightly with the movement of the canoe. Ma'eva moved closer and tilted his mother so she could lean against him.

"Anali is human," Iuti began . . .

But Ma'eva's touch had wakened Anali. She straightened. "Of course I'm human," she said. "Who says I'm not?"

"The Storm Caller." Ma'eva giggled. Iuti warned him with a look and he immediately sobered. "I think she thinks you're a sea mimic, Mama."

"Me? A mimic?"

"But you changed," Tarawe said. "You were a parrot fish, and that black, shiny thing, and . . . and you're Ma'eva's mother."

Anali patted Ma'eva's knee and smiled up at him.

"Anali was gifted with the mimics' sea-changing magic many years ago," Iuti said. "She either did them a kindness and was repaid for it, or she tricked them into giving it to her in some mimics' game. Ma'eva would never tell me which."

This time, Anali patted Ma'eva's cheek. She smiled as her look slid past Iuti's to Tarawe.

Tarawe's eyes narrowed. "If you're really human, then you know what strong and healthy humans look like. Why did you change into that ugly body?"

"Tarawe!" Iuti said.

Anali pushed away from Ma'eva and leaned close to Tarawe. She poked Tarawe's mat-wrapped chest with her gnarled finger. "You take a good look at this ugly body, youngster. You remember it. Because this is what you're going to look like someday—when you're as old as I am now. If you live that long."

"But why don't you—"

"Tarawe, this is Anali's real body," Iuti said. "She can change her sea form any way she wishes, just like the mimics, but when she becomes human, she must take her own form. As a human she grows old, just as she would have had she never turned to the sea. This is the only human form she has, Tarawe."

Instant contrition shone in Tarawe's dark eyes.

"I'm hungry," Ma'eva said.

Anali immediately sat back and looked around for her bag. Ma'eva pointed it out in its place on her chest and she tugged it open. "I have some bread in here someplace. Now, where did I put that . . . ?"

"Bread?" Tarawe said. She lifted her confused look to Iuti, but again Iuti could only shrug. The workings of Anali's personal bag were far beyond her ken. She remembered being astonished by it as a child.

"Human?" Tarawe mouthed, and Iuti nodded.

The sudden sweet fragrance of freshly baked bread brought both their looks back to Anali. She lifted a fat loaf of dark, brown bread from the bag. Ma'eva took it from her and carefully broke it into four pieces, handing the first back to his mother, the second to Iuti. He grinned when he offered Tarawe her share.

"It's a little heavy," Anali said. "You'll probably want some fresh water to wash it down. Now where did I put my purse?"

Tarawe blinked and almost smiled. She pointed to the bag, still hanging around Anali's neck.

"Oh, yes," Anali said, and began rummaging through her rumpled sack again. She pulled out her drinking calabash and handed it to Tarawe. "Drink as much as you like, dear. It's quite full." She turned to Ma'eva. "Did I tell you, son, that the Storm Caller refilled my water gourd?"

Ma'eva nodded. "The Storm Caller is a very well-mannered human," he said around a mouthful of bread.

Iuti smiled and lay back on the deck. Anali's bread, wherever it came from, was delicious. It was rich and heavy, full of small nuts that crunched between her teeth. She closed her eyes, almost too tired to chew.

"Ser Iuti?"

Iuti opened her eyes. Tarawe was kneeling beside her on the outrigger deck. Ma'eva and his mother were talking quietly together near the bow of the canoe. "Did I fall asleep?" Iuti asked.

"Aye," Tarawe said. "I woke you because I think you need to drink something."

Iuti noticed then that the sun was far ahead of the canoe. She had slept through almost the entire day. Tarawe handed her one of the water logs and she drank gratefully. "You take good care of me," she said.

Tarawe shrugged, but looked pleased.

"Ser Iuti," she said after a while.

"Aye."

"Is it true about the sea mimics? They're all male?"

"Aye."

Tarawe sighed.

"It makes things more difficult, doesn't it?" Iuti said. Perhaps it was the added rest that allowed her to feel calmer about their situation than she had before. "I have to hide from my brothers long enough to have *two* children. A male for Ma'eva and a female for me."

"If this one's a boy, will Ma'eva . . . ?"

Iuti smiled. "Yes. We agreed along ago that if one received a child, the other should, as well. We'll have two together."

"Will you go to live in the ocean then?" Tarawe asked. "Like Mama Ana?"

"Mano's sweet breath, no!" Iuti laughed. "I may be a sea person, but I am not one of the sea*folk*. I like walking on dry land."

"Mama Anali said she hasn't stepped on dry land for almost twenty years," Tarawe said. "Do you think that's true?"

Iuti shrugged. "Probably. From what Ma'eva has told me about her, which isn't much, she gave up being a land person long ago. She's very happy living all alone out here on the sea."

"Where is Ma'eva's father?"

"He was killed in an underwater rockslide shortly after Ma'eva was born."

Tarawe glanced cautiously over her shoulder toward where Ma'eva and his mother sat. Anali had her hand on Ma'eva's knee and they were laughing. "Her bag has magic in it," Tarawe said softly.

Iuti remembered suddenly how little *good* magic Tarawe had seen in her short life.

"She brought out another whole loaf of bread after you were asleep," Tarawe said. "And bananas! Little, fat round ones, with red skins. They were good. And her drinking gourd"—Tarawe's voice dropped even lower—"is full every time she takes it out, even though I only refilled it that once."

She frowned. "Why did she get so upset when I refilled it, Ser, when it refills itself every time she puts it in her bag?"

"I think she was just startled. You repaid a kindness with an unexpected kindness. I don't think she's had that experience very often among other humans."

Tarawe looked relieved. "I thought I'd broken it," she said. Her mouth twitched into a small smile.

They were silent for a time, watching Ma'eva and Anali. The sea mimic had braided his mother's hair into thin plaits all around her head. At the end of each white strand, he had affixed an iridescent parrot fish scale.

"They really love each other, don't they?" Tarawe said.

"Aye," Iuti replied.

"I wish . . ."

"What?"

Tarawe shook her head. "Nothing. Here, I saved some of the bread for you. You should eat, and drink some more water."

There was a touch of sadness in Tarawe's voice, the echoing sound of deep personal loss. She wishes her own mother were here, Iuti thought. Tarawe's mother had been stripped of her soul by the sorceress Pahulu and her still-living body traded to the Teronin warriors years before. Tarawe, who had witnessed the treachery, had at one time been willing to take on the entire Teronin army single-handed to take her revenge. Iuti was sorry for the girl's loss, but relieved that she no longer sought to destroy those who had destroyed her mother. She took the bread Tarawe offered and sat up.

Ma'eva immediately left his mother and scrambled to her side. The outrigger dipped dangerously low, and both Iuti and Tarawe threw themselves toward the hull to bring the canoe back into balance.

"Ma'eva, you have to be more careful," Iuti said. "You're going to capsize us one of these times."

He laughed. "We'd just get wet, friend Iuti. We could always turn the canoe over again."

"We'd get wet, *and* everything in the canoe would sink to the bottom of the sea," Iuti said. "We could get along if we had to without the water logs and the sail, even without the paddles, but if my brothers or some other danger should find us, I'm going to need my shield and swords."

Ma'eva sucked in a sharp breath. He looked quickly at Tarawe and when Iuti looked that way, she saw that Tarawe was biting her lower lip.

"What?" Iuti said. What now? she thought.

Tarawe took a deep breath. "I dropped one of your swords overboard, Ser. This morning, while we were trying to catch . . . Mama Anali."

"It was my fault," Ma'eva said.

"Mine, too," Tarawe said quickly.

Mano's sharp doubled teeth!

"We should have been more careful."

Iuti wasn't sure which of them said that. It might even have been Anali. She sighed and took another bite of bread. She chewed slowly.

"I guess I could go back and look for it," Ma'eva offered, clearly not wanting to go.

"That would be more dangerous than doing without it," Iuti said. "I'll devise some other weapon."

"You might want to devise it quickly, warrior woman," Anali said.

Iuti glanced toward the bow. "What?"

Anali was standing up straight, staring back the way they had come. Her hands were tight around her bag. "We're about to have visitors," she said.

Iuti followed her look, then slid immediately into the hull. Taking care not to bang her injured leg, she pulled her shield and her remaining sword from the weapons rack.

Tarawe was beside her in an instant. "Ser, you mustn't kill—"

"Tarawe, I will do whatever I must to keep us alive." She held the girl's look for a moment before turning back to watch the eastern sky.

It was filled with swiftly approaching birds.

‌‌ Chapter 7 ‌‌

TARAWE stared at the billowing cloud of birds. She felt a fierce pride in the airfolk's presence, even while their ominous approach sent chills down her spine. She knew Ser Iuti was right to prepare against them, for there was no telling what they intended. That it was something serious was made clear by their great number and by the enormous distance they had come. Tarawe wondered if her gull was among them.

"How do you suppose they found us?" Iuti said. "The sky out here has been as empty of flyers as the sea is empty of land."

"The taste of the Storm Caller's magic was strong in the sea at the place where you turned west," Ma'eva said. "That's how I knew to come this way. The birds probably ate seafolk along the way to follow the taste of your path." He shivered.

Iuti turned to Anali. "It might be safer for you to return to the water, Mother Ana."

"And leave the protection of these two to you?" Anali said. "Don't be so smug, warrior woman. I've faced down a bird or two in my lifetime."

To Tarawe's surprise, Iuti smiled and dipped her head in a small bow. It was something Tarawe had never seen Iuti do before, and now she'd done it twice to Ma'eva's strange, speckled mother.

Mama Anali began rummaging in her bag again.

"Ma'eva, guard your mother," Iuti said. "Tarawe . . ."

"I'll watch your back, Ser," Tarawe said quickly. She didn't want to fight with the birds, she didn't want to hurt them, but she knew if anyone could control their movement through the sky, it was she.

The closest of the birds were near enough now for Tarawe to feel them moving the air. Because there was no wind, the birds

were forced to pump their wings almost continuously. Tarawe
sent a questing breeze toward them.

"They're tired," she said, when it returned to brush lightly
across her cheeks.

"Birds don't usually come this far from land," Ma'eva said.
"Especially not the little ones."

"I wonder how they survived so long in the air," said Iuti.

"There's my gull!" Tarawe cried. "Oh, look how tired she
is. Her poor wing looks like it's broken again." She cupped her
right hand and lifted a strong, steady air current up under her
friend. The bird caught the current awkwardly, then steadied its
frantically pumping wings. It spread them wide and soared along
the current toward the canoe.

"Careful," Iuti said. "Don't bring them all in with her."

The birds near her gull, mostly giant gulls, had immediately
dropped into Tarawe's air stream. They soared close beside and
behind her friend. Tarawe tightened her wind and the great gulls
suddenly dropped into empty air. They began pumping their
great wings again while Tarawe's gull swooped almost grace-
fully toward the canoe.

"Let's just go faster and stay ahead of them," Ma'eva
suggested. He sounded frightened.

Tarawe's gull was close enough now for her to taste its wea-
riness on the incoming breeze. "If they're all as tired as she is,
they'll start falling from the sky in exhaustion soon," she said.

"But—"

"We might as well face them, Ma'eva," Iuti said. "We have
to do it some time. They're not just going to go away."

"If we were in the water, *we* could just go away," Ma'eva
muttered.

Tarawe glanced at Anali and was startled to see that the old
woman had donned an elaborate shell-and-feather headdress. A
wide band of tiny yellow cowries circled her head, serving as a
base for feathers even longer than Kuwala had worn. Anali's
feathers were brightly colored—scarlet and azure, green and
brilliant as a freshly uncurled ti leaf. There was a design worked
into the front of the headband, but Tarawe couldn't see what it
was. Anali's head was hanging forward on her chest, rolling
gently from side to side with the movement of the canoe. She
had fallen asleep again.

"Look out!" Ma'eva called.

Tarawe turned back in time to stop the wind from carrying
her gull right into the outrigger struts. Instead of just riding the

current passively as Tarawe had tried to teach her, the gull was attempting her own landing on the canoe. Because of her crooked wing, she was thrown off balance and into a tangle of her own webbed feet and wings.

Tarawe scooped the gull inboard and set her down on the deck. The bird was shivering with exhaustion. Her newly mended wing hung limp when Tarawe lifted her into her lap. Feathers fell out in Tarawe's hand as she stroked the bird back to calm.

"What are you doing here?" she asked. "Why did you follow us so far?"

The bird laid its head on Tarawe's knee and stared up at her with one dark eye. It said nothing.

"Well?" Ser Iuti asked.

Tarawe shrugged. "I guess she doesn't want to talk right now."

"Mano's teeth," Iuti muttered.

"She probably isn't supposed to," said Ma'eva. "She's only a messenger bird and she's already gotten in trouble for talking to us before. Older gulls don't like the younger ones to talk to humans."

"Here comes an old one now," Iuti said. "Be careful."

Tarawe turned toward a sweep of wind and the frantic slap of wings as a large gull braked for landing. The giant seabird, larger even than her own, swept onto the deck. A second followed, landing precisely on the tip of one of the outrigger struts. Then a third and fourth. Their combined weight tipped the canoe.

"Hoi!" Iuti shouted, and waved her shield in the air before another gull could land beside his cousins. "If you want to rest on the canoe, spread your weight," she called. The fifth gull screeched and lifted heavily away. It turned in a wide circle and swept back with a handful of others to perch on the bow and stern posts and along the sides of the main hull. The canoe settled deeper in the water, but leveled again.

Anali had been wakened by the movement and the screeching gulls. She shouted at a frigate bird who landed just in front of her. "Watch those great wings, you idiot bird. There's no need to knock us all overboard." She slapped her hand along the side of the hull. "Settle down, all of you. Stop that noise or you can go sit right out there in the sea and talk to the fish."

To Tarawe's amazement—and from her expression, to Ser Iuti's as well—the birds quieted immediately. The next bird to land did so in the water. It splashed down, its webbed feet out-stretched, its wings spread wide. It took a few frantic flaps to balance itself, then its wings slid back along its sides. The gull floated like a great fat cork on the gentle swell. The rest of the gulls, and other large and much stranger seabirds, followed, until the water around the canoe was dark with bobbing birds.

Then the little birds descended. Their tiny wings slipped and slapped against the quiet air. They twittered and shrilled as they landed on the backs of their larger waterborne cousins. When Iuti lowered her shield, many of them landed on the canoe. They rustled and chattered, whispered and whistled. They fussed with their feathers and skittered here and there along the hull and the outrigger, looking for places to roost.

Finally they settled. The afternoon became suddenly still again.

"Well?" Iuti said again. She looked very strange, standing sideways in the hull, her legs spread for balance, her sword and shield at the ready. She looked fierce with her white hair tied into a warrior's knot and her face scarred with the marks of the mighty shark god.

All around her, the birds sat staring up at her. They were all the colors of the rainbow and of so many different sizes and shapes, Tarawe couldn't count them all. One, with a single, bobbing green feather growing from a fuzzy blue crest, tilted its head one way, then the other, then back again. A tiny black and yellow o'u lifted from the deck and landed on the tip of Iuti's sword. Iuti cursed softly and shook it away.

"Ask them what they want," she said. She was looking at Tarawe.

Tarawe swallowed hard and glanced around at the largest of the gulls. "What do you want?" she said. It came out in a squeak.

"Wadywant!" a brilliantly plumed parrot squawked. The o'u chittered and tried again to land on Iuti's sword.

"Mano's teeth," she muttered as she shook it off again.

"Manoteet!" the parrot squawked.

Iuti groaned. The gulls remained still.

"That's no way to talk to birds," Anali said suddenly. She leaned forward on her seat—a handful of small birds fluttered away—and shook her finger under the nearest gull's beak.

"You answer the warrior woman's questions, do you hear me?" she shouted. The feathers on her headdress bobbed and bounced in time with her finger. The gull backed away, lost its footing on the seat, and almost toppled into the hull before regaining its balance.

The gull who had landed on the highest outrigger strut spread its wings and dropped to the deck beside Tarawe. It squawked a challenge to Anali. Anali squawked back and was answered with a long, teeth-jarring screech. When it ended, Anali lifted her look to Iuti. "They want the pearl," she said.

"Perl!" the parrot screamed.

"Be quiet!" Anali shouted.

"Kwait," the parrot whispered.

Tarawe's gull moved and she stroked it absently.

"They know we don't have the pearl," Iuti said. "Tell them we're not going back to get it. That we wouldn't go back even if the humans weren't there. We won't help them steal a flying dolphin's egg."

Anali eyed her for a moment, then glanced at her son before screeching again at the birds. Tarawe pressed her hands over her ears to dull the clamor of the airfolk's response. Even the little o'u chittered angrily. It was sitting on the tip of Iuti's sword.

Iuti noticed it, frowned, but this time left it where it was.

Anali looked at Ma'eva again. "They say you promised them the pearl, son."

"Ma'eva promised them the Great Pearl," Iuti said before Ma'eva could speak. "He did not promise them an egg. If they want that, they can go get it for themselves."

Tarawe started at that, then realized Ser Iuti had only said it because she was certain the birds couldn't get the egg on their own. They wouldn't have asked Ma'eva for it if they could have gotten it out of the clam without help. The birds shuffled and whispered and ruffled their feathers.

"Tell them," Iuti said, "that as soon as we can, Ma'eva and I will return to Kala and harvest all the pearls there. Together they will be worth much more than the Great Pearl ever would have been. The birds can have them all."

"They never wanted pearls to begin with, warrior woman," Anali said.

"The bargain they made with Ma'eva was for a *pearl*, Mama Ana."

Anali sent a questioning look toward Ma'eva.

He nodded cautiously.

"We will repay them with *pearls*," Iuti said. "As soon as we can."

The birds didn't wait for Anali's translation. They rose all at once in a wild tangle of feathers and beaks and claws. They shrieked and cried in obvious fury. The wind of their sudden flight swirled around Tarawe, whipped her hair from its knot and tangled it around her face. Her gull tried to rise with the rest, but its wing didn't work right and it fumbled and foundered back into her lap. Tarawe bent over it to protect it from its angry cousins.

"Get out! Get away!" Anali shrieked even louder than the birds. When Tarawe looked, she saw the old woman waving her bony arms in the air. She looking like one of the birds herself with her wild headdress and flying hair. The fish scales at the ends of her braids spun and twirled, sparked with iridescence where they caught the sun's rays.

The birds screamed their defiance.

"Tarawe, down!" Iuti cried.

Tarawe instantly flattened herself over her gull. Swift wind edged with sharp claws swept across her back. She gasped in sudden pain, but twisted around quickly to send a gust of wind after the screeching seabird that had attacked her. The gust caught it just in time to sweep it from the arc of Iuti's sword. Iuti had been trying to knock it away with the flat of her blade, Tarawe saw, not the sharp edge that would most certainly have taken the bird's life.

She met Iuti's look for an instant before ducking again at Anali's shout. A blur of gray feathers streaked between them. Tarawe's gull wriggled and tried to pull away. She let it go, but again it was unable to lift itself from the deck. It stumbled over its own wing and Ma'eva caught it before it could tumble into the sea.

"Idiot bird," he said fondly. He straightened the poor gull's weak wing and set the bird carefully in the middle of the deck.

Another gull swept toward them from the front of the canoe. They all ducked from its path, then ducked again as yet another bird followed.

"They're trying to make us turn around," Ma'eva called. He crawled to his mother's side and tried to protect her with his body, but she insisted on facing the birds on her own.

"Get away!" she shouted over and over. Her feathers and her shells and scales bobbled and clattered. The birds swerved around her waving arms. One came close enough to scrape its beak along Ma'eva's shoulder before Iuti could knock it away with her shield. It tumbled into the water, fluttered and rolled and righted itself, then launched again to return to the attack. Tarawe's gull was screeching as loud as the rest.

The canoe dipped and swerved as they ducked and twisted away from the birds. The outrigger float slid underwater almost to the depth of the bracing struts.

"We have to stop them, Tarawe," Iuti called as she batted another seabird away from Ma'eva. "If they can get us in the water, we'll have no defense. They could easily take the canoe and we're too far from land to swim."

"I won't let you drown—" Ma'eva began.

Iuti leapt forward to thrust her shield between the sea mimic's back and an onrushing saber bird. Its long, sharp beak snapped as it struck the hard metal, its neck twisted at a terrible angle. It tumbled and fell into the water beside the canoe. If it had struck Ma'eva, it would surely have killed him.

I have to make them stop, Tarawe thought. Tears scalded her cheeks. I have to use my magic against the birds, and I promised I would never do that. She cried a warning to Iuti while ducking away from sweeping wings herself. Something sharp and hot scraped across her already stinging back. Her gull, stranded in the center of the outrigger, screeched and squawked.

Tarawe lifted her right hand to turn the wind against the birds.

Suddenly a great shock slammed through the sea and the air. Tarawe was knocked onto her side. She turned to see a dark sleek form leap from the water near their canoe. A dolphin! It spun and arced through the air, them slammed back into the sea with an enormous splash. The birds scattered at the explosive appearance of the sleek, gray sea creature, but as soon as it disappeared beneath the waves again, they swarmed back.

"Get down, Tarawe!" Iuti shouted.

The dolphin leapt a second time, from right beside the canoe. It turned and twisted, high in the air. Salt spray showered over Tarawe. She stared up at the shining, silver-blue creature.

At the top of its arc, the dolphin paused as if suspended by the air itself. Then suddenly it snapped open thick, wide wings. Tarawe felt them catch and hold the air. She caught her breath as the magnificent dolphin slid forward on air currents so slight even the birds hadn't been able to use them. The birds stopped screaming and scattered from the flying dolphin's path.

The great dolphin flew in a wide circle all around the canoe, its wings pumping slowly with the same smooth motion as the manta rays that Tarawe had seen playing in sandy shallows. The larger birds swooped toward the dolphin, trying to divert it from its course as they had been doing with the canoe. The silent silver creature slid through them as if they weren't even there.

Tarawe watched in awe. *It flies like the wind!* she thought.

She stood slowly and turned in a circle to follow the dolphin's path. Four times the dolphin circled them, each time forcing the furious birds farther away. They squawked and cried and dove at the dolphin without effect. Those caught inside the circles rose quickly to flee over the top of whatever barrier the dolphin was laying and disappear into the cloud of their cousins.

When the last of them was far from the canoe, the dolphin folded its wings in a single, smooth move and dove back into the sea. It rose once more, lifted high enough to stand on its tail, then twisted and crashed sideways back into the water.

Tarawe shouted and laughed aloud as the spray of its fall drenched her again. The water tasted as sweet and as welcoming as the air.

And then it was gone.

"Mano's sweet breath!" Ser Iuti murmured.

Ma'eva released a very long, very audible breath. He was huddled against his mother. She had him wrapped tightly in her thin arms.

Tarawe stared after the dolphin. She wanted to follow it into the water, to hold it in her arms like Anali held Ma'eva. She wanted to fly high into the sky astride its shining, silver back. She laughed and hugged herself and, for a moment, felt nothing but joy. The great dolphin terrified her. It teased her with its strength and power. It made her feel wonderful.

She sat down on the edge of the outrigger, leaned her forehead on her knees, and hugged herself again, still laughing.

"Ana, watch for the birds," she heard Ser Iuti say. Then the warrior woman was beside her.

"Tarawe, what's wrong?" Ser Iuti laid a hand on Tarawe's back, then snatched it away. "By the gods, they cut you to shreds."

"I want to *fly!*" Tarawe whispered into her knees. Hot tears turned cool as they slid down her legs. She kept her right hand cupped tightly. "I want to fly!"

Someone shook her. A cold, wet hand touched the scratches on her back and suddenly Tarawe jerked upright. Ser Iuti was beside her, staring at her with deep concern. "Tarawe, what are you saying?" she said. "What's wrong?"

Tarawe caught her breath as fiery pain shot across her back. She remembered then that the birds had raked their beaks and claws through her skin. The cuts stung like the hot touch of fire coral. How could she have forgotten? The dolphin, she thought, and smiled.

Ser Iuti's hand circled her head in the motion she used when she was searching for hidden sorcery.

Tarawe looked again toward the place where the flying dolphin had disappeared. The water was glassy smooth again. The only birds she could see were far away.

"It's there," she said.

"What?"

"The magic."

Tarawe finally looked up to meet Iuti's worried stare.

"Are you hurt?" Iuti said. "Other than your back, I mean? I feel no sorcery around you, but you look—"

Tarawe shook her head and was immediately sorry for it. The motion sent fire racing across her back again. "Ooow!"

Iuti sat back. "Well, at least *that* sounds normal. Anali, do you have any healing salve in that pouch of . . . ? Ah, good."

Tarawe turned carefully to see Anali smoothing dark-green paste over Ma'eva's shoulder. Anali tossed a tiny pot, the same color as its contents, to Iuti. Iuti sniffed it and winced. "It smells like rotting seaweed," she said. "Are you sure this won't do more damage than good?"

"Spoken like a true human," Anali returned, and she and Ma'eva both laughed. Tarawe had no idea why they thought that was funny. She sucked in her breath while Iuti washed her torn back with seawater. Then, while Iuti spread Anali's foul-smelling salve over the cuts, she whispered a pain spell she'd learned from an injured warrior on Fanape. Neither the salve nor the spell took the sting from her back.

Iuti laughed softly. "Girl, it's a wonder you haven't turned yourself into a sea cucumber the way you play with all your borrowed spells." She tossed the salve pot back to Anali, who immediately began looking around for her bag. Ma'eva pointed it out, still hanging from her neck, and Anali stuffed the pot back inside.

"Didn't I say it right?" Tarawe asked, surprised that Iuti had even noticed her whispered attempt to end her pain.

"You said it perfectly," Iuti laughed, "and had you been saying it for Ma'eva, it would have worked just fine. That's a man's chant, Tarawe. It has no effect on women."

"Oh." Tarawe glanced back at Ma'eva. He was grinning

again and gathering up the feathers that lay scattered over the deck. He didn't seem to be in pain at all. "Did you . . . ?"

"Anali did it for him," Iuti said. "Come. Listen now, and I'll give you a proper female chant." She lifted Tarawe's hands and spoke a soft song into her palms. She closed Tarawe's fingers over the words, and the sting of the birds' gashes disappeared. Tarawe felt as if cool water had washed the cuts away. She sighed in relief.

"You can still make them hurt," Iuti said. "Be reasonable how you move while they begin healing. You do know a decent healing chant, don't you? One that won't put you into deep sleep? I don't think any of us should sleep too deeply for a while yet."

Tarawe nodded and mumbled a simple healing chant to aid her body in healing itself. Iuti nodded her approval, then began looking around.

"What a mess," she said.

The canoe was covered in a thick layer of feathers and bird droppings. Even the tips of the outrigger spars glistened with pasty white splotches. Tarawe looked for the birds again, but the only one near them was her own gull, huddled in the middle of the deck with its head under one wing. The rest were far behind, disappearing now into the darkening eastern sky.

"It doesn't look like they'll be coming back," Iuti said. "Not tonight anyway. We might as well clean this up. Anali, do you have . . ." Iuti stopped, shook her head, and smiled. Anali was asleep, leaning back against the high carved bow. She had taken off her headdress, but the scales tipping her thin braids still spun in the wind caused by the canoe's movement.

Ma'eva had collected a handful of feathers, green and blue ones, the colors his mother had been when she'd taken the form of a parrot fish. "Shall I sweep the rest into the water?" he asked.

"The water close to us is already littered with the things," Iuti said. "They're being carried along with current just like the canoe. Let's gather all of them together in one place, then I'll set a weighting spell on them so they'll sink. Who'd expect birds could lose so many feathers and still fly?"

"We shouldn't . . ." Tarawe began.

Iuti turned to her.

"We shouldn't sink them," Tarawe said, although she wasn't entirely sure why. "They're bird feathers. They . . . belong in the air."

Ser Iuti looked at her in that way she used when she wasn't sure whether Tarawe was just being stubborn or was actually saying something important. "What do you suggest we do with them? Spread out like this, they make a wide marker around us. We'll be much more visible both from the air and from under the water."

"Maybe that's why the birds dropped so many," Ma'eva said. "They're much too tired to follow us tonight, especially after attacking us and being chased by the dolphin, and there aren't many surface fish out here to give them the taste of our path like before. They'll need a strong marker to find us tomorrow morning."

Tarawe began turning the water just a finger's depth below the surface, swirling the floating feathers into small whirlpools. When they were gathered into neat piles, she sent a light wind skimming across the surface to push the piles into a single mass beneath the outrigger.

"I'll put a water shield around them so the birds can't follow their taste," she said.

"What will you do with them all?" Iuti asked.

Leaning over, Tarawe picked out a deep-red quill, half the length of her arm. She ran her fingers along its shaft to squeeze away the water. It dried quickly under her stroking fingers and began spreading into a scarlet plume. She laid it in her lap and leaned forward to lift another—a small, gray gull's feather.

"Tarawe . . . ?"

"It flew like the wind," Tarawe said softly as she stroked the feather dry. "It flew just like the wind."

She paid no attention as Ser Iuti checked her one more time for hidden sorcery.

Chapter 8

IUTI didn't know what to think about Tarawe's sudden, compelling interest in the feathers. The experience of seeing the flying dolphin had obviously affected the girl in some strange way, but Iuti could detect no evil nearby. She would have preferred sinking the bird feathers and being done with them, but as long as Tarawe kept them hidden beneath the outrigger, there was no real danger in bringing them along.

There was danger, however, in ignoring the presence of the birds themselves. There was no guarantee the dolphin would return if the birds chose to attack again in the morning.

"Ma'eva, come help me reconstruct a sail," she said. "If Tarawe will add some wind to this current, we can move much faster. I want to change directions for a while, too, to throw the birds off our trail. We've been going due west for so long, they're sure to look that way for us first—if they look for us at all."

"They'll look," Ma'eva said. He looked up from where he was piling feathers beside Tarawe. He had cleared much of the deck and splashed away most of the droppings. Tarawe's injured gull was sleeping at middeck.

"I've never seen the birds so angry," Ma'eva said. "I was afraid they might even try to kill us."

"One of them did try to kill you," Iuti remembered suddenly. She leaned over the side of the hull. Yes, the dead bird was there, carried along in the current like the feathers, but too heavy to have been swept up in Tarawe's gentle breeze. She lifted the limp body by its broken neck. Its long beak had been snapped in two when it hit her shield. The upper portion of the long spike still dangled loosely from the base.

Ma'eva pulled in a sharp breath. "A saber bird! I had an uncle who was killed by a saber bird." His look suddenly grew soft and he lifted his admiring gaze to Iuti's. "Ah, friend Iuti, mother of my child, you have saved me once again." He cocked his head to one side and grinned.

Iuti laughed. "You're as silly as a father sea mimic," she returned. "What shall I do with this? Are you hungry?"

Ma'eva wrinkled his nose. "Not *that* hungry."

"Tarawe," Iuti called. She had to say it twice to get the girl's attention. When Tarawe looked up, Iuti asked, "Do you want these feathers, too?"

Tarawe stared at the bird for a moment. "Is that the one who tried to kill Ma'eva?"

Iuti nodded.

"Throw it away," Tarawe said. She went back to cleaning her feathers.

Iuti cut away the rest of the saber bird's beak and dropped it into the weapons rack before throwing the bird far to the rear of the canoe. It fell beyond Tarawe's current and was left quickly behind.

Iuti and Ma'eva studied the remaining pieces of her mother's sail before weaving them together into another, somewhat smaller mat. It wouldn't be as strong as the original, but it would do. They had to move Anali before they could set the sail at the bow. She woke, blinked once, and began helping as if she'd been working with them all along.

"It's a little ragged," she said when the sail was set and spread, "and a little small for this canoe, but it should do. What are you going to use for wind?"

They all looked at Tarawe. The girl started, as if feeling their gazes, and turned toward them. She stared up at the great triangular sail. "When did . . . ?" She looked down at the piles of feathers surrounding her. "Oh. I was supposed to be cleaning the canoe."

Iuti smiled. "The feathers need to be cleaned, too, if you're going to keep them. But we could use some help with the wind. A strong breeze to the northwest would be most useful, and a turn of the current as well."

"Are you going to try to trick the birds?" Tarawe asked. She stood, wincing slightly as the movement jarred her back. The green paste had dried along the line of the cuts and, like that on Ma'eva's shoulder, had begun to flake off. The skin underneath looked pink and healthy. By morning the birds' scratches should be nearly healed. Iuti reminded herself to ask Anali what the paste was.

"Aye," she said. "The dolphin didn't set any kind of lasting shield that I can sense, so if the birds find us again, we may well be on our own. In any case, I prefer caution."

Tarawe looked around at the twilit sea. The sun had just set with its usual brief flash of brilliance and the sky was rapidly turning dark. "We should leave this current flowing west," she said, "with a few feathers scattered along its trail. If we paddle away from it instead of using magic to set a wind, the birds won't have any way to know we left it. Then we can set another current and raise the wind later."

Ma'eva looked up from where he was sorting tiny green feathers along his thigh. "You see, Mama? I told you the Storm Caller was smart for a human. She understands about the wind and the birds."

"If you know so much," Iuti said, "why didn't you suggest this course to me sooner? We could have been on our way by now."

Ma'eva looked down again to concentrate on the feathers.

Anali laughed. "Because it never occurred to him until the Storm Caller said it. It's a good plan, warrior woman. I think we should use it."

"Aye," Iuti said. "Come, Ma'eva. Take up a paddle. You're young and strong and very *human*. You'll make a good paddler."

Ma'eva gave her a surprised look. "But I'm injured!"

Iuti grinned at his plaintive tone. They all knew how Ma'eva hated to paddle. He would do almost anything to avoid it.

"Those scratches are all but healed, son," Anali said. "Get over here and act like a man."

That one made even Ma'eva laugh.

"Not you," Iuti said when Tarawe started to join them in the hull. "You just keep all those feathers from flying away."

Tarawe looked around at the piles of dried and drying feathers. "How? I've been using my wind to keep them onboard till now, but we really shouldn't use any wind at all if we're going to fool the birds."

"I suppose you could set another shield around them," Iuti said, not fully trusting that idea. A shield still involved magic, and if the birds were as determined as they seemed, they might find a way to detect it.

"For heaven's sakes, child, put your feathers here in my purse," Anali said. She lifted the thong from around her neck and passed her rumpled bag to Tarawe. Tarawe immediately began stuffing feathers into it.

"Mama!" Ma'eva said. "What are you doing?"

His mother looked at him coolly.

"But you *never* take off—"

"The Storm Caller refilled my water gourd," Anali said. "How can I not offer her aid when she needs it?"

Ma'eva stared at her, then back at Tarawe and the magic bag. It changed shape, but grew no larger, as Tarawe pushed handful after handful of feathers through its narrow neck. Finished with all the dry feathers, she scooped the last of the wet ones from the sea and stuffed them in, as well. When the last long plume had disappeared, Tarawe cinched the bag and handed it back to Anali.

"Thank you," Tarawe said. Anali nodded very formally and hung the bag back around her neck. Ma'eva let out a long, tight breath.

"Don't ever do that again," Iuti heard him whisper to his mother.

Tarawe heard it, too. "Why?" she asked.

Ma'eva turned to frown at her. "Because without it, she doesn't even know how to *swim!*"

Iuti felt her own jaw drop as wide as Tarawe's. She'd always assumed the source of Mama Anali's mimicking power was part of her person. Was it possible the extraordinary magic was carried in her *bag*?

Anali frowned at her son. "Now you see why I stay away from humans so much of the time, boy. I've kept that secret for more than thirty years."

Ma'eva caught his breath and slapped both hands over his mouth.

Anali sighed and patted his knee. Then she shifted her look to Iuti. Her expression turned hard. "Well, now you know, sharkwoman. But don't think you can take it away from me. Only I, or a true sea mimic, can take it off my neck—and even if you got hold of it, the magic wouldn't work for you."

"Mother Ana, I would never take—"

"Yes you would, warrior woman," Anali said. "If you needed it badly enough, and if you thought it would *work.*"

Iuti started to speak again, but Anali stopped her with a lift of her hand. "Don't lie, Iuti Mano. Not to me and not to yourself. You're carrying what might be the last child of your line, the only child of Ho'oma'eva's. You'll do *anything* to survive."

Iuti couldn't hold Anali's gaze. She turned her look away because she knew what Ana said was true. She *would* do whatever she had to to survive. Why else was she risking the wrath of the entire population of airfolk to sail this empty sea? She jumped as a small hand patted her arm. Anali had come to squat beside her.

"There's no shame in being honest," the old woman said. "I'd feel the same myself if it were my child's life at stake." She smiled and leaned close. "To tell you the truth, dear, I've done a lot worse than steal an old lady's purse in my lifetime. *That* one wasn't always easy to protect."

She nodded toward Ma'eva. He was still sitting with both hands tight over his mouth. Iuti had never seen him so contrite.

"He looks like he could use some protecting right now," she said.

"Aye." Anali sighed and patted Iuti's arm one last time. "Mark my words, warrior woman, your children will need your patience your whole life long." She left Iuti to clamber forward again.

"Come on, Ho'oma'eva," she said. "Let's get this boat turned north before the sun comes up. It's not your fault you told them about my purse. I never should have taken it off in front of you."

"You should never take it off *ever*!" he said from behind his hands. Ana pulled them from his face.

"I won't do it again, dear. Now pick up that paddle and get us moving. You, too, mother of my grandchild, or do you plan to wait for the birds to catch up and give us a push?"

Iuti glanced at Tarawe, who was staring after Anali with a look of total astonishment. Ana never even looked at Tarawe while she was giving her warning, Iuti thought. She wondered if Mother Ana had been trying to make a point or if she didn't know the girl's history of stealing other people's magic.

Or maybe she has reason to trust Tarawe more than she does me. The thought came unbidden. Iuti moved to the stern seat and took up the steering paddle, wondering again about the significance of Tarawe refilling Anali's drinking gourd.

As Iuti was about to slip her paddle into the water, she saw a small movement inside the hull. A flicker of color. She leaned forward quickly and pulled her sword from the weapons rack. A tiny flurry of feathers followed the blade into the air.

"Mano's sweet breath," she murmured. A yellow-headed o'u fluttered upward, circled her once, and then settled on her sword. She shook it off and the bird landed instead on the deck beside her. It tilted its yellow head toward her and chirped.

"I think that o'u likes you, friend Iuti," Ma'eva said. "It's the same one who was flying around you before."

"It must have fallen asleep inside the weapons rack," Tarawe said. "Look, it's so tired it can hardly stand." She lifted the small creature and set it beside her own sleeping gull. A move, Iuti was certain, that was designed to inform her that she was not to kill the thing.

"If we're going to take those two with us," Iuti said, "they'll have to be tethered. We can't take the chance that they'll fly back to tell the others of our plan."

"My gull can't fly at all," Tarawe said, "and this little o'u could never fly so far on its own. It would fall and drown before it found the others. And it's way too small to find food out here."

"If they're coming with us, Tarawe, they have to be tethered." Iuti said it firmly this time.

Tarawe looked for a moment as if she were going to argue, but then she glanced at Anali. Anali said nothing, but Tarawe turned back to Iuti and nodded. "What shall I tie them with?" she asked.

Iuti sliced a pair of thin, braided strands from Kunan's necklace. She handed them to Tarawe. "Tie the birds to each other for now. We'll work out something better in the morning."

She paused again just as she was about to slide her paddle into the water. "Ma'eva, are you planning to help?" she asked.

Ma'eva hefted his paddle, ready to plunge it into the sea. "Aye, friend Iuti. I may not like paddling, but I'm very good at it."

"Well, it works better if we're both facing the same direction, father of my child. Turn around and face the bow."

Ma'eva looked around him in confusion for a moment, then scrambled to turn around in his seat. Tarawe giggled. "I think I'd better help," she said, and this time Iuti didn't stop her from taking a place just behind canoe center. She lifted two of the remaining paddles from the bottom of the canoe, studied them for a moment, and dropped one back.

At least I have one sensible crew member aboard, Iuti mused.

Iuti began paddling with the current, setting a careful pace and calling the beat to the others. Even Anali dipped a paddle in the water from time to time, although she rarely matched the cadence of the others. When their rhythm was well established,

Iuti held her paddle against the side of the canoe and twisted it against the current. The canoe began to turn.

She guided them so smoothly from the swiftly moving current that their movement barely slowed when they left it. Only gradually did the effort of pulling the full weight of the canoe through the water begin to tell. Tarawe continued to match Iuti's cadence without missing a stroke, and Ma'eva surprised her by paddling on without complaint. Anali soon fell asleep, leaning forward against the upright sail spar.

Iuti took their bearings by the stars and aimed the bow due north. She wanted to get as far away from Tarawe's original current as they could before using any magic again. The night was quiet save for the soft splash of their paddles and the quiet creaking of the canoe's lashings. The o'u chirped once, cheerfully. Iuti hissed at it and it immediately tucked its head under its wing and was still.

They paddled until the stars showed it to be past midnight. Iuti's shoulders had begun aching with the strain of paddling. She would be glad when she could take the time to heal herself properly. Her leg felt like it was burning inside, and her strength was nowhere near whole. In the moonlight, she could see that one of the dark lines across Tarawe's back had split open and was bleeding again. She called a halt.

"This is far enough," she said, hoping she was right.

The others lifted their paddles from the water. Tarawe laid hers across her lap and leaned forward over it. Ma'eva turned around on his seat. When he saw that Tarawe wasn't watching, he changed his skin color so that he looked like a gaily painted Lowtown whore. He grinned and blew Iuti a kiss, looking as rested now as he had when they started. Anali snored softly at the bow.

Iuti returned Ma'eva's silent tease with one of her own, a hand signal that made his brows lift very suddenly and his grin widen with welcome. He'd fall into the water with me right here, she thought, laughing, and under any other circumstance, I'd be glad to do it. She was relieved, however, when Tarawe yawned and pushed herself upright. The colors disappeared from Ma'eva's skin, although the grin remained.

"You're a good paddler, Storm Caller," he said.

"So are you," Tarawe replied. She rubbed her arms and would have scratched her back, but Iuti stopped her before her hand could reach the healing cuts.

"One has broken open," she said. "Say the pain spell again.

That should stop the rest from itching. Nothing is very clean on this canoe right now, so it's best not to scratch."

Tarawe mumbled into her hands and immediately looked more comfortable. She looked up and around. "There's a nice breeze here," she said.

"There is?" Iuti said.

"I don't feel anything," said Ma'eva.

Tarawe lifted her right hand, laughing lightly. "Well, it's a very small breeze." She twisted around to face Iuti. "But I could use it to draw other winds near. Enough to make the canoe go without calling unnatural winds from the outside."

"Do it," Iuti said. Tarawe's understanding and control of the wind was becoming markedly more precise. For one with so little formal training, she was astonishingly adept. It was as if the air spoke directly to her. The sail ruffled as a quickening breeze brushed across it. Ma'eva lifted his mother from her place near the sail's base and laid her on the outrigger deck. She was truly asleep this time. She didn't wake.

"West?" Tarawe asked.

"Northwest," Iuti said. "We need to put as much distance as we can between us and our earlier path."

Tarawe nodded and hauled the sheet. The canoe dipped forward slightly and the outrigger lifted as the sail caught the wind. The sweet sound of rushing water slid along the sides of the hull. Tarawe laughed and played the sheet as if the sail were an extension of her own arm.

Iuti let them run for another hour before suggesting to Tarawe that she add a strong sea current to their speed. A quick scoop of the Storm Caller's left hand sent the canoe skimming ahead. The outrigger lifted entirely from the water, and they sang across the starlit sea. After another hour, they turned west again.

Iuti found it impossible to sleep, even after setting a mild healing spell. So she took the night watch. Ma'eva willingly curled up on the deck next to his mother and was asleep in an instant. Tarawe took longer to settle.

"Ser Iuti?" she said after a time.

"Aye."

"Do you think it was the same dolphin?"

Iuti had been asking herself the same question ever since the great creature had appeared. "I don't know," she said. "I've never seen one before, so I don't know how to tell them apart."

"Do you think it knew who I . . . who we were?"

"Are you still worried about the flying dolphins being angry with you over the storm deaths?" Iuti asked.

"Well . . ."

"If they're angry with anyone, it must be me," Iuti said. "Mano Niuhi caused the terrible battle that killed them, and he and I are still kin despite my brothers' ravings about Mano's lost power."

"I wish we hadn't tried to take the egg," Tarawe said.

"So do I."

"Do you think it will come back?"

"Tarawe," Iuti said, concerned more by the unexpected eagerness in the girl's voice than by her obvious fear. "I have no answers to your questions. Take your rest now, so that at least one of us will be alert tomorrow. If the dolphin comes back, I'll be sure to let you know."

Tarawe grew still, but she lay awake a long time, staring out at the empty sea.

Dawn came after what seemed much too long. Anali and the o'u were the first to wake. One chirped just as the sun touched the eastern horizon. The other hiccoughed. "Oh, dear," Anali mumbled, "I never should have eaten that sugarfish. I hope it doesn't give me gas."

Iuti watched in amusement as Anali muttered and mumbled and fussed in her bag. Finally she pulled out a handful of bananas and a loaf of sweet-smelling nut bread. A tiny green feather was stuck in one end of the fragrant loaf. Ana picked it off and carefully stuffed it back into her bag.

Iuti stretched and yawned.

Ana looked up at her movement. "You look terrible, warrior woman," she said. "Didn't you sleep well?"

"I didn't sleep at all, Mother."

Anali grew immediately indignant. "You need your sleep, mother of my grandchild."

"Aye," Iuti said, "but sleep wouldn't come, so I sat watch instead." She tested the sheet, but Tarawe's wind ran as strong and steady as it had the night long. The sail remained full and taut.

"Are you hungry?"

Iuti laid a hand on her stomach and smiled. "One of us is."

The o'u chirped again. It fluttered its wings but didn't try to lift from the deck. Anali scattered a handful of crumbs under its beak before passing the bread to Iuti.

"She doesn't seem eager to leave," Iuti said. "She was awake most of the night, but she hardly moved."

"You've always had a way of collecting odd companions, sharkwoman," Anali said around a mouthful of banana. She tossed the thin red skin overboard. "I remember when you had Ma'eva convinced he was first cousin to a three-legged starfish."

Iuti grinned. "How did you find out about old Cousin Three Legs? He was supposed to be a secret." She glanced at Ma'eva. "Oh . . ."

Anali waved away her suspicion. "I didn't need Ma'eva to tell me what was going on at Kiholo reef back in those days. All the reef folk kept an eye on you two for me." She spread more crumbs for the hungry bird. "You must understand, mother of my son's child. Sea mimics are highly treasured among the seafolk. They are watched over with great interest and care throughout their lives. Little that they do in the sea is done in secret."

Iuti's look moved to Tarawe. "Little they do on land is secret either, Mother." She stretched her leg forward in the hull to ease the ache in her calf. She felt no sickness growing within the deep cut, but it was healing very slowly. Without Tarawe's suturing, it might well not have healed at all.

"The time will come, warrior woman," Anali said, "when you'll have to let that girl go." She, too, was watching Tarawe.

Tarawe lay with her head on Ma'eva's knee, her cheek cupped in her right hand. Her hair had fallen from its knot and lay in a a pool of shining black across Ma'eva's lap. The wind caused by their swift passage lifted the long, sleek strands into a feathered fan around her face. Her expression held an innocence Iuti knew Tarawe no longer had.

"She is free to go whenever she chooses," Iuti said, hoping as she said it that Tarawe would not choose to go soon. She had come to love Tarawe in a way she'd never expected. The girl was more than just a companion. She had become almost like kin. No, Iuti thought. I must not claim her as kin. She faces enough danger without that added burden.

When Iuti turned back to Anali, she found the old woman leaning against the sail line, her head hanging forward on her chest. She was quietly snoring again, with her arms wrapped protectively around her precious bag.

The o'u fluffed its wings and fluttered to the end of its tether.

It settled as near to Iuti as the strand of Kunan's hair allowed. It cocked its head to one side and stared up at her.

Iuti stared back. "You're not the oddest of my companions," she told it.

✿ *Chapter 9* ✿

THEY traveled for thirty-two days across the Empty Sea. Ser Iuti marked each morning with a notch cut into the gunwale. Sometimes they stopped, while Ma'eva and his mother explored the depths below or swam back along their path to see if they were being followed. There was no sign of either the birds or Ser Iuti's brothers. The doldrums were so complete that either would find the journey across the broad sea a long and difficult one.

Tarawe suspected they themselves couldn't have made it without her wind and water magic and the ever-present food supply in Mama Anali's purse.

Tarawe couldn't believe at first that the ocean could go on for so long. She kept watching for some small island to appear, or the distant hazy outline of mountains like they had seen when approaching the eastern mainland. She sent out questing winds to search for the taste of plants or trees or even coral near the surface of the sea, but only the taste of clean air and water returned.

They traveled north three times to take them farther from the false trail Tarawe had laid. Otherwise, they sailed west, judging that course no more dangerous and marginally more interesting than simply circling in the endless sea. "As long as we've come this far, we might as well find out if there's anything on the other side," Ser Iuti had suggested during the early days. No one disagreed.

Tarawe loved the vast, vacant ocean. The water was endlessly calm and curious. The sky, although free of all but occasional drifting clouds, was filled with subtle currents and temperature changes.

She practiced with her wind and water magic until she could

lift a single strand of Ma'eva's hair, twisting and turning and tying it into knots, without Ma'eva even noticing. Mama Ana caught her wetting her braids once with drops of seawater scooped up in little wind whirls and would have scolded Tarawe if the girl hadn't quickly asked for a drink of water. By the time Anali had searched through her bag for the calabash, she had forgotten all about the scolding.

Tarawe never touched Ser Iuti's cloud of white hair. A few of the long strands had begun to turn dark again. The effects of the greenwort paste Iuti had used to change its color were beginning to wear away. It would be many months before the warrior woman's hair turned entirely black again.

When she wasn't playing with the water or the wind, Tarawe cleaned the feathers the birds had left behind. She stripped strands of sennit from the canoe's decorative prow and retwisted it into fine, strong thread. Then, with Ma'eva's help, she wove a blanket of fine mesh and tied the multicolored feathers to it. She used the feathers as they came out of Anali's bag, making no conscious attempt to create a design with the many shapes and colors.

"It looks like a seasick parrot," Anali said.

"Or a milimili's cape," said Ma'eva.

Or wings, Tarawe thought. She tried once to make the blanket fly by lifting it with her wind, but it was much too unwieldy and blew off the outrigger into the sea. Ma'eva had to dive in after it and help her drag it back aboard. It took a long time to dry out. After that Tarawe set it up as a colorful umbrella to shield them from the sun.

The flying dolphin did not return, but occasionally schools of true dolphins paced the canoe. They leapt and dove, sliding under and around the swiftly moving vessel without ever coming near enough to touch it. One, with a silken smooth infant at her side, rode the canoe's bow wave for all of one morning. Tarawe had to restrain herself from jumping into the water with them.

They were joined at times by other strange seafolk, alone or in pairs, sometimes in schools of enormous size. They circled and nudged the canoe as if it were something they'd never experienced before. Sometimes, when he judged it safe, Ma'eva joined them, flickering and changing until he was the strongest or the strangest or the most colorful among the curious creatures. When he returned to the canoe and his human form, he shared stories of wonder and danger in the waters beneath the canoe.

It was a good time. A calm time. Mama Ana told stories of

her life among the seafolk. She taught Tarawe to sing silly songs and how to braid shells and fish scales into her hair. Ma'eva flickered from one form to another, mimicking all the creatures of the sea and delighting them with his ready laughter. In deference to Tarawe, he accepted a length of green cloth from Anali and kept it wrapped around his waist whenever he took his human form.

Even Ser Iuti smiled more and more often. As her stomach began to swell, she loosened her trousers and sewed herself a padded vest, using knotted sennit and layers of woven matting from the sail. She spent long hours stretching and bending and practicing with her sword.

Sometimes the little o'u, freed after many days from its tether, rode Iuti's shoulder while she practiced her warrior's dance. It made Tarawe laugh to see the tiny, delicate creature taking part in so fast and fierce a dance. Despite Iuti's quick movements, the o'u was never caught by her swinging blade.

Tarawe's gull also roamed the canoe freely. Its wing had been damaged permanently by its long, arduous flight, and it could fly only with the aid of Tarawe's wind. After Tarawe explained to the gull that her indiscriminate, pungent droppings were inappropriate to such a small living area, the gull became more appreciated by the rest of the crew. Once the birds were freed, Iuti had made a gift of their tethers to Tarawe; she tied them like bracelets, one around each wrist.

Tarawe's only frustration was being forbidden to call storm winds close to the canoe. She tried it once, but at the first sign of rising swell, Ser Iuti ordered her to stop.

"It's much too dangerous," she insisted.

"But—"

"I know you think you can protect us," Iuti said, "but what if the canoe is damaged? Or what if *you* are hurt? Then what would we do? You'll get your chance to play with the storm winds again, Tarawe, after the child is born and safe. For now, keep them away from us."

To Tarawe's disappointment, although not her surprise, Ma'eva and Anali wholeheartedly agreed. So, as the days passed, Tarawe played only with the few natural clouds that drifted near their path. She created squalls far to the north of the canoe, with waterspouts and crisscrossing waves, and winds that lashed at frenzied seas. She sent questing breezes into the storms to carry back the taste of her storms. She grinned often at their sweet, strong power.

Late one night, while they were sailing under a full white moon, Tarawe tasted something new on the wind. A bitter taste, unlike anything she'd ever experienced before.

"Ser Iuti?" she said when she was sure the change was truly on the wind and hadn't been caused by an indiscretion by the gull.

Ser Iuti didn't look up from where she was lashing the sharp jaws of several parrot fish around the end of a paddle. She had already carved away the flat paddle itself to create a straight pole and secured the sharp beak of the saber bird to the point. It was a wicked-looking weapon, although no worse than the war club studded with shark's teeth she had once carried. Still, it made Tarawe uncomfortable. Iuti braced the new spear against the gunwale with her feet, keeping the four sennit ties taut in both hands and in her teeth.

"I think we should stop the canoe, Ser."

That brought Iuti's look up. She took the ties from her mouth, still holding them taut. "Why?"

"There's . . . I smell something, Ser. On the wind. I need to stop to see which way it's coming from."

Without questioning Tarawe further, Iuti knotted the loose ties around the base of the spear and slid it into the weapons rack. She untied the sheet and luffed the sail. Tarawe slowed the wind and current, and they waited in silence until the canoe drifted to a halt. The sudden cessation of water rushing along the canoe's sides made the night silence seem almost loud.

"What's wrong?" Ma'eva whispered. The change in motion and sound had wakened both him and his mother. They sat hand in hand on the deck, staring at Tarawe and Iuti with wide eyes.

"Something . . ." Tarawe sniffed. "I don't know what it is, but it wasn't there before." She dunked a finger into the sea and lifted it to the wind. She didn't really need to; the breeze brushing past the stalled canoe was obviously coming from the west. She felt a hint of moisture in the air, although there had been no clouds in the sky when the sun went down. Only a vivid red sunset over an empty ocean.

"I don't smell . . ." Suddenly Iuti wrinkled her nose. "Yes, I do. Tarawe, are you sure that idiot gull didn't—"

"It's sulfur," Anali said in a voice even quieter than Ma'eva's had been.

Iuti turned to her. "Sulfur! How can there be sulfur in the middle of the ocean?" She, too, spoke in a lowered voice, although not as low as Anali and Ma'eva. There was enough starlight to see that they were still alone on the sea. "Are you sure?"

"I grew up downwind of the Ilimar hot springs," Anali said. "I'd recognize that stink anywhere."

"What are hot springs?" Tarawe asked.

Ser Iuti stood and stared toward the west. "They're places where steam and hot water seep out of the ground. People sometimes use them as healing sites. They soak in the hot water and inhale the fumes."

"There are places like that at the bottom of the sea," Ma'eva said. "They taste terrible and sometimes strange creatures live there."

"It's coming from the west," Iuti said. Suddenly she looked startled. "There's a *breeze* coming from the west! That's the first true wind we've met since we set sail on this sea."

Ma'eva grinned. "Maybe we've reached the other side."

"If we have, it's still a long way off," Iuti replied.

They all stared toward the west again, where the moonlit sea stretched empty to the horizon. Tarawe tasted the wind again. It definitely smelled of moisture along with the vague stench of the thing Anali called sulfur. Tarawe wondered if sulfur was some magical element, since Ser Iuti had said it was used in healing.

"We might as well keep going," Iuti said at last. "We'll have moonlight right up until dawn, so there won't be any time when we can't see what's ahead of us. Even if it's nothing but a return to more normal seas, a change would be nice. This flat calm wears on the soul after a while."

"I thought you were prepared to stay out here until your child was born," Anali said.

Iuti shrugged and grinned ruefully. "I'll stay out here if I have to, but if there's firm ground up ahead, I'd just as soon go stand on it."

"Just so you stay near the water when your birthing time comes," Anali replied. "If that's a boy you're carrying, he needs to be born in the water, or brought there immediately after. Did Ma'eva explain . . ."

"Aye, Mother," Iuti said. "I know the danger."

Tarawe stared from one to the other, wondering of what danger they spoke. Before she could ask, Ser Iuti took up the sheet again and asked her to reset her wind and water current.

"Do you want to go fast again?" Tarawe asked.

"Can you think of any reason we shouldn't?" Iuti answered.

Tarawe looked toward the west again. "I guess not. There's nothing out there." A hint of moisture in the air hardly constituted a threat. If anything, it provided even more of a reason to continue sailing toward it. She scooped the wind and water back to the west.

Tarawe slept fitfully for the rest of the night and was glad when dawn arrived. There was still nothing on the western horizon, but the almost imperceptible swells over which they had traveled for so long had grown deeper. A faint acrid tinge of sulfur remained on the still morning air even though the easterly breeze had disappeared. Tarawe wondered if Anali smelled it, too.

Ana looked tired, as if she hadn't slept well either, or at all. That seemed impossible considering how easily she nodded off at almost any other time. Tarawe crossed the deck to sit beside her. Anali offered her bread and bananas. Tarawe ate hungrily. Her appetite had grown considerably since she'd left Fanape. She wished, as she had so many times before on this journey, that Anali carried pounded breadfruit in her bag, and coconuts. Tarawe missed the sweet soft meat found inside fresh drinking nuts most of all. She noticed that her feathered sun shade had been taken down. It was not folded on the deck as usual, which meant it had been put back into Anali's purse.

"It's still with us," Anali said before Tarawe could ask about the sulfur smell. "It was on the air all night, strongest just before the wind shifted at dawn."

"Maybe there's a submerged reef somewhere ahead," Iuti said, scanning the horizon. For the first morning in many days, she was not smiling. She had finished knotting the parrot fish's jaws onto her fighting stick and was scraping the handle smooth with a piece of broken shell.

Anali grunted. "I think I'll take a swim," she said.

She started for the edge of the canoe, but Ma'eva stopped her. "I'll go look," he said. "You stay here."

Anali blinked up at him, obviously startled at his tone. It held none of his usual playfulness. "You stay here," he said again. This time it was clearly an order. He brushed his fingers across Ser Iuti's cheek, accepted her touch in return, and slipped overboard. As quickly as he submerged, he flickered and re-formed.

"Hmmph, smart boy," Anali said, watching him. "A giant barracuda is exactly the form I'd have taken." Ho'oma'eva disappeared into the deep, swimming west. Tarawe sent a handful of questing wind after him.

"Something doesn't feel right," she said.

"Slow us down," Iuti replied. Tarawe slowed the wind and stopped the current altogether. Her questing wind returned much sooner than she had expected. As it slid across her cheeks, she caught her breath at the rich, earthy smell of fresh soil and foliage.

"Ser, there must be land—"

Ma'eva's head broke the surface just ahead of the outrigger. "There's land ahead! And humans in canoes! They're all—"

"Mano's bloody teeth!" Iuti cried. "We've been fooled by a simple hiding spell." She shouted a call into the still, empty morning, and all around them the air shivered. Abruptly the sea ahead was not empty at all, but filled with a mountain higher than any Tarawe had ever seen. Clouds lay like a necklace all around the upper slopes, revealing dark, sharp peaks at the summit. Surf spumed along sheer cliffs at the mountain's base. Thick, dark jungle clung to its sides.

And the water surrounding the canoe was filled with canoes!

Birds! Tarawe thought in that first instant, then realized the creatures aboard the canoes were only humans decked in feathered headdresses much more elaborate than Iuti's kinsmen's had been. Tarawe stopped her wind instantly. She quickly brought up a back wind to keep them from drifting farther forward.

"Tarawe, take us back!"

It was too late. By the time Tarawe turned to look aft, a pair of canoes had crossed their path and cut them off from an easy retreat.

"Shall I push them—"

"No," Ser Iuti said. She was standing at the center of the hull, her sword in one hand, her new fighting stick in the other. Ma'eva lifted himself swiftly aboard and rewrapped the cloth around his waist.

"They've done us no harm so far," Iuti said, "and they could have. Drop the sail, so we can see all around."

"They're well armed," Ma'eva said as he and Tarawe quickly did as Iuti asked. The canoes surrounding them bristled with spears and knives. When the sail was furled and lying along the length of the hull, he said, "Mama, you get ready to go in the water, just in case."

"I'm not leaving my grandchild," Anali said. She reached into her bag and, for once without rummaging, pulled out a pair of short knives. She strapped their sheaths to her wrists and straightened, eyeing each of the canoes in turn. The warriors surrounding them, if warriors they were, stared back.

Their faces were painted in red and black—streaked, jagged lines of crimson laid over an ebony base. They wore knotted and woven armor in more styles than even the southern army had used—and each wore a headdress that was thick with gray and black feathers. Or something that looked like feathers, Tarawe saw as the birdlike people moved closer. They didn't move quite like the real thing.

"Tarawe," Iuti said softly. "Take the stern seat. Keep us from drifting into any of them, or them from hitting us if you can, but don't make your use of magic obvious."

"Aye," Tarawe replied, and scrambled to do as Ser Iuti said. She held the steering paddle in the water as if controlling the canoe's drift while she pulled a current up from beneath them and sent it spreading away in a circle at the surface. Their own canoe remained still at the center, but the nearest of the dark-faced warriors' vessels lifted and settled and stopped moving toward them. Tarawe quickly added a bit of chop to the nearby water to disguise the current that protected them.

"Why don't they speak?" she asked.

Ser Iuti looked around at the gathered canoes. There were twenty or more. The largest carried a crew of eight, the smallest held only two. It was the small canoe that approached the closest. "It could be courtesy," Iuti said. "Or challenge. I've seen it done both ways."

"Well, there's one way to find out," Anali said.

"Ana, don't—"

But Ana was already on her feet, fists on her hips. She stared hard at the nearest canoe. The man at the bow stood abruptly. His small craft wobbled for an instant before the woman at the stern quickly brought it back to balance. The warriors in the other canoes whispered and murmured among themselves.

"Well, birdman," Anali called. "Are you going to invite us ashore or not?"

"Mano's teeth!" Iuti muttered. "Anali, sit down!"

"Mama, you shouldn't—"

Suddenly the small canoe surged forward. The man flung his feathered spear toward Anali. Iuti knocked the spear down with her own, while Ma'eva pulled his mother clear. The spear landed with a clatter beside Tarawe's gull. The bird, startled from sleep, screeched and spread its great, useless wings.

The attacking canoe stopped. The man grabbed the bow to

maintain his balance while Tarawe grabbed the gull before it could topple overboard. A hush spread across the assembled canoes.

Then, suddenly, a great shout went up.

"Maan! Maansusu!" The painted warriors began clapping and pounding the sides of their canoes. They shouted and cried out. "Maansusu!" One by one, they jumped up to twist their bodies into grotesque forms. Two of them threw spears at the man who had attacked Anali, but he dodged them without harm.

A moment later, a long, haunting call lifted from the nearby mountainside—a conch shell being blown from somewhere far back in the trees. The dance ended as abruptly as it had begun. The warriors dropped into their seats again and made an elaborate point of laying down their weapons. They gestured and grinned and waved Tarawe and the others through a pathway they opened to a small beach. The beach lay at the base of a steep, narrow valley, one of only a few along the rugged coast.

"By all the gods of Ilimar," Anali said. "What do you suppose *that* was all about?"

"I don't know," Iuti said. "But I suggest you don't antagonize them again, Anali. Let me do the challenging from here on. I've had more experience dodging spears."

"They seem friendly enough now," Ma'eva said.

"It looks like they want us to go ashore," Tarawe added.

She studied the surrounding canoes once more, then the beach toward which they were being urged. It was bordered on both sides by sheer, stone cliffs; Tarawe had never seen stone so black. A small stream spread across one side of the beach and into the sea. Clouds shrouded the upper end of the valley. The knowledge that they had come so close to this great, high island without seeing it sent a chill down Tarawe's back. She held the gull tightly, afraid to let her loose again. Who knew what these strange people might do if the bird startled them a second time?

"There are others gathered on the beach," Iuti said. "Some even better decorated than these. Chiefs, no doubt. I suppose we'd better go meet them."

"I'll paddle," Ma'eva said, surprising them all. He grinned at their looks of disbelief. "I *am* a man, after all," he said, "at least for now."

Anali smiled and nodded her approval, but Iuti's look of concern deepened. "Friend sea mimic," she said, "take great care when we reach the land. If any killing needs doing, you leave it to me. That goes for you, too, Tarawe."

Tarawe nodded. She had no intentions of killing, ever again, if she could avoid it. Without the healer Ho'ola to help protect her mind from the painful thrusts caused by violent death, she would become helpless in a very short time. Tarawe never wanted to experience that horror again.

Ma'eva saluted Iuti with one of the many hand gestures the two of them exchanged when they didn't want Tarawe to understand what they said. "I make a fine human male, mother of my child," Ma'eva said, "as you well know, but I have no wish to remain in this form forever. I promise to take very great care not to kill while I'm on dry land."

Ser Iuti actually laughed in answer to that, although Tarawe knew that both she and Ma'eva took the matter seriously. Anali had explained earlier that while they were on land, sea mimics were not allowed to kill humans. If they did, they became fully human themselves and lost the ability to make the sea change.

Ser Iuti remained standing at the center of the canoe as they paddled toward the shore. The painted warriors in the nearby canoes watched her warily, particularly after she laughed. Tarawe understood their caution. Ser Iuti was an impressive sight when she stood at full attention with a weapon in each hand. When she smiled while doing it, it made even Tarawe want to take a step back.

The conch was blown again as they approached the small beach. Then again when their canoe's hull first touched the sand. Tarawe held the canoe steady while Iuti stepped onto the outrigger. A handful of warriors stepped forward. Like the others, their faces were painted red and black. Each of them carried a short spear painted in the same colors.

"Ceremonial weapons," Iuti said softly.

But still deadly, Tarawe thought.

"It might be an honor guard," Anali said. "They used to do that back in the mountains."

"Most likely it's another challenge," Iuti replied. She was quiet for a moment, while warriors from the other canoes splashed into the shallow water and pulled their vessels ashore. "Stay on the canoe until I tell you to come," she said when it was clear everyone was waiting for some movement from their canoe.

"Friend Iuti, are you sure—"

Iuti leapt lightly from the outrigger into knee-deep water.

Instantly the waiting guard began hurling their spears.

❧ Chapter 10 ❧

IUTI sidestepped the first of the spears, then moved quickly away from the canoe so no one aboard would be struck by the others. The first lance struck the canoe hull and splashed into the water behind her. She ducked away from another cast and knocked the third and fourth away with her sword.

A chieftain's challenge, she thought. This was a test of her wit and dexterity. Some of the southern islands had this custom, although in this case, judging by the accuracy of the warriors' throws, the game was being played in deadly earnest. She dodged another red and black missile, glad that she'd maintained her training ritual during their long voyage. Her pregnancy had changed her balance enough so that she might not have survived this passage otherwise. Her injured leg felt strong, but the dull pain she'd felt for so long turned sharp again as she twisted and crouched away from the spears.

She counted ten casts before she reached the beach. Two from each of the guards. She slipped through the barrage without being struck.

As soon as she stepped onto dry sand, the attack stopped. Standing straight, she lowered her own weapons, but held herself ready for whatever challenge these unexpected islanders might offer next.

Someone applauded.

"Well done, stranger. You stroll the chief's path like a true south islander despite your obviously not being one."

Iuti looked toward a narrow ledge on the side of the cliff. A man sat there, one leg hanging over the edge. He wore knotted armor much like the others, but his face was unpainted and he wore no headdress. One of the chief's guard yelled and threw a stone his way. He ducked away easily.

"Bring your companions ashore, lady warrior," he called. "You've established your right to do so. If you wait too long, the rules might change."

"What rules?" Iuti asked. One of the guards began sidling closer and she turned a slow look his way. He stopped. When she continued to hold his challenging stare, he stepped back.

"What difference does it make if you don't know what they are to begin with?" the man on the ledge replied with a laugh.

"How do I know I can trust you?" Iuti countered.

"You don't. But I, at least, am willing to speak to you before you've been formally welcomed," he grinned, "—or killed. Everyone will be eager to talk with you after that happens."

Iuti studied him for a moment, then motioned to Tarawe and the others to come ashore. As quickly as they stepped into the water, island warriors dashed for the canoe. Iuti mumbled a quick shielding spell to protect the vessel, but discovered that one had already been laid. Either Tarawe or Ana had done it even quicker than she. The approaching warriors cursed and kicked angrily at the water around the canoe. They could touch the canoe's outer edges, but they couldn't move it or reach inside the hull, not that there was anything aboard but the paddles and the empty water logs for them to steal.

The man on the ledge applauded again.

"He's a brazen one, isn't he?" Anali muttered as she moved to Iuti's side. Ma'eva moved to stand beside his mother. Iuti was surprised to see that he carried the spear that had landed on the canoe. Ma'eva usually disdained the use of human weaponry. Tarawe brushed a hand across Iuti's back to let her know where she stood. The girl has the mind and reflexes of a warrior, Iuti mused, despite her inability to kill without harming herself in the bargain.

Ana spoke again. "He's right, though. You danced the chieftain's path as well as I've ever seen it done. I think you won some respect there. Gods, but this sand is hot on my feet. I remember now why—"

"Be still, Ana," Iuti said softly. Ana had lived away from humans for more than thirty years. She was likely to do or say anything. Iuti preferred having at least some control over what they shared with these strangers.

There was a flurry of motion behind the line of guards and they parted to allow a very tall, thin woman to walk through. She was followed by a man slightly taller. Both wore elaborate capes and headdresses covered with silver and black feathers.

Real feathers, Iuti noted with interest, although they were old and matted. Those that hadn't turned brown with age were gray and white—gulls' feathers. Many looked singed, as if they'd come too close to fire. The sharp claws of carrybirds were strapped to the backs of the pair's hands.

"Give me Maansusu," the woman demanded.

Iuti stared at her.

"She wants the bird," the cliff man called. Again someone hurled a stone his way. Again he dodged it without seeming to move.

"Tarawe, did you bring—"

"Of course," Tarawe replied. "I couldn't leave her alone on the canoe. But I'm not giving her away. Nobody wearing gull feathers is going to eat *my* bird."

Iuti sighed. That idiot bird was likely to get them all killed. No one, not even Iuti herself, was likely to get it away from Tarawe if she didn't want it to be so.

"Give me Maansusu," the feathered woman demanded again. She held out her hands. The insides of her arms were covered with thick, puckered scars, many of them burn scars. Some were too evenly spaced to have been made accidentally, others gave evidence of less ordered violence in this woman's past.

"Isn't it customary to be offered guest right before demands are made on our possessions?" Anali said. She was standing on one bare foot, rubbing the other on the side of her leg. She steadied herself by gripping Ma'eva's arm.

The island woman glared at Iuti. "What kind of chieftain are you that you allow your underlings to speak before you do?"

"Are *you* a chieftain?" Iuti replied. "Should I feel obliged to speak first to you?" It was an insult of great dishonor. The woman's garb and demeanor clearly defined her as being in an elevated position among this strangely silent group. Only the man on the cliff laughed at the jibe. All around, warriors fingered their weapons.

The island chief rose to her full height. She matched Iuti's stare. She said nothing, and after a moment, the fury in her eyes changed to cunning. Her jaw remained tight, but she smiled. "You are either very brave or entirely foolhardy," she said, "to risk the wrath of the Chosen One so soon after your arrival."

She tossed her head; the feathers in her headdress dipped and bobbed. "But I forgive you your ignorance. Come, join us in the village where food and drink are being prepared. Your old mother here is welcome to her guest right." Her look slid across

Ma'eva's broad, dark chest, then past Iuti to Tarawe. "As are the rest of your companions."

She stared at the gull in Tarawe's arms for a moment, then turned and swept back through the guards. The man who had stood by her in silence ran an insolent look over Ma'eva before turning to follow. To Iuti's complete surprise, the guards and most of the onlookers followed.

They were left alone on the beach except for a group of obviously curious children. The children wore skirts of ti leaves and headbands of moss and fringed leaves. One had daubs of red and black paint on his cheeks. They whispered and giggled together as the adults filed back into the jungle.

"I don't think that big male likes me," Ma'eva said when the adults had all disappeared.

"I don't think any of them like any of us," Anali replied. "Except for Tarawe's bird. They seem to like her well enough."

"I'm not giving her away," Tarawe said.

Anali patted her hand. "Of course you're not, dear. I wasn't suggesting that you should."

"I wonder what they want with the gull," Ma'eva said. "That Chosen One and her male looked like birds themselves. Very old and dusty birds."

"It's not a good idea to stand there on the beach after the Chosen One has offered hospitality," the man on the cliff called.

Iuti sheathed her sword. She settled her hands on her hips and stared up at him. "Do you remain on that cliff because you hold some exalted position or because you're afraid to come down?"

He laughed. "You're a bold one, aren't you? Who are you anyway? What brings you and your strange little group to Tahena's friendly shores? You don't look storm-blown, for all that your sail has been cut to pieces. And I'll wager you're not bird worshipers despite that fine gull you carry."

Bird worshipers, Iuti thought. That would explain the costumes these people wore, and their interest in the gull, but . . .

"I've seen no birds near here but our own," she said. If there had been sea birds flying near this isle, Tarawe would surely have noticed them despite the hiding spell.

"There are none save for the occasional straggler that survives crossing the Empty Sea," the man said. "The original birds were wiped out generations ago for the use of their feathers and their meat. Some of the first settlers brought dogs and pigs that rooted up the nests and ate the eggs. It's a rare day we see a live bird on Tahena. You've brought us quite a prize."

Tarawe's grip on the gull tightened. It clucked its disapproval, sending the approaching children scampering back. Their eyes were wide with wonder. If what the man said was true, some may never have seen a live bird before.

Iuti had a sudden thought. "Tarawe," she said softly. "Where is the o'u?"

"I have her, Ser. She's hiding under the gull's wing. She wanted to join you when you were dodging the spears, but I held her back."

"You didn't answer my question," the man on the cliff called.

"Keep her hidden," Iuti said even more quietly than before. Aloud she said, "I am Iuti Mano. I hail from the western isles, although I've spent much time on the eastern mainland of late."

The man sat up straighter. "You are from the shark clan?"

Iuti nodded. If he thought her still protected by the sharks, there was no reason to inform him otherwise. There was no way he could know of the events at Fanape. "And you?" she said. "You speak with the accent of a south islander, and you have their build."

"Slight, you mean." He laughed. "I'm one-legged, too, Iuti of the shark clan, but I can outrun anyone on this island, yourself included I have no doubt. Don't take me for granted."

She waited.

The man turned to look the way the islanders had gone, then back at Iuti. "My name is Nikivi. I have no clan here. That's why I sit on this cliff instead of painting my face and stuffing feather moss in my hair like my bird-worshiping neighbors. I came here, storm-blown, twelve years ago and have sought a way to leave ever since. I live by my own rules."

"And change them as it suits you," Iuti said.

"Of course," he replied.

"I didn't lie to you about accepting the Chosen One's hospitality, though," he added. "She'll grow impatient soon. If any of you want to survive the day, you'd best go eat her food." He pulled his foot up onto the ledge.

"Wait," Iuti said. "Tell us why you haven't been able to leave this isle."

He smiled slightly. "The Empty Sea stretches as far to the west as it does to the east. It's only by evil chance that I survived to reach these shores at all. Without a strong canoe and some mighty magic to power it, the Empty Sea cannot be crossed." His look slid back to the water and their canoe.

"Are there others like you?" Iuti asked. "Others who came here unwilling and wish to leave?"

"The last outsider to wash ashore came five years ago," he said. "The poor bastard never made it past the chieftain's walk."

His look shifted to Tarawe. "A word to the wise for the little girl who thinks she's guarding your back. There are few healthy young women on this isle, girl. So hold on to your bird. Hold on as long as you can, because once they take it from you, you'll be fair game. The shark's sister may be strong enough to pick her mates as she wishes, but you'll be a brood hen in no time. From the look of fire in your eyes, I don't think you'll like it."

He saluted them in the way of southern chieftains and backed out of sight.

"What did he mean, Ser?" Tarawe asked immediately. "What is a brood hen?"

Iuti stared after the ill-spoken Nikivi. She'd noticed that there were more men than women in the party that greeted them, but had not thought it significant. She'd been surprised, in fact, to see so many women among the warriors. She remembered now, though, that there had been no women at all waiting on the beach. Those strong enough to defend themselves become warriors, she thought. The rest serve any men who want them. It was a pattern she'd seen before.

"He means the men will seek your company," she said.

Tarawe went pale. "Like Pali?"

Iuti laid a hand on her shoulder. "There are always men like Pali."

"Ser, they can't . . . I can't . . ." The gull protested Tarawe's tightened grip again.

"I won't let them harm you, Tarawe."

"You don't understand," Tarawe cried. "I *cannot* let a man do that to me. I *must* not!" Her eyes filled with tears and she shuddered, just as she had before when she'd spoken of Pali.

Anali slid an arm around Tarawe's shoulders. "We won't let anything happen to you, dear. In fact, I'll show you a few tricks of my own for keeping unwanted men away. After you've learned those, I'll teach you how to attract the men you *do* want."

"I don't want *any* man!" Tarawe said. She looked up at Iuti.

Iuti met her look as best she could while still watching the children. They were creeping closer, their wide eyes still on the bird.

Tarawe shifted the gull into her left arm and raised her right hand. "It's something . . ." She looked down at her hand. She closed it into a tight fist. "It's something about the wind, Ser. I can't let a man touch me."

"Ayiii," Iuti said softly. She wrapped Tarawe's small fist in her own. The healer Ho'ola had once suggested that Tarawe's untapped, unparalleled power might be heightened by her youth, her innocence. Her virginity, Iuti thought. Is *that* the price she must pay for the use of her magic—to remain apart from men forever? Gods, but she wished she could find a peaceful home for this sweet child.

"I won't let it happen, little sister," she promised.

She turned and stamped her foot. The boy with the paint on his face had come close enough to reach out and try to touch the bird. He scuttled and scrambled away. Tarawe pulled the gull close again.

A conch blew, far back in the jungle. Its echoing note held long and empty on the still air.

"If I thought we could escape safely," Iuti said, "I would urge you all back onto the canoe right now. But most of their fleet is still in the water, and if they have the magic to set so large a hiding spell, they must have some way to keep travelers here after they've been caught by the deception."

She looked at Ma'eva. "You and Anali could still get away by going into the water."

"Don't be silly, girl," Ana said before Ma'eva could reply. "If we hadn't intended staying with you, we wouldn't have come ashore in the first place."

"Ma'eva?" Iuti asked, although she knew he wouldn't leave her side—not while she carried his child.

Ma'eva smiled. "I'm hungry, friend Iuti," he said, "and I smell both roasted breadfruit and taro on the air."

"If we could escape the Demon Drummers, we can escape these feathered people, too," Tarawe said. "If we have to." She had returned to that deep calm she employed when she knew she could not change her situation. She tucked a wriggling handful of black and yellow feathers back under the gull's wing.

They followed the others inland along a narrow path. It led steeply uphill, and after the first few steps, Ma'eva lifted his mother into his arms and carried her. The children flitted through the jungle shadows in total silence. The village was not far from the beach, but the jungle was so dense, and the thatched roofs of the houses so skillfully laid, that there had been no hint of the place from below.

Another deception, Iuti thought. Another challenge to new-comers to the isle. She set her mind to memorizing the sizes and shapes and smells of the place. She suspected there were others hidden in the forests, just as she was sure there had been armed and ready warriors watching them all along their route.

A circle of coconut fronds and wide, smooth banana leaves had been laid on the open ground at the village center. Garlands of flowers, interspersed with wooden bowls and calabashes, were set atop the leaves, and the containers were all piled high with food. This feast had obviously been prepared in advance.

"They must have been watching our approach since dawn," Anali muttered.

"I told you I smelled taro," Ma'eva whispered. "I hope they know how to cook it right."

Iuti almost laughed. Ma'eva wouldn't know properly cooked taro from poorly cooked sand crabs. He ate anything that wasn't poisonous to whatever form he was in at the time. She sent him silent thanks for providing her with an excuse to grin as she stepped into the clearing.

The Chosen One glared at her from across the circle. It was obvious she was not pleased by their delay.

"What do you suppose they want from us?" Anali said as Ma'eva set her back on her feet. She patted his arm in thanks. "If it's just the bird, I'd think they would have tried to kill us by now."

"They did try—" Ma'eva began.

"Sit there," the Chosen One's male companion shouted. He pointed to the right side of the circle. Red and black-faced warriors backed away from the site. Iuti led her small group to the place and sat cross-legged in the spot nearest, but still not near, the Chosen One. Tarawe sat beside her, the gull still tucked tightly in her arms. There was some hesitation, then a whispered comment from Anali that Iuti could not hear, before Ma'eva sat beside Tarawe and Anali took her place at the end of the line.

"Why do you allow that old woman such license?" the be-feathered man demanded.

Iuti turned her look to the Chosen One. "Why do you allow your consort such ill manners?" she asked.

The man's face darkened with anger, but the Chosen One smiled, coolly. "It's clear you've met formal challenge before," she said. "You meet it well. We shall enjoy your presence."

Iuti wasn't sure how to respond to that, so she grinned again. It caused a rustle of comment among the gathered warriors. The Chosen One lifted a hand and the whispering warriors quickly dispersed to places around the circle of food. Only those with painted faces sat on the leaves. The others spread out behind them. A woman, heavy with child, peered from behind a wide-boled coconut tree until a curse and a hurled stone drove her back out of sight. Iuti saw no sign of Nikivi.

Another movement of the Chosen One's hand brought a dozen or more youngsters into the center of the circle. They carried more food. After placing it before the seated warriors, they sat on their heels and waved woven fronds over the food to keep the flies away.

"They should have been doing that all along," Anali muttered. "I'd forgotten how dirty life on land could be." Her feelings did not stop her from enjoying the feast, however. She ate from each of the dishes near them, and when a bowl of bright-red mountain cherries was passed her way, she took two handfuls. After inspecting each of them carefully, she tucked the two largest into her bag and ate the rest with relish.

Tarawe, too, ate eagerly of everything offered, although she waited for Iuti's approval before she dipped into each new dish. Iuti detected no taint of sorcery or poison in the food. She noticed with some humor that Ma'eva seemed to actually be enjoying the roasted taro root.

The islanders were not silent during the meal. They spoke quietly, but only among themselves. The Chosen One spoke not at all. She, like the others, ate heartily, watching her visitors all the while. Most often, her gaze rested on Tarawe and the gull. She sat up straighter each time the bird ate from Tarawe's hand. Finally she waved away the dishes of proffered food, sat back, and belched loudly.

Anali, who had fallen asleep leaning against Ma'eva, was startled awake. She blinked around in confusion for an instant, then glowered at the warrior sitting next to her. He had been about to take the last of the mountain cherries from the wooden bowl. He looked for a moment as if he would defy her, but formal guest right prevailed. He offered her the remaining fruits.

She scooped them out of the dish and into her mouth without comment.

The Chosen One laughed. "Your old mother eats like she's never seen food. Didn't you feed her on that fine canoe of yours?"

Iuti finished swallowing a last bite of roasted fish, wiped her hands on the leaves beside her, and answered with a belch as deep and satisfying as the Chosen One's own. Tarawe stared at her in amazement. Ma'eva grinned. It was he who had taught her the trick to making such a noise.

"What shore is this?" she asked. "To whom should we offer thanks for this fine meal?"

"This is the Isle of Tahena," the Chosen One replied. "The sacred land of Haku 'Aina. We are the landmaker's servants, set here to care for her domain. What brings you so far into the Empty Sea?"

Landmaker? Iuti thought.

"We came to talk to Haku 'Aina," Anali said before Iuti could answer.

Stunned silence met her words. Even Iuti was surprised. Did Anali know of this Haku 'Aina, or was she just testing? Iuti suspected Anali knew all about ritual challenge and had faced it successfully many times. She found it harder to believe the old woman knew anyone named Haku 'Aina

The Chosen One stared at Anali. "Only one who has earned the right can speak to the landmaker, old woman." She pounded a fist on her chest. "*I* am the Chosen One. If you have a message for Haku 'Aina, speak it to me."

"Young woman, our message is much too important to be given to a *servant*," Anali said.

One of the warriors jumped to his feet. It was the same painted man Anali had challenged on the canoe. He stalked across the open center of the circle to stand before her.

"You lie, old woman," he said. "You have no message. No one outside the Empty Sea knows of this place. You never heard of Haku 'Aina before coming ashore here."

Ana glanced up at him. "You'd be surprised at how much I know," she said, and smiled. She's lived away from humans for a long time, Iuti thought, but she hasn't forgotten how to handle them.

"Who are you?" the Chosen One said.

Ana lifted her chin. "I am Anali of Ilimar. Daughter of my

mother and mother of my son. And who might you be, bird-woman?''

The Chosen One glared at her for a moment. Then she shifted her look to Tarawe. ''Who are you?'' she demanded of the girl. ''How is it Maansusu eats from your hand? You aren't strong enough to have captured so large a bird on your own.'' Her glance flickered back to Iuti.

''I didn't capture this bird,'' Tarawe said. ''She's my friend, not my prisoner.''

The Chosen One's eyes opened wide. An excited murmur passed through the assembly.

''I'm not going to give her to you,'' Tarawe said.

''Why did you bring her then?'' the Chosen One demanded. ''There is only one reason for Maansusu to visit this isle, and that is to act as sacrifice to Haku 'Aina. The Chosen One is the only one with the right to carry the bird into the landmaker's domain. Bring her to me.''

Tarawe didn't move. Her hands looked calm where they rested on the gull's back, but Iuti knew Tarawe was prepared to defend the bird if she had to. It was strange how attached she remained to the creature, even after its kin had all but declared war on her and the rest of their small group. There was no hope now that the gulls would agree to becoming Tarawe's family totem. Iuti laid one hand on her fighting stick and shifted to be sure her sword was within easy reach.

The man who had come to stand before Anali spoke again. He pointed one of two spears he carried toward her. ''You know nothing of this place. You know nothing of Haku 'Aina and our customs. You lied, old woman. I challenge you to speak the truth.''

He thrust his spear forward, but long before it could touch Ana, before even Iuti could react, Ma'eva brought his own spear up and knocked the painted shaft away. ''I won't let you harm my mother,'' he said.

Anali beamed.

A hush spread over the gathering.

The warrior glared, first at Ma'eva, then again at Anali.

''Your challenge has been met and you have lost a second time, Pulani,'' the Chosen One's consort said, laughing. ''Go, sit down and cry on your mate's shoulder. If it's still there to cry on.''

A ripple of laughter followed his words. The laughter doubled when the woman who had been with Pulani in the canoe leaned over to spit in one of the bowls from which he had eaten. Pulani blushed. The color was apparent even through his paint. He frowned and grabbed up his spear. The laughter renewed as he started back across the circle.

Carefully now, Iuti thought. Watch him carefully.

Suddenly Pulani stiffened. He spun around and cast his spear directly at Ma'eva.

⚞ *Chapter 11* ⚟

SER Iuti flicked her fighting stick up to knock Pulani's spear away. It clattered into the food dishes before the Chosen One, and an immediate cry of protest arose. Tarawe expected Pulani to try a second time to kill Ma'eva—he carried a second spear. But then she saw the hilt of a knife protruding from his chest. His look was one of total surprise. He crumpled slowly to the ground.

There was an instant of silence, then a rush of excited chatter throughout the clearing. Tarawe even heard women's voices from back in the trees. No one moved as Anali rose and walked to Pulani's side. She rolled the body over with her foot.

"I won't let *anyone* harm my son," she said. She reached down and yanked her blade free. She wiped it clean on the moss that circled the dead man's forehead and slipped the knife back into its sheath. Then she returned to her place in the circle.

Ma'eva slid an arm around her shoulders. She patted his knee.

The Chosen One frowned, staring at each of them in turn. "The man guards the old woman, the warrior woman guards the man, and the old woman makes the kill. Which of you is leader of your strange tribe?"

Her look stopped at Tarawe.

Tarawe soothed the excited gull with a stroke of her right hand. The bird was trembling under her fingers. The o'u wriggled where it was trapped beneath the gull's broad wing.

"Each of us guards the others," Iuti said from beside her.

"Do you suppose these people always try to kill their guests during a welcoming feast?" Anali asked.

"In all the lands I've visited, this is the first time I've seen it done," Iuti replied.

The Chosen One's gaze never left Tarawe.

111

"It is you, isn't it?" she said. "I should have guessed it from the beginning. You're no youngster brought on this voyage to fetch and carry. You are the reason for the voyage itself. That's why you carry Maansusu. I commend you, sorceress, for your clever disguise."

Sorceress! Tarawe was more than startled. *Disguise?* She bit back a laugh, but could not stop a small smile. The gull shifted under her hands.

The Chosen One smiled in return, obviously satisfied that she had spoken correctly.

"Mano's teeth," Ser Iuti muttered. "That's all we need, for them to think you're a sorceress."

Tarawe glanced up at her. "Well, I am—sort of."

The gull grew more and more restless. She held it tighter, trying to stroke it to calm. It struggled to escape her grip. The o'u poked its tiny head into the open, but Tarawe shoved it back out of sight before it could chirp and bring attention to itself.

Anali leaned close. "Well, for the gods' sakes, don't boast about it, girl. Not here, where you don't know what spirits might be lurking about, listening for—"

The ground moved.

Anali stopped abruptly. She glanced around in confusion as the leaves on which they sat began to shiver and tremble. A low rumble echoed through the forest, and women's voices cried out in the distance. The gull suddenly thrashed in Tarawe's hands. She turned her face away as its wings swept open and it stumbled forward out of her lap.

A great cry went up as the gull screeched its terror of the trembling earth. Tarawe could feel the bird's fear even through her own.

"Maansusu!" the islanders cried. "Haku 'Aina!" Many of them had already jumped up and begun striking the strange bird-like poses they had used on the canoes earlier. Some of them lost their balance and fell to the trembling ground. The gull shrieked in accompaniment to their cries and strange movements.

It could only have been an instant, but it seemed forever before the earth settled again. As quickly as it was still, the island warriors dashed forward toward Tarawe and the others. Not toward us, she realized instantly. Toward the gull! Before she could mumble the words to a shielding spell, Ser Iuti was on her feet guarding both her and the bird.

"Stay back," Iuti warned the approaching warriors. The Chosen One's consort was the nearest to her. He carried a knife in each of his claw-backed hands. "Tarawe, calm that creature."

The gull shrieked again and spread its wings. It would have taken to the air if it could, but its damaged wing caught in the tangle of leaves and food bowls. It stumbled and fell awkwardly to its side.

An even louder cry went up from the islanders. "She is hurt. She's injured! Maansusu has been harmed!"

If Ser Iuti had not stood between them, Tarawe was certain the islanders would have killed her. They screamed their hatred, brandished their weapons like furious children, and spat in her direction. When the Chosen One's consort reached too close, Ser Iuti smacked his hand away with the broad side of her sword. She shoved the blunt end of her fighting stick into another man's crotch. He sank abruptly to the ground.

Then, suddenly, the Chosen One was there herself—facing Iuti, glaring at Tarawe.

"You have broken Maansusu's wings," she shouted. "How dare you—"

"I didn't—"

Ma'eva laid a hand on Tarawe's arm to stop her from saying more. He leaned forward and scooped the gull into his strong arms. To Tarawe's relief, the gull seemed to welcome his touch. "I broke the gull's wing," Ma'eva said. He stroked the bird's ruffled feathers, then handed it back to Tarawe. The gull reached up to rub the side of its head across Tarawe's cheek.

The Chosen One stared in amazement—at Ma'eva, at Tarawe and the bird, and finally at Iuti. She sucked in her breath suddenly and stumbled back as the o'u, who had escaped in the confusion, fluttered upward toward the tip of Ser Iuti's sword. The tiny, brilliantly colored bird chirped a challenge of its own.

Tarawe could feel Ser Iuti's surprise at the o'u's sudden presence, but the warrior woman allowed the bird its chosen place at the tip of her weapon.

"Who are you?" the Chosen One asked. Her voice was husky with uncertainty and, for the first time, with fear. "What are you? Why did you come here?" She stared and stared at the tiny o'u, then back at the gull.

"As my good mother has said," Ser Iuti replied, "we came to talk with Haku 'Aina. We would be honored if you would take us to her."

Tarawe had not thought the Chosen One could look more shocked, but she did. All the islanders did. The Chosen One's

male companion sucked in his breath and looked darkly at
Ma'eva; he was rubbing the knuckles of his left hand.

Suddenly the Chosen One smiled with the first honest smile
Tarawe had seen since they arrived on this strange isle. "You
must bathe and rest while we prepare the offerings and the processional. Then I will lead you into Haku 'Aina's domain."

"We don't need a processional," Iuti said.

"The path between here and the lava fields is dangerous and
tiring," the Chosen One replied. "Rest and cleanse yourselves.
Then we will take you." It was clearly not a courtesy she was
offering. It was an order.

"I could use a good bath." Anali sighed. She wiped a runnel
of sweat from her cheek. "This dry air is wrinkling me up like
an old woman."

The Chosen One turned to her. "You will bathe in the Chosen
One's own pool." A babble of excitement accompanied her
words. The Chosen One's male companion glared at Ma'eva,
while the o'u glared around at them all. The bird flitted back to
Ser Iuti's shoulder as she moved to sheathe her sword.

Five painted warriors led them from the village. They climbed
uphill again until they reached another clearing bordering a rushing stream. Tarawe thought this must be the washing place, but
the guards waved them across a pile of stones that created a
makeshift bridge across the water. From the looks of the barren
shoreline, the water must have run much deeper here in the
recent past.

Ma'eva lifted Anali onto his back to carry her across the slippery rock trail. "My balance isn't all that bad, son," she muttered, but she didn't resist the ride.

As Tarawe made her own careful way across the bridge, she
knew Ma'eva had been right to keep his mother safe from falling. The water ran steeply downhill just below where they
crossed. If anyone were to fall here, he or she would fall a long
way. Ser Iuti insisted their guides stay well away from them
until they had all crossed safely.

Across the stream, the trail led uphill again. Several times,
Tarawe was sure they must have reached the washing pool.
There were a number of likely looking places, but they were
always urged on.

"When it rains higher up the mountain, they must get great
floods down this stream," Iuti said. "This valley is so narrow
and steep, all the drainage would have to come this way. I hear
waterfalls both above and below us." Tarawe sent a questing

breeze to study the clouds that clung to the hillside above them. They were all water-laden, but none was raining at that moment. She whispered her find to Ser Iuti, who nodded in thanks.

Finally they reached a place where the ground was level. The stream had flattened into a large, deep pool, with a great wall of water falling into its upper end. The cliff over which the water flowed was high and sheer; along its sides, dense growths of brilliant green ferns sparkled in the constantly lifting spray. The roar of the cascading water was unlike anything Tarawe had ever heard.

"Ayiii!" Ana breathed. "I'd forgotten places like this existed."

Tarawe stared at the falling water in wonder. She'd never seen such a thing. The waterfall was like a giant ocean wave continuously crashing down. The sound was rich and wet, and enormous. She grinned and would have slid into the pool immediately if Ser Iuti hadn't stopped her.

Their guides motioned for them to enter the pool. "We will guard Maansusu while you bathe," one of them said. "Fresh clothing is being brought from the village."

Ser Iuti ignored him.

"Ma'eva," she said quietly. "Check this place for underwater currents. There's a lot more water coming in here than shows downstream. I don't want any of us to get sucked into an underground river."

Their guides—their *guards*, Tarawe reminded herself—were standing well back from the edge of the pool, but were watching them closely. Ser Iuti ordered them farther back.

"Aye," Ana said. "There were far safer-looking places where we could have stopped on the way here. I don't like the looks of that waterfall. I don't like the looks of these bird worshipers, either. I wouldn't be surprised if they try to kill us the first chance they get."

Ho'oma'eva slid into the water and immediately submerged, diving deep into the center of the pool. Two of the guards stepped closer to watch, but Iuti again ordered them back. Suddenly Anali, too, splashed into the water, waving her arms and shouting at the cold—distracting the guards from the slight flicker of Ma'eva's underwater change. As quickly as Tarawe realized what Ana was doing, she stamped into the shallows herself.

The guards demanded that she leave the gull on the shore;

they seemed almost panicked in their fear for the bird's safety, but again Iuti forced them back.

Tarawe took care not to go any deeper than her knees. She had grown up on an atoll, where there were no such things as rivers. She had seen only one in her entire life—the great Veke River on the eastern mainland—and she couldn't imagine such a thing here. But if Ser Iuti thought there might be one under this pool, Tarawe wasn't going to take the chance of falling into it. The gull wriggled in her arms.

Ser Iuti gave a soft laugh as Anali splashed to the center of the pool. She thrashed and splashed and made enough racket to hide ten changing mimics. "This group is never short of a distraction when one is called for," Iuti said.

Tarawe came to stand beside her. "Are we going to try to escape?" she asked.

Ser Iuti's gaze never stopped moving. She watched the guards and the shadows behind them, her eyes shifting with each small movement in the surrounding jungle. "I think we must," she said. "If we can find a way. So far the only ones of us that have really impressed them have been you and the birds. I think returning to the village would be a mistake. I don't know who this Haku 'Aina is, but I suspect we'd be better off talking to her alone, if we have to talk with her at all."

"Do you think Mama Ana really has a message for her?" Tarawe asked.

"I doubt it," Iuti said, "but I'm sure she'll think of something to say if they happen to meet."

Ma'eva had surfaced beside Anali, and they splashed together for a moment before returning to shore. The island guards whispered and pointed as Ma'eva walked into shallow water. He had left his waist wrap somewhere in the pool.

"Come swim," Ma'eva said. "The water is cold, but very clean. I like swimming in fresh water when I'm a—" He glanced at the guards. He smiled at them. "—when I'm in such a friendly place." The guards grinned in return, falsely cheerful, and encouraged him back into the water.

"Stay close to the surface," Ma'eva said under his breath. "You were right, friend Iuti. This is a very dangerous place for humans to swim."

When Tarawe began moving into deeper water, the guards called out in concern again. "Leave Maansusu on the shore," one cried. "Stay with her, sorceress, if you don't trust us to watch her alone. You can take turns with your bath."

"The gull is a water bird," Iuti said. "She will bathe with us." She lashed her fighting stick onto her back and walked into the water at Tarawe's side, still watching all around.

"Your clothes and weapons—"

"They need cleaning, too," Iuti called back.

The island warriors cursed and complained and followed them right up to the water's edge. They did not enter the pool.

"Those fools really expected us to leave the gull ashore with them," Anali said. "Or at least to separate. They must not get many outside visitors here if they think us that gullible." She laughed at her own joke.

The gull screeched once, when its feet first touched the cold water. It flapped its wings, then folded them against its sides and floated contentedly within the circle of Tarawe's arms. "This water is *cold*!" Tarawe said. She felt instantly chilled, all the way to her bones. Even her teeth felt cold.

"Let's cross to the other side and get away from these bird people," Anali said. Tarawe was surprised to see that the old woman didn't seem to mind the cold. Chill bumps had lifted along Ser Iuti's arms, though, and the o'u had taken perch at the tip of her hair knot.

"There are guards there, too," Iuti said. "See? There by the breadfruit tree. And behind the large pandanus. They've been using hiding spells, but they're not very good at it. I wonder how they can hide this whole island when they can't even hide themselves."

"Maybe Haku 'Aina helps them," Tarawe said.

They had reached the center of the pool and she stopped to stare around. Tarawe found it hard to tread water. Her feet were going numb. Her hold on the gull became one more of support than control. Ma'eva stayed close, warning them when they drifted too near the dangerous underwater currents.

Anali cursed. "I guess we'll have to go back down with them. Ho'oma'eva says there's a cave behind the waterfall, but the two of you could never get into it."

"Why not?" Iuti said quickly.

Ma'eva grimaced. "The force of the waterfall is too great. The only way I got through was by changing into a stone crab, and even then, I thought my shell was going to crack under the strain. True humans could never make it. You'd be crushed."

Tarawe quickly turned to face the great waterfall. Would her water magic work here? She had never used it anywhere but on the open sea. She held the gull in her right arm and lifted her left hand.

"Don't let them see you," Iuti said quickly. "If it works, we'll try to escape without them knowing how we did it. If it *doesn't*, it might be better if they don't learn right away that you're not quite the powerful sorceress they think you are."

Tarawe frowned at that. She may not be a sorceress in the way these people thought, but she held powers even Ser Iuti couldn't match. She cupped her hand under the water and focused her attention on the base of the waterfall.

"Friend Iuti?" Ma'eva said.

"Aye."

"What are we going to do inside the cave, if we get there?"

Tarawe tried to stop the great waterfall from reaching all the way to the stone floor of the pool. Nothing happened. The pressure of the falling water was too great. She tried turning the water into a whirlpool at the fall's base, to suck the water away from what felt like the deepest and safest place to swim under. Again, nothing changed. This was very different from moving the ocean water where she had natural currents and wind and waves to work with. All the natural movements here forced the water to fall with greater force.

"I don't know," she heard Iuti say, "but it's better than staying with people who are intent on stealing Tarawe's bird and no doubt killing us in the bargain. I'm certain they intend for at least some of us to die in this pool."

Tarawe stared up at the roaring wall of water. "I can't stop it. It's too strong."

The echoing single note of a conch shell being blown sounded from somewhere far uphill. "What now?" Iuti muttered.

A shout came from the shore. The guards began waving frantically and calling them back. "Bring Maansusu! Maansusu! Bring the bird back quickly!" One of the men splashed into the shallows, arms outstretched. He, like the others, turned a frightened look toward the waterfall.

A rumble deeper than the waterfall's roar trembled through the air. For a moment, Tarawe thought the earth must be moving again, but then she heard one of the guards shout, "Floodwater! Bring Maansusu back! Hurry!" Tarawe sent a questing wind, no simple breeze this time, racing upslope.

"Rain!" she cried an instant later. "It's raining uphill, the river is starting to flood."

"To shore!" Iuti said immediately.

But Tarawe couldn't pull her eyes from the cascading water. "I know I can move it," she murmured. "I have to be able to move it."

"Tarawe, come!" Iuti called. The roar of approaching water grew louder. It echoed through the narrow canyon. The guards on shore screamed and shrieked for the safety of Maansusu.

Tarawe thrust the gull into Ma'eva's hands. He immediately handed it to his mother, who stuffed it squawking and screaming into her bag.

"I don't have to stop it," Tarawe cried, understanding suddenly what she had to do; the flooding stream above them was loud enough now to keep her words from reaching the shore. "I don't have to even slow it."

She pointed to the top of the waterfall with her open hand. Focusing on a single spot of water, she followed its smooth slide over the lip of the falls and down. As it fell, it shattered into frothing foam. Tarawe began slowly spreading her fingers and the plummeting drops moved farther and farther apart. The spume became less concentrated.

"Come!" she shouted, and began swimming toward the spot where her controlled water would land. To her relief, Ser Iuti and the others followed without question. She was certain they couldn't see her slight change in the plummeting wall, but they trusted her enough to come. She held her fingers rigidly apart as her water touched the surface of the pool, then motioned the others to dive under at that place.

Anali took Ser Iuti's arm and dove deeply with her, directly into the falling spume. Tarawe saw a flicker just as Ma'eva circled her waist with his strong arm and followed.

When they turned from their dive to swim under the falls, it was like being struck by a pile of stones.

Tarawe cried out at the impact, and would have choked if Ma'eva had not held her tight and blown a strong breath of air into her lungs. He tasted like the sea. Tarawe kept her fingers spread far apart, even after she was sure it had made no difference at all in the force of the falling water. She could see nothing at all of Ser Iuti and Anali. She couldn't even see Ma'eva through the maelstrom of churning water. Her hands and feet had lost all feeling in the frigid cold.

By the gods, she thought in numb despair. This time I've killed us all!

🦐 *Chapter 12* 🦐

JUST as Tarawe was certain they would all die, the crushing weight lifted. She was tumbled into black, still water, colder even than before. She opened her eyes, but the darkness didn't change. Something strong and hard pulled at her arm, something else yanked at her hair.

Her face broke free of the water and she gasped in frigid air. She choked and coughed, doubling over on herself until she thought she would burst from the strain of drawing breath. At last her lungs began to clear. She heard other coughing then—Ser Iuti, she thought—and splashing. Someone was swimming raggedly nearby. Had they lived through the waterfall after all?

"This way," a voice said. Something pulled at Tarawe's arm again.

"Ho'oma'eva?" It came out in a whisper. The word sounded enormous in the total darkness.

"Of course, friend Storm Caller," the sea mimic replied. He had to shout above the waterfall's roar. She could almost hear his grin. "Who else would it be?"

Tarawe shuddered, not wanting to think about that. She heard Ser Iuti cough again. "Is she . . . Ser Iuti, are you all right?"

The coughing continued, but Anali's cheerful voice answered. "She'll be fine as soon as she catches her breath, child. Gods, but it's dark in here. Ma'eva, where is that ledge you said was here? This mother of my grandchild is heavy."

"It's just ahead of you, Mama," Ma'eva said. "Be careful, you're going to bump—"

"Ooow!"

Ma'eva's hand dropped from Tarawe's arm. "Ayii, Mama. I forgot you can't see. Let me help—"

"Oh, go away, boy. I've cracked my head harder than that right out in the open sea."

"Mother Ana, you can let go of me now." Ser Iuti coughed again. "Tarawe?"

"Where *are* you all?" Tarawe wailed. Her voice echoed eerily through the cold air. She jumped as Ma'eva's hand touched her arm again. She gripped it tight with her opposite hand. "Don't leave me alone, Ma'eva. I can't see, either. I'm afraid."

Another hand touched her, fumbling in the darkness. Then she felt Ser Iuti's strong arm slip around her shoulders. Tarawe hugged her tight.

"Where are we?"

"In the cave," Ma'eva said, "behind the waterfall. Your magic worked, Storm Caller."

"Are you sure?"

Ser Iuti laughed lightly. "Either that or we're in the land of warrior's dreams, girl. I don't know many warriors who would agree to stay in a place like this, before or after they were dead, so I presume it must be the cave. It sounds huge, Ma'eva. What can you see?"

"Shadows mostly," Ma'eva replied. "It's dark in here even for me. It tastes awfully big, though."

A scrabbling sound came from nearby. Tarawe tensed. "Now where did I put my . . . Oh, here it is." Anali's mutterings were barely audible over the din of the falls. "Ouch! Get out of my way, you idiot bird, and stop eating my bread."

Light flared suddenly; it flashed directly in front of Tarawe's face. She was blinded again, this time by light.

"Hoi, Mama. You should warn us next time," Iuti said. As Tarawe's vision cleared, she saw that Ser Iuti, too, was blinking away the brilliance of Ana's light. To Tarawe's surprise, the light was only a small flame cupped in Anali's hands.

"Haven't you ever seen a flint light?" Ana asked. Ser Iuti was staring at her hands.

"Flint! I thought it was . . ."

"Magic?" Anali laughed into Ser Iuti's puzzled pause. "Warrior woman, you've been consorting with too many sorcerers. *I'm* no firemaker that I can bring flames out of nowhere. Now climb up here out of that cold water before my grandchild freezes."

"I think we'd better get your grandchild higher than that," Ma'eva said. "The water is rising. Some of the floodwater must be coming through here. Probably from back in the cave some-where.''

"Lift the light," Iuti said.

Tarawe looked around then and was as startled by the dimly lit cave as she had been by the darkness. The ledge to which they clung was barely wide enough for Anali to squat with her bag. The gull sat beside her preening its feathers. Its dark eyes looked angry.

Anali's small light reached upward along a shiny black wall until it dimmed into nothingness. The ceiling was too far away to see.

"The ledge looks as if it leads upward and away from the falls," Iuti said. She lifted Tarawe from the water, then climbed up after her. "Let's see where it goes. Ma'eva, aren't you com-ing with us?"

"I'll go see where the water's coming in first," he said. He flickered and disappeared.

"I wonder what form he's taken to explore these dark wa-ters," Iuti said.

"Probably a ghost fish," Anali said. "He's always liked playing with those silly creatures down in the deeps."

"How can he see?" Tarawe tried to ask, but her lips were so cold she couldn't get the words out. She had so little feeling in her legs, she was sure she was going to fall. She felt very hungry all of a sudden.

"Walk ahead with the light, Ana. We'll follow." Iuti laid a hand on Tarawe's shoulder. "Mano's teeth, child! You're as cold as ice. Ana, do you have any dry clothing in your bag?''

"Dry clothing won't do her any good if we don't get higher in a hurry," Ana said. "The water's up around my ankles al-ready. Here, girl . . ." She pulled something large and bulky from her bag and wrapped it around Tarawe's shoulders. It was the feathered blanket Tarawe had made on the canoe.

"Come now. Quickly."

Tarawe followed Anali up the incline as best she could, clutching the blanket around her with one hand, trying to use the other for balance against the slick, wet wall. Ser Iuti kept a hand on her shoulder to steady her.

"It narrows here," Anali said. "Wait. Let me put my sandals on first. My feet aren't used to this hard ground." Tarawe held back while Anali negotiated a narrow crossing, then moved for-ward again when Ana held the light back for them to see. Their path took them around a bend, and then another. The roar of the great waterfall receded.

"I wonder how far this cave goes," Iuti said, no longer having to shout.

"A long way, judging by the sound of it," Anali said. "Listen, you can hear water running all around. There must be lots of smaller falls leading from one chamber to another."

"The air is fresh," Iuti said. "There must be openings to the outside somewhere."

"Aye, openings big enough for air to get through," Ana muttered. They rounded another corner.

"There are steps here. Natural ones. Probably an old rock fall."

Iuti's grip on Tarawe's arm tightened as she started up the rough steps. The stones' edges were worn smooth. A lot of water must have passed over them since their original collapse.

Tarawe shivered under her blanket. Ana had wrapped it around her so that the feathered side touched her skin. She concentrated on the feathers' smooth, silken touch to help her control her fear. The darkness and the slow, sluggish air closed around her. She wished she could see the sun. Even a simple star would do. Anything that gave evidence of an air-filled sky overhead.

"I don't like being inside the ground," she whispered. "There's no wind here."

"Hoi, Mama!" Ma'eva's voice boomed through the darkness. "There's light ahead. Around a bend just ahead of you. Be careful, though. The passage narrows and you'll have to climb up. There's a waterfall beside where you'll climb." His words bounced and echoed all around.

"Are the floodwaters still rising?" Iuti called.

"They've started to drop again. This is a fine cave, friend Iuti. There are many strange creatures living here. Some of them are friendly."

"Mano's teeth," Ser Iuti muttered.

"Well, leave them alone," she called. "Follow us up the path. It sounds like you're far below us now."

"I'll jump the falls and meet you above," Ma'eva said.

"That boy is *so* much like his father," Anali muttered.

"If he gets himself lost in here, I'm never going to forgive him," Iuti replied.

Anali chuckled.

Tarawe was beginning to warm inside her blanket. The feathers brushed and tickled across her legs and arms. She could feel her feet again. They hurt. Her stomach growled and she wished they could stop long enough to eat and to unwrap the soggy matting from around her waist.

The splash of falling water grew louder again as they approached the falls Ma'eva had warned them about. "I don't see any light," Iuti said.

"Well, there's not much use going back, even if all he saw was a reflection of our fire," Anali said. She rounded a corner and stopped. "Oh, my!"

Peering around her, Tarawe caught her breath. They were facing another wall of falling water. It wasn't nearly as wide as the great falls outside the cave, nor as high. But a solid, narrow column of water plummeted like rippled stone straight down into a darkness too deep to see. A rough wall of jutting rocks led upward just beside the falls to an opening that showed dim, white light. The wall was slick with moisture—with spume from the falls and trickling water oozing through cracks in the stone.

"Oh, my," Ana said again.

Something flickered halfway up the falls. A dark smudge slid down, disappearing in the rush of water. Then another flicker came from far below. Something bright flashed in the water, leaping upward against the current. It flickered, darkened, and slid back. A flicker, then the flash leapt upward again, reaching higher this time. Another flicker and darkness fell back.

"It's Ma'eva," Anali said. He was leap-frogging up the waterfall. He skipped upward in one form, indistinct because of the darkness and the motion, then slid back in another. Then he changed and leapt up again. Each time he gained another arm's length against the current.

Anali smiled and squatted to watch. Iuti slid both arms around Tarawe and Tarawe leaned back into her warmth. She was surprised at the solid round shape of Iuti's stomach. It was bigger than it had looked under the padded vest.

It took Ma'eva many tries to crest the upper lip of the falls, because the current there was strongest. But at last, a flash of silver flipped over the edge and out of sight. Anali clapped her hands in delight. Then she stood and frowned, and looked up again at the path they would have to climb if they wanted to follow Ma'eva. Her shoulders sagged.

"I don't suppose you have a coil of rope in your bag," Ser Iuti said. She, too, was staring up at the nearly vertical wall.

Anali shook her head. The fish scales tipping her braids flashed iridescent in the small firelight.

Tarawe could feel Iuti's disappointment right through her arms. It was doubtful even the warrior woman, with all her strength, could negotiate the slick vertical passage. Getting Anali up without a rope would be impossible.

"Couldn't you jump up, Mama Ana?" Tarawe asked. "Like Ma'eva?"

Ana looked over the edge to where the waterfall roared into darkness far below. "I can't change as fast as Ho'oma'eva. I'd land right at the bottom, flatter than a land-stranded jellyfish."

"Maybe if you changed into something small, one of us could carry you up," Tarawe suggested.

"I can only change when I'm fully submerged," Ana said, "and I can't change small enough to fit into my water gourd so that you could carry me." She shook herself and turned back to face them. "I'll go back and wait for you at the cave mouth. Go on. You two get started up. I'll stay to watch until you're safe. You can come back and get me later."

Ser Iuti unwrapped her arms from around Tarawe. "We're not going to leave you behind, Mother. There's no way to get you out through the cave mouth either, not without exposing ourselves. We'll think of something."

"Hoi!" Ma'eva's voice came from above. "Are you there?"

"We're here," Iuti called.

"It's nice up here, friend Iuti. Come up and see."

"We can't, Ma'eva. The trail is too steep. It's wet and dangerous; we'd never make it up there without falling."

"Ayiii." Ma'eva's quiet sigh slid down with the rushing water.

"Did you find any other passages out of the cave below?" Iuti called.

"Many, but none so promising as this," Ma'eva said. All the playfulness had left his voice. He sounded tired. Tarawe wondered if he'd been hurt jumping the falls. "Most lead to tunnels that are filled with fast-running water. You and the Storm Caller could never get through."

This time it was Iuti who sighed. "Is there anything up there you could use for a rope, Ma'eva? Is there any sign you might be near the surface so you could go outside and find something to help us climb?"

"There's nothing, friend Iuti. Only more cave. It tastes like it goes on forever."

The cave grew silent then, save for the sounds of running, falling, dripping water. Tarawe looked down to see Anali's head nodding. She laid a hand on her shoulder to keep her from tumbling off the ledge.

"Ser Iuti?" she said.

"Aye." Ser Iuti sounded tired, too.

"Couldn't Ma'eva turn into a rope?"

"What?"

"Not a real rope. But something long and thin that—"

"Ma'eva!" Iuti shouted. Anali started awake. "Is there something up there you can hold on to to lower yourself over the edge?"

"Oh, he mustn't try—"

Iuti cut Anali off. "Not as a human. As an octopus, Ma'eva. You could take the form of that giant creature you were when you came to our canoe in the Empty Sea. That way you could hold on above and reach down to help us climb at the same time."

She was answered by a bright flicker. Something moved at the top of the falls, then a dark lump began lowering itself slowly, sinuously down the rough, wet, stone wall. The lump uncurled into thick tentacles that slid like sea snakes down the slick stone.

"We'll have to climb partway up to reach him," Iuti said. "Tarawe, you'd better put that blanket back in Mama Ana's bag. And the gull, too, if you can do it without knocking the two of you off the ledge."

Tarawe had forgotten all about the gull. She turned to see it huddled just behind Ser Iuti's feet. Its head was tucked under its damaged wing. "How did she get up here?" she asked. She was sure Iuti hadn't carried the bird.

"She walked, just like the rest of us," Iuti said. She glanced back up the falls again. "Could you lift her up there on the wind?"

Tarawe tested the air for currents that she might use, but found that her wind magic had little effect on the still air. She shivered. "It doesn't work very well in here," she said. "This isn't a wind place."

Then she looked around again. "Where's the o'u?"

Iuti lifted a slow hand to her hair knot. "I haven't seen her since we came into the cave. I hope— Well, there's nothing we can do for her now. If she's in here, she'll find us eventually. If not, she'll have to avoid the bird worshipers on her own." She motioned for Tarawe to remove the blanket.

The gull refused to follow the blanket into Anali's bag. It screeched and spread its useless wings in defiance. Ser Iuti held

Tarawe back from trying to reach it. "It's no use," she said. "She won't go back into the bag without a fight, and we can't afford a struggle here on this narrow ledge."

"We can't leave her," Tarawe said. She felt ashamed that she had left the bird before without even thinking of it.

"Hand her up to me," Ma'eva said. His voice was deeper than before, strange coming out of the shadows of the wall. The tip of a long tentacle lifted from the wall and stretched toward them.

"Don't try to change enough to talk, Ma'eva," Ana said quickly. "You might slip and fall. I'll take care of the bird."

She turned to face the gull. It eyed her darkly.

"Listen, bird," Ana said. "You either let me hand you up to Ma'eva without a struggle, or I'll wring your neck right now and throw you down there to feed the cave creatures."

Tarawe held her breath while the two of them stared at each other.

"Get over here," Anali growled.

Slowly the gull ducked its head. It waddled between Iuti's, then Tarawe's legs, and sat again in front of Anali. "That's better," Ana said. She patted the gull's back and motioned Iuti up the trail. "Better send her first. She's smart enough to believe I'll do what I say, but I don't know how long she'll remember."

Iuti eased past them all and carefully climbed the first few arm lengths up the steep wall. Her hands and feet slipped on each of the wet stones. When she reached a secure place just below Ma'eva's dangling tentacle, she called for the bird. "I guess this is as good a test of Ma'eva's strength as any," she said as Ana handed the quiescent bird up to her.

"Don't drop her," Tarawe whispered.

Ma'eva coiled the tip of one tentacle around the bird. He lifted it away from Iuti and up. After a moment, he transferred the gull to another long arm. After a second transfer, he lifted her out of sight over the cliff's edge. A loud squawk followed.

"You next, Mama," Iuti said when Ma'eva reached down again. This time two tentacles pulled from the wall. Anali set her small light on the ledge and Tarawe braced her from behind as she reached up to grasp Iuti's hand. She had to climb several steps up the treacherous slope. It was clear they could never have made it to the top without Ma'eva's help. Tarawe wasn't sure they could make it now.

Iuti pulled Anali up to her own height, then Anali reached eagerly for Ma'eva. He coiled one pink-tipped arm around her

wrists to pull her higher, then slid another tentacle around her
waist. She laid her cheek against his mottled red skin, as trusting
of his strength as if they'd been standing on solid ground. He
lifted her almost as easily as he had the bird. Very quickly she
disappeared over the edge of the waterfall. A moment later,
the gull screeched again.

Carrying the light in her teeth, Tarawe climbed to where she
could reach Ser Iuti's outstretched hand. Iuti pulled her up beside her. The ledge on which she stood was much narrower than
the one from which they'd just come. Tarawe carefully set the
light into a niche in the wall.

Then she looked up, toward the tentacles uncoiling above her.
She shuddered at the sucking sound they made as they peeled
from the wall.

"He'll hold you tightly," Iuti said. "But he won't hurt
you. The bulk of his body is hanging over the cliff, so don't
struggle. You might loosen his hold." Ser Iuti looked at her
carefully. "Tarawe, can you do this thing?"

Tarawe closed her eyes and whispered the calming chant her
mother had taught her just days before the Teronin warriors had
taken her away. It was the only chant her mother had ever given
her freely, openly. All the rest, she'd let Tarawe learn on her
own, simply by listening and watching. The calming charm
worked as it always did, like a soft breeze brushing away her
tension. Quiet slid over her with greater warmth than the feathered blanket had held. She opened her eyes.

Ser Iuti smiled slightly. "Good girl," she said. "I'll see you
up top."

Tarawe reached up to Ma'eva's waiting arms.

His touch wasn't nearly as bad as she had expected it to be.
The rows of suckers, still wet from the wall, pulled against the
skin of her wrists and arms as Ma'eva pulled her into reach of
his second arm. But they released gently and smoothly once he
had grasped her securely around the waist. He had coiled the
great tentacle around her twice, she saw. She was heavier than
Anali.

The rippled bag that was Ma'eva's head in his octopus form
lay pressed against the wall an arm's length below the cliff edge.
His eyes were mere slits in the mottled skin. She couldn't tell if
he was watching her or not. One of his upper arms slipped on
the wet rock, slid sideways, and steadied again.

As Ma'eva passed her from one arm to another, always higher
up the cliffside, she could feel the tension of her own weight

pulling him away from the wall. She gripped each new tentacle tightly, then released it quickly when she was passed on to the next. Ma'eva was trembling by the time he lifted her over the top and set her gently down on solid dry stone again.

Immediately his body sagged, still clinging to the wall. His color had paled almost entirely to gray. "Oh, Ma'eva," Tarawe said. "You look so tired."

She called out. "Ser Iuti. Ma'eva needs to rest before he carries you up."

"Aye," Iuti called back. Her voice sounded very far away. "Rest and eat, Ma'eva. I'm tired and hungry myself, although I don't know how that can be, so soon after that big feast. We haven't been in here all that long."

To Tarawe, it felt as if they had been in the cave for at least as long as they'd been on the canoe. Her own hunger was a gnawing pain deep in her gut. How can I be so empty after eating so much? she wondered. She woke the dozing Anali to explain Ma'eva's need for food. Without question, Anali pulled bread and bananas from her bag.

Ma'eva crawled back up over the cliff. He flickered, and changed back into a man. He looked paler than Tarawe had ever seen him, as he took the bread from his mother with trembling hands. It looked as if it were all he could do to eat it. "I thought I was stronger than that," he whispered.

His mother ran a hand along his arm. "You're very strong, son. You did a good job. Now you eat and sleep. We can explore the rest of this cave later."

"I have to bring up friend Iuti first."

Suddenly Ana looked around. Her eyes opened wide. "You left my grandchild below?"

"Just until I can rest, Mama. Friend Iuti is safe."

"Is my grandchild well?" Anali shouted.

"Well and kicking," Ser Iuti replied. "And *hungry*! I wish I'd brought a slab of pork and taro with me. Those bird worshipers might be devious, but they cook well."

Tarawe brushed her fingers along Ma'eva's arm. He met her look and grinned weakly. "You *are* very strong," she said.

Ma'eva's deep golden color had begun to return. He stood and stretched, rubbing his arms and legs. "I think I stretched myself taller," he said. Then he frowned.

"Friend Iuti," he called.

There was a slight hesitation. Tarawe hoped Ser Iuti hadn't fallen asleep and slipped off the ledge. If she had done so without crying out, they would never know. "Aye," the reply finally came.

"I'm going to come down for you now," Ma'eva called. "But I won't be able to lift you like I did the others. You're much heavier and I don't want to take the chance of dropping you and our child. You'll have to climb, but I can guide you and hold you against the wall."

"I can climb," Iuti said. "I'll have to do it slowly, though. My stomach is big enough now to change my balance. It feels bigger here in the dark than it did outside. I must have eaten more at that feast than I thought."

"Can I help?" Tarawe asked.

"Only if you know a way to catch us if we fall," Ma'eva said. He flickered and changed, and crawled back to the cliff's edge. He anchored four of his thick tentacles around rock outcrops at the top of the cliff and lowered his body over the edge. The tentacles tensed and tightened. The sounds of scraping rock lifted from below.

✎ Chapter 13 ✎

It seemed forever before Iuti reached the top of the treacherous cliff. Ma'eva held her right wrist securely as he led her up the sheer rock face. He set her fingers in places where she could manage a tenuous hold, but her feet slipped constantly on the slime-covered stone. Ma'eva had lifted the light into a high niche and the shadow cast by Iuti's swollen stomach prevented her from seeing safer steps.

Cool spray from the falls settled over her face and arms, chilling her along with her fear. She was very afraid. More afraid than she ever remembered being before, though she'd been in at least as great a danger many times. It's the child, she thought. Before, if I killed myself, I killed only myself. Ma'eva's grip tightened on her wrist and she smiled in the darkness. It was Ma'eva's presence that made her fearful, too. She didn't want to pull him down with her into death.

Strange thoughts for a warrior, she mused as she felt carefully for another handhold. She flinched as her stomach scraped against the wall. She was glad she'd loosened the ties to her padded vest; she doubted she could have maneuvered her growing bulk otherwise.

Finally the rock wall ended. Ma'eva wrapped a second full tentacle around her swollen waist and lifted her over the edge onto flat ground. She collapsed, unable even to thank the great ruddy-brown mimic who had brought her to safety. She wondered if they *were* safe yet.

Tarawe's anxious face hovered a hand's width from her own. "Are you well, Ser? You look so pale. How can I help you?"

"Food," Iuti whispered. She felt so hungry she was afraid she would faint before she could eat. Why am I so weak? she thought. I'm not *that* pregnant.

131

Tarawe's face disappeared, then returned almost immediately. "Here's bread, Ser. And a mountain cherry. Mama Ana brought it from the feast." She helped Iuti sit up enough to eat and then drink from Ana's water gourd. Iuti was vaguely aware of Anali doing the same for Ma'eva, although the old woman looked almost as tired as her son.

"Why are we all suddenly so exhausted?" Iuti muttered.

The food brought an almost instant return of energy. Not a great deal of energy, but enough to allow Iuti to sit up on her own. She was surprised at how awkward the move was. She loosened the ties of her vest again and sighed in relief.

She realized suddenly that the light had changed. The soft orange of Ana's flint light had been replaced by a cooler, whiter glow. It came from a narrow opening just above where they sat.

Another climb, she thought. Even if it led outside, she doubted she could make it now.

"Do you want more?"

Tarawe slid another chunk of Ana's nut bread into her hands. Iuti ate it ravenously. Tarawe grinned and stuffed a piece into her own mouth. "I thought it was just me," she said. "I can't remember being so hungry."

"It must have been farther through that cave than we thought," Iuti said. "Are you warm enough now?"

Tarawe shrugged. "Sort of. It was scary down there, Ser." She looked up and around. "It's scary up here, too."

"It's not as frightening as that village was," Anali said. "At least no one in here wants us dead."

Tarawe looked up and around again, as if wondering if that were true.

"I hope the ground doesn't start shaking again," Ma'eva said. "It's fun when that happens under the ocean, but I think it might be dangerous in here." He scooped up a handful of loose stones and tossed them into the swift current that ran beside them. In an instant they had tumbled over the edge of the falls.

Iuti looked up toward the light. "Have you been up there, Ma'eva?"

"Just for a look," he said. "It's very strange."

"Is it safer than this place?"

Ma'eva glanced back along the course of the river. It flowed from the yawning black mouth of yet another branch of the cave. Watermarks along the sides of the walls made it clear the river ran much higher through this chamber at times.

"I think so," he said.

Iuti sighed and forced herself to stand. Tarawe steadied her. "Let's move on, then." She stood with one hand on her stomach, the other on her lower back, suddenly knowing an appreciation for all the pregnant women she had once thought so clumsy. No wonder they move so cautiously, she thought. If unborn babes are this active and heavy at five months, they must be a dreadful burden at nine. She stared up at the climb ahead.

"At least it's a gradual slope," she said. "I think we can make it. Once we reach the top, if it looks safe from flooding, we'll stop and take a long rest. Ma'eva, you'd probably better go first again. Even tired, you're still the strongest among us."

Ma'eva grinned at the compliment. The meal—she'd seen him eat two full loaves of Ana's ever-present bread along with a full hand of bananas—had revived him remarkably. "I'll always be strong enough for you, Iuti Mano," he said.

"Come, Mama. You climb beside me and I'll help you up."

Anali nodded, smiled as if she hadn't just fallen asleep again, and joined Ma'eva at the base of the slope. "Where's that idiot gull?" she said suddenly.

Tarawe pointed. The gull was scrabbling its way up the slope on its own. It reached the top just as Ma'eva and Ana began to climb, and screeched in triumph. At least Iuti hoped it was triumph, and not some horror it had spotted in the lighted chamber. She urged Tarawe after the others.

After making sure her weapons were still secure on her back, she climbed quickly after Tarawe. Something about the bird striking out on its own made her uneasy. The broad, rocky shelf on which she stood no longer felt safe. "Mano's teeth," she cursed as she overbalanced in her hurry. She forced herself to slow.

"Ser, come quickly," Tarawe called suddenly. "There's a strong wind coming from the river cave. I think—"

A rumbling roar cut her off.

"Floodwater!" Ma'eva shouted.

Iuti scrambled up the loose stones, scraping her knees and hands. She felt Ma'eva's hand lock onto her arm, and she grabbed Tarawe's as they clambered over the upper edge of the slope. Looking back, she saw a wall of water smash through the mouth of the river cave. It slammed into the walls of the chamber they had just left, swirled and roiled, and as suddenly as it came, drained away over the falls.

Iuti collapsed again, this time into Ma'eva's arms. He held her tight until her shaking stopped. When it did, she was aston-

ished to find that she had been crying into his warm and welcoming chest. By the gods, she thought. I've turned into a sniveling—

She looked up to meet Ma'eva's look. He grinned.

—mother, she thought. I've turned into a sniveling mother.
She returned Ma'eva's grin and kissed him fully on the mouth.

"You've saved me again, friend mimic," she said, and they
both laughed in extraordinary relief.

"When you two finish telling each other how wonderful you
are," Anali said, "you might want to turn your attention this
way and decide what we're going to do about all *this*."

Oh, gods, Iuti thought. What now?

She turned, and caught her breath in amazement. The
chamber they'd crawled into was ablaze with light. The floor,
the ceiling, the walls—and all the strange posts in between—
shimmered in a bright white glow. Iuti moved carefully away
from the edge of the slope they'd just climbed and stared
across the sparkling room.

Great pillars rose from the floor and stretched to dizzying
heights. Where they attached at the ceiling and the floor, the
pillars were wide and round, like great mounds of thick, white
foam. At their centers, the soaring pillars narrowed. Some to
a mere hand's width, some to thread-thin, sparkling lines.
Others . . .

Iuti stared and stared.

Others didn't connect at all, but she could see where they
would, or could, someday. The air was as still as if it didn't
exist.

"What are they, Ser?" Tarawe whispered. She was staring
across the room as dumbfounded as Iuti.

"They're cave drippings," Anali said. "I've seen such things
in the Ilimar mountains, but never all lit up like this. It looks
like the light's coming from the stone itself." She reached toward the nearest of the pillars.

"Be careful," Iuti said. "Don't break it."

Ana laughed and slapped the side of the broad post soundly.
"I couldn't break this rock with a hammer, warrior woman."
She pulled her hand back and stared at her palm. It glowed
softly.

"Magic!" Tarawe whispered. She stepped back. Ma'eva
grabbed her before she could fall back down the way they had
come.

"Rock?" Iuti asked. Gingerly she touched the pillar herself.

It *was* stone—or something as hard as stone. She stared up to where the pillar narrowed, a full warrior's length above her. "Is it like this all the way up?"

"If it wasn't, I expect it would all come crashing down," Anali replied.

Tarawe caught her breath again and Iuti laid a reassuring hand on her shoulder. "At least there's no water here, to wash us away in our sleep," she said. "And sleep is what we need most. Mama Ana especially." Anali was sliding down the side of the glowing pillar, her eyes closed, her mouth open in a quiet snore. Ma'eva eased her to the ground.

"Do you think she'd mind if I wake her up long enough to give us some food?" he said. "I'm hungry again."

"So am I," Iuti replied. Then she frowned and looked back the way they had come. "How can we be hungry, Ma'eva? We ate only a few minutes ago." She turned a questioning look toward Tarawe.

"I'm hungry, too," the girl said in a small voice.

Quickly Iuti whispered a discovery chant, a spell to search for hidden sorcery. Something wasn't right. It hadn't been right since they entered the cave. Tarawe held her right hand out, palm forward. She met Iuti's look and shrugged. "I don't feel anything on the air, Ser. Just a very soft wind."

"I don't feel anything either," Iuti said. "That means whatever's happening isn't directed specifically at us. I wonder who else's magic we've stumbled into. I hope it isn't a trap set here by those bird people."

Ma'eva took a step toward her. He was staring at her stomach. "I think we more than stumbled, mother of my child," he said.

Iuti look down. Her belly protruded farther now than her breasts, and her breasts were far larger than they had been. The ties to her vest were straining again.

"Mano's great gray grandmother!" she breathed. She laid a hand on her stomach. The child kicked against it. Carefully she lowered herself to the ground. It was covered with tiny, glowing pebbles. Stones in the shapes of teardrops. The air in the sparkling room was blessedly warm.

"What's happening to me?" she said. No wonder she'd been off balance during the climb. She was twice the size she'd been when she entered the cave. Ma'eva squatted beside her. He slid his hands across her swollen belly. The child kicked him, too.

"It's growing, friend Iuti." He looked as delighted as he did startled.

Tarawe knelt and brushed Ma'eva's hands away. She released the ties to Iuti's vest. Iuti sighed with relief as the tight garment stretched open. Tarawe whispered something into her palms and laid them on the great mound of Iuti's growing child.

"Ayiii!" she said softly. She looked up. "This baby is moving and kicking. It's much bigger than it was before."

"I can see that," Iuti said. "I can *feel* that. What does it mean?"

Tarawe studied the shape of her body carefully. She examined her breasts, her stomach, even her ankles, although Iuti could think of no reason for that. Finally Tarawe laid her ear on Iuti's stomach and listened.

After a moment she said, "I guess it means you're going to have it sooner than we expected."

Ma'eva slid his hand into Iuti's. "When?" he asked. Fear touched his eyes as he looked to Tarawe for her answer. "She must be near the sea when it comes."

"Oh, not anytime soon," Tarawe said quickly. "It'll be at least another couple of months. I think."

"Tarawe, are you sure?" Iuti said.

Tarawe looked back at her stomach. "Well, not completely, but my mama was a midwife and she used to let me watch when she examined the women who came to her. Your baby feels big, but not big enough to be born yet."

"It's very important that we be near the ocean when it comes," Iuti said. She started to get up. "If it comes now—"

Tarawe pushed her back. "It's not coming now, Ser. You'll know for yourself when *that* time comes." She turned to Ma'eva. "Why does she have to be near the water? Can't sea mimic boys breathe air?"

"Sea mimic boys are born completely human," Ma'eva said. "They can breathe just fine if they have to."

"Then why—"

"If my son isn't born in the water, or put there very soon after, he'll never learn the sea change. He'll be locked in his human form forever." Ma'eva's eyes grew dark. They reflected the strange sparkling light of the glowing pillars. "I will only have one son in my lifetime, Storm Caller. If this is he, we *must* be near the sea when he is born, or he will be lost to me."

Tarawe glanced at Anali. "Couldn't you just give him a magic bag like Mama Ana's?"

Ma'eva smiled and shook his head. "There is only one bag like Mama Ana's, and its magic is something even the sea mimics don't fully understand. Only an adult can use it, and then only if they know the sea well.''

Tarawe took a deep breath.

''Well,'' she said finally. She glanced somewhat fearfully around their strangely lit haven. ''The first thing we have to do is eat again, and rest. If we try to go on now, you could get overtired and the baby might come early. Then we'd really have trouble. After we've all had some sleep and can think straight again, we can start looking for a way out of here. We've climbed up a long way. We must be near the surface someplace.''

''I'll go look now,'' Ma'eva said.

Iuti tightened her grip on his hand. ''Stay,'' she said. ''Tarawe is right. We all need food and rest.''

''But I—''

''If you must do something now, take the first watch,'' Iuti said. Her stomach growled loud enough for them all to hear. ''And please, get me something to eat.'' Ma'eva scrambled to do her bidding.

It was the child that woke Iuti, kicking hard and steadily against her bladder. Iuti groaned and rolled onto her back. ''Oh, gods,'' she said when she saw that the huge shadow of her stomach was not a shadow at all. She tried to take a deep breath, found it was impossible, and pushed herself up heavily. Ma'eva was sprawled beside her, looking older, quieter than she remembered. Anali was still snoring beside the great stone pillar.

''Tarawe?'' Iuti called softly.

''Aye'' came the instant answer. ''I'm here.'' Tarawe's face appeared around the side of one of the stones. She had smears of light on her cheeks and clothing. She grinned. ''This is a wonderful place, Ser. There are lots of small air currents. I must have been too tired yesterday to feel them.''

Iuti looked down ''Yesterday?''

Tarawe crossed quickly to her side. Her eyes widened when she took in Iuti's size. ''The child is at least another month along,'' she said after examining Iuti again. She glanced at Ma'eva. ''I think we'd better find a way out of this cave.''

She reached across to wake Ma'eva, but Iuti stopped her. ''Wait until after I pee,'' she said. ''As awkward as I am now, he's bound to make me laugh, and I'm afraid I'll burst.''

Tarawe helped her to a place beside one of the pillars. She had just begun to wet the glowing pebbles when the ground shivered. A rumble sounded from somewhere below, and Ma'eva and Anali came instantly awake.

"Floodwaters," Ma'eva said.

Iuti pressed her hands against the wall and the pillar to keep her balance. She'd half woken to the sound of floodwaters rattling through the lower cave several times during the night, but she didn't remember the ground moving like this. She finished what she was doing, the ground settled, and cautiously she returned to the others.

Anali, as usual upon waking from a long sleep, was busy rummaging in her bag. A loose feather drifted up. It slid away on some small air current to settle against the side of one of the pillars.

"Leave it," Tarawe said. "As a small payment for our night's rest."

Iuti glanced at her, surprised that the girl would suggest such a thing. She'd been extraordinarily careful with the feathers until now. She'd not let a single one fall into the sea.

"It's a gift from the wind to this windless place," Tarawe said softly. Her right palm was pressed to one of the glowing pillars.

"By the seven gods of Ilimar! What happened to you?" Ana exclaimed when she finally looked up and caught sight of Iuti. "How long was I asleep?"

"Something is making the time move faster," Ma'eva said after assuring her she'd not been asleep for three months.

"There was an old witch in Sandar City who claimed to be able to do that," Anali said, "but I never thought it was true."

"There are those who can work such magic," Iuti said. "But I know of no reason why it should be happening here."

"Maybe this is one of those places where time doesn't exist," Tarawe said. "Remember, Mama Ana? You said the seafolk had rumors about such places?"

"I did?" said Ana.

Tarawe nodded.

"Well, I think we should look for a way out of here then." She turned to Iuti. "You look like you could drop that child any minute."

'There are fresh air currents coming from that way." Tarawe pointed across the chamber. "They smell like outside air. We could follow them."

"We'll eat along the way," Iuti said. Ma'eva eagerly agreed. He was as ravenously hungry as Iuti and Tarawe. Anali quickly broke a loaf of bread into four pieces. She handed each of them a mountain cherry, as well.

"Where did these come from?" Tarawe asked. "You only put two in your bag and we ate those yesterday."

Anali grinned and patted Iuti's stomach. "Two is all it takes to make three, dear."

Ma'eva laughed. "It's a good thing you didn't have a second gull in your bag, Mama. We'd be up to our knees in birds by now."

Tarawe looked confused for a moment, then frowned at them both. She scooped up the gull and began threading her way through the pillars.

"I keep expecting something to jump out at us," Iuti said as they walked. She tried to stretch and rub her back at the same time.

"We have enough trouble now, warrior woman," Anali snapped. "Don't go calling up more."

"Aye, Mother." Iuti laughed. She glanced at Ma'eva and was surprised when he didn't return her grin. She forced herself to grow serious again.

On the far side of the lighted chamber, they came upon two wide vertical cracks in the wall. "The freshest air is coming through this one," Tarawe said. "Shall we—"

"Yes," Anali said before Iuti could.

"It's dark in there," said Tarawe.

Iuti picked up a handful of teardrop-size pebbles. Like the rest of the stones in the room, they cast their own soft glow. "Let's try these," she said. "There's not much oil left in Anali's lamp. We might need it later."

Each of them scooped up a handful of the tiny stones. Anali hesitated, then stuffed a pair of the lighted stones into her bag. She shrugged at Tarawe's questioning look. "You never know, girl. It might work."

Iuti started to turn sideways to move more easily through the narrow opening, then realized it made no difference. She stayed as close behind Tarawe as she could, holding her handful of light high to help them all see.

"How are we going to find our way back if this leads us nowhere?" Anali asked. "It might, you know. This could be an endless maze with no way out."

"Don't call up trouble we don't already have, Mother," Iuti reminded her.

They passed many small side cracks; from some of them, Iuti

caught a faint whiff of sulfur. The air grew close, and damp and warm. Finally they came to another open chamber. This one was much smaller than that they'd been in before. Two passages large enough for them to pass through opened on the far wall. Water dripped along the wall between the openings and disappeared into a narrow crack in the floor. A thin veil of steam lifted from the dark hole. The smell of sulfur was strong enough to make Iuti sneeze.

"This one has the freshest air, but we'd have to crawl," Tarawe said. She glanced at Iuti with concern.

"I can manage," Iuti said.

Tarawe held the gull under one arm and crawled into the dark passage. Ma'eva brushed a hand across Iuti's cheek before she slid into the hole behind Tarawe.

Suddenly the gull screeched. Iuti saw the edges of its wide wings beyond Tarawe's shadowed form.

"Oh! Go back! Go back!" Tarawe screamed suddenly. She began scrabbling backward. "Hurry, Ser!"

The gull shrieked and dashed forward, away from Tarawe. Tarawe cried out and stopped. Iuti grabbed her foot to keep her from going after the bird. The gull shrieked again and a flurry of feathers filled the darkened passage ahead of them.

Iuti's foot bumped something. Anali, she thought. The old woman was almost as awkward on land as Iuti now was. Iuti wanted to draw her sword against whatever danger approached, but there was no room in the low passage. She couldn't even get her weapons off her back. She crawled backward as quickly as she could, keeping a hand on Tarawe all the while.

Finally she felt Ma'eva's hands guiding her backward out of the hole. She yanked Tarawe after her, pulling her clear just as a blur of feathers burst from the opening. Tarawe threw her hands over her face to keep from being struck by the gull's sharp beak and flailing wings. The bird thumped to the ground, thrashing and rolling, fighting something hairy and white.

Not hairy, Iuti realized as another fat white creature wriggled from the hole. As big around as her thumb and longer than her hand, it looked like a segmented grub with many, many hair-thin legs—and a wide-open mouth glistening with teeth. It had no eyes that Iuti could see.

Tarawe screamed and pointed. More of the grotesque grubs were crawling out of the hole from which they had just come. Iuti and the others backed toward the passage through which they had come earlier.

The gull screeched again, then clamped its beak solidly around the white grub's head. Something cracked, and the grub went suddenly limp. The bird spat it out and dropped it. Iuti kicked it back toward its kin. They paused, then began tearing at their own dead cousin. Like *my* kin, Iuti thought. Like sharks in a frenzy.

Iuti tried to set a protective shield around the grubs, but nothing happened. Her war magic had no effect. She tried setting a warding spell around their own small group, but with the same result.

"We'll have to go back," she called.

The gull squawked and screeched and dove at the grubs, trying to force them away. More and more tumbled from the tunnel. The feast provided by the dead one wouldn't hold them back long. Already a handful had started again toward Iuti and the others.

"They must be following our heat," she said. "Or our smell. We need to get somewhere where there's room to either fight or avoid them." One of the grubs caught hold of the gull's damaged wingtip. Iuti sliced it in half with her sword; it didn't let go. She shuddered.

Glancing back, she saw that Anali had already stepped back into the vertical crack. Tarawe was moving her right hand frantically, but her wind magic was having no effect that Iuti could see. Ma'eva gave Iuti a look of despair as he waved Tarawe after his mother.

"We'll find a way out," Iuti promised before turning back to stamp hard on the nearest pair of wriggling grubs. One burst under her boot. The other kept coming. A sick-sour stench lifted from the floor. The gull flew an arm's length into the air, flapping its wings frantically. It ripped the head off another of the grubs.

When she falls, Iuti thought, and she knew the poor bird would soon fall, she's going to land right on top of them. There were tens of the grubs, hundreds of them, wriggling and tumbling over one another. More kept coming.

Iuti reached out but there was no way she could help the bird. Ma'eva yanked her backward toward the crack.

"Don't leave her!" Tarawe screamed.

✥ Chapter 14 ✥

SOMETHING white flashed high on the opposite wall. Oh, gods! Iuti thought. They're starting to fall from the ceiling.

Suddenly the flash of white swooped toward her and she saw that it wasn't a grub at all. It wasn't even white. It was yellow!

"The o'u!" she cried.

The tiny bird chirped as it swept past her face and darted back toward where it had appeared. The gull shrieked and clawed at the air, trying to stay aloft.

"Ma'eva, wait!" Iuti shouted when he tried to pull her into the tunnel again. The o'u darted toward her and away, back to the same place as before. The second tunnel! Iuti thought. The one they had chosen not to take because the air had been fresher in the other.

The o'u swept toward her again. It landed for an instant on her shoulder, then sped back toward the hole in the opposite wall. Its tiny chirps were barely audible over the shrieks of the terrified gull.

Iuti reached back and grabbed Ma'eva's arm. She pointed. "Over there," she shouted. "Into the other passage."

"There might be more—"

The o'u flashed into sight again. "She must have come from outside. We have to trust her!" Iuti cried. "These creatures can follow us anywhere in the maze. They'll catch us eventually, wherever we go."

Understanding touched Ma'eva's eyes. He began looking around for a way to reach the other side of the small chamber. Iuti was the only one of them wearing boots. There was no way the others could get past the grubs in their bare feet, and it was too far to jump.

Iuti yanked her shield from her back. She scooped the grubs

back to create a path at least partway across the chamber. She couldn't kill them or move them fast enough to keep them away.

"Give me the spear," Ma'eva said. As quickly as it was free of her back, he grasped one end with both hands. "Put me over there on that ledge. You throw. I'll catch," he said. He began to flicker and change.

"What—"

Ma'eva's arms and legs split back into tentacles, much smaller this time than before. They wrapped tightly around the tip of the spear. His torso and head turned ruddy brown and rippled.

Suddenly Iuti understood his plan. Before his change to an octopus was fully complete, she had lifted him across the chamber to a ledge beside the o'u's passage. He released the spear and Iuti let it fall into the grubs. They swarmed over it.

The o'u swooped at Ma'eva, chirping a challenge. It flapped to a frantic stop as Ma'eva began flickering again. A much larger octopus formed on the ledge. Its fat long tentacles snaked along the walls to gain a strong hold.

"Tarawe, come—"

"I'm here," Tarawe said. "Save my gull, Ser!"

"You first," Iuti replied. Before Tarawe could object, Iuti grabbed her by the waist and threw her across the short distance to Ma'eva. Three long arms stretched out to catch her. Tarawe didn't even have time to cry out before she was inside the second tunnel.

"Oh, my!" Iuti heard Anali say.

A sharp pain pierced through Iuti's right calf. She looked down to see that the grubs had reached her feet. They were tumbling over her boots. One had climbed high enough to reach her skin. She grabbed Ana up off the floor.

When she turned back to Ma'eva, she saw that he had snagged the gull. It must have finally fallen. A handful or more of wriggling white grubs hung from its feathers and skin. Ma'eva tossed it back into the tunnel with Tarawe and reached for his mother. Iuti almost dropped her as another grub sent its fiery teeth into her leg. She steadied herself and threw Ana toward her son.

It was not as clean a throw as the first, but Ma'eva caught her and swept her up into the dark tunnel. Iuti stamped her feet, trying to dislodge the grubs. They clung to the stiff leather almost as easily as they clung to her skin. She used her sword to scrape them away before more could reach her legs. Then she rammed the sword into its sheath and took a running jump toward Ma'eva.

Ma'eva caught her outstretched arms and swung her toward the dark opening. She cried out when she saw that she was going to strike the wall beside it instead. Tarawe and Anali both reached out to stop her before she hit. She saw Tarawe grimace as if she'd been hurt, then felt her strong, small arms pulling her to safety.

"My leg," she gasped, but Ana was already at her side, cutting the wriggling, gnawing grubs away from her skin and her boots. Tarawe was doing the same for the gull. Iuti wanted to force the pain and her sudden exhaustion away with darkness, with healing sleep, but knew they couldn't stay where they were. She glanced back toward the roiling pile of ravenous creatures. They had already begun to tumble and turn their way. It was all Iuti could do to keep from retching.

Tarawe touched her arm. "Can you walk, Ser?"

"I'll fly, without wind if I have to, to get out of here," Iuti replied.

A slight smile touched Tarawe's lips. Then the o'u flew between them, chirping madly. Iuti pushed herself to her feet and followed Ana, who followed the bird. Tarawe, carrying the now-silent gull, came next, and Ma'eva brought up the rear. They were quickly back into pitch darkness. Their light pebbles had been left scattered among the grubs.

"Watch your eyes," Anali said, and suddenly the narrow passage flared with light.

"I hope it wasn't the light that attracted those things," Ma'eva muttered. Iuti shuddered. She never wanted to see another grub. Not for as long as she lived, or at any point thereafter. Her leg stung as if she'd been poisoned.

"Tarawe," she said. "I'm going to set a healing spell for my leg. One that will cleanse it of whatever foul thing those creatures might have injected. Listen carefully in case any of the rest of you need it later." Or if *I* do again, she thought, and can't do it for myself. "You might want to say it for the gull, too." Iuti wondered if the bird was still alive.

She felt dizzy with pain.

And hunger.

Oh, gods! she thought. It must be happening again. She sang the healing chant quickly, then laid a hand on her stomach and hurried after Ana. The o'u flitted back to ride her shoulder for a moment before returning to lead them on.

Iuti, ducking and scraping through low places, squeezing her large stomach through others, wasn't sure how long they walked.

It didn't matter. The passage of time in this cave had nothing to do with reality. All she wanted to do was get out.

They ate twice more before the bird led them from the narrow passage into a low-ceilinged, almost perfectly round cave. Only the floor was level. The entire thing looked to be made of solid black rock.

"Look," Tarawe cried. "There are roots hanging from the ceiling."

"We must be just beneath the surface," Anali said. "This must be the way out. What a smart little o'u."

"Put out your light, Mama," Ma'eva said.

Iuti tensed and reached over her shoulder for her sword.

"I think there's light ahead. I can see it better if we're in the dark," Ma'eva went on. Iuti dropped her hand in relief. Tarawe slid her arm around Iuti's waist as Anali doused her lamp. The girl's small, trembling hand rested on Iuti's stomach.

"I don't like the dark, Ser," she whispered. "Not this kind of dark."

"I don't either," Iuti agreed. She covered Tarawe's hand with her own. The child kicked them both.

"There," Ma'eva said. He took Iuti's free hand and tugged. She followed, although she could still see nothing but blackness. She walked hunched over to keep from cracking her head on the ceiling. "It's night," he said. "That's why it's so dark in here. The opening is just ahead."

"Why don't we light the lamp again?" Tarawe asked.

Iuti understood Ma'eva's caution. He would have made a good warrior, too—if he hadn't been a sea mimic and forbidden to kill other humans while on land. "There might be someone out there," she told Tarawe. "A light would draw their attention to us. We've come safely this far. We don't want to grow careless now."

"We must go straight downhill to the sea, mother of my grandchild," Anali said. Her voice lowered suddenly. "Oh. Oh, my. I can see the stars."

Two steps later, Iuti could see them, too. And after Ma'eva pushed aside hanging vines at the opening of the cave, she saw the moon. Near full, but very low in the sky. She sent the others ahead of her out of the cave. They went only a few steps before squatting to hide in the thick foliage. Iuti paused, then turned back to face the total darkness of the cave.

"All honor to whatever beings inhabit this mountain," she sang softly. "I give thanks for a safe passage through it."

And, she added silently, I pray to all the gods in existence that I never have to pass through it again. She stepped outside to join the others.

The open night air felt like silk across her skin, light and clean and free. Tarawe's right hand moved and a spiral of rotting leaves lifted from the ground beside her. Tarawe grinned and opened her hand, then turned her face to the sky. The leaves tumbled back to the ground while coconut fronds chittered and whispered high above. Watching Tarawe's return to the open air was like watching night change to sudden day. Her eyes glowed with pleasure and her small form moved as lightly as if she herself were made of air.

"Is that the rising or setting moon?" Anali said.

Iuti studied the stars. "Setting. We must have been traveling south through the mountain. Look, there's firelight down below. There must be people at the water's edge."

"Hmmph," Anali said. "I was hoping that was just reflected moonlight. Well, it doesn't matter. We have to go down."

Tarawe ran a hand across Iuti's stomach. "The baby hasn't moved into the birthing tunnel yet. We still have some time. Maybe we should—"

"We have to get to the water," Ana snapped.

Iuti lifted a hand to stop them from arguing. "I agree we need to go downhill. But if Tarawe says there's no need to rush, there likely isn't. She hasn't been wrong yet. We'll move quickly, but with caution. Tarawe, why don't you make a basket for that bird, so you don't have to carry it in your hands." The poor gull had been so badly injured by the grubs that it could no longer even walk.

Tarawe turned immediately to the task. She stripped a freshly opened coconut frond from a low-growing palm and began weaving it into a carry-basket.

"What about the people on the shore?" Ma'eva said.

Iuti touched the hilt of her sword. "I may be swollen with child, but I'm still a warrior and Tarawe can still control the wind. I warrant we can make our way through any defense these bird worshipers might offer."

"Once we reach the sea, I can protect you, friend Iuti," Ma'eva said. "Mama can, as well."

He paused and smiled. "It would be fitting for my son to be born at the center of the Empty Sea while his mother and her helper are guarded by circling sharks." There had been a time when Iuti refused even the idea of Ma'eva taking the shark's form. Mano Niuhi did not take well to being impersonated by the sea mimics, and the great shark god's wrath was one even the capricious mimics were careful to avoid.

But now Mano Niuhi was gone. If Ho'oma'eva chose to protect her and their son with the shark's form, then so be it. It might even be comforting, Iuti thought, for she and the shark had been allies for much longer than they had been enemies. Despite what her brothers believed, she was still the sharks' kin.

"The ground may be treacherous," she said when Tarawe's basket was finished and the gull rode safely on her back. "There are probably cracks and holes covered over by this thick growth. We'll seek a path downhill, but until then, walk carefully."

They discovered very soon that they couldn't walk at all through the dense brush. The ground was more uneven than Iuti had expected. Tough vines tangled through the bushes and shrubs, sometimes reaching waist high. The luxuriant growth was impenetrable.

"Give me your sword, Ser," Tarawe said, handing the gull to Ma'eva. "I'll chop them away." She held out her hand to Iuti, then quickly dropped it back to her side. "Oh, I'm sorry, Ser. I should never have demanded your weapon like that."

Iuti laughed. "My sword is yours, little sister. And your manners are impeccable. You are forgiven for the demand."

She pulled her sword from its sheath and soon Tarawe was hacking a way through the dense jungle growth. She slipped once and almost slid into a deep crevasse, but Ma'eva caught her by the hair and pulled her back. After that, they slid Iuti's fighting stick along the ground before them, straddling it so that if the ground dropped away suddenly again, there would be something to catch them. They made slow, painful progress.

Finally they came to a place where the undergrowth thinned. Giant breadfruit trees spread their branches far above and the deeply shaded floor of the jungle became bare of all but a thick mat of drying, dying, decaying leaves. They still used the stick for protection against falling into unseen holes, but they moved forward much faster. Their movement through the forest became silent again.

When the moon set, their path became almost as dark as it had been inside the cave. They stopped to rest and eat—it was a natural hunger Iuti felt this time—and to wait for the dawn light. After eating, Anali promptly fell asleep against Ma'eva's side. The o'u settled on Iuti's right shoulder and tucked its yel-

low head under its wing. Even asleep, its tiny claws clung to
her tightly.

"How is your gull?" Iuti asked when she saw that Tarawe
did not immediately close her eyes. The girl looked at the heap
of mangled feathers that huddled at her side.

"I think she's sick from those creatures' poison," Tarawe
said. "I said your chant for her, but I don't know if it's working.
I don't think she'll ever get strong enough to fly again now."
She stroked the gull's back. It shivered slightly.

"She is a brave bird," Iuti said. "Without her, we never
would have escaped the grubs. I give her great honor."

Tarawe whispered Iuti's pain spell into her palms and laid
them on the gull. It rustled its feathers for a moment, then settled
again.

"My wind magic didn't work in the cave," Tarawe said.

"Nor did my war magic," Iuti replied.

Tarawe blinked up at her, then glanced back the way they had
come. Then she reached into her basket and lifted out a pile of
fresh ti leaves she'd gathered while they were still in the thick
jungle. She began tying the stems together and slitting the long,
wide leaves into a thick fringe.

"What are you making?" Iuti asked.

"A shirt," Tarawe said. When she had a full strand of shredded ti leaves made, she tied it around her chest. The leaves,
shining and thick, fell like long grass almost to her knees. Only
the patched edges of her trousers showed. Without showing a
finger's breadth of skin, Tarawe pulled the torn remnants of her
earlier covering from underneath. The woven matting was torn
and crumbling. She buried it under the rotting jungle leaves,
then wriggled her shoulders and sighed in relief. Iuti laughed
softly. Tarawe's insistence on remaining fully clothed was a
constant source of amusement to her.

"Ser Iuti?"

"Aye."

After a long pause, Tarawe asked, "Do you ever miss your
mother?"

Sudden pain clutched at Iuti's heart. "Oh, aye, child."

"Will she ever forgive you for killing the shark?"

Iuti leaned back against the tree and stared up at the stars.
"Maybe. If enough time passes before we meet again, and if I
can give her a granddaughter to raise. She was furious when
Mano and I agreed to bond. She'd cut her own warrior's career

short to bear children and it took her six tries before she got me.
I think . . .''

Iuti ran her fingers down along the scars on her cheek. ''I
think when she called Mano Niuhi to help the southern army,
she intended to bond with him herself, and leave me home to
bear and care for the next generation. If she finds me any time
soon, and still carries that anger, I think she will try to kill me.''

Tarawe slipped her hand into Iuti's. She leaned her head on
Iuti's shoulder. She said, ''Sometimes I miss my mother, too.''

They sat quietly together until the sky began to lighten. Then
they woke Anali and Ma'eva to begin their march again. The
o'u chirped and flew into the trees.

Suddenly Tarawe stopped. She stared at Iuti. ''Ser, your hair!
It's turned dark again!''

Iuti reached up to release her warrior's knot. Long, straight
ebony folds cascaded across her shoulders.

''Ayiii,'' Ma'eva said softly. ''You look young again, mother
of my child.''

Months before, Iuti had used greenwort paste to bleach her
hair white. Now the effects were entirely gone. Her hair had
returned to its own natural black. She fingered the thick strands
for a moment, wondering what else might have changed while
they were in the cave, then rolled her hair back atop her head. I
wish I felt young, she thought.

Tarawe played with the wind as they walked. She spun leaves
off the ground and rustled those still hanging in the trees. She
grew bolder and sent small air currents into Anali's hair, twisting
her thin braids into knots and then untangling them again.
Ma'eva laughed at the jest while Anali glanced around in confusion. Finally Iuti ordered Tarawe to stop.

''There may be other people in this forest,'' she said. ''If
there are, I'd like to be able to hear them before they hear us.''

Ma'eva stopped laughing immediately. The air around them
returned to dead calm.

The grove of giant trees ended too soon. They were about to
return to the jungle trek when Iuti had a sudden thought. She
cursed herself for a fool for not thinking of it sooner.

''Tarawe,'' she said, ''can't you use your waryvine spell on
these vines? It would be a lot easier than cutting our way
through.'' And a lot quieter. Iuti couldn't see or hear anything
unusual, but as the sky brightened, she found herself growing
more and more uneasy. Something did not feel right.

Tarawe's eyes went wide. "I forgot all about the grabber vine spell."

The charm was a simple one. Tarawe had learned it from a visiting warrior on Fanape before Iuti had taken refuge there. It had proven invaluable to them more than once. Tarawe brushed her hands across the vines blocking their path, sang her spell softly, and a path began opening swiftly and silently before them. Tarawe met her look and grinned sheepishly.

"I think we were in that cave too long," Iuti said. "Our brains must have grown senile."

Anali sniffed.

They hadn't gone far before Iuti was forced to call another halt. "I have to rest," she said. She hated being the one who held the group to such a slow pace. Even Anali, who looked much older now than she had two days before, moved with more agility. But there was nothing Iuti could do to change her situation. Her body, strong as it still was, simply could not move as quickly and effortlessly as it once had. She wondered if her advanced pregnancy would have been any easier to manage if it had taken her a full nine months to reach it. Probably not, she decided finally. There was simply no way around the bulkiness.

"Was Ma'eva this heavy before he was born?" she asked Anali. She rubbed her lower back with one hand as she leaned against the smooth trunk of a paper palm for support. Tarawe and Ma'eva had gone ahead to scout the best path downhill.

"I wouldn't know," Anali replied. "I never went ashore after the sixth month. In the water, he never weighed much of anything. Are you thirsty, dear? Now where did I put my water gourd?"

Iuti smiled and pointed out Anali's ever-present bag.

"Friend Iuti." Ma'eva's soft voice called her attention back to the jungle. "Come quick. That cliff man is up ahead."

Iuti pushed herself away from the tree, too quickly; she overbalanced and had to reach for Ana's arm to catch herself. "Mano's teeth," she muttered. "I'm as awkward as an over-stuffed blowfish."

"He's sleeping," Ma'eva said when they reached him. They eased along the path Tarawe had spread until they reached a small clearing. A narrow but deep stream ran nearby. Nikivi lay sprawled on his side on a pile of dry leaves, well above the stream's flood line. He hadn't been lying about being one-legged. His left leg ended in a stump halfway down the thigh. He was wearing a thick-soled sandal on his right foot. A spear

with a metal tip and a sling with a pile of stones lay near his
right hand.

Iuti motioned Tarawe to close the vines behind them so their
path wouldn't be obvious, then sent her and Ma'eva to guard
the very obvious path that led from the clearing downhill.

"Come, Mother Ana," Iuti whispered then. "Let's see what
this fellow knows about those lights down below."

Ana smiled grimly. She checked the knives at her wrists again.
They stepped from the shadows and squatted across from each
other, one on each side of Nikivi. Iuti tapped his shoulder with
the flat of her sword.

Nikivi jerked awake, reached for his weapons, then froze when
he felt Iuti's blade touch his chest. She pulled it back slightly.

"Fair morning to you, South Islands man," she said. "What
are you doing down off your cliff?"

Nikivi looked up at her, confused for a moment. He stared at
her hair and then back at her face. He sucked in his breath and
lifted his hand in a warding sign.

"I . . . I did you no harm, warrior woman," he stammered.
"You have no cause to harm me!"

"You did us no good, either," Anali muttered.

Nikivi's look jerked toward her, then darted around the clearing until he spotted Ma'eva and Tarawe. He groaned and formed
the warding sign again. His eyelids flickered and his eyes started
to roll up.

Iuti grabbed him by the front of his knotted armor. It was old.
From its smell, she judged he had been wearing it for a long
time. "Don't faint on me, island man, I want to talk with you."

Nikivi trembled under her hand, clearly terrified. He half
choked on each intake of breath. "Wha . . . what do you want?"
he whispered at last.

"I want you to tell me what those people are doing down at
the shore."

Confusion touched his eyes. "Why are you asking me?"

Iuti pulled him upright. "Because you're the one we found
sleeping all alone out here in the jungle, Nikivi. What's happening down on the beach?"

He stared at her stomach. "Y-you're pregnant!"

"So I am," she replied.

He reached out, but Iuti grabbed his wrist before he could
touch her. He looked much more surprised at her touch than he
had at her size. "By the gods, *you're alive!*" he exclaimed.

"Well, of course she's alive," Anali snapped. "What did

you think she was. A ghost?'' She stopped suddenly, then laughed. ''That's *exactly* what you thought. Ho! I never expected to be mistaken for a spirit in *this* lifetime.''

''But you were caught in the floodwaters!'' He continued to stare wide-eyed at Iuti. ''I was there. I saw you in the pool. All of you.'' He looked around at them all. ''You couldn't have survived being washed down the gulch. No one has *ever* survived that.''

Iuti lifted a brow. ''How often are people given that opportunity?''

He swallowed hard and scooted back a bit. She let him go, but kept her sword balanced lightly across her knees. His look slid toward his own weapons. ''Don't,'' she said softly.

He straightened. ''Any newcomer the Chosen One considers a possible threat is taken to that pool. If they get sucked into the underground river, or washed downstream by one of the floods, a death feast is held in their honor. Then they're forgotten. Those lucky enough to bathe and get out of the pool safely are allowed to become permanent residents of the island.''

His look passed over them all again. ''How did you do it? How did you escape? You didn't make it out of the pool before the floodwater hit. I know that. We searched for you for weeks downstream, at every opening of the underground channel, but never found more than the man's loincloth and a few feathers. The Chosen One was furious about the bird being lost. It was never supposed to be taken into the water.''

He glanced toward Tarawe. ''Did you save the gull, too?''

Tarawe said nothing. The gull was hidden in the basket on her back, but it was clear from Nikivi's look that he believed the bird safe.

If the search went on for weeks, Iuti thought, then we must have spent more actual time in the cave than it seemed. She remembered that Nikivi had seemed surprised to find her pregnant but had said nothing of the time it had taken her to get that far along. Was it possible that five months of true time had passed during what seemed like only two days to them?

Nikivi was staring at her again. ''The rumors about you must be true.''

''What rumors?'' Anali asked.

''The ones that say Mano Niuhi's bonded sister can never be killed.''

If Iuti could have, she would have been on him in an instant, her knee in his belly and her sword at his throat. Instead, it was

Anali who flicked a blade under his chin. Iuti climbed to her feet slowly.

"How can you have heard rumors of the shark god's sister?" Iuti demanded. "You claimed no one had come to this isle for more than five years." She had bonded with Mano Niuhi ten years before, but her reputation as a warrior had not grown large until many years later. There was no way word of her exploits could have reached Tahena if Nikivi had not been lying before.

Nikivi smiled. Ana pricked his chin and he grew serious again. "Where have you been hiding all this time, Iuti Mano? Didn't you see the arrival of the Western Islands' war fleet?"

"War fleet!" Iuti stared at him. "How can a war fleet have crossed the Empty Sea?"

"It took them a long time," Nikivi said. "They spent many months paddling across the dead calm waters. They had a wind caller with them, who took advantage of every errant breeze. They say they ate from the sea, but none will admit to how they caught enough fish to feed so many. Seven of the largest canoes were filled with nothing but water. Even so, they were more than thirsty when they arrived."

"When did they come?"

"Five days ago. They began searching for you the moment they stepped from their canoes."

Iuti caught her breath. "For me?"

Nikivi smiled again, despite Anali's knife. A look of cunning crossed his features. "You have visitors, Iuti Mano," he said. "Your kinfolk have come to call. It was their lights you saw on the beach last night. Theirs and the bird worshipers'. They've hired everyone on the island to search for you."

Iuti turned in shock to stare downhill. The shore was now hidden behind the jungle growth. She laid her hand on her stomach.

Nikivi said, "The entire shark clan is here, Iuti Mano—"

She turned back.

"—and every one of them is looking for a taste of your blood."

≈ Chapter 15 ≈

SER Iuti's entire body shook at Nikivi's words. Her shoulders sagged. Tarawe took a step forward, afraid Iuti might fall, but then the warrior woman straightened. She lifted her chin and suddenly looked strong again.

"Well, I don't intend to feed them," she said. "Get up, South Islands man."

Anali prodded the cliff man with her knife and he immediately reached for his spear. Ser Iuti put her foot on it. "How badly do you want to survive this meeting?" she asked.

Nikivi stared up at her. "I need my walking stick to help me stand."

Iuti returned his stare coldly. "Ma'eva, take the tip off this man's *walking* stick. He doesn't need *that* to help him stand."

Nikivi cursed as Ana passed the spear to Ma'eva. The sea mimic's hands flickered for an instant while he snapped the spear off just below its metal tip. He handed the blade to his mother, who stuffed it into her bag, then gave the broken stick to Nikivi.

Nikivi grabbed it and pushed himself up, muttering and cursing all the while. "I'm not your enemy, warrior woman," he said when he was upright again. To Tarawe's amazement, he stood as straight as if he had two good legs reaching all the way to the ground. It appeared he needed the stick only to get up.

"You would do better to make a friend of me," he said. "You won't find many others on this isle."

"Why would *you* want to befriend me?" Iuti asked.

"I have no great love for my bird-worshiping neighbors," he said. "And they have none for me. If I can find a way off this island, I will take it. Like I told you before, I play by my own rules."

"Well, for now, my newfound friend, you will play by mine."
Iuti took a slow breath and pressed a hand to her lower back.
Tarawe wasn't sure, but it looked as if Iuti's stomach was hang-
ing lower than it had been before.

"What is the fastest way to the sea?" Iuti asked.

Nikivi pointed toward the path Ma'eva and Tarawe were
guarding.

"And the safest?"

"There is no safe way now," he replied. "You'd do better
to hide up the mountainside, although I doubt it would help for
long. There is a woman of power among your visiting kin who
claims she can find you wherever you might hide. They say it
was she who convinced the birds to lead the fleet here."

"Birds!" Tarawe heard herself say.

Nikivi's sly look turned her way. "Aye, small sorceress. The
birds have returned to Tahena. All the birds in existence it
seemed when they first started to arrive. More gulls than I've
ever seen, and seabirds beyond counting—even landbirds,
though how so many crossed the Empty Sea safely, no one
knows. The bird worshipers have gone mad with joy. The Chosen One claims it was she who called the airfolk back to Tahena,
by using your gull's feathers that washed down the river."

By his look, Tarawe suspected he didn't believe the Chosen
One or the feathers had anything to do with the birds' return.

The o'u chose that moment to flutter from the trees and light
on Ser Iuti's shoulder. It chirped rapidly. Nikivi cursed and
would have moved back if Anali had let him.

"Let me go, Iuti Mano," he said. "I've done you no harm
and told you all you asked. Now that you've been discovered,
I want no part of you. The bird worshipers will claim I've been
helping you all along. They've already accused me more than
once since your kin came. I have enough problems of my own."

"What do you mean, discovered?" Anali demanded. "No
one has discovered us here. We're as alone now as we were
when you woke. Speak clearly, island man, or you'll be short a
tongue as well as a leg." She nicked Nikivi's chin again; a thin
trickle of blood ran down his neck and under his knotted armor.

"The bird!" He pointed at Iuti's shoulder. "The bird will tell
them where you are. They've been paid to find you, too, Iuti
Mano. Or they will be when you're caught."

Anali harumphed. "That little thing isn't going to give us
away. She's the one who—

The o'u left Iuti's shoulder and swooped toward Ana. It hovered just before her face, flapping its tiny wings and chirping frantically. Anali waved a hand at it. "Slow down, bird. I can't understand a thing you—"

Ana went suddenly pale. "Wait," she said to the bird. "*Who* did you say sent you?"

"What is it?" Ser Iuti asked.

Suddenly Nikivi turned and ran. He moved as smoothly and swiftly as if he had two good legs. Iuti started after him, but she clearly would not reach him before he reached the trees. Tarawe dashed forward and scooped a stone from Nikivi's own pile. She flung it after him.

"Yeeow!" Nikivi stumbled and fell forward as the stone struck the back of his right knee. He lay groaning and clutching his one leg. He turned paler than Anali as he looked up to meet Iuti's stare.

"You can't blame me," he said quickly. "You'd have tried to get away, too, if you'd been in my place. You can't blame me for trying."

Iuti kicked his stick away from his reach. "If you've heard one rumor about me then you've heard others," she said. "Consider the one that deals with my patience and what happens to those who abuse it."

"I'll watch him, Ser," Tarawe said. Anali had squatted on the ground and was rummaging through her bag. Iuti nodded at Tarawe, caught Ma'eva's eye for a moment—he had stayed near the downhill path—then walked back to where Anali sat. The o'u was perched on Nikivi's pile of stones, still chirping frantically.

Ana pulled her feathered headdress from the bag and tied it around her forehead. Tarawe heard Nikivi suck in his breath as the brilliant feathers caught and held the sunlight.

"Now," Ana said to the bird. "Tell me exactly what happened. And don't shriek it this time. I can hear you, I just can't understand you."

The o'u chirped and chittered and fluttered its tiny wings.

"What is she saying?" Iuti asked.

Ana took a deep breath. "I think I'd better talk with Tarawe's gull."

"*Ana!*"

Ana looked up at her. Her eyes had darkened in concern. The spots and splotches on her weathered skin stood out clearly. "She says the flying dolphins are looking for you, too."

"*What?*"

"She says she was feeding in some berry bushes down below when a flying dolphin flew over and—"

"Over *land*! That can't be—"

"They can do it for a short time when the need is great enough," Anali said. "It takes them days of rest to recover the strength they lose."

"But—"

"Do you want to know what she said or not?" Anali snapped.

Ser Iuti stopped and stared down at her. Finally she sat cross-legged at Anali's side. "Tell me," she said.

Mama Ana nodded. "The dolphin called the o'u into the sky; it knew somehow that your little friend knew where you were. It told her to bring you a message from all of its kin."

Iuti waited in silence while Ana took a deep breath. Even Nikivi remained still.

"They ask that you give them back their egg," Anali said at last.

"Mano's bloody teeth, Anali!" Ser Iuti's voice was abruptly angry. "I don't *have* their damnable egg! You know that. Tell the o'u to tell the dolphins that."

"She already told them," Anali said. "It seems, though, that your kin are in possession of the egg, as well as another *true* pearl they found inside the Great Clam."

"How did they find the clam?" Ma'eva asked. "How did they even know it existed?"

"The birds led them to it. After they lost our trail on the Empty Sea, they returned to Kala Atoll. By that time, Iuti's brothers had returned, and the birds demanded that they pay your debt. The humans waited until they had the egg in their hands before telling the birds they wouldn't give it up until you were found. The birds began searching the Empty Sea while your kinfolk gathered their fleet and followed. It took them all these months to find this place."

Tarawe thought of the great gray dolphin who had stopped them so easily from harvesting the pearl themselves. "Why didn't the flying dolphins stop them from taking the egg?" she asked. "As they did us."

Anali sighed. "They tried but were too late. The men used no magic to find or to open the clam, so the dolphins had no warning." She lifted her look to Iuti's. "Your brothers smashed the shell into pieces and left the clam to die."

"Ayiii," Ma'eva said softly.

"Those sea slime brought the egg with them across the Empty

Sea," Ana went on. "They threatened to smash it just as they had the clam shell if the dolphins impeded their way. Now they are promising the egg to anyone who finds you."

Iuti glanced across the clearing toward Nikivi. "Is this true? Is the dolphin's egg the price my kinfolk have put on my head?"

Very cautiously Nikivi nodded.

"Gods, but I'm tired of fighting wars of greed and revenge." Ser Iuti sighed.

"Are there any other kind?" Anali asked.

"Does this path follow the stream?" Ma'eva said.

They all looked toward Nikivi. He nodded.

Ma'eva met Iuti's look. "I'll go ahead to be sure it's safe." He turned and was gone in an instant. Tarawe didn't need to hear a splash or see a flicker to know the sea mimic intended to scout the path in one of his water forms. Good, she thought, he can travel much faster that way. They would have more time to hide or to get away if someone was coming uphill.

Iuti grunted slightly and leaned forward as far as her stomach allowed.

Tarawe wanted to go to her but was afraid to leave Nikivi. She looked around until she saw a hanging vine. She turned the onshore breeze to swing the vine close enough to touch. Then she muttered the grabber-vine spell. Nikivi stared in wide-eyed horror as the vine began twisting around his arms and his leg. When he started to call out, she said to him, "If you make any noise that draws the others to us, I'll release the vines before they see you and tell them you've been hiding us all this time."

Nikivi met her look and his lips closed tight. Tarawe made sure he was securely tied, then hurried to Iuti's side.

"Are you well, Ser?" she asked softly. She explained quickly what she had done with Nikivi, then slid her hands over Iuti's stomach.

"Something happened," Iuti said. "I felt it move just now, in a different way from before."

"The baby has moved, Ser. It's dropped into the birthing tunnel."

Iuti met her look bleakly. "How much time do we have?"

"Most women would have at least a week or more, a few days, at least. But . . ." She shrugged.

"But the time change in the cave may have altered even that," Iuti finished.

Tarawe nodded. "I'm sorry, Ser. I wish I knew more, but

even my mother couldn't always tell exactly when a baby would come.''

"Tarawe," Ser Iuti said. Her voice dropped to a whisper and she laid a hand on Tarawe's cheek. She looked directly into Tarawe's eyes. "I want you to promise me something."

"I'll do anything you say," Tarawe replied.

Iuti's hands remained steady on her cheek. Her skin was warm and damp. "If this child is born before we reach the sea," she said, "I want you to promise me that you will take it to the water immediately. Don't wait for anything, not even for the afterbirth to come. Tie the cord, cut the babe free, and take it to the sea."

"Oh, Ser, I could never leave you before—"

"Listen to me, Tarawe, We *must* save this child, no matter what else happens. Male or female, it makes no difference. Take it to the sea. Ma'eva has told me that there will be other sea mimics to help you even if he and Ana cannot. The mimics always know when and where one of their own is being born."

Ser Iuti's face tightened for a moment. She took a shallow breath and blew it out slowly. "Promise me, little sister. Give me your word, for I trust it above all others."

Tears stung Tarawe's eyes. Her mother had exacted such a promise from her once, a promise to leave her alone in the hands of her enemies. She'd done it to protect her only child, Tarawe understood that now. "I don't want you to die, Ser," she said.

Iuti surprised her by smiling. "I'm Iuti Mano, remember? Sister to the shark god. Nothing can kill me, so the rumors say." They both knew that wasn't true, but finally, reluctantly, Tarawe nodded.

"All right," she said. "I promise. But if it happens and someone hurts you while I'm gone, I'll come back and find them. I won't kill them, Ser, but I'll make them wish I had. I'll make them *all* wish I had."

"You would not do me honor by starting a war of revenge, Storm Caller," Ser Iuti said.

Tarawe watched her for a moment, then pushed back and stood. "We need to go before you have that baby right here," she said.

"Aye." Iuti pushed herself up with much less ease. "I love this child," she said, "but I'll be glad to get my warrior's agility back." The o'u fluttered up from the rock pile to settle on her shoulder.

"Mother Ana, tell friend o'u to . . . Mama Ana?"

Tarawe smiled and gently shook Anali awake. Iuti stopped

Ana before she could remove her headdress. "I want you to talk to the o'u again," she said.

Ana blinked up at the bird. The o'u cocked its head and blinked back.

"Tell her to tell the other birds that Ma'eva and I intend to keep our bargain with them," Iuti said. "But if my kin find me first, they will never get their pearl."

"How can you be certain of that?" Ana asked. "Despite your warlike nature, those of Mano's clan are generally known to keep their word."

"Mano's kin are sea people, Ana," Iuti said. "Once my brothers have me in their hands, they will either return the egg to the flying dolphins or, if necessary, destroy it. They would never give it to the birds."

Ana watched her for a moment. "You, too, are a sea person, Iuti Mano. If you convince the birds your kin won't give them the egg, what makes you think they'll believe *you* would?"

"Tell them what I have at stake," Iuti replied. Tarawe bit her lip to keep from protesting Ser Iuti's words. Surely she would not give—

Ana chittered sharply to the bird. The o'u fluttered up at her voice, settled again to listen, then chirped in return.

"She wants to know what to tell the dolphins," Ana said. "She's terrified of them, and they're waiting for her to return with your answer."

"Tell them about Ma'eva's child," Iuti said.

Ana nodded. Her lined face was a mask of sadness. The trade was entirely unfair to both the sea mimics and the flying dolphins. They were both slowly disappearing from the seas, and neither wanted to see the other go. Ana chittered again, more softly this time. Then the o'u darted from Iuti's shoulder back into the trees. Anali stuffed her feathered headdress into her bag.

Nikivi let out a long sigh. "I would never have guessed it was the old woman who was the sorceress."

Anali eyed him with disgust. "You land folk credit every sensible skill to sorcery. You'd do better to just open your eyes a little wider. Now, how can we best get down off this mountain?"

"I told you before," he said. "The path leads directly to the beach. But there are guards there, just as there are at the base of every valley on the eastern side of the island. If you want to avoid them, you'll have to cross just downstream from here and head west into the lava fields."

"How long would it take to reach the sea if we go that way?" Iuti asked. She had her hand on her stomach again.

"In your condition? Two days, at least, to reach a place where you could get down the sea cliffs," Nikivi said. "That's if the landmaker doesn't object to you crossing her private domain. She's been restless ever since you first came. Even more so since your kin arrived."

"Who is this landmaker?" Iuti asked. "The Chosen One spoke of her. She said she was going to take us to the mountain to meet her."

Nikivi snorted. "The Chosen One was planning to kill or maim any of you who survived the pool. Then she was going to take the *gull* to meet the landmaker."

"Why?"

"A live bird is considered the most valuable sacrifice the bird worshipers can offer Haku 'Aina," Nikivi said. "Any storm-blown bird that has the misfortune to discover this isle is eventually caught and taken to her. Usually the offerings are no more than a few old, sometimes even fake feathers, stuck into various food gifts."

"What happens to the birds?" Tarawe asked.

Nikivi shrugged. "Usually the ground opens and swallows them. Sometimes it opens and swallows the islanders who brought the bird, as well. Then a new Chosen One has to be selected. The women on Tahena compete for that honor from the time they're born. That's why your arrival caused such a stir. Three women! Two of you young enough, one certainly strong enough to meet the ritual challenge rites. If you hadn't slowed your canoe when you did, they'd have killed you before you even realized the island was here."

Tarawe remembered the sulfur smell that had caused them to slow their passage. She wished she had paid more attention to it then. They might have avoided this place if she had.

"The ground opens?" Iuti asked.

Nikivi frowned. "Haven't you felt the earth moving? That's Haku 'Aina showing her displeasure. When she's irritated, she can shake the ground right out from under you. When she's *angered*—" He shook his head as far as the entangling vine would allow. "—she can open her mountain and pour her fiery blood right across your feet." He glanced down at the place where his left leg should have been.

"How can we appease this spirit?" Iuti asked. "What would we have to do to travel safely across her land?"

Nikivi glanced toward Tarawe. "You could offer her the gull." Tarawe glared at him.

Iuti pulled her shield from her back and began lacing it to the ties of her opened vest. "We'll take our chances downhill. There can't be too many guards here in this one valley. We'll find a way to slip past them, or we'll fight them. I'm in no mood, or condition, to confront some angry island spirit."

She finished lacing the shield across her chest and stomach. It didn't look comfortable, and it would probably add to her imbalance, but if she had to fight, it would protect the child. Anali pulled another set of knives from her bag. She fastened them at her hips, then slipped on a tunic of overlapping fish scales. Tarawe picked up Nikivi's pile of stones and stuffed them into her pockets.

When they were ready to move, Tarawe untangled the vine from Nikivi's leg, leaving a loop around his ankle. She left his hands securely tied behind his back. He eyed her darkly again. Ana cut the vine free of the jungle and jerked Nikivi upright. She kept a tight hold on the loose end of his tether.

"If you oppose us, or try to escape, we'll kill you," Iuti told him. "If you help us, but we get caught, Tarawe will release you and we'll tell them you captured us first and earned the pearl. If we escape, we will take you with us."

Nikivi's eyes brightened in surprise, then grew cunning again.

"Do we understand each other, Nikivi of the South Islands?"

"Aye, Iuti Mano," he said with a grin. Ana prodded him, and he preceded her across the clearing to the path. Iuti motioned for them to go first.

"Ser?" Tarawe said before entering the path.

"Aye."

Tarawe hesitated. "Ser. About the dolphin's egg. You mustn't give it to the birds."

Ser Iuti laid a hand on Tarawe's shoulder. "Tarawe, our debt to the birds is, as it has always been, the Great Pearl. If they choose to misunderstand that to mean the flying dolphin's egg, that is their own business."

Tarawe let out a long, soft breath.

Iuti smiled. "I had to say it that way to the o'u, because even though she helped us find our way from the cave, she's still one of the airfolk. We can't be sure her loyalties are really with us." She glanced down the path. "Also, Nikivi was listening." She closed her eyes for a moment.

"Are you all right, Ser?" Tarawe asked.

"Just tired." Iuti straightened. "Let's get started."

The path was much less difficult than the way they had traveled before, but it still wasn't easy. Tarawe kept glancing back to be sure Ser Iuti wasn't falling behind. After the first few steps, Iuti pulled her fighting stick from her back and used it as a walking stick. Ahead of them, Ana kept a tight hold on Nikivi's tether. He walked as easily as if both legs touched the ground. The sight made Tarawe shiver.

They had just reached sight of the bridge Nikivi had spoken of when Ma'eva burst from the center of the stream. "They are coming, friend Iuti!" he called. "Your brothers! They are on the path just below! I missed seeing them on my way downhill, because they were using a hiding spell. But one of them stopped to pee into the stream. I came back as soon as I tasted him."

"We'll have to go back," Iuti said. She sounded as tired as Tarawe had ever heard her. Despair was in her voice. Tarawe knew Iuti couldn't travel much farther. She certainly couldn't travel any faster.

"Are they below the bridge?" Tarawe called to Ma'eva.

"Aye, but not far," he replied. He scrambled up the steep floodbank of the stream.

"Get to the bridge, Ser," Tarawe said. "Hurry. Get across before they get there."

"What—"

"Go," Tarawe shouted.

Ma'eva had reached Iuti's side. He flickered for an instant. His shoulders and thighs swelled. Then he scooped Iuti from the ground. Anali and Nikivi ran ahead of them to the bridge.

Tarawe lifted her right hand to the sky. "Come," she called to the wind. "Bring rain. Hurry." She scooped the water-laden clouds down the sides of the valley. When they were thick and dark, almost overhead, she called the rainwater down. It fell suddenly, in pounding torrents, sounding almost like the great waterfall at the entry to the cave. Tarawe ran for the bridge.

It was only a plank walkway, so narrow that Ma'eva had to put Iuti down and walk behind her to balance her on the way across the gully. The planks were tied together with ropes, and a single additional rope served as the only hand guard. The bridge swayed dangerously, but by the time Tarawe reached it, Iuti and Ma'eva had stepped onto solid ground on the opposite side.

Ana cut Nikivi's hands loose and pushed him onto the bridge. He protested briefly, then started quickly across when Ana poked him with her knife. A shout rose from the path below. They had been seen.

The stream had already begun to rise with gathering rainwater. Tarawe pulled the clouds closer and started across the bridge after Ana and Nikivi. Surely if the ropes had supported Ma'eva and Iuti, it would hold three smaller people. The planks grew slippery with spray and the approaching rain. Tarawe spared a quick movement of her left hand to hold the rain back from the bridge. Nikivi screamed and pointed upstream, then slapped both hands back around the guide rope and slipped and slid his way forward as fast as he could move.

A shout came from behind Tarawe. A conch began to blow, over and over—a flood warning to those downstream. Tarawe didn't look back. She could feel the wall of floodwater gathering just upstream. She could taste it on her wind, smell it on her air. Her foot slipped, and she was left dangling from the guide rope for an instant. She scrambled back up onto the slippery foot bridge.

She tried to pull herself forward, but the guide rope went suddenly slack under her hands. Someone behind her had cut it free.

The roiling face of the flood wave appeared—and struck. Tarawe screamed as she was washed into the torrent.

❧ Chapter 16 ❧

MA'EVA flickered and changed and snaked long sucker-lined arms out to catch Tarawe. His form change wasn't even complete before he had Tarawe's wrist tightly wrapped with the tip of one tentacle. She had not let go of the slack rope, and he used that and another arm to help pull her ashore. The rushing floodwaters had kept her from slamming into the side of the gully, but she was limp, coughing and choking, when Ma'eva finally pulled her to safety. Iuti nearly wept in relief.

Anali helped Tarawe to her knees and bent over her while she emptied her stomach onto the mossy ground. Ma'eva flickered back to his human form and returned immediately to Iuti's side. He took the sword she had kept pressed to Nikivi's throat and urged her to sit back and rest while she could.

"You don't need that sword," Nikivi said. He was staring at Ma'eva in awe. Through the rain, the men on the other side of the river might not have recognized Ma'eva's change, but Nikivi had witnessed it clearly. "I won't run away now." He wiped rainwater from his eyes.

Ma'eva ignored him. He retied Nikivi's hands, then returned Iuti's sword to her sheath. Iuti reached up to touch his cheek. He moved his head, rubbing his smooth, wet cheek across her palm, and smiled.

Then he grew serious again. "Are there paths from the beach up this side of the valley?" he asked Nikivi.

Nikivi shook his head, blinking against the rain. "There's only this one. It's the formal processional path to the landmaker's domain."

Ma'eva walked back toward the bridge, which was somehow still intact. No one could cross it while the floodwaters still washed over it, but at Iuti's nod, Ma'eva cut the bridge free of the bank. It swung out and down with the foaming river, shattering in the torrent into splintered pieces.

Finally Tarawe pushed Ana away. She turned to stare at the flooding river. Then she looked up toward the sky and lifted her right hand to the wind. The pounding rain slid upslope from them and across the river to strike the shouting, cursing warriors. They moved quickly back from the edge of the gully.

Iuti could hear Kuwala's curse even across the roar of the flood. He alone remained near the bank, screaming and shaking his fist. Three of Iuti's other brothers were there, and at least ten of her cousins and uncles. She did not see Anele among them. How was it that they had been in this very valley? What had led them to her?

"How long will the flood last?" she asked.

Tarawe glanced at her. She had a wide, bleeding scratch across her right cheek. "Until late afternoon at least," she said. "I've already called more clouds from the other valleys. Your brothers won't be able to cross the river for many hours, Ser."

"What about upstream?" Anali asked. She pulled her green paste pot from her bag and began smearing the healing salve on Tarawe's cheek. Tarawe backed away from the smell, then stopped and allowed Anali to finish.

"They'd have to climb a long way to get higher than my rain," she said. "They're more likely to go down and around to the next valley by sea. They could catch us there if they move fast enough. We'd better get going while we can."

"There is no next valley," Nikivi said. They all turned toward him. "Beyond here, the lava fields begin."

"Are there other ways there besides this path?" Iuti asked.

He shrugged. "There are others, but this path is the shortest and simplest way. Once you're in the lava fields, you should be safe. It would take the gods' own good luck to find anyone hiding out there, and we don't have much of that on this isle." He glanced at Tarawe and then Ma'eva. "People make their own luck here."

"If my mother could find this island, and then this valley just as I emerged into it," Iuti said, "she can find me anywhere. We need to reach the sea before that happens."

"Your mother?" Ma'eva said as he helped her up.

"Nikivi said there was a woman of power among my kin," Iuti said. "It has to be my mother. Only she could have gathered the forces to bring an entire fleet across the Empty Sea. Only she could have sung the seafolk into the fishermen's nets along the way. Only she could have known I was here in this valley today. She must have called in all the shark clan's debts to convince a wind caller to accompany her here. Be careful of that, Tarawe. Someone else might try to take control of your clouds or your wind.''

Tarawe held her palm to the sky and pressed her fingers closed. ''These clouds will stay where they are until I release them or they're empty,'' she said. From the look on her face, Iuti didn't doubt that they would. Her mother's wind caller was likely in for a big surprise if he or she tried to start moving the Storm Caller's wind.

They made better time than Iuti had expected. The jungle path was steep, leading them up over the ridge of the valley, but it was wide enough for Ma'eva to walk beside her and offer his support when she needed it. Ana walked ahead carrying Nikivi's tether. When it was clear that she was beginning to tire, Tarawe took over as the cliff man's personal guard. Nikivi began walking much faster than before. Ma'eva called them back to keep pace with the rest.

They stopped to rest more often than Iuti wanted, but less often than she needed. Ana patted her hand at one such stop and said, ''If you do this again, dear, you really should consider just spending the entire nine months in the sea. It's much easier.''

Iuti laughed and gave Ana a hug. ''You are a treasure, Mother Ana. You must be much more tired than I, and still you find ways to make me smile.''

''Hmmph!'' Ana muttered. ''This is the first time I've walked on dry land for decades, and the mother of my grandchild thinks I'm tired.'' She closed her eyes and fell asleep against Iuti's side.

At late afternoon, they came to another bridge. Like the other, it was made of breadfruit planks, strung together with coconut fiber rope. It led across a deep chasm directly into the mouth of a large cave.

''What's wrong?'' Nikivi said when they all stopped to stare at the cave. He looked back at them in confusion.

''What's in there?'' Tarawe asked. Her right hand twitched at her side.

''Nothing. It's just an old lava tube. It leads through the hill to the edge of the lava fields.''

Iuti walked to the end of the bridge and looked down. She shuddered. The crack fell deeper than she could see. Steam rose in curling plumes from the sides and the invisible bottom of the chasm. The whole pit stank of sulfur. The ground shivered slightly.

"Is there any other way?" she asked.

"Not unless you want to trek through the jungle around the ground crack and then climb over the top of the ridge," he said.

Iuti looked up. The sides of the ridge were almost vertical and the crack ran as far as she could see both up and down the valley. She sighed. "Mama Ana, put a knife to our good guide's throat and let him lead us through this cave," she said. As tired as Anali was, Iuti knew she could trust her to kill Nikivi in an instant if something should go wrong. Both Ma'eva and Tarawe would kill him, too, if it became truly necessary, but Iuti wanted to protect them from being placed in that personal danger.

She looked directly into Nikivi's dark eyes. "If we meet anything in that tube other than clear air and a smooth floor, you won't live to see the other side."

Nikivi held her look. "There's nothing to fear in there, Iuti Mano. The tube's not even long enough to get fully dark. Nobody on this island would be fool enough to go into a *true* cave. Dreadful things happen in caves here, things few humans have lived to tell about. I wouldn't even go through this tube if it was night."

He turned a cool look on Ana. "Not even with your bloody knife at my throat, Grandmama."

"Aye," Iuti said after a moment. "Only a fool would go into a true cave here." She nudged Nikivi's shoulder and urged him across the bridge. Ana released one of his hands so he could hold on to the guide rope. Ma'eva crossed with them to protect Anali, then started back for Iuti.

"Do you think he's telling the truth?" Tarawe asked.

Iuti nodded. "I hope so." A sensation of tightness passed over her stomach. She closed her eyes and spread her hands over the firm mound of her child.

"Ser Iuti?"

Iuti blew out a slow breath. She opened her eyes to find Tarawe staring at her wide-eyed. Tarawe slid a hand across Iuti's stomach, but the tightness had passed.

"Ser, is it—"

"We need to keep moving, Tarawe," Iuti said. "I don't think we have much time left."

"Oh, gods," Tarawe breathed. "Ma'eva, hurry!"

Iuti crossed the bridge slowly and very carefully, hoping all the while that the tightness would not return before they reached the other side. More than that, she hoped the earth would not shake again. Ma'eva and Tarawe flanked her closely. When they reached solid ground again, Ma'eva slipped his arm around Iuti's waist and practically carried her through the cave.

Just as Nikivi said, it never grew entirely dark. By the time the light from the valley side faded, they could see the glow of late-afternoon sunlight ahead. Tarawe immediately darted ahead.

"Oh, Ser!" she called. "It's beautiful!" She came running back to help Anali. "It's like that cavern of light we found. All sparkling and shining. The wind tastes *good* out there, except for that strange sulfur smell." She laughed. "If sulfur places are good for healing, Mama Ana, this landmaker's home must be very healthy."

Nikivi stared at her as if she had completely lost her mind, but Iuti smiled at Tarawe's enthusiasm. It served to lighten her own increasingly dark mood. The birth day of her child was not supposed to have been like this. She should have been on a safe beach somewhere, or far out at sea, surrounded by seafolk and people she loved. It should have been a day of celebration and joy.

Ma'eva brushed his hand across her scarred cheek and stepped with her into the sun.

The lava fields were, indeed, beautiful. Fractured stone, as black as night in the shadows but shimmering so brightly iridescent in the late-day sun that it made Iuti squint to look at them, spread clear to the western horizon. Downhill from where they stood, the lava stretched to the edge of the sea. Shades of gray and black and silver that Iuti had never imagined existed flickered and flared over the great expanse of overlapping lava flows. It looked both welcoming and entirely forbidding.

"This is the driest, most desolate stretch of land I've ever encountered," Anali said. The ground trembled. Nikivi sucked in his breath in concern, but the ground did not open to swallow them.

"I like this place," Tarawe said. "The wind is free here. This is better than in those valleys where the air is trapped in among all the trees and plants and can hardly move for all the water it has to carry. The wind likes to be free." She lifted her hand and a sulfur-laden breeze circled them.

"Carefully, Tarawe," Iuti warned. "Too much of the sulfur can harm us, and we don't want to disturb the spirits of this place unless we have to."

"There is only one spirit that matters," Nikivi said. His eyes had grown cunning again. "If you want to appease her, you should give me the bird. I'll take it to one of the offering pits and give it to Haku 'Aina in your name, while you rest here. I can be back by morning, then I'll lead you to the sea."

"We can find our own way to the sea now," Anali snapped. "We don't need you to lead us to it."

"But . . . ." He looked toward Iuti. "You need to find a place where you can get down the sea cliffs. After I—"

"Nikivi, we're not going to give you the bird, and we're not going to let you go off on your own to tell the others where we are." Iuti turned to Tarawe. "If we can get to the cliffs, can you—"

"I can bring a sea wave up to lift us off, Ser," Tarawe said quickly.

Iuti paused while her stomach muscles tightened, pressed all around the mound that was her child, then relaxed again. When it was finished, she pulled her weapons from their sheaths and laid them on the shining lava.

"Ana," she said. "Do the same."

Anali frowned, but Ma'eva prodded her forward. "We don't have time to argue, Mama. My child is coming."

Anali gave Iuti a startled look, then quickly complied with her order. She didn't look pleased, but she laid her four knives beside Iuti's sword and fighting stick without comment. She glared at Ma'eva when he reminded her of the metal tip he had broken from Nikivi's walking stick. When it was set with the others, Iuti lifted her hands, palms open, to the shimmering fields.

"Honor to you, Haku 'Aina, and to all the spirits of this place," she called. "We give you greeting and ask your permission to walk freely from here to the sea. We intend no harm."

She waited for a moment, half expecting the ground to begin moving again, or some dark stone goddess to rise from the lava fields to confront them.

After a moment, she lowered her hands.

Nikivi stared at her. "Is that all you're going to do?"

"There's nothing more I *can* do," Iuti said as she resheathed her weapons. The effort of bending over to pick them up left her all unbalanced again. Tarawe and Ma'eva each took one of her arms. She shook them away. "I'm not that far gone yet," she said. "Ma'eva, go walk with Anali. Traveling across this stone isn't going to be easy. Tarawe, you can stay with me, but both of you keep an eye on our guide. I can walk, but I don't think I can run right now.''

"He'd be easy to trip out here in the open," Tarawe said. "My wind wouldn't have any trouble at all catching him. Shall I untie his hands?"

"Aye. We're all going to need our full balance. If you fall, Nikivi, I'm not stopping to pick you up."

"How do you walk so well with only one leg?" Tarawe asked as she loosed Nikivi's bonds.

He looked her right in the eye and said, "Magic, little girl. Very powerful magic."

"That's what I thought," Tarawe said. She left him staring as she returned to Iuti's side.

The sun-gilded lava was as treacherous to walk on as it was awesome to look at. Its shining crust crunched under Iuti's boots, collapsing at times into small pockets with razor-sharp edges. They were soon forced to stop so that Tarawe could wrap her feet with cloth from Ana's bag and pieces of woven matting cut from Iuti's vest. Ma'eva formed thick, dark calluses on the bottoms and sides of his feet.

"I saw a man with feet like this once," he said. "He was a coral walker and very strong. He'd have lived longer if his head had been as hard as the soles of his feet."

Tarawe continued to play with the wind as they walked. She brushed cool breezes past their faces and sent scudding gusts ahead to scrape loose stones from their path. She laughed and talked with her gull, describing the surrounding air currents and the heat vents she could feel in the distance to the poor basket-bound bird.

"She's a true child of the air," Anali said as they watched Tarawe soothe the bird.

The earth trembled from time to time—Nikivi made a warding sign and turned his terrified stare toward the cloud-shrouded mountaintop each time it happened—but the ground never shook enough to make them fall. Iuti decided the spirits must had been satisfied with her request to cross their land.

When the way became very difficult, Ma'eva carried Anali ahead, then came back to assist Tarawe and Iuti. They stopped more and more often as the contractions in Iuti's stomach grew more frequent and more intense.

"I never expected to have your child in the middle of a stone desert, friend mimic," she said after one such stop. She took slow breaths to calm herself.

Ma'eva ran a palm across her stomach. "I thought we'd still be playing at Kala," he said. Then he grinned. "It doesn't matter. We're close to the sea now. I can smell it. Our child will taste the water soon."

As the light faded and they climbed downhill, it became more difficult to see the best path to the sea. Sometimes they were forced to pass between great outcroppings of thrust-up lava walls. Then they couldn't see the ocean at all. It was almost dark when Iuti noticed the outline of trees ahead and somewhat to the west.

"It's a kipuka," Nikivi said. "An island of unburned forest in the hardened lava. That one is a very ancient place. Going there is forbidden even to the Chosen One."

"We have no intentions of going there. We want only to reach the sea," Iuti said.

"You'll never be able to get down the cliffs," Nikivi replied. He glanced at Ma'eva. "Not even with *his* help. They're too high and sheer."

"We'll get down the cliffs safely," Iuti said. She tried to imagine being lifted from the clifftop by one of Tarawe's great waves. The image ended abruptly when her stomach tightened again, with much greater force than the time before.

"I hope I can *make* it to the cliffs," she muttered when it had passed.

"Ser?"

"I'll keep going until I have to stop," Iuti said. "Remember your promise if I can't make it all the way to the sea. I can always catch up later. Ma'eva, wake up Mama Ana and let's move on."

A short time later, the sun set. The sky grew brilliantly orange, then quickly faded to dark as the sun sank behind the sea. "Now what did I do with my bag?" Anali said. "I have a light somewhere—"

"There's enough moonlight to travel by," Iuti said. "If we carry a light, we'll make a beacon of ourselves for anyone else who might be out here."

"Ma'eva and I can keep us headed toward the sea," Tarawe said. "And my wind can tell us if there are any deep cracks or rough places ahead."

Nikivi stared at them. "You are *all* sorcerers. I never thought you would survive the day, but you have escaped the shark clan and now walk across the landmaker's home with impunity." He came to stand close to Iuti. "Take me with you when you go, warrior. Don't leave me here on this cursed isle. I'll be your servant for the rest of your days if you'll—"

The ground trembled. Nikivi fell to his one knee and promptly tumbled over onto his side. "Forgive me, Haku 'Aina!" he cried. "I did not mean to insult you!" He cowered with his arms wrapped around his head until the shaking stopped.

"Look there!" Tarawe said.

An orange glow had appeared between two outcroppings of lava not far from where they stood. "Ayiii!" Nikivi cried. "The landmaker walks!"

"Get up," Iuti said when the glow neither brightened nor approached. "Ma'eva, help him stand. Nikivi, if the landmaker walks, then it is time for us to do the same. Whether I take you with us or not depends on what you do between now and the time we leave." When Nikivi hesitated, she added, "Your other choice is to remain here on your belly, alone."

He stared toward the glow, then at Iuti. Then he allowed Ma'eva to lift him to his one foot. He followed closely as they began crunching their way across the crusted stone again.

Looking behind them, Iuti saw other patches of fiery orange light. They reflected eerily against the night-dark lava and the sky. The smell of sulfur was strong when the wind blew toward them from the mountain. Tarawe pulled up a clean sea wind to keep it away. Time and again, Iuti had to stop while her stomach contracted. Finally she was forced to lean on Ma'eva and bend forward against one of the contractions' strength.

"We must hurry," Ma'eva said when she had caught her breath again.

"Maybe we should stop here, Anali said. "Once the child has come, we can move it quickly to the water and then come back for—"

"Ser Iuti!" Tarawe called softly. "There are lights down by the shore. It looks like torchlight."

"Nikivi, could it be the bird people?" Iuti asked.

He shook his head rapidly. "The only places the bird worshipers go are the offering sites, and when they're there, they don't use torchlight."

"Whoever it is is coming this way, Ser," Tarawe said. "They must be following the shortest way from the shore to the cave we came through. We have to move before they get close enough to see us in the moonlight." She slipped a supporting arm under Iuti's.

Mano protect us, Iuti thought. "Let's go into the trees. Without lights, they won't be able to see us."

"You can't go to the kipuka!" Nikivi cried. They ignored him. He stayed close to them, though, when they began to move—as afraid of being left alone in the dark lava fields as he was of the island of trees ahead.

"How could they have known where we would be coming down?" Anali asked. "How could they even know we were coming down?"

"Even without knowing about the child, my mother knows I would head for the sea as soon as I could," Iuti said.

"Don't talk," Tarawe snapped. She urged Iuti on as quickly as she could move across the torturous lava.

Again and again, Iuti was forced to stop. Her muscles contracted with such force that she was afraid she would drop the child where she stood. She resisted a strong urge to push.

"Tarawe, it must be coming soon," she gasped finally. They were just a few warriors' lengths from the trees. "I don't know if I can—"

"Your waters haven't broken yet, Ser. You can make it to the trees."

Iuti caught her breath again as another contraction nearly doubled her over. At its end, she felt flooding warmth running down her legs. She laughed softly. "Tarawe, my good friend and soon-to-be midwife, I think the last barrier has broken."

At Tarawe's order, Ma'eva lifted Iuti and carried her to the trees. Another contraction struck just as they reached them. She clung to Ma'eva until it passed.

"Over here," Tarawe called. Ma'eva carried Iuti into a small clearing and set her on her feet at the base of a giant tree. It was no kind of tree she had ever seen before, and it made Iuti laugh that she would even notice such a thing at a time like this. She had no strength at all in her legs. She sank directly to the leaf-matted ground. Ma'eva knelt behind her to support her back.

Tarawe ripped away Iuti's trousers and Anali wrapped her with a sheet of dark cloth. It smelled of the sea. Iuti laughed again.

"Why are you laughing, Iuti Mano?" Nikivi asked. His voice was tight with terror. "We're going to die here in this place. Your child will be born a monster. Haku 'Aina—"

Why *not* laugh? Iuti thought.

"Hush about your spirits, South Islands man," Anali snapped. "Now, where did I put my . . ."

Iuti didn't hear the rest. It was time. Her child was ready to enter the world. Iuti could no longer resist the urge to help push it free. Not if Haku 'Aina herself had walked into the kipuka just then could Iuti have denied the birthing of this child. She bore down with all the strength she possessed.

Tarawe's hand slid across her stomach. "That's good, Ser," her sweet voice said. "It's coming. I can see the head."

But it wasn't enough. Iuti collapsed back against Ma'eva. He wiped her forehead with his cool, smooth hand. "You are very strong, mother of my child," he said. She had time to smile before it began again.

"It has lots of hair, Ser!" Tarawe laughed. "It's shining and black like Ma'eva's when he takes a fur seal's form."

Iuti squeezed Ma'eva's hand until she was afraid she would crush it. She tried to loosen her grip but could not. Ma'eva's hand never moved in hers. She sank back again, panting for breath. The work of pushing the emerging child free was like none other Iuti had ever done. No warrior's battle, not even her final struggle with Mano Niuhi had taken such all-consuming strength and concentration.

"I'll never again think a woman weak who chooses child-bearing as her life's work," she said, meeting Anali's look. Ana's thin chin lifted. Fierce pride shone in her eyes.

Iuti's eager child gripped her attention again. She could taste its overpowering desire to be born. "Honor to you, sweet babe," she whispered as she bore down again. All welcome to your coming presence in this world. The last was said silently because she had no breath for words.

Suddenly the baby's head slipped free. She felt it, warm and wet between her legs. The pressure abruptly ceased. Tarawe leaned forward and Iuti felt the child turn.

"Once more now," Tarawe said as calmly as if she'd been birthing babies all her life. She's become such a strong, powerful child since we left Fanape, Iuti thought. Then she laughed. Tarawe was no longer a child. Iuti wondered if Tarawe had ever truly *been* a child. She heard a small cough that could only have come from the babe.

"Push now, Ser," Tarawe said. "There are only the shoulders to go."

The effort it took was not quite as great as that Iuti had needed before, but it still took all of her strength. She pushed until, at last, all at once, the child slid free.

"It's a boy!" Ma'eva and Anali sighed in one voice. The

child coughed once, then let out a soft but full-throated wail. Iuti laughed again as Ma'eva leaned forward to lay his cheek against hers.

"Honor to you, mother of my child," he said. "You have given my people life."

Tarawe set the tiny, squirming baby in Iuti's arms. It turned its mouth to her breast and Iuti knew a moment of joy so intense it left her breathless. Surely there could be no greater moment in life than this.

"Ayiii!" Nikivi groaned quietly.

Iuti forced her look up.

"It's Haku 'Aina! She's found us!"

There was light glimmering near the edge of the trees.

"Oh, gods," Iuti whispered.

It was torchlight!

☙ Chapter 17 ☙

Ma'eva slid out from behind Iuti's back. She thrust the baby into his hands. "Go," she said.

"Not yet." Tarawe stopped Ma'eva with a look. "Mama Ana, I need your knife." She tied something dark around the birthing cord, then used Ana's blade to cut the baby free. Anali quickly wrapped another length of green cloth around the child.

"Go now!" Iuti insisted. She could hear lava crunching under heavy steps. A man's voice cursed softly. A woman's voice ordered him to silence. It was her mother's voice.

"Go," Iuti said again.

Ma'eva brushed a hand across her cheek—his own cheeks glistened in the dim light—then turned and ran with Anali and the child into the trees. Iuti pushed herself upright and moved back so that she could lean on the wide tree trunk. Tarawe scooped up the birth-stained cloth and rolled it into a bundle. She kicked leaves across the place where Iuti had lain. A strong, warm breeze washed the scent of the birthing from the clearing and toward the sea.

"They need you to get the baby off the cliff," Iuti whispered. "Go, Tarawe. Hurry."

Tarawe shook out another strip of cloth and pushed it into Iuti's hands. "Wrap this around you," she said, glancing back to where the lights were now moving in among the trees. The shadows of many men showed in wavering firelight. The ground shivered again. If this was truly a sacred place, Haku 'Aina was not likely to be pleased by this second intrusion.

Tarawe helped fold the cloth around Iuti's waist, then bent to whisper in her ear. "Fair winds, Ser. I'll come back for you." There was no time for more. Tarawe disappeared like a wraith just as Kuwala's huge form stepped into view. Pali was close at his back.

They trod into the clearing and stopped. A slow smile spread across Kuwala's face. "Hoi," he said softly. "So you've finally been forced to stop and face us." He unhooked his war club from his belt.

Iuti's fist tightened around the hilt of her sword. It lay beside her, covered with damp leaves, although she didn't remember placing it there. Her fighting stick rested under her opposite hand. She found the touch of her weapons comforting, but she did not want to fight with her mother and her brothers. Not here. Not now, while her soul still soared with the joy of her son's birth.

"What happened to your friends, cousin?" Pali growled. "Did you and that fat belly of yours become too much for them to carry?"

"It was stupid of you to think you could defy our vengeance by getting yourself pregnant," Kuwala said.

Iuti said nothing. Her other brothers and cousins emerged from the trees. Ka'ave, Kumaro, Malu. She met each of her brother's looks. Malu ran his fingers along the edge of his sword, and spat.

Anele came last—and behind him, their mother. A chill ran down Iuti's spine. Her mother was dressed in full warrior's garb. A tunic of overlapping tortoiseshell covered her upper body. Her legs were hidden by dark, loose trousers, armored across the thighs and shins with ornately knotted pads. She wore the full feathered crest that proclaimed her the matriarch of the shark clan.

Her hands were empty, but her strung bow was slung across her shoulder and a full quiver of arrows hung at her back. She wore knives at each wrist, like Anali's. Iuti knew there were more hidden inside her clothing.

During Iuti's childhood, her mother's formal warrior's garb had been used only for ceremonial occasions. The last time Iuti had seen her mother dressed in it was the day the clan had bargained with Mano Niuhi for his assistance in the Teronin War.

Her mother was flanked by Anele and the sallow-faced Gala, the shark clan's chief sorcerer. The sorcerer's dress was a parody of her mother's, consisting of an oddly knotted vest, daubed here and there with red paint, and ceremonial knives at his wrists. Iuti doubted the vest would stop even a clumsy blow of her sword. It was the sennit whisk in his gnarled hands that presented the danger.

As a child, Iuti had been terrified every time Gala pointed his whisk her way, until her mother finally assured her that she had forbidden the sorcerer to harm her only daughter. Gala smiled slightly as Iuti met his look. He lifted a woven basket from his back and one of the cousins hurriedly laid a thick mat on the ground. Gala carefully placed the basket on it. The flying dolphin's egg, Iuti thought. A small spot of iridescence showed through the woven coconut fronds. Aye, the sorcerer would be the one to carry it across the treacherous lava.

Her mother and Gala left the egg at the edge of the clearing and came to stand before Iuti.

"Greetings, Mother," Iuti said. She did not offer welcome. The lie would have been too great, the insult too enormous.

Had her mother come with any sign of forgiveness, any evidence that she would welcome or even consider a peaceful end to the shark clan's shame, Iuti might have spoken otherwise. But the long-unused warrior's garb, the arrows on her mother's back and the sorcerer at her side, the look of cold fury in her eyes—all declared an unyielding stance of intended revenge.

Iuti knew that she had no hope of surviving this meeting. In all her imaginings since she'd been forced to kill Mano Niuhi, she had never imagined such hatred as she saw now in her mother's and her brothers' eyes. To escape, Iuti knew she would have to kill them all.

Even if that were possible, she wouldn't do it. She would not kill her mother or brothers to save her own life. Her soul was worth more to her than that. The only thing she could do now was prevent her vengeful kinfolk from discovering her child. The longer she stayed alive, the longer her son had to reach the sea and safety. *Hurry*, Ma'eva, she urged silently.

Iuti's mother's slow look slid down her body. "You've grown since I saw you last," she said. Her voice was dark and husky. It made Iuti's heart ache.

"It's been more than ten years, Mother. I was little more than a child when I left Kiholo." Iuti heard the same dark coldness in her own voice. Am I becoming my mother? she wondered.

Her mother's gaze rested on her stomach. "Now you carry a child of your own."

Iuti sent silent thanks to Tarawe for hiding the evidence of the birthing. Seated as she was, wrapped in Ana's cloth, she looked almost as pregnant as she had an hour before. She laid one hand on her stomach in the move that had become automatic since she first learned of the child's presence. Her stomach was soft now, its touch brought her fierce joy, and piercing pain. She should be holding her child, cleaning and caring for it. She knew it was too soon for her milk to be ready, but her swollen breasts ached with the need to suckle her son.

Mother, she wanted to cry. Rejoice with me. Your grandchild is born!

"How did you find me here?" she asked.

Her mother lifted a thin brow. "You are a child of my body, daughter. I followed your taste on the wind."

Iuti shook her head. "No. The wind would never have led you to me. Not while I was traveling in the company of the Storm Caller."

Her mother laughed. "The Storm Caller! So that's who the girl is. How wise of you not to reveal her identity to your brothers. How stupid of them not to have recognized her at once. Their orders were to kill your friend the Storm Caller without hesitation."

Iuti remained silent.

Her mother pointed to her torn vest. "I followed my sail, daughter. It was generous of you to clothe yourself in it. You saved us much time searching on this isle. You see? Even *you* are not always wise."

Iuti stared down at the shreds of woven matting she had used to make the protective vest. She'd recognized the sail as one of her mother's making, but had never thought—

Mano's teeth! I might as well have sailed straight home to Kiholo and surrendered, she thought. How could I have been so careless? She remembered suddenly that Tarawe had used bits of the padding to protect her feet from the sharp lava.

"Where were you hiding until this morning?" her mother asked. "Your trail led us to the river pool, where the bird worshipers claimed you died. Then it disappeared entirely until I sensed you high in the neighboring valley this morning. You must have devised a strong hiding spell. Why didn't you stay within it?"

Iuti said nothing. These were not the questions her mother had followed her all the way across the Empty Sea to ask.

Her mother watched her for a moment, then motioned to one of the cousins. He spread a finely woven mat on the ground. She stepped onto it and sat cross-legged, facing Iuti. She laid her bow on the ground before her and rested her hands on her knees.

When she was settled, Gala squatted beside her. He flicked his whisk several times around the place where he sat. The ground shivered slightly.

"I have been told," Iuti said to him, "that this grove of trees is sacred to the spirits of this land. It might be wise to disturb them as little as possible."

Gala glared at her. He lifted the whisk again, but her mother motioned for him to stop.

"Do you fear the land spirits now, daughter?" she said. "You who were once a child of the sea."

"I fear them no more than I ever did," Iuti replied. "But offering respect rarely causes harm. You taught me that."

Her mother's eyes darkened. Her hands tensed on her knees. "Where is your respect for *me*, daughter? Where was your respect for your *clan* when you murdered Mano Niuhi?"

"I did not murder the shark god," Iuti said. Something moved in the shadows beyond the clearing. Another cousin, Iuti thought, patrolling the small copse of trees.

"You broke our family's trust with Mano," her mother said. "You threw away the protection he had given us for generations. You killed him!"

"It was Mano who broke the trust," Iuti said. She was surprised at how calmly she could speak of Mano now. "It was he who turned to evil and tried to force me into turning with him. Would you have had me lose my soul just to keep his *protection*?"

"The decision to break the bond with the sharks was not yours to make," her mother said. "What you did affected our entire clan. You should have returned to Kiholo so that I—"

"Mano's teeth were ripping at my flesh, Mother. I had no time for a journey to Kiholo." The movement in the shadows shifted again, too stealthily to be one of her kin. Foolishly none of them was acting as a guard to the outside. They no doubt thought their numbers and strength would protect them against anything that might come. The shadow was probably only Nikivi. He had disappeared as soon as the torchlight had reached the trees.

"You killed our family god," her mother insisted. "You broke the bond our clan has had with the sharks for generations. You *shamed* us."

"Is it the shame that concerns you?" Iuti asked. "What shame would the shark clan have faced if I had allowed Mano to continue down the path to evil? What shame if I had *helped* him down that path?''

She took a deep breath. "If Mano Niuhi had killed me that day, he would have gained the means to destroy the entire world. There never would have been an end to war; Mano would have made peace impossible. He fed on the deaths, Mother. He sat at the back of my mind and fed his hunger with each of my kills. Whenever the killing began to slow, he offered his *protection* to anyone who could cause human conflicts to arise again. *That* is the shark clan's shame, Mother. That we fed him for so long without even knowing.''

Iuti looked down at her left hand. She could still feel the deadly dark thrust of her sword as it slid through Mano Niuhi's gills and then on into his great brain. He had been her brother, more than her brother. He had led her to many victories before that final defeat.

"The only honorable thing I *could* do was kill him," she said.

Her mother stood abruptly. Gala scrambled to his feet, as did others among her kin who had sat down to rest. Her mother scowled when Iuti did not join them on their feet.

"Stand when your mother rises," Kuwala ordered. Pali muttered a curse. Malu touched his blade again.

"I cannot," Iuti said. "I mean no disrespect." She could have stood, she felt strong enough to do it now, but the birthing was not yet finished. The ground offered more support if she should have to defend herself while the afterbirth came. Already she felt an intermittent tightening in her stomach as her body prepared to expel the last of her too-brief pregnancy.

Her mother looked at her sharply. "You *cannot*?" Her eyes slid across Iuti's stomach again.

"I . . . injured my leg," Iuti said quickly. She didn't want her mother to examine her and learn the child was gone. She uncovered her right leg instead.

Iuti had never expected to thank the gruesome cave grubs for attacking her, but her kinsmen's startled reaction to the sight of her leg gave her good reason. Great welts had risen where the grubs had sunk their teeth into her skin; her entire leg was swollen and discolored by the effects of their poison. The scar that ran the length of her calf was once again livid red and Tarawe's stitch marks showed clearly.

The healing spell had taken away much of the pain and Iuti knew the leg was strong and healthy inside. But her kinfolk did not. Even Kuwala seemed to relax a little, believing no doubt that she would be easier to guard with so disabling an injury.

"What kind of wound is that?" Anele asked. "I've never seen so strange a thing." Ahh, Brother Anele, Iuti thought, you should have become a healer instead of a warrior. He'd never been given that choice. The shark clan's sons were always warriors.

"The scar is yours," she said. "Your sword struck me on the canoe at Kala. You drew first blood, brother."

He frowned and, for a moment, Iuti thought he almost looked sorry. Then Kuwala smirked and said, "If it had been *my* blade, it would have killed you and we'd have been done with all this."

Anele turned away and walked to the edge of the clearing. He sat beside the basket containing the dolphin's egg. Iuti glanced around at the others. "The other marks were caused by some very hungry and malevolent spirits of this place. I urge you to caution."

Gala flicked his whisk toward her leg while her cousins murmured. Iuti's mother stepped back onto the mat. She sat again.

"This pregnancy," she said, waving one hand toward Iuti's stomach. "When did it begin?"

Iuti ran a hand across her stomach. The shadow in the trees moved again, closer to where Anele now sat.

"Was it before or after Kuwala told you of my decision about the clan's future?" her mother demanded.

Iuti took a deep breath. "It began before Kuwala and the others came to Kala." Then she met her brother's look. "I was not told that it was our *mother's* decision to end the clan."

Her mother sent Kuwala a frown before returning her attention to Iuti. She sat watching her in silence for a moment. Behind her, the prowler in the shadows moved yet again—toward the basket bearing the flying dolphin's egg! Iuti's first thought was to give the alarm. What if it was some trickery of the birds? Or Haku 'Aina? But no, this place belonged to the landmaker. If she wished to take anything on it, she would not skulk around in the dark to steal it. She would just open the ground and swallow it.

"Has it been easy for you, daughter?"

Iuti started. "Easy? What— Oh, the pregnancy." A warm, tickling breeze brushed across Iuti's cheeks. A thin, brown arm reached out from the shadows beside Anele.

Oh, gods! *It was Tarawe!*

"It has given me a new appreciation of the women who choose

to do it more than once," Iuti said. She must hold her mother's attention. She must not stare at the trees.

Her mother laughed softly. "Yes. Yes, it is good that you have learned that. I was afraid you might never have the opportunity when Mano took you off to the wars. Or that you would be too old or disabled to understand the sacrifice when it finally happened to you. Nine months taken from a warrior's life is a great price to pay for a child."

Her mother was reminding her of how many times she had tried before finally bearing a daughter to carry the clan forward. She was reminding her of the warrior's life she had forsaken to accomplish that feat. It was your life, Mother, Iuti said silently. I didn't ask to be born. I honor your decision, but I take no responsibility for your choice.

"The time passed much more quickly than I expected, Mother," she said.

Tarawe set a second basket beside the one carrying the dolphin's egg. It was the basket in which she had carried the gull. It looked almost identical to the other. Her hand shifted to the container carrying the egg.

"I was fortunate that I never felt any sickness," Iuti said. She forced herself not to stare at the place where Tarawe was lifting the egg to safety. "I hope the birth comes as easily."

Again her mother laughed. "Mano's children are always born easily, daughter. It's only when the mother has acted foolishly during her pregnancy that difficulties arise."

Suddenly Anele's hand shot out. He grabbed Tarawe's wrist, held it for an instant—Iuti saw them exchange looks—then let it go. Tarawe and the basket disappeared instantly. Anele shifted the new basket into the exact place of the old.

"I do not expect . . . difficulties," Iuti said, almost unable to speak in her relief and her continued dread that Tarawe would be caught. Anele met Iuti's look and she was forced to close her eyes to keep from giving herself away. Honor to you, brother, she told Anele silently. He might stand by and watch her be killed, but he would not deny the flying dolphin's egg its rightful place in the sea. Like Iuti, he must believe their mother capable of destroying it.

"You look tired," her mother said. "Trekking through the jungle and across this cursed lava is not—"

The ground shook hard—a single, solid jolt. Iuti pressed both palms flat on the ground to keep her balance. More than one of

her cousins lost his footing and fell. The feathers on her mother's
crest wavered and bobbed.

"Mano's teeth, Mother!" Iuti exclaimed. "Do you want us
all to die? This place belongs to the landmaker. It is not cursed
in *her* eyes. She could kill any or all of us in an instant if she
wished. Keep your curses to yourself."

"How dare you speak to our mother so!"

Kuwala swung his war club at Iuti's head. She whipped up
her fighting stick and deflected the blow before it touched her.
The jolt to her arm felt almost as strong as the one that had
shaken the ground.

"Enough!" their mother cried as Kuwala lifted his club for a
second attempt. "This is not the way it will be done, Kuwala.
Stand back from her."

Iuti stared at her mother. "How *is* it to be done, Mother? Will
you pierce my neck with one of your poisoned arrows? Will you
cut out my heart with one of your ceremonial knives? Or will
you just give me to Gala, who no doubt thinks he can draw away
some of my warrior's power before I die?"

Gala muttered and flicked his whisk.

Her mother watched her coldly.

"Will you kill me before or after your grandchild is born,
Mother?"

Her mother took a long breath and sat back again. Kuwala
muttered a curse. "Be still, Kuwala," their mother said. "All
of you be quiet. This is a matter between my daughter and me.
You have found her for me. Your duty to the clan is done."
There was another round of muttering before silence came.

Iuti's stomach tightened suddenly. She had no time to disguise
it. She pressed a hand to her waist and bent forward. She felt
moisture between her legs.

Her mother leaned toward her.

"What is it, daughter?" she asked. "Ah. Ahhh. Is it time for
the last of the shark clan to be born?"

Suddenly she laughed aloud. "You've been in labor all this
time! How clever you are to have kept it hidden, even from me.
Ahh, Iuti Mano, you were always my pride. So strong and
clever. There was a time when you could have had my soul if
only you had asked. But did you really think you could outlast
me here? Did you think when I saw you pregnant, I would kiss
your cheek and walk away to let you have this child alone?"

Iuti's stomach tightened again and she couldn't help pushing,
just as she had with the child. Something soft and wet passed

from her. A small stain showed on the front of her cloth wrap. Her mother laughed again, and when Iuti next looked up, she found her mother and Gala flanking her.

"You would have had this babe right in front of us without saying a word, wouldn't you," her mother exclaimed. "You make me proud, daughter. But there is no need to hide longer. I will help you now." She motioned to the sorcerer and together they began unwrapping the cloth from Iuti's waist.

"Don't uncover me before my brothers," Iuti said. She held the cloth tight around her. *Hurry, Tarawe!* she thought. *Take my son to the sea!*

"Do you fear to be shamed before these men?" There was a hysterical edge to her mother's laughter that Iuti feared much more than her words. "*You*, who shamed us all?"

"You shame *yourself*, Mother, by acting this way. Send them away, into the trees. Tell them, at the least, to turn away. Anele—"

Gala yanked the cloth away.

There was an instant of silence. Then both her mother and the sorcerer screamed.

"You lied!" her mother cried. "You had the child before we came!"

Gala grabbed up the bloody mass of the afterbirth, spat into it, and threw it back to the ground. Before he could dishonor it further, Iuti laid a warding spell over it—a strong spell that she had learned to use while Mano was still protecting her mind. The afterbirth dissolved and drained quickly into the ground. Gala cursed and reached into his waist pouch for one of the foul-smelling powders he always carried. Iuti flung a shield around him and he staggered back.

"Haku 'Aina," she murmured as her mother hurriedly set the sorcerer free. "Forgive this desecration of your land."

Her mother slapped her, hard, across the face. "How dare you speak to the spirits of this place when you have defiled your own family here!"

She turned to Kuwala and the others who had gathered near, weapons in their hands, horror on their faces. Only Anele remained apart. He stood with his head bowed, staring at the ground. He had moved well away from where Tarawe's basket lay. "Go after them!" her mother ordered. "Find the child!"

"*No!*" Iuti shouted so loud they all stopped to listen. "There is no need to follow the child. It is a boy! It cannot carry the shark's line to another generation. Only I can do that. Kill me, and leave the child alone."

"Do you expect us to believe you now?" her mother demanded. "The child *must* be a girl or you wouldn't have gone to such lengths to protect it. No son would ever mean that much to you." Even Kuwala glanced darkly at their mother for that. Listen to her, brothers, Iuti begged them silently. Listen to the evil in her voice. She is not the kind woman she once was. Her mother's voice sounded like Mano's during the last days of the Teronin War.

"Did Mano Niuhi turn you, too, Mother?" she asked. "Did he sink his desire for human blood so deeply into you that you would kill a sea mimic's son to take revenge on me?"

"A sea mimic!" Anele's look snapped up. Her brothers and cousins looked suddenly unsure of their anger.

"Ahh, you are so clever, Iuti Mano," her mother said. "How better to protect your daughter than to claim she's a mimic's son? Gala, you held the child's blood sack. What is it? Male or female? Human or mimic?"

The clearing grew quiet as everyone looked to the sorcerer. He stared down at his bloody hands. He licked one finger, then lifted his look to Iuti.

"It is a sea mimic's *daughter*," he said.

"Liar!"

"Find her! Bring her to me!" Iuti's mother screamed.

"It is a mimic, Mother! You *must* not—"

Kuwala struck Iuti on the side of her head. She fell back, stunned. Kuwala and Malu quickly bound her arms and tied her securely to the tree. When they finished, her mother ran her hands over Iuti's vest. "There isn't enough of my sail here to account for it all," she muttered. She looked up and around, then took a pinch of the powder Gala offered and blew it into the air.

"That way," she said, and pointed toward the west.

Why did Tarawe go west? Iuti thought. Why didn't she go directly downhill to the sea? Iuti watched in dread as her brothers and cousins disappeared into the night.

"It is a mimic's son," she said again when they were gone. "If you stop him from reaching the sea quickly, he will never be able to make the sea change. You will deny him his birthright. If you kill him, the mimics—"

"I will decide what to do with the child after I've seen it with my own eyes," her mother said.

"There's no time to bring him back here," Iuti insisted. "If you delay him, it will be too late."

"You should never have left the sea while you were carrying a mimic's child," her mother said. "If it's truly a boy and he loses his birthright, it's on your head, not mine." Her voice had grown calm again. It was suddenly much more frightening.

She pulled the knife from her left wrist sheath. It was short and thin. A knife of stealth, Iuti thought, and suddenly realized something about her mother that she had never known before. "You worked as an assassin," she said. "That's why you carry only silent weapons."

Her mother smiled.

"How can you kill your own child, Mother? Your own grand-child?"

"I'm not going to kill you, Iuti Mano," her mother said. "I won't even kill your daughter unless I have to. Certainly not before she becomes a woman. I will take her, though, to raise for myself. You won't mind my taking her, will you? In ex-change for her life?"

"My child is a sea mimic's son," Iuti said again.

"I wouldn't want to risk losing my soul by deliberately killing my own kin," her mother said as if Iuti hadn't spoken.

Do you have a soul? Iuti wanted to ask.

"Mano should have chosen me," her mother said. "I had finally birthed a girl child to carry the shark line on. I had raised you to womanhood and was ready to return to the warrior's way." Her eyes turned suddenly dark again, with fury. Iuti had seen the same look in Mano's eyes the night she had killed him.

"But he took you instead!" her mother went on. "He carried *you* into war and made a legend of *you*, instead of me. And in the end, *you* chose to break the bond I had given up so much of my life for. You chose to break it for us *all*."

She nodded to Gala and the sorcerer began chanting softly.

"What are you doing, Mother?" Iuti asked. "What can you hope to gain here?"

"It's good that you gave your brothers an excuse to leave us," her mother replied. She smiled again, and a chill ran down Iuti's back. She tested her bonds, but they held no slack.

"Only Anele would appreciate what I intend to do," her mother said, "and of course, he would try to stop me. He's the only one of your brothers with kindness in his heart. He stood up for you. Did you know that? Even after you killed Mano

Niuhi. I gave him honor for speaking his mind clearly, even though he was so clearly wrong. He's always been a fool.''

She laid the blade of her knife along the palm of her right hand.

"Kuwala is wiser, of course, but he sees no other course than to kill both you and the child outright.''

She closed her fingers around the sharp blade, cutting into her own skin until blood welled in her palm. It dripped onto the already bloodstained cloth lying at Iuti's side. "Kuwala has no subtlety,'' she said.

"Mother, what are you doing?''

Gala leaned forward and blew a puff of foul-smelling dust into Iuti's face.

She coughed and gagged. Her stomach cramped suddenly—a hard, sharp clench. She tried to cast a warding spell around herself, but it had no effect. She pulled against her bonds, but her strength was suddenly gone.

"Mother, what are you doing?'' she said again. Her stomach felt as if it were aflame. She gasped for breath.

Gala began chanting louder. He blew another puff of dust into Iuti's face and flicked his whisk over her legs. Her mother slid her bloody hand across Iuti's thigh.

"I'm going to castrate you, daughter,'' her mother said softly. "I am going to destroy your future children and leave you alive to wonder who they might have been.''

"Oh, gods, Mother, no!''

The bloody hand moved again.

"You are the *last* of the shark clan's line, Iuti Mano.''

Iuti screamed as her mother's silent blade slid to the very center of her soul.

❦ Chapter 18 ❧

SER Iuti's scream echoed like a death wail across the lava fields. Tarawe wanted to turn back, but knew she could not. She had to get both Iuti's child and the flying dolphin's egg to the sea.

She had taken a great chance returning for the egg, but even Ma'eva had agreed they couldn't leave it behind. Even without the sea mimic's approval, Tarawe would have gone back. She'd been responsible for the deaths of two of the magical flying dolphins; she wasn't going to be responsible for the loss of one of their precious eggs, as well.

The earth trembled and shook as Tarawe ran, not enough to cause her to lose her balance, but enough to let her know that the spirits of this strange place were unhappy. Tarawe sent her wind ahead of her to study the terrain and to sweep as much loose debris from her path as possible.

She had gone west after leaving the clearing, then thrown her tattered sandals far upslope. A gusting wind carried them well beyond the landing place the strength of her arm alone could have achieved. Then she wrapped her feet in thick layers of ti leaves torn from her shirt.

She could tell from their lights and the noise of their clumsy movement across the lava that Iuti's kinsmen were following the sandals' trail. She hoped it would gain her enough time to catch up with Ma'eva and Ana at the shore. The basket with the egg bounced and bobbled on her back. It was much heavier than her gull had been.

The sulfur fumes were strong and the glow of orange showed more and more frequently across the broad stretch of lava. The moon was high enough to let her see, but jagged, twisted shadows haunted the land all around. Once, when she jumped across a narrow crack, Tarawe felt searing heat and saw bright red deep below, as if the earth itself were burning. The heat caught at her wind and sent it soaring high into the sky. Tarawe cooled the air and spun it back down again.

Suddenly one of the spots of glowing orange began to grow larger. The light lifted high into the sky and spread until it lay like a wavering wall between Tarawe and the sea. She could hear the rumble of sea waves crashing beyond the eery light. She sent another questing wind to search for Ma'eva and Anali. Their tastes came from straight ahead.

As she came closer to the light, Tarawe saw figures moving in the red glow. Strange figures, posing in grotesque shapes. The bird worshipers! What were *they* doing here?

Then she saw Ma'eva.

He was on his knees, at the center of the dancing, posturing bird worshipers. He was hunched over a cloth-wrapped bundle that had to be the child. The Chosen One herself stood guard over him, while her consort danced and posed with the rest. Creeping closer, Tarawe saw that a bloody wound darkened the left side of Ma'eva's face. The Chosen One's consort darted toward him, arms outstretched, claws flashing in the light. Ma'eva flickered and the birdman danced back.

Tarawe saw no sign of Anali. She sent another questing wind, but before it could return, she heard a scraping sound in the lava to her right. She backed carefully away, far enough to circle a stone outcrop so that she could see the place from which the sound had come.

"Mama Ana!" she cried softly.

Anali started, then let out a long sigh of relief. "Thank the gods, child. You've found us before it's too late."

Tarawe scrambled across the jagged stone to Ana's side. "What happened?" she asked. "What are they doing?"

Ana shrugged. "They think he's a spirit come back from the dead, just like Nikivi did when he first saw us. They're trying to force him into the firepit as a sacrifice, so Haku 'Aina will make the earth calm again."

She glanced toward the wall of orange that separated them from the sea cliffs. "I'd jump into the fire myself if I thought it would do any good. Even if we can get Ma'eva free, I don't see how we can reach the sea from here."

Tarawe stared at the line of orange blocking them from the sea. "Is that really a firepit? I see no flames."

"It's a fire much hotter than flames," Anali replied. "The

stone itself is burning underground. The glow is the reflection
of molten stone on the smoke and steam clouds. See? It's coming from that deep crevasse. We'll never get across it in time.''
Tarawe remembered the crack she had jumped over. This barrier
was much wider and stretched a long way in each direction. She
wondered if the landmaker had set it there deliberately to keep
them from escaping.

"Well, the first thing to do is get Ma'eva and the baby free,"
she said. "We're close enough to the water now. I'll wrap the
baby in my wind and carry him over the fire wall. Ser Iuti said
there would be other sea mimics waiting to help him."

"Aye, but—"

"Come on, Mama Ana. Ma'eva is already hurt. We have to
hurry."

"I can't come with you," Ana said. Tarawe heard tears and
deep, deep anger in her voice. "My hip is hurt. I can't move
from here."

"Oh, Mama Ana," Tarawe said. "Where—"

"It doesn't matter. Save Ma'eva's son, Storm Caller. Even if
you can't get him to the sea, don't let them kill him."

Tarawe cupped her hands around Ana's and whispered Ser
Iuti's pain spell into Ana's palms. "Don't bother with me, girl,"
Ana said, but she sighed in sudden relief.

Tarawe looked back at the posturing bird worshipers, wondering if they were close enough to the cliff's edge for her to
call up a wave and wash them all into the sea. It was an impossible idea. Even if the distance was not too great, a wave large
enough to sweep through the landmaker's wall and back again
would be too dangerous even for a sea mimic to manage. Many
of the bird people would surely be killed, and if the death thrusts
caused Tarawe to lose control of the wave, Ma'eva and the baby
might be washed into the landmaker's pit. Then all would be
lost.

The Chosen One's consort screamed and rushed at Ma'eva.
Dressed in all his tattered feathers, he looked like an angry bird
darting at its prey. The claws strapped to the backs of his hands
flashed in the light.

Like a bird! Tarawe thought. Quickly she said, "Ana, give
me the blanket, the one I made with the feathers. If I can distract
the bird worshipers, Ma'eva might be able to escape."

Ma'eva flickered into a partial form change, but this time the
birdman didn't stop his mad rush. He raked his claws down
Ma'eva's back. Ana gasped.

"Quickly," Tarawe said.

Ana fumbled in her bag and pulled out the feathered blanket. Tarawe slung it around her shoulders like a cape and fastened it with a length of Kunan's hair. She had used the other strand to tie off the baby's birthing cord. You've served us well, Kunan, she said silently.

Ana handed Tarawe her feathered headdress. Its colorful feathers matched those of the cape. "Take it," she said. "It might help."

Tarawe fastened the headdress around her forehead. Then she sent another call to the wind. *Bring me the birds*, she told the restless air. *Bring all the airfolk here, but don't let them fall into the fire.* She sent a call to the high winds, those that kept the clouds wrapped around the summit of the mountain. *Bring me the clouds*, she called. *Bring me the cooling rain.*

"Wait," Ana said before Tarawe could turn and go. "Take these." She reached into her bag and pulled out a handful of tiny, glowing lights.

"The cave pebbles!" Tarawe cried. "Your bag turned them into more!"

Ana's small smile did nothing to hide her fear and her pain. She whispered something over the tiny teardrops, kissed the very top one, and threw them at Tarawe. They struck the feathered cape with the soft, musical sound of the deep sea. Where they touched the headdress and Tarawe's multicolored cape, they clung. They lit the shifting feathers like a sparkling, starlit night.

"Go now, Storm Caller," Ana said. "I'll follow if I can."

Tarawe used her wind to fold the feathers over the lighted pebbles so she wouldn't be seen too soon, then moved as quietly as she could across the lava. The ground trembled and shook, but her wind kept her from falling. She had a sudden image of Nikivi walking so securely on just one leg, and wondered for a moment if it was the wind that kept him balanced. She knew that it couldn't be; she would have felt it. The touch of the moving air had become so familiar to her, it was as if she and the wind had become one being.

Just as Tarawe reached the mound where the bird worshipers danced, the Chosen One's consort darted forward to strike Ma'eva again.

Tarawe sent a swirl of sulfur-tainted air between them. The birdman was knocked from his feet. His shabby headdress fell off; its shells clattered against the stone. He grabbed for it, but

Tarawe sent another scudding gust to tumble it right to the edge of the glowing firepit. The Chosen One screamed in rage at her consort's clumsiness.

Before either of them could reach the fallen headdress, Tarawe stepped up on the mound. "Let the mimic go!" she cried. The wind caught her words and spun them around and around the open space. They caught in the heat of the firepit and sailed high into the sky.

The dancers, already stunned at seeing the Chosen One's consort lose his balance, turned. They stared. Then abruptly they screamed, "Haku 'Aina!" They threw themselves to the ground and pressed their faces to the stone. Only the Chosen One remained standing.

"Haku 'Aina! Haku 'Aina!" The dancers cried the landmaker's name over and over.

Tarawe wrapped herself in a light breeze that lifted and shifted her feathers so that they glittered in the scattered light of the cave pebbles and the glow of the firepit. If these strange people wanted to believe she was Haku 'Aina, that was fine with her, although she had no intentions of claiming the title herself. The real Haku 'Aina was already upset enough. The ground trembled steadily.

Ma'eva lifted his head slowly. He stared at her, just as the others had done—just as the Chosen One was still doing. The woman stood up very straight. She walked slowly forward.

"Who are you?" she demanded. She had to say it three times before her voice could be heard over the cries of the prostrate dancers. One by one, they grew silent and listened.

"Who are you?" the Chosen One demanded again. She came close and stared down at Tarawe. "You're not the landmaker! Who are you?" Her consort looked up cautiously, then slowly crawled close enough to the firepit to reach his headdress. He clutched it in both hands as he stood and took his place at the Chosen One's back.

The Chosen One's cool look ran down Tarawe's body, from the tall feathers of her headdress, down the length of her cape to her ti-leaf–wrapped feet. The bird woman's look lifted to Tarawe's face again, and suddenly she started in recognition.

"You are the sorceress! The sorceress who brought the first bird!"

Tarawe nodded in agreement. She *had* brought the bird. She could feel many of the gull's cousins coming on her wind.

"Are you a spirit?" the Chosen One asked. She spoke boldly,

but her hands trembled where they clutched the front of her own faded, feathered cape.

"I am alive," Tarawe said.

"How could you have hidden from us all this time?" the Chosen One asked. "There is nowhere on this island we didn't search. No one can survive the river floods."

Tarawe wished Iuti Mano was here to answer the bird woman's questions. The warrior woman would know what to say, what to reveal and what to keep secret. Tarawe could think of no answer but the truth.

"We walked through a cave. A strange place with waterfalls, and glowing stone pillars, and time that passed without our knowing."

The Chosen One caught her breath. The dancers near enough to hear struck sudden poses. "You found the Cave of Lost Time?"

"Is that what it's called?" Tarawe asked.

"How did you escape?" The Chosen One's hands were shaking now. "The legends claim that that cavern is guarded by spirits so powerful Haku 'Aina herself cannot always control them."

"A bird led us to safety," Tarawe said.

The dancers let out soft cries of amazement and edged back farther. The Chosen One's voice trembled. "A bird?" Her look slid down Tarawe's cape again. Tarawe ruffled the wind through her brilliantly colored feathers. The glowing stone teardrops glistened. She smiled. That was something Ser Iuti would do.

"And the wind," she said.

The Chosen One shivered. The ground shook and she glanced fearfully back at the firepit. "We must dance again," she said. "We must make sacrifice and seek the landmaker's wisdom."

"There is no time to dance," Ma'eva said. Tarawe thought she saw a faint flicker through the folds of green cloth he carried. Ma'eva looked back at the glowing wall of heat and fire that separated him from the sea.

"Be silent, Spirit!" The Chosen One's consort raced forward to rake his clawed hands down Ma'eva's back. A blast of wind slammed him away.

"Storm Caller, no!" Ma'eva called. Tarawe's wind had blown the birdman directly toward the suddenly flaring firepit. Tarawe caught her anger in time to stop him from falling in. A shiver slid down her arms as she realized how close she had come to killing him. The glaring orange subsided to a wavering glow again, although it seemed brighter than before.

I cannot lose control, Tarawe thought. I must not.

"Ma'eva is not a spirit," she cried. "He is a sea mimic. You saw him change."

The bird dancers pulled their looks back to Tarawe. Then they turned to stare at Ma'eva. He carried the child in Anali's cloth, tied close to his chest. One of the dancers reached out to help the fallen consort back from the edge of the pit. The ashy flavor of scorched feathers slid across the air.

The Chosen One continued to stare at Tarawe.

"He carries his newborn child," Tarawe said to her. "We must help him get the babe to the sea before it tries to make its first change. If he's not in the water by then, he'll lose his birthright and remain human forever."

A soft exclamation of surprise whispered across the dance ground.

"There is very little time," Ma'eva said. He wiped a runnel of blood from his neck, then stumbled and almost fell. Tarawe sent a supporting wind to help him.

"A sea mimic?" the Chosen One said at last. Her fingers ran along the edge of her cape as she spoke.

"You saw him change," Tarawe said again.

"The spirits of the dead can change," the Chosen One snapped. She turned to Ma'eva. "Haku 'Aina's land has been desecrated! By you, whatever you are, and by that warrior woman's kin. A sacrifice has to be made!"

"I will do it, Chosen One," Ma'eva said. "I will give whatever honor you wish to Haku 'Aina. My body, or my soul if need be. Only take my child to the sea, quickly."

Tarawe took a step toward him, but the Chosen One moved between them. "There is no way past the landmaker's fires now, sea mimic," she said. She stood straighter; her fingers no longer trembled, but Tarawe could see she was disturbed by the presence of the child.

"Give me the baby," Tarawe said. "I can send it on the wind—"

It was the wind that warned her. Tarawe flicked her right hand in time to deflect the spear that had been aimed at her back. It tumbled to the stone and the bird dancers all scrambled back. This was not one of their red and black ceremonial spears. It was long and sleek—ironwood. Gray feathers circled its steel tip.

A second spear streaked through the air, this time toward Ma'eva. With a flick of her fingers, Tarawe lifted it past him and let it drop into the firepit. The light flared and the ground shook hard—so hard that the Chosen One almost fell. Tarawe dashed past her to Ma'eva's side as Iuti Mano's kinsmen swept into the light.

The bird dancers tried to resist the attacking warriors. They thrust at them with their short, ceremonial spears. They hurled stones and curses, trying to prevent the invaders from crossing their dance ground, but they couldn't match the shark clan's weapons or their warriors' skills. The Chosen One and her consort remained close to Tarawe and Ma'eva, protecting them as if they were allies, although Tarawe knew it was because they wanted them as sacrifices.

Tarawe spun her wind into the struggle, deflecting blows and tripping the attackers when she could. She flung Nikivi's stones into the melee, injuring one after another of Iuti Mano's kin.

But she could not stop every move of every warrior without taking the chance of killing some of them. One by one the bird people began to fall back toward her and Ma'eva, and the firepit.

Suddenly there was a change in the air. A bird streaked down from the night sky. The o'u! Tarawe had never imagined it could fly so fast. The o'u stopped and hovered before Tarawe's face; it chirped once in question.

Tarawe pointed. "The kipuka," she said, and the o'u raced away.

The other birds came then, the gulls and the saber birds, the great and small seabirds for which she knew no names—and all their landbound cousins. They slid from the sky on the lines of Tarawe's wind and instantly began attacking Kuwala and the others. The great, green parrot perched on a jutting stone and screeched echoes to each of the shark clan's war cries.

The bird dancers cheered and cried out in welcome. Had the Chosen One not ordered them to continue fighting, they would have begun dancing and striking their own strange bird poses again. The Chosen One met Tarawe's look and grinned fiercely.

Tarawe did not smile back. She felt a small touch of death as one of the birds died at the tip of Pali's sword. He, too, was grinning, enjoying the taste of death. Tarawe did what she could to help the birds, but they fought more efficiently without her confusing air currents. Still, many were injured or killed. Tarawe expected to suffer with each of their deaths, but the ice-cold death thrusts didn't come.

They're fighting their own battle, she thought as she watched them. My wind only carried them here; it isn't forcing them to fight. The birds and the bird dancers began pushing Iuti's kinsmen back.

Tarawe knelt beside Ma'eva. "Give me the baby," she said. "It's light enough for the wind to carry it over the firewall. The other mimics can help it when it reaches the sea."

Ma'eva untied the cloth from around his chest and laid the child in Tarawe's arms. The baby's small fist slipped outside the wrappings and Tarawe saw it flicker softly. Ma'eva tucked it back inside the cloth. The wind smelled of approaching rain, but the air around them was hot and dry. The heat from the firepit had grown intense.

Tarawe glanced up at the sky. Dark clouds were gathering, scudding toward her from the mountain heights. *Hurry*, she said to them. Then she turned back to Ma'eva. She raised her right hand and turned the air between them into a tight spiral. It swirled and circled until it had formed into a visible cushion. Quickly Tarawe laid Ma'eva's son onto the wind. The baby flickered ever so slightly.

"Hurry," Ma'eva whispered.

Tarawe pulled the basket from her back and laid it beside the child. Then she said to the wind, *Go. Take them both to the sea.*

The wind turned and lifted. She strengthened the circling column of air, and the child and the basket rose toward the night sky. Hope touched Ma'eva's eyes. The bird dancers, even the Chosen One, called out in wonder. Kuwala cursed and cried out in protest. The ground shook.

Then, abruptly, the circling wind stopped. The child and the basket plummeted through empty air.

≈ *Chapter 19* ≈

TARAWE scooped her wind back under the falling baby and basket. She caught them only a handsbreadth from the hard stone. Ma'eva snatched the baby back to his chest as the wind began to flail and thrash. It whipped at Tarawe's hair as she carefully lowered the basket to the ground.

A wind caller's doing, she thought, and that made her very angry. Her feathered headdress and cape spun around her. The birds and the dancers were blown back from the battle. Even Ma'eva was hard-pressed to remain standing.

Tarawe stood into the wind and shouted, "These winds are mine! Begone!" She sent a sudden gust toward the hidden wind caller, then lifted her right fist high. She opened her hand, palm down, and the wild wind stopped, all at once. The night became abruptly silent, with only the hiss and crackle of the landmaker's firepit and the distant rumble of crashing surf left to be heard.

The birds took flight along currents Tarawe sent their way, while the bird dancers cowered near the edge of the pit. When Kuwala and his men tried to follow them, Tarawe dropped a wall of gusting protection between them and the dancers.

"Again, Ma'eva. Quickly," she said. She brought another spiral of wind up under the egg.

"Give me my granddaughter!"

Tarawe turned toward the Chosen One, but it was not she who had spoken. The bird woman was staring open-mouthed toward the edge of the dance mound. A chill ran through Tarawe as Ser Iuti's mother stepped into the light. There was blood on her hands and on the front of her armor. Her dark eyes flashed in the light from the fire wall.

"That child belongs to the shark clan," she said. She made a motion with her left hand and the wind caller tried again to move the air. Tarawe sent another strong gust that way, and the interference stopped. She spun her wind cushion faster.

Iuti's mother lifted the bow from her shoulder. It seemed a slow and casual move, but before Tarawe realized what had happened, an arrow was splitting the air between them. She stopped it a handsbreadth from her own heart. Ma'eva snatched the baby back into his arms an instant before a second arrow pierced the air where it had lain.

"Give me my granddaughter," Iuti's mother said again.

"This child is my son!" Ma'eva shouted.

"She belongs to the shark clan."

"He is a child of the sea!"

The bird people murmured and muttered. One reached out with her spear to touch the gusting wind barrier. The spear was whipped away and she quickly snatched her hand back. The ground shook hard and the dancers shifted their fearful looks from Tarawe to the glowing pit behind them.

Another arrow was in the air almost before Tarawe realized it. With a quick word, she dropped a protective shield around the place where she and Ma'eva stood. The arrow struck the shield and skewed to one side. It clattered to the ground.

Iuti's mother lowered her bow and frowned. The sorcerer flicked his whisk toward the shield and muttered something to her. "I see my daughter has shared some of the shark clan's secrets with you, youngster," Iuti's mother said. She signaled with her left hand again and Kuwala called a spell into the night.

Use no war magic with these men, Iuti Mano had warned.

Suddenly Tarawe realized her mistake. She tried to drop the shield, but it was too late. Kuwala's locking spell had sealed the shield tight. She and Ma'eva were safe now from outside harm, but they were trapped inside a prison of Tarawe's own making. Tarawe muttered the release spell Ser Iuti had taught her. The shield thinned for an instant, then Iuti's mother strode forward and touched the barrier with her own hand. It locked tight again.

"She taught you more than you should know," she said coolly. "Now, give me the child or I'll drive you all into the firepit." She closed her hand into the invisible fabric of the shield and shook it. Tarawe stumbled and almost fell. With the help of her kin, the woman could easily push both Tarawe and Ma'eva into the pit. Tarawe had seen Ser Iuti move a shielded man so. She tried again to break the spell.

"I will never give you my son," Ma'eva said.

Iuti's mother stared at him, then at Tarawe, obviously startled that she had heard Ma'eva's voice. A locked shield was supposed to leave those inside sealed into silence. Iuti Mano didn't teach me *all* that I know, Tarawe told the woman silently, wishing the small change she'd been able to achieve could offer her some advantage.

Iuti's mother smirked before returning to the edge of the mound. She motioned for her sorcerer to come forward and put down the basket he carried. "This is a flying dolphin's egg, mimic," she called. "I will trade it for my daughter's daughter."

The bird worshipers called out in sudden protest. "The egg is *ours*!" the Chosen One cried. "We found these intruders first."

"We bargained for the shark's sister," Kuwala shouted. "We found *her* on our own."

"We took this egg from the great clam's shell at Kala, mimic," his mother said as if there had been no interruption. "This is a true child of the sea. It has no ties at all to the land." She ran her hand over the top of the basket; a glimmer of pearly iridescence shone through the small openings in the woven fronds.

"If it dies before it's born, its parent will die of a broken heart and *two* magic dolphins will be lost." She picked up a large, sharp stone from beside it.

"Ayiii," Ma'eva moaned softly.

Tarawe tried again to break through the locked shield. Again she was stopped, this time by a move of Kuwala's hand. Pali stood at Kuwala's side, grinning. Blood dripped from the sword in his hand. The blood of my birds, she thought, and she forced herself to hold tight to her anger. If she had not feared the loss of power his death thrust would have caused, she would have used her wind to kill Pali where he stood.

Ma'eva pulled the covers from the baby and held it up. "This is my son, mother of the mother of my child!" he cried. "Look at him and know that he is male."

The sorcerer began chanting loudly and waving his whisk. He whined and he wailed and he finally shrieked, "It is a girl! He holds a girl child!" For just an instant, the child appeared to be female. Ma'eva clutched it back to his chest and rewrapped it in the cloth. It flickered faintly.

"Give her to me!" Iuti's mother cried. She lifted the rock above the basket. "Or I'll destroy the egg!"

Only Anele and Tarawe didn't react. The sorcerer began

chanting loudly while Kuwala and his brothers and cousins stared
in horror. The bird dancers screamed and posed. Even the Chosen One lifted her chin to the sky and shrieked a high chittering
note. A conch shell was blown, a long, mournful note that echoed and echoed across the lava fields.

The Chosen One ran toward the basket, reaching for it with
her clawed hands. The sorcerer flicked his whisk and she froze.
A look of great pain spread over her face. She crumpled to the
ground. A gull swooped down toward the egg, but was thrown
by the unseen wind caller across Tarawe's head. Before Tarawe
could catch it, it tumbled into the glow above the firepit. It
hovered for moment, Tarawe heard its silent scream, before
bursting into flames and falling straight down. The bird worshipers posed and the ground shivered.

"Give me the child, mimic," Iuti's mother shouted.

"You know it is male and belongs to the sea," Ma'eva returned.

"You promised the dolphin's egg to the birds, mimic. They
told me that. If it's destroyed, you can never pay your debt and
the birds will despise you and your child forever, as will the
dolphins."

Again Ma'eva moaned. "What can I do?" he whispered.

"Wait," Tarawe said so softly that only he could hear.

"Then I will give you the dolphin's egg as a birthing gift,
mimic. In pieces!" Iuti's mother smashed the stone down onto
the basket. It clunked against something hard and slipped from
her hands. She lost her balance and fell onto the jagged lava.
The earth trembled and the conch blew again.

Iuti's mother jerked upright and began tearing at the basket.
She screamed when it fell open. A scattering of large, iridescent
fish scales tumbled away to reveal a tree-hardened copra nut.
She screamed again, picked up the coconut, and dashed it against
the shield. It bounced harmlessly away. She glared at Tarawe.

"*You* did this!"

Tarawe nudged the basket with her toe. "Open it," she said.
Ma'eva squatted. He caught his breath, cried out softly in relief,
then lifted the great, glistening egg for them all to see. A smaller
pearl, the size of Ma'eva's fist, remained in the bottom of the
basket. The Great Pearl, Tarawe thought. The true pearl that
was supposed to have gone to the birds.

She felt the shield waver. For a moment, she thought Iuti's
mother would lower it so that she could reach the egg, or the
child. Tarawe prepared her wind to lift them away quickly, but

when she tested the shield again, it had steadied. It was stronger now than before.

Ma'eva sat the flying dolphin's egg back gently and pressed his tiny child's hands to the sides of what they had once thought was only a pearl. Then he began to cry, for there was no way now that they could get the egg or his child safely to the sea. The baby's skin no longer flickered. When Tarawe looked down, she saw a network of fine silver cracks spreading around the egg.

"Oh, gods," she whispered. "I have failed you both."

Iuti's mother called to her sons and nephews to push the shield into the pit, but only Kuwala and Pali started forward. The others were too horrified by her attempt to destroy the flying dolphin's egg. Their relief at seeing the egg safe did not lessen their dismay at what had been attempted. Like Anele, they had been willing to use the egg to find Iuti Mano, but they had never imagined their matriarch capable of destroying it.

The Chosen One crawled back toward the firepit.

The air changed again. The birds were returning. The great gulls, and the saber birds, and the parrot. "Perl!" screeched the parrot. Ma'eva held the true pearl up, and the parrot screeched again. A gull swept through Tarawe's shield and snatched it from his hand.

Suddenly a bird much larger than all the rest came. It was strong and powerful, silver gray, shining in the firelight. The air moved in great shocked waves at each slap of its wide wings.

It was the flying dolphin!

Tarawe hurriedly closed the egg into the basket again. She lifted it high as the giant winged sea creature swept near. "Take it!" she cried, and heard Ma'eva shout, "Take your child, good friend. Fair winds!" The bird dancers screamed in terror. Then, when they realized what Tarawe was offering the great flying creature, they howled in protest.

But the dolphin did not take the basket. It circled, then swept close and snatched the cloth-wrapped child from Ma'eva's arms.

"No!" Ma'eva cried. "No! It's too late for mine!"

The dolphin soared upward with a single slap of its great wings and disappeared into the cloud-filled sky.

Ma'eva cried out in despair. He flickered and changed—into a fur seal, a giant land crab, a sharp-toothed sea boar. He changed into all the creatures he could be while standing on dry land. He flickered and changed until at last he cried out in his human voice, and dissolved back into his human form. His skin was dark. His face was lined with grief. He collapsed to the ground and hugged his arms around his knees.

"Now our children are both lost to the sea," he moaned.

The basket moved in Tarawe's hands. The flying dolphin's egg was about to hatch.

It began to rain.

Softly at first, then harder as the clouds Tarawe had called down from the mountain began emptying their dark bellies over the desolate land. The rain slid down the invisible walls of Tarawe's prison, leaving the air inside warm and dry.

"I can't even cool you with my rain," she said to the egg. "What can I do?"

The shield moved. Tarawe stumbled and fell beside Ma'eva. With Kuwala and Pali's help, Iuti's mother and the sorcerer were dragging them toward the firepit. Anele and the others tried to pull them away, but a flick of Gala's whisk sent them staggering back. Tarawe and Ma'eva fought the forward motion, but even when Ma'eva flickered and changed into a much larger man, they could not resist.

At first the bird dancers called out in protest. Then, suddenly, the Chosen One began posing and shrieking her shrill call into the sky again. The others quickly followed, dancing and posing and calling out to Haku 'Aina that their sacrifice was about to be given. They don't care who forces us into the pit, Tarawe thought, as long as we fall, and the egg falls with us. The rain pelted down, dousing the dancers' feathers—the false and the true—making them wilt and droop.

Tarawe turned her wind against Iuti Mano's kin, but Gala and Iuti's mother had set some magical protection about them. The slow, steady movement continued. Tarawe could feel the heat of the firepit even through the shield.

Rainwater sizzled on the hot stone bordering the pit. Larger and larger steam clouds rose from the landmaker's underground lair. The reflection of firelight on the low-hanging clouds colored the dance mound livid orange.

Suddenly the shield disappeared. It vanished so abruptly that Pali fell face forward onto the hot stone at Tarawe's feet. Ma'eva kicked him away. Tarawe and Ma'eva scrambled away from their attackers as a warm, welcoming presence appeared between them. Iuti Mano! The warrior woman's sword flashed. Blood flew. A wide gash opened in Kuwala's shoulder, and he and Pali quickly backed away.

"Ser Iuti!" Tarawe cried. "Oh, Ser, I thought you were dead."

"Not dead, little sister," Iuti said. She was pale. Her black hair hung in rain-slicked strands across her shoulders and breasts. Her eyes looked empty of all feeling. She still wore Anali's cloth around her waist. It was bloodstained, but she had rid herself of the treacherous vest. When she turned to follow her mother's and her brothers' movements, Tarawe caught a glimpse of the dark tattoo the Demon Drummers had impressed on her back.

Iuti's mother shouted something that Tarawe couldn't hear and the sorcerer flicked his whisk toward them. Tarawe slid slivers of wind between the snapping sennit strands and tied them into heavy knots so that they could no longer carry the sorcerer's dark magic beyond his fingertips.

"Not dead yet," Ser Iuti said.

Nikivi was with her. He held Anali in his arms and seemed to be having no trouble standing on the trembling ground. Anali's eyes were closed, but her hands were clutched tightly around the neck of her precious purse.

The sorcerer tossed a strange-colored powder into the air. Tarawe swept it up and away before its taste could taint her air. Gala screamed and cursed in fury. He threw down the ruined whisk and began chanting loudly. Tarawe yanked the knot from his hair and retied it before his face, shoving the ugly gray mass between his teeth.

"The dolphin took your baby, Ser," she called. She clutched the basket with the egg close to her chest. She kept her right hand free to touch the wind, although she no longer needed it to give the wind direction. Moving the air had become as easy for her as breathing. Easier.

"I saw," Iuti said. Tarawe spared a brief look toward Ma'eva. He touched Iuti's cheek with his fingertips. Then he snatched the fighting stick from her left hand and blocked a swing of Kuwala's club.

"The egg is hatching," Ma'eva said. "Help me decide, mother of my son. Which is the crueler act? To destroy the egg now and break its parent's heart, or let the child be born here in the air where it will gain a bird's mind and soul?"

The birds circled and dove along Tarawe's turbulent air currents, adding their protection to Iuti's sword and Ma'eva's fighting stick. When the bird dancers tried to come close, it was the birds who forced them away. A pair of small sweetbirds was struck by a red and black spear and tumbled into the hot glow.

"If the egg hatches here, all the dolphins will be lost," Iuti said. Her voice was flat, emotionless. "We must either crush it, or give it to the firepit and let it burn. It is the only gift we can give the dolphins in return for their kindness to our son."

You cannot kill it! Tarawe wanted to scream. She tested and tested the wind, but could find no sign of the dolphin returning. Why doesn't it come back? she thought. And then remembered. Because it could not. It had the strength for only one pass over the land—and it had already made two. It had had one chance, and it had chosen to save the sea mimic's child rather than its own.

I will not let them kill it, Tarawe promised. She tied the woven basket to her waist. The Chosen One saw her and rushed forward.

"The egg must be given to Haku 'Aina!" she cried.

Pali swung his sword to the side as she passed him. It caught the claws on her right hand and sliced them away. She turned and brought her short spear up hard into his stomach. He folded over it for an instant, then straightened and ripped it from her hands. She staggered back as he lifted his sword to plunge it into her chest.

A flurry of black and yellow prevented the blow. The o'u flew directly into Pali's face, throwing him off balance. Pali grabbed at the bird with his free hand, swung at it with his shield, then with his sword. The tiny o'u flitted and flittered away from each of his attempted blows. It darted up toward his face, then down and to the side, drawing his sword into unbalanced swings. It slid under his arms, circled, and snatched at his face and hair.

Tarawe realized that the tiny bird was flying the paths of the killing fields Ser Iuti had practiced with her weapons on the canoe. Its moves were so smooth and precise that Tarawe could almost see the flash of Iuti's sword slipping and sliding through the air.

The o'u pushed Pali back and back. Kuwala ran toward them but was knocked to his knees by a sweeping gull. Pali began to panic as he felt the heat of the firepit close behind his back. His attempts to avoid the bird grew wild and uncontrolled. Kuwala shouted a curse. His mother screamed at the sorcerer to stop the attack, but the sorcerer was still trying to pull his tangled hair from his mouth. Kuwala's curses had no affect on the o'u.

Tarawe glanced at Iuti, wondering if the warrior woman would stop the bird from killing her kin, but Iuti watched her cousin's fate as emotionlessly as she had acknowledged the fate of her son.

"Shall I stop her, Ser?" Tarawe felt compelled to ask.

Iuti shook her head. "This war is between the bird and Pali. Pali killed the o'u's mate back on Kala. That's why she hid on the canoe after we left the other birds behind. She knew my kinsman would find me eventually, and she wanted to be here when he did."

In the end, it was not the bird that killed Pali. Just as Pali reached the edge of the firepit, the Chosen One's consort darted forward and pushed him over the edge with a jab of his short, ceremonial spear. Pali's shrill scream was echoed by the high-pitched warbling of the Chosen One and the low, moaning cry of the conch.

The light flared for an instant, then the ground trembled. Had it grown quiet before? Tarawe couldn't remember. She held the egg tight and took a step closer to the pit, studying its edges carefully. There had to be a way. She could feel angry waves reaching high up the sea cliffs on the opposite side of the pit.

Iuti put a hand on her shoulder, holding her back. She shrugged it off and moved closer to the fire. She blew the steam away from the pit's edges so that she could see. Her eyes watered with the heavy, burning touch of sulfur. She pulled more rain down from the sky. Lightning crackled along the upper edges of the fire wall.

The firepit narrowed just beyond where she stood. A ledge of stone jutted toward her from the opposite side, as if the land underneath had dropped away at some time in the past. She looked up and down the crack. A lava tube, she thought. Like that they had passed through on the cliffside. But this one's roof had caved in. She could see molten stone running like a river only a warrior's length below.

It was too wide to jump across, too hot for the wind to lift her and the egg safely to the other side—and she dared not let the egg out of her hands. The cracks in the shell had widened. Any sudden movement could cause it to split.

Come! she called to the wind.

Come! she called to the waiting, straining sea waves.

When she could feel the wind and the water answering her call, she shouted, "Come, Haku 'Aina! Come to the surface so that the Storm Caller can give you honor."

"Tarawe, what are you doing? Stand back!" It was Ser Iuti's

voice. Metal struck metal, then Tarawe felt the birds swooping down to help Iuti protect her back.

She stepped to the very edge of the pit. Only Pali had gone closer. The ground trembled and shook. The fire roared and crackled. Steam rose in great plumes all around. She thrust the stench of sulfur away.

Tarawe stared down at the molten stone, which had begun to rise like a river in flood. She urged it silently toward the surface, toward the cool rain and the gusting wind. She sent a strong wall of wind along the surface of the molten stone, scooping the lava up into a wave. When the wave was high enough to splash against the upper edges of the pit, she called again for Haku 'Aina.

The Chosen One darted close and posed. She cried out in her shrill chittering shriek and the conch echoed a long, solitary note. Then it grew very silent. For a moment, only the sizzling rain could be heard, and the rising waves crashing higher and higher up the sides of the seacliffs in answer to her call.

Then, almost imperceptibly, a deep rumble rose from inside the glowing firepit. The ground trembled. It shook harder and harder. Kuwala stumbled and was driven back toward his mother by the birds. Iuti put a hand on Tarawe's shoulder, but Tarawe pushed it away. Her wind would not let her fall. She took another step forward.

The bird worshipers remained near the edge of the pit. They posed and danced, chittered and squeaked, imitating the movements of all the birds that had followed Tarawe and the others across the sea. Despite the ground's shaking, none of them fell. None even wobbled in their strange, one-legged stances. All of Iuti's kin, except for her mother and Kuwala, scrambled to the far edge of the dance mound.

The rumble from the pit suddenly turned to a roar. At the far edge of the dance mound, flames shot high into the air. *Not flames*, Tarawe's wind told her quickly. *Molten stone! Haku 'Aina!* The soul of the land was exploding into the sky. The bird dancers screamed and cried, and called out in welcome.

Tarawe held the dolphin's egg tight to her chest and called out again to the wind and the rain and the sea.

ᨀ Chapter 20 ᨁ

"HAKU 'AINA," the bird dancers cried. They posed and danced and threw their painted spears into the fountain of liquid stone. Sizzling, rain-brushed cinders—shattered stone, cooled and hardened by the touch of wind—began falling from the sky. Iuti forced herself to stay back from Tarawe. The girl flicked her right hand and the searing heat and tumbling cinders were blown away from the dance mound.

A lick of saltwater, the leading edge of what must have been a great sea wave, slid up to the brink of the far side of the crack. Iuti stared, stunned, as it inundated the place where Tarawe's lava wave was throwing its splash. The seawater crackled and hissed across the hot stone, turning to steam before it had time to drain away. More liquid stone splashed. It formed into hardened lumps along the water-cooled edge of the pit.

Tarawe called out again to Haku 'Aina. As if in answer, the molten river rose higher; its surface was now only an arm's length below where Tarawe stood.

Where the rain touched the river's fiery orange surface, it cooled and turned to a dark crust, then shattered with the continuing movement of the viscous liquid beneath. Tarawe's wave threw the solid pieces of crust onto the bank before they could be swallowed by the river again. The lava splash cooled and darkened further, turning black with only an occasional glimmer of orange showing from deep inside.

Another sea wave swept over the newly made land. It sizzled and steamed. The mound of stone grew higher. Tarawe's hands moved ever so slightly. The outcrop of new land began stretching toward them across the fiery pit.

"She's building a bridge!" Ma'eva cried.

Another and another sea wave struck, each deeper than the

one before. Tarawe stood straight as her wind and water molded the molten river splash into a growing arch across the landmaker's pit.

The feathers on her cape shriveled from the heat and began bursting into tiny flames. The rain doused them, one by one, before Iuti could act. The molten river rose and the heat increased. Ana's teardrops of light popped free to spin, sparkling into the building of the bridge.

"Come up, landmaker!" Tarawe called. "Show me your fiery face."

The burning river rose to fill the firepit. Lava oozed over the edges of the pit, cooled and hardened. The river sank back a handsbreadth.

She knows, Iuti thought. The landmaker knows that she will turn to hard stone if she flows outside the crack. Does she know she's being deliberately called up? Deliberately being used to build our escape? How can Tarawe do such a thing?

The fountaining lava at the far end of the dance mound flared again, then settled into a slightly lesser display. Iuti understood then that the fountain was the source of the molten stone in the river. The bird wordshipers struck grotesque poses in its red-orange glow.

Tarawe took a step to one side, into a puddle of rainwater. The ti leaves she had wrapped around her feet had begun to smolder.

A face began to form in the steam clouds. A young woman's face, an old woman's. Or was it a man's? Iuti couldn't tell. It flickered and flowed and folded over on itself. Long fiery-red hair lifted like flames high into the night sky. The bird worshipers dropped to their bellies and pressed their foreheads to the ground, then jumped up and began posing again.

Tarawe continued to stand at the very edge of the molten river. She had, in fact, stepped forward onto new land that the cooling, crusting edges of the river had just formed. She slid the flying dolphin's egg into the basket at her waist and lifted both of her arms to the emerging landmaker.

"Welcome, sister," Tarawe called. "Join me in the air and the water, and be at peace. Let our powers rest together as kin."

It was a warrior's greeting, worded in Tarawe's own personal way.

The face in the cloud turned. It looked down. Eyes the color of burning gold shifted to stare at the place where Tarawe stood. Lips as deeply red as fresh-spilled blood parted.

"You are no kin to me, human." The voice was like flames across dry kindling. It flashed and was gone.

"I am the wind. I am the water. We are sisters," Tarawe called. Her voice was like cool water poured over a burn.

The Chosen One cried out and the conch shell blew. The flaming figure in the sky turned back to the dancers. The Chosen One lifted her arms, pleading. "I have brought the birds back to Tahena, Haku 'Aina. I have brought you sacrifice."

The ruby lips smiled slightly. "*You* did not bring the birds, faithful one. But I am pleased with your service. Come, join me."

The bird dancers called out honor and congratulations as the Chosen One and her slightly less eager consort moved toward the firepit. A finger of flame licked out and touched them. They stumbled and fell, struggled to their feet and fell again, this time at the very edge of the pit. The flames reached for them again. Their capes and feathered ornaments dropped away just before their charred bodies tumbled into the molten river.

"Ayiii!" Ma'eva said softly. The bird dancers screamed and posed in pleasure. By the time the river's flow reached the place where Tarawe stood, the Chosen One and her consort had disappeared.

Iuti turned back to Tarawe. Her arms were still raised. Her fingers still moved ever so slightly. The bridge she was constructing had reached to within an arm's length of where she stood.

"Will she step onto it?" Ma'eva said. "Will she dare?"

The landmaker's face shifted and folded; it disappeared for an instant. When it returned, it was the face of a young woman again. The eyes turned to stare at Anali.

"You claimed to have a message for me, sea woman," Haku 'Aina said.

Anali's mouth turned very round. She blinked.

"Well?"

Suddenly Ana straightened. She was still in Nikivi's arms, but she lifted her head proudly. "I bring you greetings from the spirits who now dwell in the Ilimar firepits," she said. That made Iuti blink. Was she making this up?

The landmaker's image grew old and older still. The scarlet skin grew mottled and the flaming hair thin. "I do not remember Ilimar," she said.

"It is a very old land," Ana said quickly. "You must have made it long ago. It's far off on the eastern mainland."

A flaming brow lifted. "The mainland! Ahh, I have not visited there in a long time. My greetings to those who now guard my land."

The fiery voice suddenly crackled young again. The golden gaze shifted to Iuti.

"You claimed to seek only safe passage across my lands, warrior woman, yet you wet on the floor of my cave without so much as a by-your-leave." Her look suddenly softened. "But you offered me honor when you fed me the blood of your son."

The fiery gaze snapped back to Tarawe. "I see you there, wind and water! I see you using your storm against me!"

"I mean you no dishonor," Tarawe said without apology; she did not slow the building of her bridge, "but I must take this egg to the sea."

She has grown to be so polite and so wise, Iuti thought. So wise and full of power.

Sea waves, one after the other, were sweeping far inland now. They reached halfway across the nearly completed bridge. They slid, sizzling and steaming, across the growing arch. The stone thickened and hardened as the cool water ran over, and around, and through it. The heat turned the water to steam that billowed through the landmaker's flaming image. Rain fell steadily while the wind forced all but the worst of the smoke and fumes away.

"My servants promised the great bird's egg to me," Haku 'Aina said.

"It was not theirs to promise," Tarawe said. She lifted the basket into her arms again.

"She's going to jump," Ma'eva said.

"Oh, gods, Tarawe," Iuti whispered. Mano, protect these two children of your sea, she prayed.

The wind swirled. Iuti felt it lift just as Tarawe jumped. Flames licked up from the river to catch at her, but they only succeeded in setting her feathered cape alight. It swept out from Tarawe's slight form, spread by the wind. The fire was doused by the rain.

Ankle-deep water swept across the perilous bridge just as Tarawe's feet touched it. Iuti feared for an instant it would wash away Tarawe's footing. Instead, it spun and swirled and grabbed at her ankles as precisely as the wind had balanced her flight.

The image of Haku 'Aina swept down to block Tarawe's path. "I can stop you!" the landmaker roared. "I can open another pit, and another and another. You will never reach the sea!"

"*I* can stop *you*!" Tarawe cried. "My wind and my waves

will tear at your land until it is nothing more than a pile of rubble lying under the Empty Sea.''

''I will build it up again!''

A wave as deep as Tarawe's knees swept across the bridge. ''I will tear it down forever and forever! Let me pass!''

The fire flared. Tarawe staggered back. Iuti ran forward, but she knew she couldn't catch the girl if she fell. Ma'eva, too, rushed toward the bridge, flickering. There was nothing either of them could do.

Tarawe's cape spread like a great set of wings. The wind steadied her before she could slip off of the still-forming span. She gasped as her feet touched newly spattered, red-hot stone. Iuti and Ma'eva were forced back by the heat.

The image in the sky flared, but Tarawe held her ground. She stepped forward and lifted her left hand high. ''Come!'' she cried to the water.

A gout of flame spewed from the river. It seared across the back of her legs. Again she staggered but did not fall. She took another, stumbling step forward.

The landmaker's steam-borne form shifted and flowed. The molten river surged and splattered so that burning stone splashed over Tarawe's feet. Still she moved forward. The wind began to swirl around Tarawe, a barrier of sorts against the spattering lava, but her cape began to burn again and the rain was not strong enough to put it out.

Come!

It was the voice of the wind this time, not the girl.

The answering roar of the enraged landmaker drowned out all other sound. The lava fountain soared higher and the river surged. Ma'eva slid his arm around Iuti's shoulders as Tarawe moved stubbornly forward across the perilous bridge. She had bent forward, her arms wrapped tightly around the basket containing the dolphin's egg.

Come! the wind called again.

The basket dropped away. It burst into flame the instant it left Tarawe's hands. Ash soared away on the wind.

A flash of iridescence tumbled away from Tarawe. A sliver of iridescent shell.

''It's hatching!'' Ma'eva cried. Another, larger piece of the flying dolphin's shell fell from Tarawe's hands into the river. It floated like a pearl as it was swept downstream.

''The time of the dolphins has ended.'' Ma'eva moaned. He held Iuti tight, weeping into the night.

But the emerging dolphin was still hidden by Tarawe's arms. She shuffled forward on legs so burned she shouldn't have been able to move. The tip of a silver wing slipped into sight, but she gathered it close and hid it just as she had done once to the tiny o'u. Another small piece of shell fell away.

"It's not fully born yet, Ma'eva," Iuti called. "There is still time left."

The landmaker's roar grew enormous. The fires soared around Tarawe and the hatching dolphin. Then:

"Ma'eva, look! The sea has come!"

It wasn't the landmaker's roar they had heard. It was the deep, rumbling bellow of a great sea wave building and then surging across the land. A wall of tumbling water raced toward Tarawe. It sliced through the landmaker's fiery chin, causing her to disappear for an instant.

A geyser of molten stone shot into the air, piercing Tarawe's defensive wind. It splashed across her back just as the wave reached the bridge. Tarawe fell. She huddled in the center of whirling wind and flames and hissing rain, protecting the partially hatched egg with a body so burned it should not have been able to hold life.

Another large, jagged piece of shell spun away.

Then the rushing sea wave struck. Tarawe's burning feathers burst into brilliant flames just as the wave front washed across her. The cape was torn away. Charred feathers swirled in roiling, steaming water. Tarawe and the egg disappeared into an ash and stone-strewn maelstrom.

The lava river surged and spewed great clots of molten stone, but the wave held its shape, hovering over the bridge.

"How can she do it?" Iuti whispered. "How can she hold the water in place so long? How can she still live?"

Something silver flashed in the roiling water.

"The dolphin!" Ma'eva cried.

The turning, tumbling figure of the dolphin pup rose toward the surface of the hovering wave. It leapt in a tiny, silver arc through the fire-laden air, then slid back into the water without a splash. Iuti squeezed Ma'eva's hand. Where is she? she thought. Where can she be? She glanced down at the racing, roaring river, but saw no sign of Tarawe. A charred feather drifted down. It was immediately swallowed by molten stone.

The dolphin pup was swimming back to the surface when Iuti looked back. It leapt again, higher than before—and paused.

"It's going to *fly*!" Ma'eva called. "Fair winds, child of the sea! Welcome!"

His sudden joy was like a knife through Iuti's heart. She had not thought she could feel more pain.

The tiny dolphin snapped its wings open. They spread, and spread. The dolphin grew in the fiery sky. Its wings spread and spread until they stretched wider than Iuti could reach. The child dolphin, no longer a pup, hovered for an instant. Then, with a great boom, it slapped its wings up, and down—and soared.

"By the very gods," Iuti breathed. She would have sunk to her knees if Ma'eva's strong arms had not held her upright. It is too much, she cried silently. It is too much to lose this child, too.

Tarawe had become her daughter, her sister, a friend she trusted more than life. Her relief for the flying dolphin's child only added to the pain of losing her own.

"Look," Ma'eva said. Then again. "Look. It's coming back."

The sea wave had finally begun to collapse. Whatever strength Tarawe had left within it was gone. It was no more than knee deep when the soaring dolphin once more touched its boiling surface. The dolphin skimmed the wave, sending a wide spray of water to each side of its sleek, silver body. It dipped beneath the surface and rose again—with Tarawe clinging to its back!

It's not Tarawe, Iuti thought in horror. Not that mangled, burned body. The remnants of charred ti leaves drifted from the sky. That cannot be my Tarawe!

But it was. The dolphin soared upward with the wind and, at last, the wave collapsed into steam. The dolphin flew through the clouds of smoke and ash that formed Haku 'Aina's image, and the landmaker shattered and disappeared. The fountaining lava and the molten river began to subside.

The dolphin circled.

It grew strangely quiet on the dance mound. The bird worshipers all stared at the sky, their poses forgotten. Iuti's kin remained huddled at the far side. Kuwala shouted a curse after the soaring dolphin, but was instantly silenced by the swooping, diving airfolk.

"Look," Ho'oma'eva whispered.

The figure on the dolphin's back sat straighter.

It's the smoke, Iuti thought. It has to be the shifting clouds of steam that make it look like she is moving. She cannot be alive.

But, high above her, the movement continued. Tarawe's bro-

ken body straightened further. Blackened flesh fell away to reveal golden brown skin. Strong, thin arms reached out to hug
the dolphin tight. Tarawe's dress of shredded ti leaves grew
whole again, and, for an instant, she wore the rich colors of her
feathered cape and Ana's headdress. She rode the dolphin with
her face lifted to the wind, her long ebony hair streaming behind
her.

Her sweet laughter slid softly across the sky.

"A bird spirit!" one of the bird worshipers gasped, and he
and the others began posing again.

"A wind spirit." Ma'eva sighed. He held Iuti's hand tight.

"I am the wind, Ser!" Tarawe called. "I am the storm! I can
fly!" She laughed once again.

The dolphin circled four times before Tarawe's shimmering
form began to fade. In an instant, she became nothing more than
a memory of thinning smoke and drifting steam. A rain of tiny,
glowing teardrops fell into Iuti's outstretched hands as the dolphin soared alone toward the sea.

"Come, friend Iuti," Ma'eva said quietly. "The birds will
soon follow the dolphin. We must use the escape the Storm
Caller built for us." He led Iuti to the edge of the pit and together
they leapt across the subsiding river to the bridge. Nikivi jumped
the small gap behind them. He still held Anali in his arms. The
old woman was asleep, or pretending to be. Moisture glimmered
on her mottled, sunken cheeks.

"Down!" Nikivi shouted suddenly. Something small and dark
and very, very fast streaked past Iuti's face. A knife. Her mother's. Iuti knew it by the taste of its passage, and she knew that
it had not been intended for her. Ma'eva gasped as the short,
dark assassin's blade sliced across his shoulder. Iuti pushed him
behind her and turned back.

Her mother stood at the center of Tarawe's bridge, a second
knife already in her hands.

"I will kill every bird in the sky, Iuti Mano," she cried.
"Every creature of the sea who has given you aid. The mimic
will be first—"

The cold, hard voice ended abruptly in a choking cough. One
of Anali's knives had struck the center of Iuti's mother's throat.
She stood there for a moment, her bloodied hands grasping the
hilt of the knife. She stared at Iuti with lifeless eyes as she
toppled slowly into the pit.

Kuwala jumped onto the bridge. He cried out in a long, shuddering wail, a death call for their mother, then threw himself

forward. He knocked Ana and Nikivi from his path and swung his massive war club around and up in a killing blow.

Ma'eva thrust Iuti away and swept her fighting stick up between them. The sharp, pointed beak of the saber bird met Kuwala's wide chest. It slid through the knots between his armor. He stumbled and fell forward, impaling himself on the long, hard blade. His club, then his lifeless body thudded to the ground.

Ma'eva flickered once, very faintly.

"Oh, Ma'eva," Iuti cried. "Oh, my good friend Ho'oma'eva. What have I done to you?"

He turned to her, eyes shimmering. "You gave me life, mother of my child."

Iuti looked down at her dead brother. Her brother whom Ma'eva had killed while he stood on dry land.

"I have cost you both your son and your life, my friend," she whispered.

Ma'eva touched her cheek. "I am not dead. Only human." His voice held the same emptiness Iuti had felt when Gala and her mother had left her alone in the kipuka.

Ma'eva touched her chest with his fingertips. His skin glistened with the heat of the firepit and his own tears. "My son cannot learn the ways of the sea. It is fitting that I . . . help you teach him the ways of the land."

"Son," Anali said quietly, "you don't know for certain that the child didn't reach the sea in time."

"I know," Ma'eva said, and his mother said no more.

"The others are coming, " Nikivi said. "We must face them, or go. There are places to hide in the lava fields. I can show you."

Iuti glanced back to where Anele and her remaining kinsmen had gathered at the unfinished end of the bridge. Two of the cousins were holding Gala, bound and gagged. The others had sheathed their weapons. Iuti straightened and forced herself to walk back to face them across the still-glowing pit. The lava river had receded to a dark orange ribbon, far below.

"It is finished," she called. "Our mother's wishes have been met. The shark clan has ended."

Anele lifted a hand before any of the other brothers or cousins could speak. "It is finished, sister," he called. "We will bury our hatred along with our dead."

"Aye," she said quietly. She had no hatred to bury. She turned back to Ma'eva, and together they walked toward the sea.

🐚 *Chapter 21* 🐚

THE edge of the sea cliff was only a short walk beyond the firepit. When Iuti and the others reached it, they stopped and stared. The cliff was gone. Tarawe's surging waves had piled shining black sand against the cliff face so deeply that it now formed a wide, gently sloping beach reaching far out to the sea. It was a single step from the cliff top to the sand.

Nikivi started to make a warding sign, but Anali slapped his fingers sharply. "Don't insult this place by naming it evil," she snapped.

The pristine beach was as black as the night had become. It sparkled like a moonless, starlit sky. Or like the lights in Tarawe's cape, Iuti thought, and she almost smiled. Tarawe would have loved knowing she had created such a beautiful place.

They walked a short way out onto the sand. Then Nikivi set Ana down. She groaned quietly, and Iuti quickly knelt beside her to study her injury. Iuti called a powerful healing spell into her hands and laid them on Anali's hip. "There's no need—" Ana said, but in an instant she was fast asleep.

Iuti tended Ma'eva's shoulder and a burn Nikivi had taken on his back, then Ma'eva left them to walk across the sand to the sea.

Nikivi sat. "I never thought you would survive this day, Iuti Mano," he said.

"Why did you help me then?"

He shrugged and reached down to rub his leg. "I told you. I live by rules of my own. I *wanted* you to survive."

She waited until he looked up. "How is it you walk so well with only one leg? You've not stumbled since we left the kipuka, and you sat just now without using your stick."

He looked startled for a moment, then he laughed. "I must

219

have grown careless in my relief.'' He laid his hand over the place where his left knee should have been. His palm curved to the shape of a man's leg.

Surprised, Iuti said a discovery word. Then another, much stronger. A third word, one she had rarely had occasion to use, brought a slight shadow. Nikivi grinned. It took a fourth word to completely dissolve his powerful hiding spell.

''I said a discovery spell when you first claimed to have only one leg,'' Iuti said as she stared at his two strong and entirely healthy legs. ''Then again when we found you in the clearing. You are a clever man, Nikivi, to set such a doubled and tripled spell. But why?''

''Strong and able visitors to this isle never remain that way long,'' he said. ''I was lucky enough to survive the bathing pool, but the then Chosen One's consort tried to kill me soon after. I escaped death at his hands three times, before I made my way into the lava fields. I hid here for many months. Until I got tired of living entirely alone. When I allowed the bird worshipers to see me again, I told them that Haku 'Aina had taken my leg. After that, they considered me harmless and left me alone.''

Iuti glanced toward Ma'eva. He was standing at the very edge of the sea. He did not step into the water.

''What will the bird worshipers do now?'' she asked. ''Will they follow us here?''

Nikivi shook his head. ''They'll ignore you as long as you stay out here. If you return to the valleys, they'll assume you're coming to compete for the honor of being the next Chosen One. The other women seeking the position will try to kill you.''

Nikivi leaned forward. ''Will you take me with you when you go, Iuti Mano? I did what I could. I stayed behind in the kipuka when your kin found you and set you free as quickly as I could. I carried the old woman here. I'll be your servant, sharkwoman. I'll be your slave if you'll free me from this isle.''

''I'll free you of this isle and then of my company as soon as we reach the eastern edge of the Empty Sea,'' she said. ''You owe me nothing, South Islands man.''

She pressed a hand to her lower stomach. The strong healing and pain spells she'd used to blunt the pain of her mother's treachery had begun to weaken. ''It would be a kindness, though, my newfound friend, if you would watch while I sleep for a time.''

Nikivi shifted and saluted. ''I am at your service, Iuti Mano.

Although I doubt you'll be in any danger while the sea mimic remains near.''

Iuti fell asleep watching Ma'eva watch the tumbling waves.

She woke to the o'u's chirping. It was sitting on the sand beside her; she could see it through a tangle of dark hair. A soft whimper and a cough brought Iuti's eyes wide open. Ma'eva was beside her cuddling their son in his arms. The baby was wrapped in shining green cloth.

Iuti sat up quickly, reaching with hungry arms. Ma'eva passed the child to her. The babe turned his tiny, groping mouth to her breast as soon as she held him close.

"Mano's sweet breath," she murmured at the first touch of his eager lips. "He is real!" She met Ma'eva's smile.

"Very real," Ma'eva said. "And strong. My cousins told me he is a good swimmer."

Iuti caught her breath. "Did he—"

Ma'eva shook his head. His smile drained away. "He reached the sea too late to make the change. He tried, they said. He tried with more spirit than any child they'd ever seen. His hands changed once, into the tips of a manta ray's wings."

Or a flying dolphin's, Iuti thought.

"They said that for an instant, his sweet face had the look of a shark, but there was nothing more." Ma'eva brushed his fingertips over the baby's hand where it was spread along the side of Iuti's breast. "They brought him to me just before dawn."

Ma'eva smiled down at his hungry son. "He is a beautiful human, Iuti Mano."

"Just like his father," she said, and wished she could cut out her tongue at the sudden pain her unthinking remark brought to Ma'eva's eyes. "Ho'oma'eva, I'm sorry. Forgive me. I did not think—"

He covered her lips with his fingers. "We are good friends, Iuti Mano. There is no need for apologies between us. I will kill again for you if need be." He stroked her cheek, then turned his look back to the sea.

"Is there a way I can give you a daughter?" he asked after a time.

A tear slid from Iuti's eye, dripped onto the green cloth and disappeared. "I cannot have another child," she said. "My mother took that gift from me in a way that I cannot repair."

She touched his arm. "Ho'oma'eva, I know you can't stay with me forever. You may be in human form, but your heart is still in the sea. If you need to go, go. Know that I will always care for our son.''

Ma'eva sat silent for a long time. Finally he nodded. He touched her cheek and the child's warm hand, then walked back across the sand to stand at the edge of the sea.

Anele came at late afternoon. He knelt in the sand before Iuti and greeted her son as an uncle.

''Will you come back with us?'' he asked her. ''Will you travel with your kinsmen across the Empty Sea?''

''Will you take me?'' she replied.

He lifted a rueful brow. He knew she couldn't cross the wide sea without a full crew of paddlers. She knew that he and the others couldn't cross without her to call the sea creatures close enough to provide food. She nodded.

''Nikivi will help you gather food and water in the valleys,'' she said. ''Bring my canoe here for me when you are ready to leave.''

The sea mimics brought food for her and Ma'eva, delicacies from the deep ocean and drinking coconuts from hidden valleys on the land. They brought gifts for the child—bright shells, colorful coral, and other treasures from the sea.

One pressed a small, perfect pearl into Iuti's hand. ''For you,'' he said. ''From the flying dolphins.''

Late that evening Iuti woke Anali, knowing she needed food as much as she needed healing sleep. The instant Iuti released the sleep spell, Anali opened her eyes and reached for her bag. The baby burped and sighed just as she was about to open it.

Ana looked up, startled. Her tired, lined face opened into a wide grin. ''Is this he?'' she cried. ''Is this my grandson? Here. Here. Come to me, boy. Ah, my lovely, lovely little boy!''

She lifted the baby from its wrappings and held him high. She turned him this way and that in sure steady hands, inspecting him from top to bottom. She touched each of his fingers and toes and the very tip of his tiny manhood.

''You are perfect,'' she said. ''You are the most beautiful boy I have ever seen. Except for Ma'eva, of course. Although . . .'' She turned the baby again and smiled at his tiny, scrunched-up face. Then she hugged him close.

''I might be wrong. I must be wrong. This old memory of mine plays tricks on me sometimes, boy. No child could be more beautiful than you.''

The baby peed down the front of her fish-scale armor. She laughed heartily and passed the child back to Iuti. ''Have you eaten, mother of this beautiful boy?'' she asked. ''You need to eat well to feed him well.''

''The mimics brought us squid and sugarfish,'' Iuti assured her. ''And coconuts to drink. This boy is eating very well. My true milk has already started to flow.''

''Well, you need more than squids,'' Anali said. ''You need fruit and bread and . . . Now where did I put my purse?''

Iuti laughed and pointed to the bag that never left Anali's neck. She rewrapped her son, sending silent thanks once again for the mimics' gift of the soft green cloth. Its shimmering folds absorbed the infant's small wettings as if they weren't there.

''Ah, yes,'' Ana muttered. ''Now where is that— Ouch! Get away from that bread, you idiot bird! Here. Get out! You don't belong in here. Look how much of my bread you've eaten.''

Iuti caught the glimmer of glowing stones as Anali lifted Tarawe's gull from the bag and set it on the sand beside her. The gull's eyes were bright, but its battered body showed all the scars of its many narrow escapes. Its feathers were as faded and broken as those on the Chosen One's cape. Great patches of bare skin revealed the ugly scars of the cave grubs' teeth. The gull's wide wings shifted once, then lay limp and useless across the sand.

''Aaaaaaaahh!''

Iuti snapped her look up at the sound. There was no one on the beach but Ma'eva and he was far off by the sea.

A breeze ruffled the feathers along the gull's back.

''Aaaaaahh! My poor, broken friend.''

''Tarawe?'' Iuti whispered. A sweet, warm breeze slid across her scarred cheek. She held the baby in one arm and lifted her other hand to the sky. ''Tarawe, is it you?''

For an instant, she thought she felt Tarawe's small hand grasp her own.

''What's that, dear?'' Anali said. She looked up from her bag. ''I'm sorry about the bread. It's all crumbled from that silly bird's pecking. Here, take a banana and some cherries. The cherries will put color into my grandson's cheeks.''

The gull's feathers lifted again. Then a strong, smooth gust of wind scooped it up from the sand and lifted it into the air. The great gull's wings stretched wide and in an instant, it had disappeared into the darkening sky.

''Oh, my,'' Anali said.

Iuti stared after the bird. ''It was Tarawe. I heard her voice, Mother Ana. She touched my hand.''

Ana patted her arm. "Aye. The Storm Caller was a nice girl. I loved her, too. Did I tell you that she once refilled my water gourd?"

Iuti smiled and turned back to Anali. She broke the crumbly bread into pieces and insisted that Anali eat. Ana picked a tiny, glowing stone from the bread.

"Look at that," she muttered. "That idiot bird made such a mess. Not at all like that nice Storm Caller." She laughed and flicked the glowing stone onto the sand. "She was so surprised when I pulled the stones from my bag last night. She thought they'd been breeding in there."

"Hadn't they?" Iuti asked, remembering the sparkling glimpse of the bag she'd just had.

"Of course not, mother of my grandson. They're *stones*! I picked up handfuls of them when we first entered the lighted cavern. They looked like something that might come in handy someday. The girl only saw me put in those last two."

"You are a treasure, Mother Ana," Iuti said. She listened, but heard no more voices on the wind.

Ma'eva joined them just at dark. He slipped an arm around his mother's shoulders and gave her a hug. When he reached out to touch his son, Iuti saw that his hand was trembling.

"Friend Ma'eva, what's wrong?"

He met her look and she saw despair in his sea-blue eyes. "I must go to the sea, mother of my son. My grief is crushing me. I must go, but I cannot." He looked up toward the mountain, then back toward the path that led to the eastern valleys. He shuddered.

Anali rubbed a hand along his perfect thigh.

"I'll have Anele bring our canoe," Iuti said. "You can take it—"

"I cannot live on a canoe!" he cried.

"Here, here, son," Anali pulled him close again. "Give your old mother another hug. I cannot bear to see you cry. Here. Let me hold you."

She sighed. "You are so much like your father."

Ma'eva pressed his face to his mother's cheek. In a move so quick, Iuti almost missed seeing it, Anali lifted the bag from around her neck and slipped it over Ma'eva's head. He jerked back.

"Oh, no. No, Mama. I cannot. This gift belongs to you."

"It belongs to you now, son," Anali said. "I have given it to you. It won't make you the same as a true mimic. The only land change you'll be able to make will be to this one human form. But you can be whatever you want to be in the sea. You belong in the sea, Ho'oma'eva.''

"You belong in the sea, too, Mama," Ma'eva said. His right hand clutched the neck of the precious bag.

"I'm an old woman," she said. "It's time I returned to the land to take care of my grandson. Take the bag, Ho'oma'eva. Its magic belongs to the sea. I'd always intended to give it back someday."

Ma'eva embraced his mother then; he held her close for a long, long time. Finally Ana pushed him away. "Give me another loaf of bread and a handful of cherries," she said. "And a hand of bananas. This mother of my grandson needs to eat properly. Then you go on. This isn't a proper place for a sea mimic to grieve."

Ma'eva took the food from the bag, much more than his mother had asked for, and cinched it tight again. He held his son for just a moment. "He is a beautiful human, Iuti Mano," he said. He met her look and smiled sadly. "He is very much like his mother."

"Fair seas, good friend," Iuti whispered. He returned the child to her arms. He brushed his fingertips across her scarred cheek, turned, and walked back to the sea.

Iuti watched until she saw a flicker in the rolling waves, and for a long while after. When he was truly gone, when she could move again, she turned back to Ana. The old woman was sound asleep, her head resting on her hand. She was using a loaf of nut bread for a pillow.

Iuti pushed the cloth back from her son's face so he could see. "This is your grandmother, Anali of Ilimar," she told him. "She is a strong and gentle woman. She can always make me smile."

The baby watched Ana for a while, then turned his face back to Iuti's dripping breast. She smiled and held him close. She stared out across the distant sea. The night air was moist and warm. The only sounds were the gently rolling surf and the infant's contented sucking.

"Ser Iuti?"

Iuti caught her breath.

"Are you well, Ser?" Tarawe's sweet voice slid past Iuti like a soft summer breeze.

"Aye," she replied softly.

"And your child?"

"He is healthy and strong. He will grow into a fine man."

There was a long silence. The night became still again. Iuti turned her look back to the sea.

Then, "I'm sorry, Ser. We tried to get him to the water in time."

"I know."

"I saw Ho'oma'eva just now. He was a shark, swimming due west through the Empty Sea."

Iuti sighed.

"Will he come back, Ser?"

Iuti thought her heart would break. "I don't know."

A breeze brushed her cheek. A fine mist fell like teardrops from the sky. Tarawe's comforting touch slid around her shoulders and warmed her like a lover's, a mother's, a sister's arms.

"Are you well, Tarawe?" Iuti asked. "Are you happy? I want so much for you to be happy."

The touch of the wind lightened, lifted. It became suddenly gay. "Oh, yes, Ser. The flying dolphins are my kin now, and my gull flies strongly at my side. I really am the wind now, Ser. I live with the clouds and the rain in the high wide sky. I made a rainbow today!"

Her joy was like cool water pouring over Iuti's pain. Iuti pressed her eyes closed and asked, "Will you come back, Tarawe?"

The wind shifted and sighed across her shoulders. "No, Ser. I cannot. But this is a good place. I have no fear here. No one can ever take my magic away, no one can ever cause me to turn it to evil. Death thrusts don't touch me here, Ser, and—" She giggled. "—I will never grow old and spotted like Mama Ana."

The wind ruffled the baby's thick black hair. Iuti looked down. The child's golden brown skin looked darker in the starlight, more like Ma'eva's. He opened his eyes and blinked up at her. For an instant, it looked as if he smiled around his mouthful of breast. His eyes were the same color as his father's.

"Do you remember when we first left Fanape, Ser Iuti?"

Tarawe's voice slid like a wraith around the night. A funnel of sand lifted and skittered across the shining beach.

"You promised you would take me to a place where I could be safe and happy."

The breeze touched Iuti's cheeks again. It tasted like sea rain and fresh ocean spray. "Aye," Iuti said.

"I am safe now, Ser."

The baby hiccoughed. Iuti lifted him to her shoulder.

"I am *very* happy."

The wind quickened and circled. Tickling tendrils of air lifted Iuti's thick, black hair from her shoulders and tied it into a tight warrior's knot atop her head.

"I must go now, Ser," Tarawe sang. "Fair winds to you and the babe."

Iuti lifted a hand to her hair, then to the departing breeze. "Farewell, Storm Caller," she whispered. "Fair winds!"

About the Author

Carol Severance is a Hawaii-based writer with a special interest in Pacific Island peoples and their environments. After growing up in Denver, she served with the Peace Corps and later assisted in anthropological fieldwork in the remote coral atolls of Truk, Micronesia. She currently lives in Hilo, where she has worked as an artist, a journalist, and a playwright. She shares her home with a scholarly fisherman, a surfer, and an undetermined number of geckos. Her first novel, *Reefsong*, was the winner of the Compton-Crook Award for best first novel of 1991.